PRAI/E FOR *THE PRACTICAL NAVIGATOR*

"A world of intrigue, suspense, sex, and murder. A riveting legal mystery. I couldn't stop reading."
—James D. Zirin, author of *The Mother Court*

"Tightly written. Superb."
—Gay Talese, bestselling author and journalist

"Who'd have thought that our favorite health and fitness master could not only teach us how to live but also write a novel? Not just a novel *but* a legal thriller. What a feat! It's graceful and smart, full of beautiful descriptions of Maine waters, sailing lore, and courtroom intricacies, with a clever plot twist, which I won't reveal. Remarkable, and kudos to Crowley!"
—Roxanna Robinson, award-winning author of *Cost*

"A most original murder mystery. Set on racing yachts in Maine, it's a well-written tale involving Wall Street lawyers; Maine sheriffs; beautiful, smart women; plus dubious financiers and a great deal of sex. Who could resist it? Certainly not I."
—Frances FitzGerald, Pulitzer Prize–winning author of *Fire in the Lake*

"No doubt about it: best work of fiction I have read in the past year."
—DeCourcy McIntosh

"Some writers are known for their ability to tell a tale. Others, their way with words. But Chris Crowley is both. His use of language is as charming as it is syncopated and quirky. And his storytelling can only be described as *page turning*."
—Bruce Turkel, brand consultant and bestselling author

"I went through it like a brush fire."
—Hamilton Robinson Jr.

"Crowley's writing is as addictively compelling as the obsessive sexuality at the heart of this beguiling blue-blooded mystery."

—Melissa Coleman, author of the memoir
This Life Is in Your Hands

"I read it in one sitting and then went right back to page one, wanting to do it all over again. The characters are so thoroughly developed, so vivid, that one wants to spend more time with them. And Crowley's writing is just superb. To somewhat misquote Nietzsche writing about Wagner: Where can we find a more knowledgeable guide to the labyrinth of the modern soul than in Crowley's *The Practical Navigator*?"

—Michael Robinson

"A riveting and sometimes ribald read!!!!!"

—Inge Heckel

"Crowley writes with such clarity, pace, and believability. I could easily picture the people, the scenes, and the venues in my mind, as fantastic as some of them were. The story, with its twists and turns, carried me forward totally willingly, and the ending ties in neatly and rewardingly with the beginning. I find myself still thinking about the characters."

—Robert Devens

"OMG! I absolutely loved the book. Great story, wonderful characters, and excellent writing. It's a winner!"

—Cathy Rasenberger

"Reading *The Practical Navigator* is like finding yourself in a riptide—the current is strong, you don't know where it is taking you, and there is no getting away until it lets go of you."

—David Bliss

"Told with wit, style, and cunning, *The Practical Navigator* is as fast-paced as it is unforgettable. Fun yet harrowing, this highly readable thriller sets a direct course for the darkest recesses of the human heart."

—Scott Lasser, author of *Say Nice Things About Detroit*

TO:
HILARY COOPER, A. P. "PETIE" MARVIN,
AND JOAN CROWLEY

Stand, stand at the window
As the tears scald and start.
You shall love your crooked neighbor
With your crooked heart.

—W. H. Auden, "As I Walked Out One Evening"

You can do business with anyone,
but you can only sail with a gentleman.

—J. P. Morgan

Ich bin dein Labyrinth.
(I am your Labyrinth.)

—Friedrich Nietzsche, *Dionysus-Dithyrambs*
(Dionysus to Ariadne, on Naxos.)

CONTENTS

PART I

PROLOGUE

July 1988, Broken Harbor

Harry's death was utterly like him: orderly, decisive, and oddly considerate. He sailed to Maine without telling a soul—left a note saying he was going on a business trip but of course he wasn't. He picked up his boat in Marion and sailed overnight to Broken Island, seven miles off the coast of Maine, near the Canadian border. It's a big boat, over fifty feet, but it has all kinds of gadgets so it wasn't hard for someone like Harry to do it alone. Actually, he wasn't entirely alone. He had stopped at the New York apartment and picked up Gus, the big black Newfoundland, to keep him company on this . . . this journey, I guess.

He got there late in the afternoon, furled the sails, and set the anchor with his usual care. Then he fed the dog and had something himself, down below. Put the dishes in the sink and opened a bottle of wine, which he took up into the cockpit. A very good bottle of wine, but he only had the one glass. It was a sacrament, I imagine; he didn't really drink.

No one was there so I can't tell, but it looks as if Harry sat there for quite a while, with Gus at his side. I see them with great clarity: there is Gus, with his huge head on Harry's lap and Harry calmly looking around, his hands working the thick black fur around Gus's neck and ears. Or I see them both, sitting up now, looking at the beach and that remarkable shoreline, the sun going down over the Cut. It *is* the loveliest place. Then he shuts Gus down below.

One imagines the intimate business of getting Gus down the steps. Harry stands at the bottom of the companionway, and gets his arms around him (a face full of fur, legs every which way; Gus's great face is interested but relaxed: they've done this a hundred times). Then he picks him up, all hundred pounds of him, and gently sets him down on the cabin sole. Sets out some water. Harry put him below because he didn't want him to see. Or more likely, he was afraid the dog would jump in and try to save him, as Newfies are bred to do.

Then, after he had lowered the guardrail on the starboard side, he got the Camden marine operator to call the sheriff, Bud Wilkerson, over in Hanson, and told him what he was about to do. Hung up before Bud could say anything, but wanted him to know so he'd come out and get the dog. Then he put on his commodore's cap—an old-fashioned hat with a small, shiny visor and a narrow crown, the kind worn in the Navy in World War I. Do you remember the photos of Admiral Sims? Like that. That was one of a number of affectations at the Great Arcadia Yacht Club of New York, Boston, and Mount Desert, of which Harry had recently been commodore. That and the pips, the four raised brass-and-enamel symbols of his rank on each epaulet. Then Harry sat down on the gunwale with his back to the water. And blew his brains out.

Here's an interesting thing. Just before he did it, he tied a float to his leg. When he shot himself, his body went over the side, as he intended. Not a drop of blood in the boat. But it floated. So my friend Bud wouldn't have to dive for it when he got there. Imagine thinking of that, in the closing moments of your life.

Well, Harry—my brother, Harry—had a weakness for order. More than a weakness, a passion. He was a subtle man, entirely capable of making his way in a dark and uncertain world. But his great passion was for order. That was the real business of his life: not making an astonishing fortune as a very young man or becoming a cabinet officer, but preserving order. Against the sweet, dark pull of the Labyrinth, as it spins away, under the city, under our lives.

CHAPTER 1

GOD'S LAUGHTER

The seeds of that passion were planted when he was a kid, in our chaotic shingle-pile house by the sea, and they were nurtured secretly, urgently, by Harry in hostile ground. Hostile because our parents were not orderly people. Charming and loving, when at all sober, but not orderly. He shaped his character against a background of drunks making speeches, playful grown-ups falling down at croquet. Lovely manners punctuated with the occasional slap, somewhere upstairs. And screams. Real, flat-out crazy-person screams.

We were a handsome family in decline. We lived in a grand house on Peaches Point in Marblehead, which was in trust so it could not be sold. But there was lawn furniture in the living room, and the gardens running down to the water had gone to jungle. The television was on in the afternoon and there was drinking all day long.

Our mother, Sarah, was very beautiful and had great charm, great style. But she was not useful. As a mother, she was not as useful as the five Newfoundland dogs that ran more or less wild around our house. And they were not useful at all, until Harry took them in hand when he was nine or ten. Housebroke them and made them mind. By the time he was fifteen, he was taking care of all of us, the dogs and me, anyway. He must have had remarkable gifts because we were all pretty well behaved and happy. He tried to take care of our mother, too. Had been trying, desperately, since he was a little boy. But that had not gone so well.

Harry finally gave it up as a bad job when he was sixteen. Suddenly lost patience, I had always supposed, and simply ran away. He told me, much later, that he talked to me about it for a long time the night he left. Explained to me why he had to go and why he couldn't take me with him. It was obvious: he was sixteen and I was six. He promised to come back and get me when he could. Which he did.

When I was sixteen and she was forty-four, our mother died of her excesses. From having been very popular, in a raffish, untidy way, our parents' lives had suddenly gone toxic, after Harry left. They became the kind of people whom one no longer saw. Solitary drinkers, alone and separate in that big house. Some people were surprised that a woman that young and attractive should drink herself to death. I was not surprised. I thought that's exactly what she had in mind. Our father died a year later, in similar circumstances. I don't know what he had in mind. He had been a heavy-drinking absence in our lives for a long, long time.

As a result, neither Harry nor I really knew him. So we were both astonished when, at his interment, there appeared, unannounced, an honor guard of Navy-enlisted men and an officer, in dress blues, with rifles and an American flag. He had won the Navy Cross, among other medals, during the war and the Navy never forgets that one. So, at the end of the service, the officer stepped forward and read the citation describing what our father had done—an act of truly extraordinary bravery and competence. The enlisted men fired their rifles, carefully folded the flag, and gave it to Harry and me. Then they disappeared as mysteriously as they had come. We knew our father had flown a fighter off carriers during the war, but *this*? What was one to make of this? I was merely surprised. Harry wept. *Harry!* That was astonishing.

Harry had been loaned a big sailboat the summer our mother died, and we sailed Down East for a fortnight. To Broken Harbor, actually, among other places. I felt as if I were coming home, not running away, and so it turned out. Those weeks and the months that followed were among the happiest of my life.

In the fall, he sent me away to boarding school. As if he were my father, not my brother. Visited every other weekend. Urged me to row, to write, to work hard. He was very popular with my friends, who thought him wildly romantic. He was more than romantic to me. He was a Hero and a Rescuer. I simply adored him all my life.

I was a bright kid—bright enough for those days, anyway— and Harry sent me to Harvard (where he had gone) and then Harvard Law School. Not the Business School: he saw I would make a lawyer, not a businessman. He was right about that, as so much else. I actually made the *Law Review*, vindicating his instinct. Once I started to practice, Harry and I were more like brothers again. I did a stint in the US Attorney's Office, then joined a big firm. I worked like a lunatic and made partner pretty fast. We assumed, after that, that we would lead orderly lives. We would marry and have children and all that, but we would always be together. And we would never hear another grown-up scream as long as we lived.

Harry and I were almost unnaturally close, like in *The Corsican Brothers*, the Dumas novel about brothers who can feel each other's pain, even when they're hundreds of miles apart. But we were very different, too. He was a Hero and a Rescuer, as I say. I was not. He saw a God-created world, lit with bright colors and certainty. I . . . well, I was a lawyer. The law is not a field for absolutists. It is not a matter of finding the Way, the Truth, and the Light. It is a matter of getting from over here, someplace, to a spot over there . . . lit only by your own intelligence and your adherence to a set of rickety, man-made rules. I confess that I think it a high calling, and I believe in those rickety rules with all my heart. Because I think that's all there is.

The *practical navigator*, Harry used to call me, with a blend of kidding and respect, because I was more practical and cautious than he. It's from the name of a book by a Salem sea captain named Nathaniel Bowditch. It was published in 1802 and instantly became the definitive work on ocean navigation. It stayed that way for the next 150 years. It was still used at the Naval Academy during World War II. Men who could navigate were said to "know their Bowditch." I actually knew my Bowditch, which was an anachronism by the time I learned it, but I liked the idea. Liked the tie to my Salem roots and to a set of rules.

My devotion to the rules was partly a matter of personal taste, but it was also philosophical. I believe that life is mostly a game, which we make up, in the *absence* of Divine Guidance. If that's right, the rules make all the difference, don't they? No rules, no game. Once little kids start running from first base, over the pitcher's mound to third, they're going to lose interest pretty soon, and want to go home. Except for this: There is no God and there is no home, there is only the game. So we better not cheat.

I used to tease Harry about his worldview and especially about his God. "If your God created this relentlessly humorless world, Harry," I once said, "I want no part of Him."

"Humorless?" Harry perked up at that. He only half listened to these rants.

"Yes, Harry. Humor is at the heart of the human condition. And your God has none! Or—if He does—it is so cruel and remote that He and I will never make each other laugh." Pause for effect. "At least, not intentionally."

Harry loved that line, laughed out loud. "You see Him giggling, do you, as He dangles us, spiders over the flame?"

"Of course. He's a psychopath." Harry nodded, considered it. But he still believed. At least until he popped that big black Sig Sauer in his mouth at the end. At that point, who knows?

I have that weapon on the desk beside me as I write, and I confess that a couple of times I have carefully put it in my mouth, to see what it was like. I didn't care for it. And it did not make me think of God.

Bud called me as soon as Harry called him from Broken Harbor, and I set out for Maine at once. Not because there was any hope, just to be there. By the time I got to the little airport in Hanson, Bud was back from Broke, with a heartbroken Gus at his side, waiting by his pickup truck—with the bubble-gum light on the cab and guns in the rear window. He shook his head, unnecessarily. "He's gone, Doc," he said, his voice full of sorrow. We'd become close in the course of the Minot affair.

"Let's go take a look," I said, and we got in the truck.

There's no coroner's office in Hanson so a suicide would normally go to the local jail. But Bud said he couldn't bear the idea of Harry going back in there again, so he just took him home. The way everyone was taken home, in the old days of "laying-out rooms" and "coffin corners." When death was more familiar. Bud wasn't a toucher, but—at the door to his house— he put his big arm around my shoulder, gave me a hug. "Awful damn sorry, Doc. Awful sad."

Harry was lying faceup on Bud's dining room table, with towels wadded around the back of his head, which was pretty bad. Gone, actually; the bullet had been a hollow point. The table was covered with towels, too, because his uniform was still soaking wet. Salt water never dries.

Harry left a note. There were two, in fact. One for his wife, Mimi, and one for me. Mine read:

My Dear Tim:

I love you very much, now as always. My only doubts about this come from the fear that you will somehow blame yourself. Do not, I beg you. There is absolutely nothing more you could have done. You have been superb, through all of this. Through our whole life, in fact. I could not have had a better brother.

You will find that I have left most of my estate to you. Please do not give it away. Get married and have children, perhaps. Lead the best life you can, after all this. I hope you will marry Cassie. Or someone like her, if that doesn't work.

I have more than taken care of Mimi and think she will be all right. But look after her. You need not marry her, as brothers sometimes do, but I care for her a great deal and hope you will keep track, at least until she remarries.

Would you be good enough to take Gus? He was never really Mimi's dog and he will do better with you.

I love you so much.

Harry

I had Harry cremated in his Arcadia uniform. He was no longer a member of the Great Arcadia, to say nothing of being its commodore. But that's all right, he was entitled to that. He was entitled not to go naked into the dark water, like the victim of a sex crime or a murder. Although he was both of those things, as well.

The undertakers didn't like the uniform. They particularly didn't like the half-inch, half-round pips on the epaulets. I think it is like metal in a microwave . . . bad for the oven. But the undertaker had his price and Harry was cremated in his uniform, pips and all. When I got the canister of ashes to pour into the sea out at Broke, there were some hard bits that rattled like stones. There are often bits of bone, I understand. But this was different. These were *the pips*.

My first thought had been to douse Harry's sailboat, *Silver Girl*, with kerosene, put him aboard, and touch her off . . . a Viking funeral. Bud had patted me on the back and said to calm down, we weren't doing that.

So we all went out to Broke in the *Betsy B*, Bud's big lobster boat—Bud, Mimi, and I. And two friends, Frank Butler and Cassie Sears, the "Cassie" Harry referred to in the note. I asked Mimi if she wanted to do it, wanted to put him over the side. But she said, "No," in that little Jackie Kennedy voice of hers, "I can't." So I took her hand in one of mine and, with the other, poured Harry into the sea. The bottom there is sandy, as I well knew, so Harry will turn to sand pretty quick.

But the pips, all melted down and looking like spent bullets, the pips will last a long time. The pips, man. A comic thread in this sad story. A line to make God laugh.

CHAPTER 2

ARCADIA

June, the previous summer, Broken Harbor

It was a little before six in the morning, and I was on the good sloop *Nellie*. There wasn't a cloud in the sky, or in my life, except that Cassie Sears, the tall blond woman tangled up in the naked sheets down below, had made it clear that she was not to be woken up under any circumstances. She was on Montana time, she said, she'd been traveling, and she was not a morning person in any case. Made me crazy, because I am a morning person. I was pretty interested in Cassie and wanted to start our day right now. I was thirty-five and had been dating ferociously forever. But my reaction to Cassie was wonderfully new, because it looked as if she may be the real deal, for which I had been looking, in a desultory way, for such a long time. You never know, of course; it's early days. But I was tentatively moving the furniture around in my head, getting used to the idea that we just *may* be together for the rest of our lives. Had anything like this crossed Cassie's mind? I didn't know but I thought, maybe. She was a remarkably loving woman, even at this early stage, and it was all coming my way. We'd see.

We met two weeks ago, on her dude ranch out in Montana. I had been trying a case in LA, which ended in an early settlement, so I suddenly had a free week on my hands. A colleague knew about this place and suggested we stop. It turned out that I liked the West a lot, and I was blown away by Cassie. By her beauty, her dignity, her easy authority, and by her grace, her remarkable warmth. Oh, and she was almost eerily smart. I am enormously vulnerable to smart women. And a smart, *loving* woman? Oh, yes!

Every move, afoot or on horseback, held my eye, as did her wonderful blond hair—a jumble of short, blond curls that went every which way—the remarkable, honey-colored skin, and the green, hooded eyes. On the second day, she loaned me some of her dead husband's clothes. That felt funny but I took it as a "tell," as they say in poker, that maybe she thought I was all right.

It was odd that a woman of thirty and a remarkable beauty owned and ran an elaborate dude ranch. Ran it herself, too, a lot of the time. Assigned the horses to the guests, with unerring instinct. Showed them how to ride Western, showed a few of them how to rope and tie, the ones who were up for it. And gave them a little taste of how to shoot from a moving horse. They did not try that, just watched in awe as she blew away tin cans with a huge revolver, trotting along, to show it could be done. No one can hit anything with a revolver. And to hit tin cans from a moving horse? *Jesus!*

At the outset, her having the ranch had been an accident of inheritance, I learned. Her husband, who was older, had shot himself, climbing alone over a fence with a loaded rifle a year before. That seems to be a near-occupational hazard for ranchers in that part of the world. Anyhow, she inherited, and instead of selling it, she had made it her life. Partly as a monument to him, she later told me. He had loved it very much, and she was devoted to him. But she loved it, too. She had grown up in the East, had gone to Mount Holyoke for a year. But she went to Montana for a summer, fell in love with the West, and transferred to the University of Montana. Never looked back. Once she fell in love with Don, the older guy, she had settled in as comfortably as if she had been born there. She kept her maiden name but she was a cowgirl now, and she threw the hoolihan. ("I ride Old Paint; I lead Old Dan. I'm goin' to Montana to throw the hoolihan . . ." Like that.)

Toward the end of that week—despite the fact that we had never so much as had a meal alone together, to say nothing of having been intimate—I took a deep breath and asked her to join me on *Nellie* in Maine. "For the summer cruise of the Great Arcadia Yacht Club of New York, Boston, and Mount Desert." I let the full name rumble out, straight-faced. She cocked her head, quizzically.

Then she repeated it, deadpan: "The Great Arcadia Yacht Club of New York, Boston, and Mount Desert?"

"Yes."

"Pretty hot I imagine."

"The queen would have trouble getting into this club."

"Okay."

I didn't quite get it. Okay, what? Did she mean, "Okay," she was actually coming? Surely not. But I had the wit not to ask that. Instead I just said, "Excellent." As if it were settled. "I'll arrange tickets."

Now her smile was warmer. "I've never been to Maine," she said. "Or slept on a boat. Or gone on a fancy yacht club cruise." A pause, then she repeated what I'd just said: "Excellent!" A huge grin this time that filled the room. She had an amazing smile . . . as big as all Montana. Felt good.

A week later, I met her plane at LaGuardia. I never meet planes in New York, believe me, but I met hers. Then we went to my place, downtown; we would drive to Maine in the morning. After settling Cassie into her section of my cozy loft and getting us drinks, I asked if she didn't want to get some rest, we would be getting up early. She said, "Yeah, but we better try this first." I didn't quite get that, either, but it turns out she meant we'd better try making love, see how that was going to go. Pretty blunt girl. I liked that, too.

Making love the first time is almost always electrifying. The wonderful business of having strangers step suddenly out of their daytime manners and their clothes and do these extraordinary things together: panting, thrusting, twisting, and crying out into each other's faces. As if they had suddenly lost their minds and wanted to climb inside each other, at least for a few minutes. I have led an unsheltered life, but I am astonished by that, every time. Such a sweet miracle. At the same time, first-time lovemaking is often bumpy and awkward, too.

Not this trip. It was an easy joy. Slick as glass. Slick as sweat on hard bodies. Hers harder than mine. She was lean and wiry, from her life in the West, throwing the darned old hoolihan. (It's the noose at the end of the lasso, by the way; I looked it up.) She was terrific at it, of course. A great rider, a great roper, and an amazing shot. A Western Star, suddenly risen in my life. *Maybe.* I say *maybe* because she had great reserve, too. Great reserve and great dignity. So it was hard to tell what she really thought.

Except for right then. As we were lying around after making love, she turned and smiled . . . that magical smile again. "This is going to be okay," she said. Meaning the trip, I guessed, not our lives together. But who knows? She was not an ordinary woman and did not move at an ordinary pace. Then she kissed me companionably, rolled over, and went to sleep. She was a terrific sleeper; she was good at everything. I later learned that it was the first time she had been with anyone since her husband's death, so it was a big deal for her, as it was for me. Good. It continued to go well on the long drive to Maine, while she told me about her life in the East and the West, her parents and her sister in Boston, with whom she was still close. I told her about my brother, Harry, and our life together. We continued to talk easily on the good sloop *Nellie*, which she took to with winning enthusiasm. She wandered around on deck in the fading light, that first evening, asked about this and that. But she really got into it when we went down below. Made sense. *Nellie*'s cabin is one of the coziest places on earth. Lots of dark, polished wood and creamy white paint. A surprisingly good galley and an open stove, for cool Maine nights. And a big double bed that pulled out to half fill the cabin, so you could lie side by side and watch the fire. Nice spot. We made love for a long, long time that night, and she was simply amazing. She was so utterly *there*. Such a rare and wonderful gift. But all the coziness of the night wasn't doing me any good this morning. Cassie slept and slept.

I sat at the top of the companionway steps, barefoot, in white pants from yesterday, with a blue denim work shirt and a big blue coffee cup. I hoped I might look appealing, in a "Hello, sailor!" kind of a way, and she'd ask me to join her, if she woke up. But she didn't. At one point she stirred a little, rolled halfway over on her back, and the green frog appeared. She had a green frog tattooed low on her taut, golden belly. I had noticed it before and admired it very much. It turned a darker green when it was wet. I would like to have gone down now and given it a thoughtful lap, see where that led. But I didn't dare; she was a formidable woman.

So I sat there, cradling the hot, blue mug and looking around at the harbor, the day, and the elegant "Squadron" of the Great Arcadia. And at *Nellie*. She was named after the yacht at the beginning of Conrad's *Heart of Darkness*. Four old friends who are going for a summer cruise are moored, in the evening, on the busy Thames at the turn of the last century, waiting for the ebb tide to take them downriver. And Marlow—the narrator and the only one who still "follows the sea"—sits by the mizzenmast (the one near the stern) and says, looking out at teeming London: "And this also has been one of the dark places of the earth." Then on to the Congo and a tale of utter darkness. Well . . .

The scene this morning was the polar opposite of the Thames, that summer in 1900. Broken Island was one of the wildest and most remote places in the country. There was an empty Greek Revival house on the other side of a hill, out of sight. But, apart from that, nothing, except a dilapidated dock and an abandoned stone boathouse on the two-mile beach. Otherwise, it was completely wild and stunningly beautiful. An Arcadia, one could almost say, of the old kind. With nymphs and satyrs in the woods, goats in the fields and, maybe, a god disguised as a bull, walking along the sandy beach. Do you remember the story?

Zeus disguised as a bull, to seduce Europa? He is wonderful looking. Enormous, of course, but as gentle as a dog, mewling and pawing the ground. He has incredibly sweet breath, too, and a group of young girls—led by Europa—is completely charmed by him. They twine flowers in his short, white horns; he rubs his great head against their young bodies. Europa climbs up on his back, the foolish girl. And in a flash, she is gone. He plunges into the waves and heads out to sea while she screams for help to her poor father. Eventually there is a child, Minos, king of Crete . . . half man, half god. Always a tricky business.

It was clear that Cassie was not going to stir for a while, so I decided to go for a row, as I did most mornings. The tender

to *Nellie* was a wooden Whitehall skiff, the kind they used to
have as water taxis off Whitehall Street, on the wild East River,
a hundred years ago. She was long and slender, with a wineglass stern, but wonderfully stable.

I settled onto the sliding seat, got balanced, and took a
hard pull with the long, curved oars. The skiff leapt away. I
rowed for perhaps a half an hour, out to the Tangles, the only
other exit from Broke. The twisty, rock-lined channel was enormously tricky, but it wasn't hard in my skiff; I drew only inches.
Halfway in, I stopped to look around and was astonished to see
a huge motor yacht with a Great Arcadia burgee and the name
Endymion in gold on the stern, in the middle of the one patch
of good water in the Tangles. Someone must have known what
he was doing, to squeeze that puppy in here. And he or his
skipper must have valued his privacy an awful lot.

Back in Broken Harbor, I stopped and stared again. At the glittering fleet, coming to life in the rising mist. At the flagship,
Java, making steam. At the hills, the beach, the granite rocks.
And always the sea, calmed in the island's arms. You may want
to get your bearings in this last, good light. It will be dark soon
enough, and we'll all have to hurry.

CHAPTER 3

JAVA

There were still no signs of life on *Nellie*, so I pulled over to *Java* to see Harry.

The very rich of the late 1800s and early 1900s—Vanderbilts, Morgans, and the like—spent huge amounts on incredibly beautiful steamers. *Java*, launched in 1920, was among the best. She was 190 feet long, with clipper-ship lines, a long, graceful bowsprit, and raked masts for signal flags and the like. When Harry found her, she was resting on a mudbank in Jersey City. When he was done, one old sailor said she was "the most beautiful thing afloat." That was about right.

I stopped halfway to Harry's cabin and went back along to the galley. I'd be waking him up; the least I could do was bring coffee. The galley was the domain of Frank Butler, Harry's cook, occasional private secretary, and friend. Harry was a bit of a collector of odd ducks. None was odder than Frank Butler. Six foot two and thin as a rail, he was imperious, insecure, and a polymath. He was also a wonderful cook.

"Morning, Timmy." Only Harry and Frank called me Timmy. As if the three of us had grown up together, which is about the way Frank saw it.

"Morning, Frank. Mercy! That smells good. What are you making?"

"Croissants," he said, as if cooking croissants were the simplest thing in the world. It is not.

"You know, it's odd, Frank. You're almost always the smartest man in the room, but it's eerie that you can cook, too. How come?"

"Work for my hands," he said, easily, "to calm my tortured mind." Made sense; his mind was tortured and cooking did calm him down. A little.

Frank—like several other lost souls in those days—had been working in a law firm's all-night steno pool when Harry met him. He came in to type a rider, to Harry's dictation. He didn't bring a steno pad, just lugged in this huge electric typewriter, plugged it in, and waited. Harry didn't say anything—didn't ask where the hell his steno pad was—just started dictating. Frank typed as fast as Harry could talk. And the draft was perfect. Nobody knows about that stuff anymore, but it was a remarkable performance, and Harry was impressed. Later, they started to talk. Then he was really impressed.

You know the expression *horse whisperer*? Harry had been a "dog whisperer" as a boy, and it turns out that he was something of a "crazy-person whisperer" when he grew up. He took great pleasure in it, at least if the crazies were brilliant, like Frank. He saw through to their essential humanity, calmed them, and drew remarkable things out of their darkness. He hired Frank as a secretary, but Frank was a little scary for an office. Then Harry had him help around the house and the yard, out in the Hamptons—not a success. Finally, he had the surprising idea that Frank might make a cook, which was exactly right. In fact, he was superb at it. Took lessons, learned everything. With that role in place, they settled down into their real connection, which was an odd but close friendship.

In the early days, Frank made me uneasy. No surprise: it turns out he had actually lived with a pack of feral dogs in Prospect Park, Brooklyn. His "Mowgli phase," he called it; he had read everything. His pronunciation was odd because he never heard educated conversation, but his vocabulary was amazing.

I wolfed down a croissant. "Jesus, that's good, Frank. No wonder Harry's getting portly."

"Fat," Frank said, not looking up from his work. "I despair."

"How did it go last night?" I asked. Cassie and I had left *Java* early. We stayed long enough so that Cassie and Harry had some time together but then left.

"Dreadful," Frank snorted. "Old men, drinking themselves stupid . . . as if they needed to be stupider. And talking repetitious, snotty nonsense until two. I don't know how he does it."

"Mimi still sleeping on the sailboat?" I asked. Harry's wife, Mimi, had been sleeping on their sailboat for a while because she did not crave the company of the yacht-club people who were Harry's friends and who tended to stay up late on *Java*. He said she was.

"Can't fault her for that," I said.

"Mostly she just doesn't want walrus goo on her good clothes." Frank saw the older members of the club as walruses.

"Harry says you did okay out west," Frank changed the subject. He was talking about that trial in LA.

"We did okay. Client's happy."

"Tweedledum this trip?" Frank asked. "Or that fucking Tweedledee?" Frank thought my work lacked moral content.

"Tweedledum, thank God."

"Ah, good. That's a relief. Want to take some stuff up to Harry?"

I said I did and Frank began preparing a tray. "Where's your girl?" he asked.

"Asleep. She's on Montana time."

"You're disgusting," he said. I wasn't sure, but I suspected he assumed that unspeakable sexual acts had gone on all night, and that's why Cassie was still asleep. Frank's grasp of the real world was uncertain and never more so than when it came to the sexual life.

"No jam?" I asked, picking up the tray.

"He's getting fat. You can have some, if you don't give him any."

"That's all right." And I headed out the door, which he held.

"Listen, take a good look at your brother, there's something going on. He's fucked up."

I stopped. "Like what?"

"I dunno. He won't tell me, but something. You ask." I said I would. As I backed out the door, Frank looked uneasy. I wasn't that worried; he was born uneasy.

Harry had a little sitting room, as well as a bedroom, on *Java* and it was perfect: dark, paneled walls, two lovely marine miniatures, brass-bound portholes, and a small porcelain stove in which a steward had already set a fire. I put the tray down on the desk, sat down in one of the little armchairs, and made myself at home. The varnished lattice door into the bedroom was ajar, but I didn't try to be quiet. A few clinks of cup and saucer and Harry began to stir. Then a grunt or two and the sound of covers being thrown back. Harry walked into the little study, a big man in a white terry-cloth robe. Ruddy-faced, blond . . . forty-six, about six foot one. And strikingly handsome. Perhaps twenty pounds overweight at 210, but he carried it effortlessly.

"'Stately, plump Buck Mulligan . . . ,'" I intoned, standing.

"Morning, Timmy." He gave me a hug and a thump. Always the same. Always nice.

"Not plump," he said, pouring himself a glass of orange juice and tossing it off. "Mercy, that's good." And he poured himself another. Perhaps he had been drinking last night.

"I am merely substantial. Which is appropriate for a man of my years." Wonderful voice, one of his major features.

"And your station in life."

"Yes. You, on the other hand"—a pause, as if he was thinking about it—"are too thin." He nodded to himself, satisfied with that pronouncement, and took a croissant. He poked around on the tray. "No jam?" he said.

"Television adds ten pounds," I said. Harry was going to be doing a lot of television soon, if our plans worked out. "Frank said to skip the jam."

"Skip the jam," he said. "*Skip the jam!* This is my last day as the commodore of the Great Arcadia Yacht Club . . ."

". . . of New York, Boston, and Mount Desert . . . ," I finished helpfully.

". . . and I am to have no jam? You go too far."

"I do not, Harry. It's Frank. And he's right. Soon you'll be on TV all the time, and you do not want to be—how shall I put it?—fat!"

"Not fat," he said, pushing the concept away slightly with one hand and popping the rest of the croissant into his mouth with the other. "More like . . ."

"More like fat," I interrupted. "And you will create a bad first impression. And, as you so often lectured me, you only make a first impression once."

"Just the one time?" he asked, concerned.

"Just the one."

"Ah." Harry nodded, defeated. He picked up another croissant and gave it a critical look. "No jam, then."

"No."

He nodded pleasantly, accepted it. Changed the subject. "Why are you here, by the way, and not in the arms of your Amazon lover? Anything wrong?"

"My Amazon lover. I guess you could say that." Harry, like Frank, had an exaggerated view of my love life. He thought I was a hound, which by his standards, I may have been.

"It's a compliment. I'm completely crazy about her. She's different"—he shrugged, probably thinking of Cassie's blond curls and her blunt manners—"but terrific. Best woman I've seen you with." I liked to hear that; I thought so, too. "Anything wrong?" he asked.

"No, she just likes to sleep in."

"Better and better. Marry her."

I grinned. Harry had been trying to get me married for years. "Just do it," he said. "Contrary to what many think, it is not the most important decision in the world." I thought that was so odd that I didn't even try to respond.

"She's terrific," I agreed, "but there are issues."

"There are always issues with you. Marry her. Work on the issues later."

"Like moving to Montana?"

He made a face; that *was* a problem. "She won't come east?"

"Oh, Lord, Harry, I don't know. We're nowhere near talking like that. But I am a little wary . . ."

"You, Timmy, are a very wary chap." All of a sudden he was not joking anymore. "It is your blessing and your curse."

"That is ungrateful," I said, declining to be serious. "It is my wariness that makes me so useful to you. God knows, you're rash enough."

He walked around the back of my chair and began kneading my shoulders. "True," he said, a bit ruefully. "Absolutely true." It was a saving convention of our relationship that we agreed to these roles: I was practical and cautious while Harry was an inspired but reckless plunger who had to be reined in at times, by me, so he wouldn't do something foolish. It gave me a certain heft in our dealings, but it was only partly true. Harry was quick as a cat, sometimes, but he didn't have a foolish bone in his body. Not one. He had not found those hundreds of millions of dollars or whatever he was worth under the Yum Yum tree.

He gave me another thump on the back and stepped away. "I do worry about you. Don't be hurt but you are too wary sometimes. And too thin."

"Ah," I said, latching onto *thin*. "That is correct. And not my fault. Last night, for instance, I ate . . ." We spoke in shorthand so he didn't wait to hear what I'd eaten.

"Yes, but then you stayed up half the night, rolling about and wearing yourself to a frazzle. Then you're up at dawn," he went on, "rowing that damn boat all over. You have to prioritize, for Christ's sake."

"All right, Harry," I sighed. "You're right. I'll marry Cassie when we get back to New York. And we'll get a dog. And I'll put on some weight." I was about Harry's height but weighed 175 . . . not enough, probably.

"What kind of dog, do you think?"

"A Newfie like Gussie?"

"Fine. Does she like to cook?"

"Too soon to tell."

"I'll lend you Frank."

"Mmm. Very handsome of you." I could not imagine a less promising idea.

He stopped and looked out the porthole at the day. "Steve Goldstone called last night," he said finally, not turning around.

"Ah . . ." I was all ears for this. Goldstone was the former CEO of a major bank and now the secretary of the Treasury. He and Harry were as close as such people get, and he was the point man on Harry's efforts to become deputy secretary.

Goldstone wasn't as attentive to us as we sometimes wished, but he was our man. "Any news?"

"Sort of." He gave a little sigh. He was venturing into an unfamiliar area where he had little control, and sometimes it frustrated him. "Goldstone is seeing him at the end of next week." *Him* was the president of the United States.

"Oh, Harry, why didn't you send for me. Pretty definite?"

"Who knows with those people, but, yes."

"That's the best! Do we get to prep him?" I meant, prepare Goldstone, tell him what to say to the president.

Harry thought for a minute, then said, "Nope, he'd resent it."

But we looked at one another for a long moment, thinking it over. Thinking over the risk of offending Goldstone by offering to tell him what to say. And the risk of letting him go in unprepared on the other.

"Not the most gifted man in the Republic," I said, tentatively, testing Harry's resolve.

"You're quite wrong about that," he said, as sharply as he ever let himself be with me. But then he went on gently: "It's just that they don't think the same way you and I do. You have to listen to the music instead of the words, when they're talking."

"You're very poetic this morning, Harry. Or is that just a polite way of saying they're dopes?"

"No," Harry said. "But they aren't easy, are they?"

"Listen," I said, "I'll put together a couple of talking points. You can decide later."

"Thanks. I'm going to go take a rinse," he said. "Will you wait for me?"

"I'll wait by the pilothouse," I said. "We can take a last look at your 'Squadron' together." That's what they called the boats of the Great Arcadia when they went off on a toot like this, *the Squadron.* The usage dated back to the early days of the Royal

Yacht Club when most yachts were basically warships, and warships traveled in squadrons. As a practical matter, Harry would cease to be commodore after the big gala tonight. I was relieved. I was afraid that the yacht club connection made him look like a lightweight to the politicians.

Was it J. P. Marquand who said, "No one cares what happens to a girl on a yacht"? Or maybe Dorothy Parker.

I was leaning on the rail by the pilothouse, looking out at the anchorage, when Harry hurried up, buttoning his elegant, double-breasted uniform and straightening his narrow-brimmed cap.

"You look like the president of Paraguay," I said. He ignored that.

"Listen," he said, "I've got to go down for colors." That meant the ceremonial raising of the American flag at 8:00 a.m. "Could you stick around? There's a meeting of the Race Committee, but it should be over in twenty minutes."

"More on Goldstone?"

"No, something else. Something troubling, as a matter of fact. If I'm not done by eight thirty, would you stick your head in?"

"What in the world could trouble a man like you on a day like this?" I asked.

"Probably nothing." And he hurried off.

On the dot of eight, the brass cannon on the stern boomed out, the American flag was slowly raised, a hundred signal flags were hoisted, and the lovely ship was suddenly "dressed" from stem to stern . . . the little flags bright against the sea and the sky. It was a breathtaking moment. J. P. Marquand wept. Or maybe it was Dorothy Parker.

CHAPTER 4

GEORGE MINOT

"If you don't like our rules, Minot, why don't you get the fuck out of the club!" Peter Osborne, until recently the head of the Race Committee, was red-faced and furious . . . almost panting. The rest of the committee was staring at him, surprised. It was a stunning sight, not just because voices are never raised within the sacred confines of the Great Arcadia but because he was not just shouting, he was beside himself.

"Get out, sir! Get out! Get out! Get out!" He was almost barking like a dog. A dog that has scented some wild creature in the yard, just outside the door. And he was going crazy because no one else could smell it or understand the threat. And this was Peter Osborne behaving like this. Not the most amusing man in the world or the most likable, really. But a solid, Greenwich-based yachtsman and investor. A "decent chap" and a fine sailor who surely knew how to behave. The last person in the world to act like this. Osborne was there—despite having rotated off the committee—because he had actually designed the course and sold the idea to the new chairman. Minot had asked that he be there.

I slipped into the room and sat down by the door, looked at Harry to see what he was going to do. But he wasn't doing anything, just sitting there, looking at Minot. Not concerned or appalled or anything, just . . . interested. Very, very interested. That was almost the weirdest part of the whole business, the fact that Harry was doing nothing.

But not the weirdest thing. The weirdest thing was George Minot himself. As ever. Even though he was just sitting there, absolutely still, almost indifferent, his enormous head tilted forward, staring at Osborne from under his fringe of curly, dark hair, with his tiny black eyes. About forty-five, well over six feet and well set up, with huge shoulders. A bull, contemplating . . . what? I certainly had no idea. I had always been baffled by him and—most of all—by his friendship with Harry. Minot was, inexplicably, Harry's friend and the commodore-elect who would succeed him in a couple of days. Harry's man, it appeared. It was beyond strange.

Not that he wasn't qualified. Minot was a remarkably accomplished and successful man. An uncannily gifted sailor, he was also a hugely successful financier—he was said to be a billionaire—and had been a generous benefactor of the Great Arcadia; in fact he had single-handedly made it the richest yacht club in the world. He also had beautiful if slightly eerie manners. But in a way, I was with poor Osborne on this one: I thought Minot was feral and dangerous. He had that smell on him. And he wasn't just a wild animal out in the yard; he was a wild animal in the house, in among us, and most people didn't seem to realize it. No wonder poor Osborne was barking so frantically. I wanted to give a bit of a yip myself.

"Mr. Osborne," Minot finally said, in his surprisingly high, almost feminine voice, "it is you who cannot live by the rules." The fingers of one huge hand ran up and down the arm of his chair slowly. "Here's what I think we should do." He leaned farther forward now, hunching his shoulders and lowering his head ominously. "I think it might be best if you left this club, and started your own. It would be a nice WASP club, of course. No Greeks or new-money people like me." A little lift of the great shoulders, as if in self-deprecation. "But the members," he went on with soft intensity, "the members would all have to be *cheats*. Like you, sir." And now he sat back in his chair. "Yes," he said. "They would all have to be cheats. That would be their bond. And you, Mr. Osborne, you would be their leader." He sat there, this enormous man, very still now. And the very embodiment of menace.

"Why, you son of a bitch . . . !" Osborne said, genuinely stunned, and he started to get up and come around the room. Minot started to get to his feet, too, and it looked for a moment as if there would be a fight. And that Osborne would be trampled.

At which point Harry stood and, with that extraordinary presence of his, stopped everything cold.

"Gentlemen, thank you for your views." That was a nice way to put it; it was scarcely an exchange of views. "George, I understand your"—he paused—"your concern. And, Peter"—turning to Osborne—"I think it was a bad idea that you urged a change like this on the eve of the Stuyvesant Cup. A very bad idea, actually." Then his voice went hard as he turned to Minot.

"But it wasn't cheating, George. Best take that back." Pause and a shrug, as if the next were just an observation. "Or one of you will have to resign. You, I imagine, George." He said it with just a touch of emphasis. No one thought he was kidding. The notion that Harry would actually see to it that George would be thrown out of the club on the eve of his becoming commodore was astonishing, even after this set-to. It was a nice index of just how powerful Harry was, and how tough he could be.

I thought it was awesome and was proud of him. I half hoped it would come to that and that Minot would go away, but no.

Minot sat for a moment; there was a real change of color as the blood rushed to his already dark face. My sense was that he was dangerously angry. But he was a realist, too, and he reckoned Harry's power to a nicety. He said, in an easy tone, as if it were the most casual thing in the world, "My apologies, Harry. Heat of the moment. Peter, I have no doubt you didn't mean to cheat. I was merely surprised, is all. I withdraw my objections. Of course, it's too late to do it differently. Sorry, Harry. Didn't mean to embarrass you." Considering that he looked as if the top of his head were about to fly off, that was a remarkably graceful performance. Harry was not the only formidable man in the room.

"Peter?" Harry asked.

"Fine, Harry," he barely managed to choke out. "That's fine. I accept, George. Forget it."

Harry waited a moment, then said, "Okay. Thanks, gents. I think that's all we have this morning." Small smile, as if this were just an agenda item. Then, "Tim, would you and George stick around for a minute." With that, the others filed out, and I joined Harry and George at the big table.

"Pretty hot stuff," I said, trying to take things down a notch. George Minot gave me an arch look, amused.

"Yes," he drawled. "The ancient drama of bad character playing itself out. Surprised to see your brother involved, though." Harry looked up sharply, started to speak, and then got up to freshen his coffee. I jerked back in my chair, scarcely believing my ears. I couldn't imagine anyone talking like that to Harry. What the hell was going on?

It was beyond odd that I didn't know more about Harry and Minot, but the fact was that there were a couple of parts of Harry's life that I did not know that much about, and Minot was one of them. Harry's first marriage and the almost-instantaneous divorce was the other. He and Minot dated back to that dark period. I assumed that it was more than a coincidence. Harry, of all people, had gone to pieces after his divorce. Drinking, drugs, and I didn't know what all. I was up in Cambridge, in law school, but a concerned friend called me and I came tearing down. For the only time in his life, Harry wouldn't talk to me and I was frantic.

Then, as suddenly as it had begun, it was over. Mimi came into his life and everything was fine again. Mimi was not exactly my cup of tea. She just wasn't smart enough, for one thing. Or maybe I was jealous of her place in Harry's life. But I was relieved at the change in Harry and grateful to her, too. I returned to my own hectic life as Harry settled into his, with Mimi. Except now George Minot was part of it, and they had some bond that I did not understand. Partly financial, I gathered; they had done at least one huge deal together, early in Harry's career. In the lives of most rich men, there is one deal at the heart of the whole thing; it is called the *whale*. I think that Minot may have been part of the landing of Harry's whale. But, whatever was going on with Harry and Minot, my guess now was that it was something else, not money. And it was important.

Harry sat back down with his coffee. "A couple of things, George," he began, conversationally. "First, I was not 'involved,' as you so unkindly put it. I heard about it for the first time last night. If you had come to me in the first place, instead of calling Osborne a crook in an open meeting, I would have fixed it."

George just looked at Harry, those little black eyes very sleepy now, languid under the heavy brows. "I didn't know you weren't involved."

"You didn't *know*?" Harry said with quick anger. "You didn't know that I wasn't involved in cheating?" Now all the tremendous force of Harry's character was brought to bear again. "You'll want to watch yourself, George," he said. Just those few words but it was very heavy. And sure enough, Minot backed down.

A long hard look and then: "Sorry, Harry. Of course it is inconceivable that you'd be involved. It's just my unfortunate manner. You know I am still finding my way in your . . . your American mores. I come from an older and more brutal culture. Sometimes I get things wrong. Luckily, I have had you, my dear friend, to steer me." Again, he was very graceful, but I didn't think there was a penny's worth of sincerity in what he'd said.

Harry gave him a wintry smile. "You made a grave mistake, George. There are times to be tough in life, but this was not one of them. It would be the work of a moment for a little group to come together over this and force you out. I won't let that happen. But this kind of thing . . ." He paused and gave George a heavy look: "This won't do. I would like you to seek Osborne out, later today, and apologize again, personally. As if you meant it. Do you get that?"

Wow, that was blunt indeed. Deliberately insulting, in fact. But, without a moment's pause, Minot accepted the rebuke. "I do. And I'm terribly sorry, Harry. I'll fix it today."

Harry looked at him for a long moment. Then, "I'd be grateful."

George nodded, then said very easily, "But Osborne is a cheat, you know, and you ought to get rid of him. In your wonderful words, he 'won't do.'"

Harry didn't say anything. With that, George got to his feet. "Was there something else?" There was not and Minot left the room.

Harry sat back down, looked at me.

"Harry, what in the world was this all about?" I asked.

He started to say something else, then shifted gears. "A long downwind finish," he said, casually. "Minot doesn't like the idea of a long downwind finish for the race today."

"A long downwind finish! Are you nuts? This business that almost led to a fistfight and throwing the vice-commodore out of the club, and it's about a long downwind finish? What are you talking about?"

"If you knew the first thing about racing . . ." I didn't. Harry was the racing brother; I was the cruising brother. He started again. "Look, some boats are good upwind, some are good downwind, as you know. The Stuyvesant Cup, like most races up here, is always two-thirds upwind, one-third down. Osborne has laid out a course that's almost two-thirds downwind."

"Who cares?"

"Minot's new *Ariadne* isn't so good downwind. He built her—at great cost—just to win the Stuyvesant Cup, in Maine waters. She's not great downwind. Osborne and I just happen to have new boats that are pretty good downwind. A coincidence"—he shrugged—"but you can see where George is coming from."

"Oh," I said. "That's not so nice."

"Dreadful. And if I'd known . . . Well, Osborne is an idiot. Maybe even a cheat, though I'd be surprised. I would have done something, but Minot got ahead of me."

"You had to back your man or agree he's a cheat?" I said.

"Basically, yes."

"But I got the sense, Harry, that Minot was deliberately picking a fight with you. What in the world is that all about? I thought he was your creature."

"Huh!" Harry grunted. "That is a profound misunderstanding; he is most assuredly not my creature. I met him through sailing, a long time ago, and admired him for that. Back in my single days, we saw each other some . . ." He paused, apparently thinking for a moment. "Saw each other socially. We did one big financial deal together, and I got him into the club. A close call, but he was such a good sailor, I thought it was all right. Beyond that, I have simply been fascinated by him for a long time. He is one of the smartest and ablest men I have ever known. And, maybe, one of the strangest. But he is not my creature. Not even close."

"So how come he's commodore-elect? He looks like a thug."

Harry waited a moment. "He has his little flaws." He smiled at that. "But he has strengths which I think you miss. Sailboat racing is one of the most complicated and interesting sports there is, and George is superb at it."

"Like you," I said.

"No. George Minot is far better than I. And—putting this little contretemps to one side—racing brings out the best in him."

"Do you like him?"

Harry grinned at that. "No, but happily he won't be my problem much longer."

That struck me as so cavalier—to leave the club with a problem like Minot—that I sat down again. "Harry, is something bothering you? Frank says something's wrong."

"Frank is ridiculous."

"Yeah, but is something bothering you? Are you all right?"

He stood up, pulled down the tails of his elegant jacket. "No and yes. No, nothing's bothering me and yes, I'm all right." He put his arm around my shoulder and walked me toward the door.

Then he stopped, as if he had remembered something, and said, "Listen, would you and Cassie be willing to race with us this afternoon?"

That stopped me dead. Racing for Harry was serious business. Friends and family were not casually invited along.

"How come?" I asked.

"Oh, I just want to work on Cassie a little. I liked her so much last night. I want to show her a nice side of our life. Make her more open to coming east. And I'd be grateful."

"Surely not because of this business with Minot?" I said. "The race course?"

"No, no," Harry said. "But I'd appreciate it." That was good enough.

CHAPTER 5

THE MINOTAUR IN MAINE

I stopped in the galley again, on my way back to the skiff, to get some croissants for Cassie. Check in with Frank after the weirdness of the morning. I told him a short version of what had just happened and asked what he made of it. He was chopping something up . . . didn't stop. But, without a moment's hesitation, he said:

"He's the fucking Minotaur, Timmy. Only question is, what is Harry doing, playing with a guy so crazy he thinks he's the fucking Minotaur?"

"The Minotaur?" I said. "That's nuts."

"C'mon, look at him," he said impatiently. "He's twice as big as he oughta be. He carries his fucking shoulders as if he's about to charge. And he's got that little curls-on-the-forehead hairdo and those menacing eyes. Cocksucker thinks he's the Minotaur. It's obvious."

I just stared, nonplussed.

"He calls his sailboat *Ariadne*, for Christ's sake. The Minotaur's half sister and the source of 'Ariadne's thread'? And he calls himself Minot, as the American version of his Greek name. Which is Saganopolis, by the way."

"I assumed he liked sounding like a Boston Minot. You know, Minots Light, out in Boston Harbor?"

"Please! He wouldn't know Minots Light if he had it up his ass!"

I paused for a moment, reluctant to look stupid to Frank, but then I just bit down: "Remind me, who's Ariadne?"

Sure enough, Frank looked disgusted. "The idea that you can graduate from Harvard College and not know the Minotaur . . . the oldest myth in the Western canon. Astonishing."

"Yeah, yeah," I said, "I know but I forget the details. Tell it. *Briefly.*"

Frank had almost no formal education, but he was a polymath and he knew some utterly unexpected things in remarkable detail. Including, apparently, Greek mythology.

"Start with Crete. As you presumably don't know, Crete was the cradle of civilization, the Minoan civilization, a thousand years before the rise of Athens or much of anything else."

"Actually, I do know that. Arthur Evans, the archeologist who found Knossos, the capital."

"Good for you," Frank said, unimpressed. "Anyhow, Poseidon, god of the sea, was the patron of Crete. One day, he sent this amazing white bull to the island, to show his gratitude to the people. It just turned up one day, on the beach, but everyone knew it came from the god. And that it was supposed to be returned to him—sacrificed to him—at once. But the king—who had a hell of a herd of his own—was so dazzled by the white bull that he couldn't bear to give it up. So he pulled a 'merchant's switch.' He hid the enormous bull with his herd and sacrificed some lesser white bull to Poseidon."

"Did the god like that?" I asked, innocently; I was beginning to remember the story.

"No, he did not. And he took a bizarre revenge. He caused the king's wife to fall in love with the bull. She went absolutely batshit and had to have him. Not, like the king, in his herd. But in her body. So she had the great craftsman to gods and kings, Daedalus, create a wooden statue of a cow. A beautiful cow . . . an irresistible cow. And it was hollow."

"Oh, no," I said.

"Oh, yes. The queen crawled into the statue . . . backed in, of course . . . to align her parts with the statue. The bull fucks the statue. *And* the queen, of course. And she *loves* it. Comes back, night after night. Cannot get enough. Until, sure enough, she becomes pregnant."

"With the Minotaur."

"Just so," said Frank. "Which is a problem. The little chap is wonderful looking . . . big and strong. But with the head and horns of a bull."

"Not so easy," I said.

"No. So the king calls good old Daedalus, just as the queen had done. And Daedalus has an idea. 'You can't kill him, because he comes from the god,' Daedalus says to the king. 'And you can't set him to learn architecture or kingship with his brothers, because he's a bull. So, let's tuck him out of sight. Let's build a paddock for him under the city. With a maze, a labyrinth, circling it—so no one blunders in by mistake. And no one can ever get out, if he does get in.' Hard to get in . . . impossible to get out."

"Genius," I said.

"Not exactly, but it was a tough problem; what are you gonna do? Anyhow, that's what they did. It was supposed to be a secret, to hide the queen's shame. But everyone knew. The creature bellowed alarmingly at night, and everyone seemed to know it was the monster and that it was the queen's. One of the midwives must have said something. Anyway, Knossos was a weird place to live, in those days."

"And Ariadne?" I asked.

"Almost there," Frank said. "The king had long been taking tribute from small towns, including then-tiny Athens. The tribute was the pick of the young men and women of the town. They were brought to Knossos where they were taught to leap up and dance on the backs of bulls for festivals and such. 'Bull dancing'—it was like a very athletic but lethal rodeo. A lot of them died in the arena. And the rest were eventually sent down to be eaten by the Minotaur."

"The creature eats people, not grass?"

"It's a myth, Timmy. He can eat whatever the fuck he wants."

"Okay."

"Everything goes sideways when a young man from tiny Athens named Theseus—the king's son—is sent, at his own insistence, to Crete, as part of the levy. He, it turns out, is a hell of a guy, and he becomes a great favorite of the crowds at these bull dances. Including the king's daughter, Ariadne. Who falls hopelessly in love with him."

"A break for Theseus."

"And he needs it," Frank said, "because soon it is going to be his turn to be sent down to the Labyrinth to be eaten by the Minotaur. He begs Ariadne to help him. And she, clever girl, does what the queen and her father before her did: she turns to Daedalus."

"Whose side is he supposed to be on?"

"Hard to say, but she had a lot of charm and he tells her the secret of the Labyrinth. Which is that there is no exit. There are lots of appealing beginnings, but they are all dead ends. Because the only way out is death."

"Like life itself," I said.

"Precisely," Frank said. "Anyhow, Daedalus tells Ariadne that the only thing for Theseus is to go down into the Labyrinth, slay the Minotaur, and *come back up the way he came in*. He tells Ariadne to give Theseus a sword and a thread. The sword to kill her half brother. And the thread, which he is to trail behind himself on the way down, to follow on his way back up."

"Ariadne's thread."

"That's it. One of the most famous metaphors in all literature. And she's one of the most beloved heroines . . . a woman who can send her lover down to the underworld and bring him back again. Huge deal."

"And it worked," I said.

"Yup. Theseus slays the Minotaur and follows Ariadne's thread back from death. Then he grabs Ariadne and the surviving Athenian kids and sails away. In some versions they burn down the city, kill the king and queen. Anyhow, everything's terrific until they stop to rest, on the way home to Athens, on the island of Naxos."

"Now I remember," I said. "There's this opera, *Ariadne auf Naxos*. Long, man; very long. And in German."

"Jesus, you saw the opera and you still don't remember the story? That's pathetic."

"I dozed a little. But I remember that Theseus just up and left her at some point . . . went home without her and there were a bunch of screaming arias from her. All in German, of course."

"Yup, she's heartbroken. And why not, after what she's done for him. But then she catches a break. Dionysus, the god of orgies and a bunch of other cool things, comes along and *he* falls in love with her, too. She must have been quite a girl, 'cause Dionysus got laid a lot. Anyhow, he falls in love, marries her, and he makes her into a goddess."

"And they live happily ever after?" I asked.

"They do, as a matter of fact."

"You know some odd shit, Frank."

"You have no idea."

I thanked him, grabbed a couple of croissants, and hurried back to Cassie. Who at last was up, sipping coffee cheerfully in the cockpit. Glad to dig into the croissants.

"Hey, baby," she said. "Pretty nice out here." I agreed and told her all that had happened and about Frank and the Minotaur story.

She gave me a puzzled little scowl. "Can you really graduate from Harvard and not know the Minotaur story?"

"Fuck you," I said pleasantly.

She smiled again and said, "Okay." And we went down below.

CHAPTER 6

THE RACE

"So where is everybody? I thought this was a race!" Cassie shouted in my ear. She'd lifted up the wet flap of my yellow slicker hat the way you lift up the flap of a dog's ear, to tease him. It was blowing hard. Harry's *Silver Girl* was a fifty-foot racer/cruiser in the Custom Fifties Division, but we were pounding up and down like a skiff. Occasionally, she would drop her sharp nose into a wave and green water would come pouring over the deck toward us. Not scary but starting to get dramatic. And there wasn't another boat in sight.

"The races I know about," Cassie went on, "you see the other guy . . . see how you're doing. Where is everyone? Or where are we?"

"A radical tack," I said wisely, nodding my head.

"Oh," she said, nodding, too. "A radical tack. Excellent . . . Feels good." She furrowed her face and craned her head around at me comically, as if by looking hard she could actually see what in the world I was talking about. Bits of her blond hair were slicked against her tanned face.

"The dumb thing about sailboats," I shouted to her, peeling a wet strand of hair away from her dark lips, "is they can't sail into the wind. You remember that." She nodded dutifully, like a little kid: she remembered that. "So, you zigzag all over the place. There's no track. You come at the mark any old which way. Depending"—I raised an instructional finger—"depending on where you think the wind may shift to. We think"—and I cocked my head at Harry, standing dramatically at the wheel above us—"we think there'll be a big wind shift, so we came way out here. We'll get a 'lift' and go whizzing by everyone."

"And we're the only ones who know this?" she asked, looking around.

"The only ones," I said.

Actually, I didn't think that Harry was doing a radical tack to catch a wind shift. I thought that he was gracefully but deliberately throwing the race. My guess was that he'd been stung by George's accusation and either wanted to win big—which sometimes happens with a radical tack—or lose definitively. He did not want it to be a matter of boat speed, which makes all the difference in a close race.

But, if Harry was throwing the race, it didn't work. The wind actually did shift our way quite a bit . . . just enough to bring us off the downwind leg a few minutes behind the two leaders, Minot and Osborne.

Most of the time, I think yacht racing is numbingly dull—probably because I don't really understand what's going on—but not that day. By the end, the wind was blowing thirty and the gusts were higher. Races are canceled if it's blowing that hard at the start, just to give you an idea. There were ten-foot waves so boats were sluing down the faces, and it was hard to keep the huge, super-light spinnakers full. One boat right behind us—its big spinnaker pulling like a train—suddenly fell off a wave and broached . . . that is, it went over so far that it dipped its sails in the water and took a long, scary time coming back up. The amazing thing about sailboats is that they tip but they don't tip over. But they do fill with water sometimes; that's not so good.

I looked at Cassie to see if that alarmed her. But forget it: Cassie was looking back, grinning. "There's one sucker ain't gonna catch us." She wiggled her eyebrows, Groucho style. Then, to Harry at the wheel, "Can we do it, Harry?"

"Nope." He grinned at her. "Not unless they do something dumb. But we'll have a mighty good view." He pointed with his chin at the two boats, now only a few hundred feet in front of us.

Cassie stood up to see better over the cabin roof. "Wow! They look as if they're gonna crash."

Harry nodded, a little smile on his lips. "They just might, Cassie old girl. They just might." Cassie stood with both hands on the cabin roof, staring through the spray at the boats, closing on each other ahead of us.

"Who wins then?" she shouted.

"Depends," he said. "Pull in that sheet a little, Bobby!" he said as softly as he could in all that wind. Whatever had made him take that radical tack, he was sailing with his usual intensity now. He squinted at the spinnaker and then said to Cassie, "Depends on who has right of way. Come here." Cassie slid back to sit at his side. Then Harry—always staring intently at the sails and the boats just ahead of us—went into all this stuff about how Osborne was on the starboard tack (don't ask), so he had right of way over Minot, who was on the port tack, like us. But of course it was more complicated than that. Minot was a little bit behind, but gaining because he had a better angle to the wind. He had a conflicting right of way to "buoy room." Room enough to get inside the final mark, and Osborne had to give way, if there was an overlap.

"But Osborne can't give way," Harry went on, "or he'll jibe."
"That's bad?"

"It'll be bad for him. He doesn't have time to do it right.
And if it happens by accident, all hell breaks loose. When you
jibe by accident, the wind gets on the wrong side of the mainsail all of a sudden, and the boom goes flying around, a hundred
and eighty degrees in a heartbeat. Maybe snaps the stays. Or
it brains someone. The boat goes out of control. Oops! Look!"

As he spoke, there was a sickening flutter in Osborne's
mainsail and the helmsman quickly veered to the right, toward
Minot. The spinnaker took a nervous dip but didn't collapse.
"That," Harry said, "was close!"

It was. And it got closer. Try to see this:

The wind is blowing like the hammers of hell, the big boats
are pounding up and down in ten-foot seas, and everyone is
shouting. The lead boats are on a thundering collision course
and we're only fifty feet behind . . . the finish line's a couple of
hundred feet away. We're all screaming toward the same buoy
at one end of the line.

"Buoy room!" Minot shouts.

"Starboard tack!" Osborne screams back. "Give way!" They
went on like that for a minute, shouting back and forth.

Now Harry, softer, on our boat: "Stay alert, boys!" Harry is
crouched low at the wheel so he can see under the sails. He's
silently signaling Bobby to keep trimming the chute. He's a big,
happy cat now, out in that howling wind.

The prows of the boats in front of us are slashing up and
down through twenty-foot arcs like battle-axes. Great screens
of spray fly up on either side as they crash down. Minot is closing fast. For both boats, it's a nice question of timing. Or geom-
etry. Or courage.

At the last moment, Minot's *Ariadne* rises up on a huge
wave and Osborne's *Scimitar* lies deep in a trough. *Ariadne*
will cut *Scimitar* in half unless they both bear off. Which, to

the roar of "Jibe-O!" and the cries of the crews, Osborne does. But not Minot. Not for two seconds. At last he pulls over hard and his boat veers right. But not quite in time. The two boats crack into each other, hard. Minot's boat made a long gash along the side of Osborne's *Scimitar*. For a moment they are stuck, like angrily rutting dogs. When the boats do pull apart, both Osborne's and Minot's spinnakers collapse. Harry edges to his left. And slips past them both.

Gun! Puff of smoke!

We win!

Our crew turns to look at him in astonishment. "Jesus, Harry!" "Nice work!" "Wow!" and so on. Harry is grinning, the happiest of all. He loves it. Cassie, too. Our crew knows Harry pretty well but even they are impressed. Then down come our sails, on goes the engine, and it's all over.

"I can't believe it, Harry!" Cassie is saying again. "That is the best thing in the world! You are great! Great!" Harry smiles, looks good. He has always been a graceful winner, Harry. Well, he's had a lot of practice.

Behind us, we can hear the purple-faced shrieks of the horrified Osborne . . . at Minot, at Harry, at the Fates. His face is contorted, and his oaths are ugly, obscene. Minot . . . well, Minot stares at him. Then he swings his boat so it almost touches Osborne's. "Steady, old boy," Minot says, in his high voice and his most sneering manner. "The commodore won't have shrieking, you know. It's not done in this club."

"Fuck you!" Osborne screams, helpless with rage.

CHAPTER 7

THE BALL

Then, without a decent interval for people to gather their wits or bank their rage, it was time for the Cruise Ball, the grand finale to the trip and to Harry's three years as commodore. I was still lolling around but Cassie had taken a shower and now was standing naked in the cabin, utterly fixed on the serious business of getting her blond hair "up" for the ball.

"You look pretty good," I said.

"I'm gonna." She was scowling at the doubtful effect she had just achieved. In the end, her curls had to be clustered and clumped and pinned down in several places with gaudy bar-rettes, of which she had quite a few. I just stood and watched. It was not so much the hair-taming, which was endearing, it was the unheeded twisting and turning of the powerful, lotioned body in the lantern light. The shifting of the small breasts, this way and that. And the darned old frog . . . he was part of it, too.

"What do you say we blow off cocktails?" I asked blandly.

"Nope," she said, not looking away from the mirror. "It's Harry's night; we're gonna be there."

"Just an idea," I said.

"Stop it." Flat, matter-of-fact.

When I got out of the shower a few minutes later, Cassie was dressed in a complicated black dress that swept the floor, with very little cover for her shoulders and bosom.

She put on her rhinestone earrings and turned around.

"How's that?"

"Astonishing," I said. And it was.

"You never asked me what Cassie was short for," she said.

"What?"

"Cassandra!" she said, and she twirled around in the little cabin, her hands over her head. "Ta-da!"

"Your secret self?"

"Yup," she said. "This is the real me. Cassandra, honey! My Nashville name!" She smiled broadly and lit up the little cabin. She was in fact a serious country singer, as I had discovered at her ranch.

"Nashville, huh?" The combination of Nashville and the name did not make a bit of sense to me, but I didn't say so. "And the Cassandra in Troy? You know about her, I suppose?"

"Yup," Cassie said. "I know all that shit. A daughter of Priam, king of Troy, poor sucker. She could see the future, like me. She was the great Truth Teller, only no one believed her. She told them not to bring the Trojan horse inside the gates but they didn't listen."

"You can see the future?"

"Sometimes. But my main gift is seeing the present. Very clearly. You'll want to remember that."

"Nice gift," I agreed, "and I will remember it."

A club launch picked us up and took us to *Java*.

Harry stood in the saloon on *Java*, beaming, the consummate host in his hour of glory. The old steamer was full of flowers, elegantly dressed guests, and white-jacketed stewards, passing drinks. Harry and Mimi were at the center of shifting groups of friends and congratulators. They positively glittered, dominated the room. He was decked out in his well-tailored dress whites, and Mimi—a tall, extraordinarily beautiful blond woman—wore a long white dress and a tiara of tiny white flowers. They looked the way royals are supposed to look and mostly don't.

"My dear Cassie!" Harry's voice was big as he saw us coming across the room . . . He held his arms wide, welcoming. "Cassie, you are . . ." He couldn't come up with words before Cassie hugged him, took his breath away. He hugged her back.

"You are, Harry," she said. "You are the great guy today." She stepped back and looked at his uniform. "And cute as a button!" He laughed, liked it. "And the amazing winner of the great Whadda-ya-call-it Race!" she added.

He lowered his voice. "Wasn't that fun?" he said, delighted, conspiratorial. "Weren't they surprised, those two? And didn't old Osborne squeal?"

"Jerk!" Cassie said, scornfully. "But it was a remarkable day. You should have seen him, Mimi." Mimi smiled, looked sideways at Harry.

"He was good?" she asked innocently.

"Amazing!" Cassie said. "Just amazing." She looked around the room. "Looks like tonight's gonna be pretty amazing, too."

"We have done our simple best," he said. "This is a real Maine night." He began a patter he must have used several times already that evening. "Everything here comes from Maine," he said, although that was manifestly not true. He steered us toward a long table of oysters, clams, and shrimp on beds of shaved ice and seaweed. "Including these sea urchins." He leaned over and gave them a dubious look. "Look nasty, don't they." He stood up. "But the Japs love 'em, and they are from Maine." He was just that much older than I that the word *Japs* didn't grate on his ear.

"And the caviar, Harry?" I asked. There was more caviar than I had ever seen before. Lashings of it in blue five-pound tins.

"Bar Harbor, perhaps?" He made a little face. "I cannot be certain."

"And this"—Harry pointed serenely to rows of Veuve Clicquot champagne bottles on ice, their pleasing, yellow labels peeking out from under white linen—"this was made in Poland Springs, Maine, under license from the Widow Clicquot." We nodded seriously, as if we believed every word, and a steward poured for us.

This was actually the pre-party before the big one on the island itself. There were only sixty or so guests for this part. For most of them, just being on board *Java* was a treat. But Harry added mightily to the effect. He had something warm to say to each one . . . told stories, made them try the sea urchin, and was gallant with the wives. Harry traveled in pretty snappy circles these days—the White House, big money, the arts. But these old sailing friends were peculiarly his people, and he went to a lot of trouble with them. Some were just sailing friends, but a few were much, much more.

Like Sammy Cameron, who came up while Cassie and I were still there. Harry lit up. "Oh, Sammy," he said, "what a pleasure!" and gave him a long hug. Cameron was a short, heavyset man in his early eighties with white hair, thick black brows, and an unmistakable air of authority. And enormous charm. "And Marcie!" He greeted the old gentleman's taller, younger wife with a hug and kiss. Sammy was a Marbleheader like us but mostly he was one of the great figures in Boston banking, philanthropy, and the arts. He was old Boston at its considerable best . . . the soul of integrity, intellectual interest, decency, good manners, the works. And he was the one who, with help from a couple of pals, had quietly taken Harry up when he ran away from home, all those years ago. Helped make him who he was.

"You look ridiculous, Harry," Sammy said pleasantly, looking at the uniform. He was done up in the same rig, of course, with special loops of braid to mark a former commodore. "But not you, Mimi," he said. He reached up a bit to kiss her. "You look stunning." He held her hand a moment, then turned to me: "Evening, Tim. Harry make you wear that costume?"

"He did. Actually had it made for me, so I wouldn't shame him at these events."

"Older brothers, boy. They're a curse, aren't they?" His voice was a bit of a growl, an old guy's voice, but warm and embracing. "This is quite a show you've put on for us, Harry." He straightened and looked around the room.

"All for you, Sammy," Harry said. "And wait till we get to the Richardson house: that's the real show. All for you and Marcie."

Sammy slipped that pleasantry as if it didn't matter to him, but I suspect it did. Harry was like a son to Sammy, who had no children.

We talked, the six of us, for a bit. Sammy went out of his way to charm Cassie, asked if she was one of the hundreds of Boston Searses. "Nope," she said. "Not as a practical matter: we were the church-mouse Searses, from out in the Berkshires."

"Dunno," Sammy said, "those Berkshire Searses were some of what they called 'The River Gods' back in the seventeenth and eighteenth centuries. Made great fortunes, trading down the Connecticut River. Judge Sedgwick, creator of the Sedgwick Pie. It was the frontier, back then, and a terrifying

one, too." Cassie understood all that. "There was a little girl
. . . ," Sammy went on, trying to remember.

"Taken by Indians," Cassie said quickly. "After they slaugh-
tered her family and everyone else. Then they returned her,
theoretically intact." A shrug at that last. "Maybe that's why I
became a cowgirl and went out west"—she smiled—"a chance
to avenge that little girl." It sounded bad but they were both
just fooling around, showing off that they knew some of the
same, old stuff. The Sedgwick Pie? Nice story: it turns out old
Judge Sedgwick arranged the family burial plot with himself at
the center and all the future Sedgwicks to be buried in a circle,
facing inward. So that on Judgment Day, when they all rose up
from the grave, they'd see nothing but other Sedgwicks. I actually know a couple of people who have been baked into that pie.
Hope it works.

"Anyway," Sammy said, conspiratorially, "I suspect they
were the best branch of the family. Certainly the bravest." Such
a graceful man. We could have settled in, but there was a polite
press of people trying to get to him and Harry so we drifted off.

"Good guy," Cassie said.

"Yup. Interesting, isn't it, how quickly one knows that with
some people?"

"Always," she said, seriously. "Always. C'mon, let's go hit
that caviar again."

At some juncture Cassie and I got separated. I was just
starting to look for her when I heard Mimi's high, sharp bark
. . . and saw her throw her head back to laugh. Cassie was
with her and a bunch of men. I smiled at the familiar sound.
I was ambivalent about Mimi, but there were some very good
things about her. Quite apart from the fact that Harry loved
her, which was all that mattered to me. She was the consummate beauty, of course: that was its own reward. And she had
a quirky flair for entertaining, which complemented Harry's
nicely. He was the grown-up and she was more like a kid. A kid

who's been thrown into a grown-up's role for some reason and having a hell of a time. She was a little self-absorbed, which is fair in beauties, but basically she was kind; I got that, too. And she was nuts about Harry. That counted for everything. Our mother had dropped that ball pretty egregiously.

Mimi was heading into her midthirties but she still had a coltish awkwardness that was pleasing, alongside all that beauty. Sometimes a note of near-hilarity would creep into her voice or her laugh that startled and warmed a room. She was an old Boston girl, with all the manners, the deep family ties, and such. But she also had this faintly manic quality. She and Cassie were at the center of a group of men, including George Minot. Everyone was laughing except George. Apparently they were laughing at something he had said. Cassie saw me and held out a hand to come over.

"Counselor," George greeted me. "I congratulate you on your good luck."

"Charm, George," Cassie said quickly. "Luck had nothing to do with it."

Minot nodded and raised his eyebrows, impressed. "Then even warmer congratulations. And I know what I'm talking about; Cassie and I met in Montana a year ago, at her ex-husband's ranch. We stayed with them for a week."

What! Cassie had known Minot before? And that hadn't come up in conversation? That was beyond odd. A tiny amber warning light went on in my head. Not so tiny, actually. I was just the least bit sick for a moment.

"My late husband," she said to me. She seemed curiously tense all of a sudden.

"In a hunting accident," George said, his face quickly becoming appropriately serious.

Cassie shrugged, clearly didn't want to talk about that. "Where's Alex? I saw you were still together."

"Alex?" George said. "She's around."

"I remember that she got around," Cassie said. It was a sharp thing to say, and her face was hard. I was astonished. She not only knew George, she held his girl in angry contempt; what the hell? George just kept smiling. She held his eye for a moment, then said, "We gotta get a drink," and she walked me away.

"What in the world was all that about?" I asked. "And why didn't you say that you knew Minot before?" I did not bear down but she could not have missed that I was very surprised indeed. Surprised and concerned.

She shrugged. "I don't know. Our connection was not a high point in my life." She took a deep breath, seemed to be deciding how much to tell me before she could let it drop. "Fact is, Don took a little shine to Alex. Went through some stuff while George watched. I think the thought was that we might all wind up naked in some kind of a pig-pile, but I didn't want to. Don was a little more open to it. Jumped right in. And paid a little price."

"They seduced your husband! The two of them? My God! What did you do?"

"I left. Took the truck and drove to Butte. When I came back, they were gone."

"Jesus! And your husband? What did he say about it? That's wild."

"It was wild all right. But I don't want to talk about it. Let's get a drink." She was more distant than I had ever seen her; the whole business was extremely odd.

"Wait a sec," I said. "You can't just drop that bomb and walk off. What happened?"

"Not telling," she said over her shoulder, and kept on walking. I waited and watched for a moment and then followed along. That was it. But I didn't like it much. I had been thinking pretty seriously about Cassie, and to have this crop up was upsetting. For example, I thought how very quickly she had agreed to come east to go on this cruise. And I couldn't help but wonder if taking another look at Minot had been the real reason. Not a nice thought. And her manner, during those few minutes we were all together, was curiously cold, unlike anything I had seen from her before. Beyond odd.

Later on, Harry, Mimi, and I were standing alone by the caviar.

Suddenly Mimi said, "Oh look, Tim, George Minot is talking with your lovely girl again." I looked up and there they were, talking intently. "You better rush over before he puts her onto one of his white slavers and ships her down to Rio."

"Is that what he does?" I asked. "I thought there was something a little off about him." I sounded a lot more casual than I felt. Underneath, I was sick with concern.

Cassie spent a surprising amount of time with Minot, but eventually the two of us stood, side by side, in a crowded launch, heading for the Richardson dock. I felt my lovely new dreams slipping away.

"What was that all about?" I asked, over the motor. "You and Minot." I tried to sound casual but I doubt if I fooled her; she was the great seer, after all.

"Chitchat," she said. "If you're toying with the idea of being jealous, forget it. The last man on earth, promise." Then a peck on the lips for me. I wasn't satisfied but that was apparently going to have to do. And, in a moment, the wonder of the next part of the night pretty much swept it away.

You can't see the Richardson house from the harbor, just the derelict dock—which had been patched up—and the stone boathouse off to the left and the path through the deep grass. Tonight, the boathouse was lit from within with kerosene lanterns, so its windows glowed like a jack-o'-lantern. And the path was lined with hundreds of "illuminata," candles set in white paper bags with sand on the bottom to weigh them down; they looked like fireflies in the field. Stewards with trays of champagne greeted us at the dock so we didn't have to trudge all the way up to the house with absolutely nothing to drink. This was Harry's staging, obviously, and it was marvelous.

We were at the head table with Harry, Mimi, and other club dignitaries including George Minot and his companion, Alexis Andrews, the one Cassie had slurred. I'd seen her before but never up close. It is not an overstatement to say I was *stunned*. She was the most seductive woman I had ever seen in my life.

Alex was tall, about five ten, slender, with light brown hair. Her hair was cut short, with almost-shaved sideburns on one side, long on the other. A clinging dress with spaghetti straps and almost no back. She looked like a boy . . . or a very chic model. A Ralph Lauren model, say . . . the kind you'd see in white bell-bottom pants on a glittering 1920s yacht. Strong, gull-wing eyebrows, gray-blue eyes, fit. She was achingly beautiful. And so sensual that you instantly thought, *That woman's a little crazy.* And wanted to know how.

It was a big table, and the flowers blocked Minot and Alex from us. I craned around a little, trying to see Alex, but couldn't. I deliberately dropped my napkin once and leaned down to pick it up and look at her. She caught me and smiled. I literally blushed.

It was a fine dinner, the music was good, and the setting was perfect. But things took a turn, as they so often do, with the speeches. Harry got to his feet and announced that, as a point of personal privilege on this, his last night, he would like to ask that he be the only speaker. "I will be mercifully short," he promised, and everyone laughed. I suspect he just didn't want to be the subject of endless, laudatory remarks; unlike most heroes, he was not vain.

He talked for about five minutes and he was good. He was at his best when he talked about Sammy and a couple of others. His affection for Sammy in particular was so clear that it felt good. Then there was the usual stuff about the cruise, old friends . . . and how wonderful we all were.

Then he stepped off the dock. "Now I would like to say just a few words, this last night of mine, about something that matters very much to me: the importance of Corinthian racing." Oh, Lord, this was going to be dull. "I happen to think that the Corinthian model does a great deal to make this place what it is, and I worry that it is being eroded." (The *Corinthian model* meant all amateurs on racing boats; you couldn't hire pros, even if they were much better. George Minot hated it and skimmed dangerously close to violating the rule. Some of his "friends" were employees of his company; no one thought their principal gifts were in accounting or sales. They were professional sailors, pure and simple, but no one could prove it. The fact that he'd pull such a stunt was part of my impression that he was basically a thug.)

"Clearly we could mount more effective campaigns for the America's Cup and so on, if we turned our backs on it and used professionals. George and I do not agree on this, and it will be up to you all to decide, not me. I just want to put in a word for the notion that what we gain in trophies we may lose in civility." He paused and looked pleasantly at George. "I think of this place as a haven of decency and good manners in a time when people gorge on material goods and individual satisfaction. We are like those monasteries that preserved books in the Dark Ages, only this place is a refuge for decent behavior. Sounds a little stupid, I know, but I really believe that." On that note, he thanked us all again and sat down.

I thought it was a pretty odd talk—cloyingly elitist, for one thing—but this crowd loved it, and they cheered him to the rafters. Harry, of course, was much loved in this room. He could have said anything.

Then George stood and tapped his glass. A few people laughed, good-naturedly, at his presumptuousness. Others fell quickly silent. Harry started to get up but thought better of it.

"Thank you, Harry," George began, with an unmistakable smirk. I remembered, with unease, how furious he had been that morning. "And forgive me, if I add just a few words. You salute the strong voices of the past but none is stronger and more honorable than yours." The words were all right, but he was off, unpleasant.

"And," he went on with a slightly theatrical tone, "a cautionary word about *gorging* in the presence of this great feast"—he gestured around the room in mock awe—"is surely appropriate." Again there was laughter but a little less of it. "You have hoped for various things, Harry. Good things. Old-money things, which is fine. Appropriate. But I hope that I will be tolerated if I spend some new money here and there. And bring an America's Cup home to the Great Arcadia!" His voice rose on that stirring note. There were real cheers from some. He held up his hand. "I know that this is a gentlemen's club and that, sadly, I am not a gentleman." He shrugged at that curiosity and people laughed. "And nowhere is this clearer than in how much I like to win!"

His face went tough at that one. "Harry, I hope you will forgive me if I break some of the old rules. Even as some were broken today." He looked around in innocent surprise when there were some gasps; everyone knew he was talking about the day's race. He raised his glass.

"To Harry," he said to the room, "I owe him so much. We all owe him so much." Then he turned directly to Harry: "I raise my glass to my good friend, Commodore Harry Bigelow." He leaned toward Harry. "And good luck to the past!" With that deliberate rudeness, he raised his glass first to Harry and then to Mimi, and sat down.

There were a few muted cheers from George's particular friends, and polite applause from the rest. I clapped politely and hoped the whole thing would quickly blow over.

Which is just what would have happened if Mimi had not stood up at that point. And hurled her glass of red wine in George's face.

"You contemptible prick!" She leaned across the table with inexplicable fury. Then smashed her glass on the floor. The room was instantly still . . . You could hear Mimi breathing hard. Then she said it again: "You contemptible prick!"

George just smiled at her . . . didn't move. Mimi stood, paralyzed in the silence. Then Harry slowly got to his feet. He calmly walked around to George's chair, knelt beside him with a napkin. And gently began to dab at his face. George closed his eyes and tipped his head back, like a child. "There," Harry said. Patted George on his enormous shoulder. "Much better."

"Thank you, Harry," Minot said softly. And the room burst into wild, spontaneous applause. Soon everyone was standing and clapping and "hear-hear-ing" for Harry. Maybe for Minot. Maybe a few for Mimi. And some in recognition of the fact that Harry had just done something remarkably graceful.

Then Harry went over to Mimi and kissed her on the cheek. He took her by the upper arm and steered her firmly out of the room.

It was quite a night after that. There was a great surge of conversation, chairs were pushed back, people in the back asked what had happened. And some heavy drinking began, the likes of which I had not seen for a long time. The dancing was manic, and there was one fight.

At one point in the confusion, I found myself dancing with Alex Andrews. It was odd: I didn't ask her and she didn't ask me. We just drifted into each other's arms. And there she was, this long, languid girl, with boy's hair on one side in a tiny slip of a dress, smiling.

"Kiss and make up?"

"Huh?"

"For George. For almost ruining the night." I couldn't say anything. "Actually, he didn't ruin the night because your brother was so amazing. You must be proud of him." I liked that. "Anyway, George was a fool and I apologize. But I think we're safely past all that. We're having some people for supper tomorrow. You and Cassie want to come?"

"I'm afraid we're going to hang out with Harry and Mimi," I said without thinking. She nodded, disappointed. We danced in silence for a few minutes and it was oddly electric, the feel of her in my arms . . . her scent. Her close-cropped hair against my cheek. I finally thought I'd better speak before I did something absurd. Like bury my muzzle in the turn of her neck. "Cassie . . . Do you know her well?"

"Yes. Some. And I like her. We were together for almost a week. You could ask her, as a matter of fact." She stepped back a little and gestured. There was Cassie, with someone I didn't know, staring at us hard. I felt as if she had caught us in bed. Alex just smiled and walked away, giving my hand a quick squeeze.

"They wanted us to come for supper tomorrow," I said stupidly, walking over to Cassie.

"Puh-lease!" Cassie snorted. "Don't mess with those two." And she jerked me up against her. We danced and she held me tight, as if I were a little kid and might run out in the road.

"You talked forever with George," I said defensively.

"That's different," she said. Oh. Glad to hear it.

Much later, Cassie and I were lying outside, behind some bushes, in the moonlight. Cassie was on the soft grass, her long dress hiked up to her waist so we could make love. Which we had just done. And now we could smell our bodies and the grass. And the air from the sea. And just a hint of the flowers, fading in the candlelit room behind us. We kissed . . . slid our wet faces against each other . . . coming down. All lovemaking sounds nasty when you write about it . . . a peril we'll face more than once in this curious story. But it wasn't nasty for us. It was magical. And it pulled me back to her. Whatever the story turned out to be with George Minot and Alex in Montana, I had the strong and wonderful sense that she was here for me. And I liked that quite a lot. Which is why the next bit was such an unpleasant surprise.

"So look," she said, pulling my mouth down firmly on hers, talking right into me. "I'm going back to Montana tomorrow."

"What! That's ridiculous. You're here for the week. We have—"

"I know," she cut me off. "I know what we have. And I like it a lot. But remember I told you how I can see stuff?"

"The Cassandra syndrome," I said. "What don't you like?"

"I like everything. I like you, in fact. Quite a lot. But I have this powerful sense that we need to separate for a while, right now. Because we're not going to happen now and we may later." I started to protest again, but she hushed me with a nice kiss. "I am giving up on us now to make us better, later. I'll come back again, I promise. This fall. And you'll see. It's just that you have some things to do first—perhaps with Alex—and so do I. Important things. I can see that clearly, all of a sudden."

"Good grief, that's crazy." Suddenly I stopped and thought for a nanosecond. "Is it about Minot?" I asked. "About you and Minot? And Alex?"

"It's you," she said impatiently. "You're a grazer, Tim. A grazer with women. At least you have been, and you're not quite done. Not done with Alex. Which is fine, but I'm going to wait, until all that is over. I see stuff; sorry."

"Grazer?! My God, Cassie! All men are *grazers*, for Christ's sake, and a lot of women, too. You can't leave on that account. C'mon!"

"Sorry, but I saw you with Alex, and it just hit me: 'he's not quite done.'"

"Alex!" I protested. "That's ridiculous." And so on. But she had made up her mind. And I was surprised to realize just how upset I was. Not because I was going to be alone for a while, but because I liked her quite a lot. *Quite* a lot. I also thought the whole thing sounded odd—as if there were more to it—and I didn't like that.

But then this shameful bit: I realized that, as upset as I was, she was partly right. And I was just the least bit excited at the notion that, somehow or other, I just might bump into Alex again, during the interim. Cassie, as if she had read my mind, shoved me off her onto the grass and said, "You idiot!"

The night was mostly over, but before we went down to the float to get a ride back, we went into the house to pick up our stuff and saw a remarkable thing. Alex and Theo Soros—Minot's business partner whom I had met a couple of times and thought of as the bumbling, timid accountant—were alone with the band in the big room, dancing. Alex looked the same as before: dreamy and beautiful, what you'd expect. But Soros was transformed. The few times I had seen him, he had been in dull clothes and moved awkwardly, with what I literally thought might be a club foot. Now, he had taken off his jacket to reveal a striking silk shirt. And he was one of the most remarkable dancers I had ever seen. He leaned, he twirled . . . his small feet flew in elegant black pumps. At one point he threw her up in the air in a spin, the way skaters do. Caught her and swirled her away again. It was astonishing. And it was perfectly clear that they were lovers. I found that astonishing, too.

I turned to look at Cassie, see what she made of it. "Bull dancers," she snorted, her eyes narrow. Before I could ask, there was a stir of people heading for the next launch and we moved out. I took a last, curious look over my shoulder and asked Cassie: "So, does she go home with him?"

"No, no. No way. It's not like that. I learned way too much about Minot and his life—and especially his man, Theo—out west. Minot was obsessing about him for some reason, even though he wasn't there. Maybe he sensed what you and I just saw. But Minot stressed that Theo is the poorest of poor relations . . . an indentured servant, really, from a tiny town in northern Greece. A distant relative more or less 'gave' him to Minot. Who discovered how bright he was and sent him off to a series of good schools. First in Greece and then in America. Theo was one of his great 'successes,' apparently. But Minot stressed that he, Minot, still owns him."

"He sure doesn't dance as if Minot owns him. Suppose he got confused in the New World, thought he was just as good as anybody? Took Alex to himself?"

"Minot would kill him."

"Do he and Alex know that?"

"Oh, yes." She nodded. Then said it again. "Oh, yes."

CHAPTER 8

FOG

I woke up around ten the next morning and felt pretty good. A little fluffy and vague from all that booze but surprisingly good. I remembered immediately about Mimi and the wine-throwing, but what had seemed so dreadful last night didn't seem so bad in the morning. I'd check in later. But in that same instant, I had a sinking recollection of the talk with Cassie and the fact that she was leaving. I looked around and she was not in the cabin. Good grief, surely she had not managed to take off already. I stuck my head up the companionway, and there she was, sitting naked in the cockpit, sipping a cup of coffee.

In this incredible fog.

Fog is the state color in Maine, but this was different . . . much thicker than I'd ever seen. And warm, which never happens. It was also wet. Fog is always wet.

"What?" I said stupidly, looking around at the grayness, nothing visible. Not a boat, not a bird. Nothing.

"Hi," she said. Then, gesturing in all directions, "How about this?" A little smile; she liked it. My guess was that she liked something new and weird, and this was plenty weird.

"Come sit," she said, patting the seat beside her. I did, and the moment our thighs touched a shock ran through us and we were into each other. We made love, ferociously, right on the wet, plastic seats in the open cockpit. At one point we managed to tumble down below . . . get in the big bed. And begin again. It was something.

When we rested, she smiled at me and said, "It's the fog, babe. Some special fog they got up here. How do you like it?"

"Like it," I said, "I am nuts about it. Talk about a boon to tourism." Pause. "Say, do you think we could try that again?"

She laughed and said, "Nope. Gotta get going. If I roll around with you anymore, it may sap my resolve. And I do have resolve, as you'll probably learn."

"I want to learn everything about you," I said. "Don't go."

"Prettily put," she said, "but I have to. I'm going now, so there'll be more for us later." The words were light but her manner was serious. She obviously meant it. The whole business was incomprehensible to me. I mean, we had really connected. Physically, emotionally . . . the works. And here she was, taking off. Because of some perceived threat that I might get caught up with Alex. It didn't make any sense and I didn't totally believe it.

"Tell me a little more about this decision to leave," I said at one point.

"Nope," she said. "There's nothing more to say. It's just the old thing: I see stuff. And now I see this."

"And you're just going to leave?" I said.

She stopped at that, sat down on the bunk, and pulled me down beside her. "Cut me some slack here, Tim," she said very seriously. "I know it doesn't make any sense to you, but it does to me. It's what I have to do. I'll—I don't know—I'll make it up to you somehow. But"—and now she drew herself up with great dignity, great force—"for now I have to leave. I am all but certain that we'll get together again."

"What if we don't?" I said.

She looked down, apparently sad but not deterred. "Then I'll have made a terrible mistake, and I'll be sorry."

I just shrugged, helpless. Cassie finished packing and said, "So, how do we get out of here, in this fog?"

I put on some clothes and got out a set of paper charts, parallel bars and so on, the principal tools for coastal navigation for almost everyone, in the 1980s. That plus the electronic Loran system, which didn't work up here. She looked over my shoulder while I laid out some simple courses. First from where we were anchored to the Cut. And then from the Cut, the seven miles to Hanson Harbor. On a clear day, it would have been easy; you wouldn't have needed to set a course. But in this fog, it was tricky. It made a difference if you had GPS or "Global Positioning System" gadgetry—brand new in those days—which I did. GPS was rare then, as I say, but I had had a very fancy one installed on *Nellie* that winter, at shocking expense. It cost a fortune and was huge. There was one on *Java*, too, the only other one in the Squadron, as far as I knew.

I showed it to Cassie. "That," I said, pointing to the screen, "is an actual government chart of where we are, here on Broke. You can zoom in"—which I did—"and the screen covers only a few hundred yards. Or zoom out . . . and show the whole North Atlantic." I zoomed back in. "That's Hanson Harbor over there, where we're going. And that's us, here in Broke." There was a little sailboat symbol marking our place in the harbor. "These are our courses, in degrees for the compass."

"Neat!" Cassie said. "And that'll take us there? Even though we can't see?"

"Yup. That and radar." I turned on the radar and showed her how that worked. Then we set out. We crawled through the

Squadron; the radar didn't really work in a crowd of boats like that. But I speeded up, once we were through the Cut.

Halfway across, we picked up another boat on the radar. It was a tiny blip that turned out to be a kid pulling pots in a big dory with an outboard. We were almost on him before we could actually see anything, but we pulled up alongside. I felt comradely, as if we were fellow adventurers out in this amazing fog, and ought to speak to one another. I asked if I could buy a lobster for my supper. Maybe make Cassie feel bad about leaving.

"Two pounds be good?" he said, in a thick Maine accent. I said it would and he dug around in his storage tank. I asked how he found his own pots in this weather. He had nothing but a radio, a compass, and a cheap depth finder.

"Oh, I don't fuss with that," he drawled. "Just grab any old pots when it's foggy. It don't matter." I laughed but it wasn't true; no one touches anyone else's pots, ever. I asked again. "Take too long to tell ya," he said. "Just *know* is all. Currents and the bottom an' such. Know where I been, o' course. And hell, I put 'em out; I *guess* I know where they're at." I guess he did.

Back underway, I started telling Cassie about the Grand Banks fishermen of the 1800s . . . how they sailed these waters, and far beyond, with no engines, no radar, no nothing but a compass and a lead line to test the depth. "And they did it all year round, too," I said. "In fog or winter gales, the guy with the lead line—that's a chunk of lead on a long line—would throw it continuously so he could tell the skipper how deep the water was. And a lot of times, they'd put tallow in a hollow in the lead so that stuff from the bottom would stick to it. Sand or mud or whatever. Tell 'em about the bottom."

"You know a lot of strange stuff," Cassie said.

"Uh-huh. The thing is, they knew the bottom so well they could look at that mud or sand or whatever—and the depth—and have a pretty good idea of where they were."

"Wow," she said, not impressed.

"You try it," I said, a little hurt. "It's trickier than you'd think."

"And you're the great guy, right?" she said.

"That's exactly right." I smiled. "And then there's 'potato navigation.' I dare say you'd like to hear about that?"

"I would," she said flat-toned, uninterested. "I would very much."

"Well, with potato navigation you go up on the bow of the boat with a sack of potatoes. Every minute or so, you throw a potato as hard as you can, up ahead, into the fog."

"Y-e-s-s," she said, waiting for it.

"When you throw a potato and you don't hear a splash, you turn the boat around real quick. 'Cause the potato's landed on the rocks."

She laughed in spite of herself. "Potato navigation. Good. You get pretty salty after a couple of days up here, don't you?"

"You could say that," I agreed. "I'm a salty old boy when I get away from the law for a while." I was beginning to speak with a slight Maine accent; it would get worse the longer I stayed. It happens every time.

We hit the entrance to the harbor right on the button, which was a small triumph, in that horrendous fog. I picked up a mooring and rowed us ashore, tied up and took her bags up the ramp. We went looking for her taxi in the fog. We couldn't see the houses any better than we had seen the boats, and there wasn't a soul around, since it was Sunday. Finally, in front of the big stone courthouse, I found a public phone and called the cab company. The woman on the phone said, "Lester ain't but a block from where you're standin'. Don'tcha take a goddamn step; he'll be right over. But I tell ya, you ain't doin' much flyin' today, that's a fact."

I repeated that to Cassie and suggested we get back in the boat, stay another day or two. She said no, she'd rent a car and drive to Boston. We had a long hug, at the door of the taxi. And then she was gone.

Back on *Nellie*, I was sad but only for a bit. I made myself a drink, cooked the lobster, and had a hell of a meal. That cheered me up, shallow creature that I am. I read for a bit and fell asleep pretty early. Slept the sleep of the just.

Which is good, because around three thirty that morning, I was wakened by someone tapping on the side of the boat and saying, with mounting urgency, "Tim, wake up!"

CHAPTER 9

LITTLE BILLY COLLINS

Billy Collins had a berth that night on *Java* and he was desperate to get back to it. Not one of the master cabins, you know, but a cabin just the same, and that was quite an honor for a guy like Billy. He had it for a number of reasons, including the facts that he wasn't a bad sailor himself, that his father was a genuinely nice man, and that his great-grandfather had been a partner of J. P. Morgan. That last one had done the trick.

Billy had gotten drunk on his own. He had made love to Sally Pringle on his own, too, if that's the term for a union consummated on the wet sidewall of an inflatable dinghy, tethered twenty feet off a sailboat in the middle of the night. It was slippery and difficult work, but Sally was terribly sick of old Ted—her husband who was passed out, back on the sailboat—and Billy was terribly keen. Together, they had managed. When they were done, Billy pulled the dinghy back to the sailboat, and put Sally back aboard. She went to bed, Billy headed off into the fog, and old Ted stayed right where he was. Billy was absolutely delighted with himself.

But half an hour later, Billy was hopelessly lost in the fog, the sexual starch was gone right out of him, and all he wanted in life was to find *Java* and go to bed. Then, quite by chance, the side of the steamer loomed suddenly out of the fog, and simultaneously, Billy's dinghy plowed into the service float. Billy almost went overboard, but he managed to lunge up and grab hold of a cleat. Then, ignoring protocol (members do not use the portside float; that's for the men working the boat), he clamored out and tied up his dinghy. He was heading for the gangway when he saw something odd.

The fog was so thick he almost missed it, but there were two other dinghies. And there was a bundle—actually a sleeping man—lying in the bottom of one of them. His butt was stuck under the seat and one bare foot hung over the side.

Billy felt a surge of sympathy for what he took to be a fellow drunk, and he stepped into the black inflatable without a moment's thought. The brotherhood of drunken men is an ancient and honorable one, and Billy felt good—a little superior but good—as he wrestled the poor fellow out from under the seat where he'd partially gotten himself stuck and turned him over.

"Come on, old boy," he said cheerfully. "No good sleeping out here in the fog." Then he noticed some funny things. First, the man he held in his arms was George Minot, commodore-elect of the Great Arcadia and not much of a drinker. Next, the body didn't feel quite right, and it smelled funny. Then Billy saw something astonishing. Someone had taken two of the pips from one of his epaulets, and stuck them to George's forehead. Billy thought for a second that they had been pasted on somehow as a gag, and he curiously lifted one off. But that wasn't it.

Somebody had punched a hole in George's forehead, and the pip was just "stuck in the goo," as he later put it. Billy said, "Uh-oh," and carefully put it back. Then he jammed Minot partway under the seat, the way he'd found him, and ran up the slippery gangway for help. Ran straight to Harry's cabin, as a matter of fact. He didn't think about it one way or the other, but clearly this was serious business: One told a grown-up. One told Harry.

Harry had sent the rear commodore, Bobby Jones, to get me; he was the one tapping on the side and telling me to wake up. By the time we got to *Java*, there were some lights on, and Harry was waiting at the top of the gangway along with several others. Harry looked somber . . . in command; Collins looked like a drunk at the scene of an accident, and the doctor looked matter-of-fact. All in their regular roles, in other words.

Harry put a hand on my shoulder. "Bobby told you?"

"Minot's been killed."

"Yup. Come take a look." He had a portable searchlight in one hand, and he led the way.

"You call the police?"

"The sheriff . . . yes. Be here in"—he looked at his watch—"pretty soon now, if he can find us. A guy named Bud Wilkerson. Met him last spring. Good guy." I grunted and we walked around the stern, under the scalloped canopy, to the service float. Harry and I walked carefully down the wet ramp onto the work float, vague in the fog.

Harry flicked on the powerful light and shone it on the body. George Minot, in his uniform without his cap, lay oddly twisted on the dinghy floor, partly under the seat. His face was side-down on the greasy floorboards and his eyes were looking into the crack. The whole thing was . . . well, astonishing. I of course knew he was going to be there, but even so, the sight of him was difficult to assimilate.

Here is a very odd thing. Standing there, looking down at Minot, I flashed powerfully back to a scene from my childhood, back in Marblehead when we found an enormous buck, dead, at the bottom of our empty swimming pool. It was one of the strongest memories of my childhood and it came rushing back to me, in the midst of this bizarre scene. Harry and I had been the ones to get it out—towed it with a truck, out to the road. So, was dead Minot like that deer? Were Harry and I going to tow his body off to the dump? I had no idea, but the image gave me the shivers. I didn't mention it to Harry; it was too strange.

There was something shiny stuck to Minot's head. "A pip?" I asked, turning to Harry. "Jesus, is that a pip stuck to his forehead?"

"Yup. One on each side," he said. "Right where his horns should be."

"Good grief, Harry, don't joke." Pause. "Frank's been talking to you? His theory about Minot thinking he's the Minotaur?"

"He may be right this time."

"Murdered, obviously," I said.

"Safe guess." Harry gave a wintry smile. "There are two bullet holes. The pips were put in after. The doc took a look."

"Why would anyone—?"

"Who knows, for Christ's sake?" Harry interrupted. He rarely swore, but he must have been shaken by this. Made sense.

We both stood silent for a moment after that. Then, just for something to say, I asked, "Collins found him?"

"Yup, little Billy Collins. He was coming back drunk from some romp," Harry said. "He saw Minot and assumed he was drunk, too. Got into the dinghy and tried to sober him up, if you please."

"That must have been amusing."

"I imagine. Anyway, he came and woke me up. I grabbed the doctor but Minot had been dead for a while. I sent for you, got Frank to take a look. Frank's eerily smart sometimes, as you know. And then I had 'em call the Coast Guard. They told me to call Wilkerson. Does that make sense to you, by the way . . . that the sheriff would have jurisdiction, not the Coast Guard?"

"Sure. All the old crimes—rape, robbery, murder—they're local. In coastal waters, you call the sheriff."

"Well, that's what we've done," he said, faintly amused. "Listen, I think you should be the point on this. Deal with the sheriff and all. 'Cause I'm going to be a suspect eventually because of Mimi and that wine business. And the pips."

That snapped my head back. "That's nonsense, Harry. No one's going to suspect you in a million years." I was seriously appalled, almost angry, at the absurd notion. "What in the world are you thinking?"

"Maybe, but I think they will and so does Frank. And even if the sheriff and his people don't focus on it, it will be in the tabloids. My chances of being appointed to the Treasury may have already gone down the tubes, with this, but being part of the investigation will help." Part of what he said did strike me as right: this was so bizarre that there was bound to be a ton of press. And everyone around was going to be tarnished. It was bad enough that Harry was the commodore of a yacht club . . . but the commodore of a yacht club where people were murdered and had pins stuck in their foreheads? Not so good.

"My notion," Harry went on, thoughtfully, "is that we try to start a little backfire by making this into another Paragon deal. What do you think?"

"Oh, Harry," I said, truly astonished. "Not in a million years. This is nothing like Paragon, believe me. This is capital murder, for God's sake. I cannot waltz into a murder investigation and take over, the way we did there. Entirely different." In the Paragon affair, the guy who had done the insider trading had laid false trails to several others, including Harry. Harry and I swamped the Enforcement Division of the SEC with cooperation and eventually took the investigation over, as a practical matter. And found the bad guy, too. A little too late for one of the conspirators, who got himself killed, but a major triumph for Harry.

"Of course it's different," Harry said. "But this sheriff's a lobsterman with a few lobsterman deputies, to start with. And even if he were a real professional, he'd need a tremendous amount of help, because the murderer is almost certainly on the cruise. And he's never going to be able to find his way through our people—in the time he has—without a lot of help."

That was true. "You're the logical guy . . . a former assistant in the Southern District and the club law officer." Yacht clubs don't have *law officers*; they don't need 'em. But Harry had made up the position so he could have my company running the club's affairs. "You have an impeccable reputation," Harry went on. "Weren't you on the Ethics Committee of the City Bar Association?" I was. "So you're perfect for a job that someone in the club has to do. It is purely incidental"—he smiled pleasantly—"that I am your brother and may have killed the poor son of a bitch. It's perfect, Tim."

I am not sure why I disliked the idea so much at that early stage, but I did. Harry saw that and said, "Look, Tim, I have not asked you for so many favors in this life . . ." I looked up sharply at that. Harry had never asked for anything.

"Yes?" I said.

"I could use your help."

And that, of course, was that. I gave him a long, somber look, but nodded. "Okay. We'll see how it goes. But this may blow up in our faces."

"Could be," Harry said, easily, now that it was decided. "We'll deal with that when the time comes." Then we heard the sound of a boat in the fog. "That's gotta be our sheriff," Harry said. "Let's get up on deck."

CHAPTER 10

THE SHERIFF

Here's a star turn for you: the sheriff arriving over the water on a foggy night, at the scene of a murder at sea. First there was the muffled throb of the big engine. Then the fuzzy, blue glow of a strobe light. Then the vessel itself, a big white lobster boat, slowly looming out of the fog. Harry was right, the sheriff was a lobsterman. He pulled up to the float fast, the way lobstermen do. Then the hard reverse, the roar of the engine, and the big swirl of water tossing the float. The stern swung in, slick as you please. He certainly knew something about boats. I wondered how he was on murder.

There were two of them, the sheriff at the wheel and a young man leaning out. The younger one tossed us lines and we made them fast. Then a couple of bumpers. That was interesting; not so many lobstermen worry about bumpers. The sheriff stopped his engine, then came over to the side of the boat and looked to see how he was tied up. First things first.

Then, "Gents, I'm Bud Wilkerson. Sheriff over to Hanson."
He was a big, nice-looking man with gray, curly hair, a ruddy
face, and one bad tooth. He was about forty-five and looked as
if he'd been on the water all his life. "That's my boy, Andy. He's
a deputy." Strong Maine accent and a gravelly baritone voice.
"Why don't you fellas tell me who you are and what we got
here?" Then, looking at Harry, "I recognize you, I guess, from
the spring. How ya doin'?"

"Evening, Bud," Harry said. "Not great, I'm afraid. We
met when I was up here planning all this. I'm Harry Bigelow,
and this is the yacht-club cruise I told you about, the Great
Arcadia."

"Yeah, I knew you was here. Meant to come out but it got
away from me. Here I am now, I guess. An' you got a murder."

"Yup, a guy named George Minot. He was the vice-
commodore of the club—the number-two guy and my successor. This"—he pointed at me—"is my brother, Tim Bigelow.
He's a former federal prosecutor and our law officer. If you
need any help navigating your way through our people, he'll be
the one to coordinate things."

Bud looked at us for a moment. Then said, "Uh-huh," and
stepped onto the float. He was dressed in jeans, a heavy plaid
shirt, and rubber boots. And on his hip, the biggest revolver
you ever saw in your life. "All right," he said. "Let's go take a
look at this poor fella." He looked at me again. "You want to lead
the way?" And I did. At the head of the gangway, Wilkerson
told everyone else to wait on deck. "Except you," he said to me.
"What's your name again?" I told him, and down we went.

I held Harry's searchlight and Wilkerson stared at Minot
for a long, silent moment. "What's that thing on his forehead?"
he asked at last.

"A pip," I said, and explained what it was.

"Jesus Christ," he muttered with disgust. "An' it's just
pounded into his skull like that?"

"No." I explained how the doctor had taken a quick look. Lifted one of the pips out. And found what was probably a small-caliber bullet hole. "The pips were just stuck in the holes after, he thinks."

"Sweet," Wilkerson grumbled. "And there's two of 'em . . . one on each side?"

"Yup. But the doc only looked under one. Before he came to his wits and remembered he was at a crime scene."

"Good for him," Wilkerson said, dryly. "Call him down here, would ya? And my boy, Andy. Get him now, but not the others." Bud went back to staring.

The doctor came down and repeated what he'd told us before. Then Bud carefully stepped into the inflatable. "This ain't gonna be like TV, ya know," he said. "We ain't got yellow tape and all that horseshit. But we'll try not to bugger things up any worse 'n we have to."

Wilkerson touched Minot's face with the back of his hand. Then he reached over and touched the outboard motor the same way. Then, to my surprise, he leaned forward and actually took a sniff of the face. "What's that smell, Doc, you know?" he asked Jeffery.

"No. I smelled it, too, but I don't know. Kind of musky . . . maybe lotion, maybe some kind of dope. It's not any poison I know about, if that's what you're thinking. Not that I'd recognize so many." Bud sniffed again, shook his head. Then he looked carefully along the oily bottom of the inflatable. He took the painter in his hand and felt it in a couple of places.

"Tell me again, Doc, when you first seen the body?" Bud asked.

"Two a.m. He'd been dead for two hours, give or take a half hour."

"Have to be a specialist to know that kinda shit, or is that pretty good?" Bud asked.

"Pretty good." He was obviously uncomfortable. "But I'm no specialist."

"So, he's murdered at midnight or a little before or after . . . somewhere in there."

"Maybe a half hour off but yes, give or take."

"Coulda been eleven?" Bud asked.

"Shit, Sheriff, I can't be precise. But, sure. I'd say later but maybe. A real forensics guy could do better."

"We ain't got a real forensics guy," Bud said. Then he got back onto the float and stood looking down at Minot. He told his son to take a roll of pictures, which he began to do with a flash camera that didn't look very expensive.

"You fellas know whose dinghy this is?" Bud asked.

"Minot's," I said. "Actually, it's off his tender, *Celene*. That's the cabin cruiser. They got a big, cruising sailboat, too, called *Ariadne* but they mostly sleep on the cruiser, he and his girl. And his partner, a man named Theo Soros. The tender is actually in his name, Soros's. The rest of the crew sleeps on the sailboat. They're moored on the other side of the Squadron, out toward the Tangles." Harry had told me all that when I asked him the same question.

"We'll go see them right quick." Bud walked over to the other two dinghies and touched their motors. "And these two?"

"That one belongs to the club," I said. "It's normally on this float. The other one belongs to Collins, the fellow who found him."

"That's the one that's warm," Bud said. "Makes sense, I guess."

Bud told Andy to put down a marker buoy where the Minot dinghy was: "So's we can look around if we have to."

"How much water are we in here?" I asked without thinking.

"Thirty foot, low tide, say thirty-five right now," Bud said at once. I suppose it was the kind of thing he'd know.

"You think he could have been killed right here?" the doctor asked. "At the float?"

"Who the hell knows," Bud said. "Any o' you hear shots?"

"None of us that're here," Harry said. "Maybe someone else."

"Maybe we'll find some shell casings down there. More likely, he was shot somewheres else and towed over here. The painter's wet and the engine's stone cold. Not that that tells ya so damn much." He looked around at the fog. "How many boats is out there?" he asked me.

"Hundred, hundred and twenty boats . . . and about five hundred people," I said.

"Jesus Christ."

"Actually," Harry said, "that overstates it a little. A few boats—maybe a dozen—already took off."

When his son was finished taking pictures, Bud said, "All right, Andy. Let's set him on the float." He told his son to stay on the float and he got back in the dinghy. He reached under Minot almost tenderly.

"Sorry, old fella," he said as he picked him up. "Take care, Andy. See nothin' drops out of his pockets. Or off his head. What d'ya call them things again?" he asked.

"Pips," I said. Bud and Andy set Minot down on his back on the float and I focused the searchlight on him.

"Well, my Jesus! Will you look at that!" Bud murmured as we all stared. One side of Minot's face was smeared with oil from the bottom of the inflatable as was his elegant uniform. We could see the two pips clearly now; they were perfectly placed on either temple. And there was a third pip through one earlobe. But that's not what Bud was talking about. He was talking about Minot's dark, uncircumcised cock, which was lolling, enormous, out of his trousers. It was tumescent and huge . . . unnatural. And through the uncircumcised foreskin there had been placed a fourth pip. As if, in death, he had been promoted to the rank of full commodore. In the Great Arcadia Yacht Club of New York, Boston, and Mount Desert.

After we'd all stared for a while, Bud knelt down and poked around the body a little. Then he stood up, told the doc to stay on the float to make sure the body didn't roll overboard in a swell, and said the rest of us should sit for a minute . . . talk about what to do next. We went up to the Race Committee room, Harry, Bud, Andy, and I. We were a solemn little group, each shaken in his own way at what we had seen.

"All right," Bud began, "we're gonna take some chances here. 'Cause we ain't got the people or time to do it right." He was looking at Harry. "Want you an' Andy and maybe a couple of your people to search this boat real careful. Look for a droolin' lunatic, o' course, with a smokin' gun. Andy, you take the point, with your gun out, just in case. An' for Christ's sake, be careful. This is a murderer we're talkin' about."

"You and me," he said, turning to me, "we'll go take a look at Minot's powerboat. See where that leads us. Time counts, o' course, so let's get going." He stood up and the two of us headed to the float.

As we walked down the gangway, Bud asked, "You got some idea where this guy's boat is at?"

"Some," I said. "Harry and I had had a look at a chart with one of the launch drivers." I gave him a compass bearing—said it was rough but ought to help. And said the boat was perhaps a thousand yards off. Bud fired up his boat—a deep, guttural throb—and we were off.

We'd barely gotten out of sight of *Java* when Bud suddenly slowed down and took the boat out of gear, as if he had just remembered something. Then he turned the engine off and we just drifted.

"You was a prosecutor, right?" he said, turning to me. That was interesting; we were going to stop and have this little talk, right here in the middle of the harbor.

"I was an assistant US attorney in the Southern District of New York for three years. That's Manhattan. I mostly did financial stuff, but I had one murder and worked closely with the FBI and the NYPD. You'd be much better off with a guy from a state AG's office, but I'll be okay on procedure, and I can ask questions."

"Better'n I coulda hoped," Bud said. Then, "Look, it ain't great, usin' you fellas for law enforcement. You know it's . . ."

"It's odd."

"I guess it's odd," he said. "But we have to do stuff like this up here, sometimes. The court cuts us some slack on conflicts or we couldn't do anything, in a small county like ours." I started to say something but he went right on. "Tomorrow, we'll have state police for a couple of days. They'll do forensics and lend me people up front, but that's it. They'll go away and it's my deal."

Then he shifted gears. "You knew this fella pretty well?" he suddenly asked.

I said I didn't. I'd never seen him except around the club and not often there. Then he asked where I'd been all night. I told him I'd been alone on my boat. And that Cassie, "the girl who came up here with me," had left the day before. "So I don't have an alibi but you're still not going to look like an idiot for using me. It'll be clear that I barely knew him."

"Yup . . . okay. Take your word for it for now. How about your brother? How about old Harry an' Minot?"

I had thought about that and my answer was artful. "They've been friends for a long time," I began. "Harry got him into the club and has supported him to be his successor as commodore. I don't think they saw each other much socially, but they did things in the club and they did some things financially, years ago. As for his maybe killing him, well . . ." I took a deep breath and stopped, as if I had to gather my wits to even consider such a thing. "He and his wife, Mimi, were together all night on the steamer, to begin with. The fella who found Minot's body ran straight to Harry and Mimi's cabin and woke them up. Obviously, you better question him closely yourself, but it's not going to amount to much.

"There is one thing," I went on, as if in an excess of caution. "There was a weird event two nights ago, at the final big dinner of this cruise. There had been a lot of drinking by the time the speeches rolled around. Harry had asked that he be the only one to speak, because it was his last night. But Minot, who had had a drink or two himself, got up and gave a toast to Harry that was maybe a little edgy. A question of whether it was okay to have professional sailors on crews. Not the sort of thing people kill each other about. I doubt if anyone would have noticed much, but Harry's wife was offended for some reason. And maybe a little drunk. She tossed her wine at Minot."

"Jesus."

"Yep, it was odd. But Harry smoothed it over, the way he does. He kneeled down and wiped Minot's face off, apologized. Everyone clapped and that was that."

"Not a big deal?" Bud asked.

"Well, it was awful damned odd, and people will certainly remember it. But murder Minot? Uh, no. Drunken yacht-club stuff at worst."

"Not serious?" Bud said.

"Not serious," I said.

"Doesn't seem exactly like that kind o' fella," Bud said dryly. "And the wife . . . she all right?"

I shrugged, helplessly. "Sure. And she was with Harry all night on a crowded yacht. Unless they did him together on *Java* and the two of 'em humped him along the outside passageway and then down the gangway and into the dinghy. I have a little trouble with that." I risked a dry smile.

"But there's one other thing you'll want to tuck away." I sounded casual but this was heavy. "Harry had a .22 on board at one time. Dunno if it's here now, but you ought to know about that. He got two Ruger revolvers a few years ago to plink at bottles. Gave one to Minot and kept one himself. They sailed together some and they both loved to plink at bottles . . . both good shots and a little competitive. You'll want to find out where they're at." Not great to have to bring this up, but it is always better to get there first with bad facts.

Bud gave me another one of his slow looks, then nodded. "Yup. Good idea." Then, without a pause, "Raise your right hand." I was completely nonplussed at that and didn't move. "Raise your right hand. I'm swearin' you in as deputy."

"Whoa! Bud, I'm anxious to help, but does it really make sense to . . ."

"Yup. We do this a lot up here, so there's at least a show o' havin' a procedure and some clear lines. Judge likes it an' so do I. Raise your right hand."

"I may be too lawyerly but I worry like crazy about future conflicts. Can't I just help out unofficially?"

"Nope. We got our little ways up here. Because of the conflicts. Everyone up here knows everyone else and sometimes it looks as if most of 'em are sleeping together on the side. So raise your right hand. We gotta get goin'." I did as I was told, and Bud administered a little oath he seemed to have made up on the spot.

"All right, old boy, you're a deputy now," he said with a little smile. "And try to remember, your only loyalty is to me and the state of Maine, okay, not to your brother or anyone else. Got it?" He wasn't smiling when he said that last.

"I got it, Bud, but that's just my point. Harry and I are joined at the hip. No one will believe that I'm not thinking about him all the time. It's how we are. We're . . ."

"Yuh, yuh, I seen that. Do the best you can, okay."

I said I would. Then I said there was one other thing we ought to talk about, up front.

"Yeah?" he said, a little impatient to get going.

"Yeah, and I hate it," I said. "It's early days, but the girl who was up here with me—Cassie Sears . . ."

"What about her?"

"Couple of things. I'm not comfortable getting into this but I am very close to her. We only just met. But, for whatever reason, I am blown away by her and think there's a real chance we'll wind up together."

"Congratulations," Bud said, a touch of irony in his voice. "What's that got to do with me?"

"Well, it may be another conflict and I want you to know about it, from the get-go."

Deep breath. "Go ahead."

"I met her for the first time two weeks ago, out at her dude ranch in Montana and invited her east, for this cruise. I was stunned that she accepted but it made some sense: we seemed to connect pretty hard, right away. But I was startled to learn, after we had been here a couple of days, that she and her late husband knew Minot. He'd been to their place out west."

"Oh, boy."

"That's right. And on the night of the dance she and Minot talked quite a lot. Later that night, she told me that she was crazy about me, just as I'd hoped. *But*, she said she was leaving. The next day. To go back to Montana."

"How come?"

"She implied that we were falling for one another but that she could see I still had some wild oats to sow. So she was leaving me to it and we'd get together in the fall . . . see where we stood."

"That sounds awful damn dumb. D'you believe it?"

"No. Well, sort of. Because I want to so bad. But if I were *you*, I would check hard to make sure she got to Boston the night before the murder. And flew to Montana the next morning. And I'd check pretty close, too. Can you do that? Oh, and by the way, you might check to see if she stopped at Just Barb's, that lobster place down in Searsport. I suggested it to her. She may not have stopped, but if she did . . ."

He just stared at me for a long moment, then said: "So let's see what we got here: Your brother has a dustup with the dead guy, the night of the murder. His wife throws a glass of wine in his face. Your brother's got a gun out there somewhere, which we probably oughta find pretty soon. And now your girlfriend turns out to know Minot pretty well . . . maybe came east mostly to see him. She talks to him a lot. The next day, she goes tearing out of town. That's the night of the murder. 'Cause you got some wild oats to sow or some nonsense. Have I got this right so far?"

"Perfect." I grinned.

"Uh-huh. Got anything else to tell me, 'up front'?"

"Nope. Other than that, we're clean as a hound's tooth. You got a way to check her alibi? So I don't go marrying a murderess some day?"

He just kept on staring at me. Then nodded. "Yeah, we can do that."

"Good. And if you feel free to tell me the result, I'd be grateful."

"I'll bet you would. You really going to marry her?"

"I think so. She's an astonishingly good woman. But maybe not, if she's a murderer."

"Makes sense, I guess. Gotta draw the line somewheres. *Jesus!*" Then he started the big lobster boat up again, headed off into the fog. It was as thick as ever. Maybe a little thicker.

CHAPTER 11

INTERVIEWS

It took a while to find *Celene*. When we did, Minot's man, Theo Soros, was standing in the stern, fully dressed. He was shaved, too, and his black hair was slicked down with some kind of oil as it had been at the dance. It was five in the morning. He did not look—or carry himself—like the lame bookkeeper I thought I'd seen in the past . . . no, no, no.

"Good morning, Counselor. What's up?"

Then, to the sheriff, "Jesus, that's quite a gun. Something wrong?"

"I'm Bud Wilkerson," Bud said flatly. "Sheriff o' Hanson County, an' Bigelow's been sworn in as a deputy, helpin' me out. We're investigatin' an incident. Who's on board?"

"Just me," Soros said. "What incident?"

"Somethin's happened to your partner, Minot," Wilkerson said. "Can we come aboard?"

Soros's eyes widened at that and he went quiet for a second. "Yeah, come on. Is he all right?"

"No, he ain't," Bud said. "When did you see him last?"

Now Soros looked scared, or at least intense. "Six o'clock last night. We better go inside."

He led us into the cabin and he sat down on one bunk, we sat down opposite. Both bunks were made up. He was not only up and dressed, he had made his bed. Fastidious guy.

"Look, I'm sorry to tell ya this so blunt an' all, but I'm afraid your friend Minot's been killed." Soros's hand slowly went to his mouth and he looked away. Then he stood up, his hand still to his face. He took a deep breath and sat down again.

"What happened?" He could certainly have been lying, but if so, he wasn't bad.

Bud gave a short version of what we knew but didn't say anything about where the body had been found or the pips. "I know this is tough," he said, "but we need you to answer some questions." Then he read him his rights, which Soros impatiently waved aside. Then Bud asked him to tell us about the last time he'd seen Minot.

He sat there for a moment, very grave. He wasn't stuck or thinking or anything, it seemed to me; he was just waiting for a moment, maybe out of respect. "George and Alex left at about six thirty to have dinner with a couple named Forstman—Fred and Patsy Forstman. On their big cruiser." I knew Forstman slightly and knew his boat, *Endymion*. It was the big cruiser that had been out in the Tangles two days ago, when I had gone for a row. It was a palatial 150-footer that could have sailed around the world. But—like most such boats—it usually sat at its mooring or a dock, waiting for an owner who seldom came. Bud asked if Forstman had come for them and Soros said no, they'd taken the dinghy. Then a little scowl, and he said, "The only dinghy, as a matter of fact. I'm stuck here."

"I see that," Bud said. "How come you're all dressed?"

"Habit, I guess. I'm on the phone most mornings to Greece and Western Europe. I'm always up by five; that's eleven out there. If you don't get hold of a lot of those people before lunch, forget it. George always insists we do our calling in the morning, keep 'em on their toes."

"Make any calls this morning?" I asked, for the hell of it.

"A couple," he said, "to Greece. About half an hour ago. Usual stuff. Through the marine operator, so it wasn't very secure, even though we were speaking Greek." Calls made through the marine operator are actually transmitted by radio. Everyone on the water can listen in and almost everyone does. Hell, I've done it myself; it's irresistible.

Bud asked when he'd first noticed George and Alex were gone and Soros said he'd woken up, once, in the middle of the night, and saw they had not come back. He wasn't surprised; it made sense that they'd stay on Forstman's boat in this fog. The only surprising thing, he thought, was that they had gone over there in the first place. Finding it must have been a trick. No radar on dinghies.

"Tell us about the day," Bud said, "up to the time they left."

"Well, they'd slept up there in the big V-berth." He pointed toward the bow. Bud asked if he could take a look, and Soros said sure. As Bud looked around, he called over his shoulder for Soros to keep talking, he could hear.

"They got in real late on Saturday night. Real late, like three or four."

"Did you come back together?" I asked, remembering that dance scene.

"No. I got home on another launch. They came in way after that. They slept until noon. Me, too, almost; no up-at-five that morning. The counselor here will tell you, it was quite a party. The next day, there was the fog, of course. So the three of us had breakfast. Lunch, really. We all sat around in the fog and read and dozed until six when they started to dress to go over to Forstman's." He didn't remember what Alex had on. But George wore his uniform. I asked if that wasn't kind of fancy for a Sunday night supper and Soros said it was but that George got a kick out of his uniform . . . laughed at himself, but liked to wear it. He had spent a fortune on it. "You know about his build, his shoulders. All his clothes have to be custom-made. But especially his uniforms, which are apt to be tight."

"You and Minot get along pretty well?" I asked. I was thinking of him and Alex, the night of the dance.

Theo paused and gave me a funny look . . . almost a little smile, and said, "Very. We are very close. He has been . . . he has been everything to me. Made everything possible."

"What do you mean?"

"We are . . . relatives." He paused, as if there was a problem translating what they were into English. "Distant relatives. George is a very generous man, and he has no children. We met when I was young and I guess he took a shine to me. He spoke to my mother and arranged to have me go away to school. First, in Athens, then a private lycée in Switzerland. Then college in this country . . . and business school. He did things like this for a few young people, and I was"—a shrug—"the most gifted, you could say. I have worked for him for the past dozen years. If it were not for him"—and he turned deliberately to Bud—"I would be perhaps a lobsterman, in Greece." A smile. "I owe him everything." I was stunned by that deliberate rudeness, but Bud seemed not to notice.

"He been actin' different lately?" he asked.

"No. Well, yes, a little. He's been very excited lately. About the races . . . the club and this cruise. He is very much *into* the club and racing, these days, as Tim will tell you." I was interested to notice that we were on a first-name basis. Actually, I was mildly surprised to hear that he and Minot were on a first-names basis; I would not have assumed it.

"You didn't kill him, I guess," Bud said mildly.

Theo closed his eyes and shook his head. "No. No, I didn't kill him."

"Any ideas?"

"None, I'm afraid. I am . . . surprised."

"How about Alex?" Bud asked.

I looked up suddenly, interested to see his reaction to that. Soros gave a rueful smile, as if that were an amusing notion. "No, not Alex," he said. "You talk to her, you'll see. I'd bet this boat on it. And a lot else besides."

"They was close?" Bud asked, coming back into the main cabin.

"Close," Soros said. "Too close to have that be a possibility."

"How about this Forstman?" Bud asked.

Soros shrugged. "I don't know him. You do, Counselor; what do you think?"

Bud wasn't having that. "I'm askin' you."

"I don't know. Doesn't seem like that kind of guy . . ."

"Okay, Mr. Soros, we gotta be gettin' over to this other boat. We'll get back to ya in a while. Let's go, Doc." Then, "Oh, listen." Bud remembered something. "I hear Minot had a handgun, a Ruger .22 he used to plink at bottles. You seen it?"

Soros thought. "No. I know what you mean but I don't know if it's on the sailboat or in the city. It's not on this boat, as far as I know." Bud nodded, thanked him, headed toward the stern.

Soros pointed us in the direction of Forstman's, but Bud knew where the Tangles were. *Endymion* was almost a mile away; Bud said we'd follow the shoreline to the Tangles. As we got back into the *Betsy B*, Soros said, "Say, get me a dinghy, will you? Or a ride ashore? I'm stuck." We said we'd try.

Endymion was quite a yacht, and as Bud would later say, Fred Forstman was "quite a boy." The boat was that enormous private yacht that I had been surprised to find, anchored, in the Tangles, when I went rowing that first morning while Cassie slept. Now here I was, going aboard, on as strange an errand as one could wish.

Like Theo Soros, the captain, a man named John Mack, was also up and dressed when we came alongside. He welcomed us aboard and Bud told him to go get the owner. Mack tried to find out what was going on . . . delay a bit before he got Forstman. Bud cut him off. When Mack turned to go, Bud said, "Tell him he don't have to dress for us, Cap. We'd like to see him in about two minutes. And, Cap, don't be puttin' anythin' over the side." Pause. "That'd be a crime, got it?" The captain said he did.

In my business I see a lot of tycoons, but Forstman was something else. We are ushered into the main saloon, a huge room by yachting standards, and there is Forstman: blond, medium height, a bit fleshy, in his late thirties. He has a tan and is dressed in fresh, white flannels, white shoes, and a baby-blue cashmere sweater. He grins and extends a hand. He is our "Host!" Big time. All these guys need desperately to be in control but Forstman is ridiculous. So cheerful—all crinkles and smiles—so very animated. And so weird.

Because, under the bonhomie and the tan, he looks absolutely dreadful. In the normal course, he's probably a nice-enough-looking guy, but this morning he's all bloated. He looks as if a dozen tiny people have been driving golf balls inside his head for hours. His merry little eyes are a mess and his color is awful. But, never mind, he's doing his best. Despite the fact that the room smells strongly of burning leaves—or marijuana—which is not what you want when the sheriff comes to call at dawn.

"Come in, come in!" he says. "You boys are up early!" A warm, two-handed handshake for me, to show we are old friends—which we are not. A more respectful but still delighted handshake for Bud. "Sheriff!" Smile, pause for a warm look. "Good to meet you!" A quick, frantic look around: *Where's that filthy steward?! Ah!* A uniformed Filipino man walks in with a silver tray. Forstman twinkles with pleasure at this agreeable development.

"Hi, Juan. Coffee, gents? I think these Danish may be today's. Are they, Juan? Good, good." To us, "Our chef makes a mighty good Danish. And there'll be fresh juice soon. Right, Juan? Guava? Orange?" A sharp look toward the steward. Then more smiles for us. "Care for a cigarette?" He's smoking like a chimney, maybe to mask that smell of burning leaves.

Then he starts sneezing. Cannot stop. "Summer cold," he says ruefully at last, wiping his nose. "The worst. Last forever." My own guess was that this one would last until he quit doing cocaine. Bud took it all in, the room, the man, the runny nose, and the sneezing. And moved on.

"Forstman," he cut in, "we're looking for a friend of George Minot, Alexis Andrews. Is she here?" Bud hadn't said a word about why we were here and Forstman hadn't asked. A little strange.

"Gee . . . ," Forstman began, as if he were trying hard to remember something that happened a long time ago. "I don't know. Well, I guess we'd have to, uh . . . How come? I mean, she was here. With George. And then we went to bed and all. I just don't know."

Bud waved away the big fresh-squeezed orange juice the steward was offering him. I reached over and took mine, drank it down. I'd had a bunch of that wine, with the lobster.

Bud said, "Let's go take a look."

"Fine!" said Forstman, delighted. I thought he might still be drunk or coked-up, but he sure was trying. I couldn't take my eyes off him.

"Perhaps she's in the master guest cabin," Forstman suggested, cheerfully leading the way. But, no, there was no one in there. Nor was she in either of the next two guest rooms—although one had been used. Then he led us—nattering away—to the master cabin, his own cabin. Forstman knocked carefully and was told, "Just a moment."

CHAPTER 12

ALEX ANDREWS

When the door opened, there was Forstman's wife, a pretty brunette of about twenty-eight, fully dressed in chic slacks, a shirt and a sweater, her hair combed and neat. And behind her was Alex. They both stood there, stiffly, their hands at their sides. Alex looked as if she had been up all night and it hadn't been easy. Even so, even with her eyes looking almost bruised with fatigue or drugs or God knows what, she was stunning. And sensual. She was wearing white bell-bottom slacks and a thin, ribbed shirt—lilac—which closely molded her small breasts. No blood. Her light brown hair was—wet. Why a shower in the short time we'd been there? Maybe to get the pesky blood off . . . who knows? But now she was standing there, with her arms straight at her sides, trying desperately to compose herself. Bud said who we were and that we wanted to talk to her.

"We need a place we can talk. This okay?" Forstman's wife said it was. Bud turned to Alex. "You might want to sit down."

She did. Bud then asked if he could take a quick look around. Alex said fine and he did. I just stood there, looking at her, a little stupidly I suspect, and she looked back at me. Then this little smile.

After his quick look around, Bud sent the Forstmans, husband and wife, off to stay in separate rooms, and told them not to speak to each other or anyone else. When Forstman began to say he wasn't sure that was appropriate and that he might want to get his lawyer, Bud just turned on him and growled, "This is serious business. Go sit where I told ya." They left without a word.

Bud sat down opposite Alex, both of them in little chintz armchairs. "Miss," he began evenly, "I'm sorry to tell ya that George Minot was killed last night." Alex sat there, stock-still. Then, slowly, she began shaking her head from side to side. Tears welled up in her eyes, but she didn't cry . . . just shook her head from side to side, very slowly. "Afraid it's true," Bud went on, then waited for her to catch up.

"He never came home," she said, finally, as if she were still wrestling with it. "He said he would and he never came back."

"No," Bud said, not unkindly. "No, he did not." His voice was gruff but there was a touch of sympathy in it. "He was killed late last night, early this morning. We don't know where. An' his body turned up in your dinghy, over at the steamboat. *Java*."

Another long pause, and he went on. "Look, I'm the sheriff, like I said. An' Bigelow, here, is a special deputy, helpin' out. We're tryin' to find out what happened. Tryin' to find the fella who done this. Or the woman." Her head jerked up at that. At the idea that someone had "done this." Or the idea that it might have been a woman. There was a touch of alarm in her eyes.

"Who?" she said.

"We don't know," he answered. "We just got here. Just got into it. And now, we gotta ask ya some questions."

But then he just sat there, looking at her and she looking blankly back at him. Then over at me and back at him, first the one, then the other. Then with a deep breath she closed her eyes and said, "Okay." Then Bud gave her the same short version of the story he'd given Soros. Only this time there was a little cry when Bud said George had been shot.

"Was he hurt?" she said. I was baffled by that; what the hell . . . he'd been killed. But Bud understood.

"No. No, he weren't beat or nothin'. As painless and quick as . . . as anythin' can be. I don't wanna talk about details but he didn't suffer none, he really didn't."

She nodded at that small mercy, nodded her head and slowly wiped her nose on her hand. "Okay," she said again. "Okay." Bud waited a moment, then read her her rights. Alex nodded to indicate that she understood, but it was clear that the whole thing had gone right over her head. Bud asked her, did she want a lawyer and she said she didn't. Which, of course, was absolutely crazy, no matter what. Anyhow, we began.

"We were wrecked from the party and slept late. Like noon or one. George was up earlier, I think, but he came back to bed. When we finally woke up, we ate and hung out with Theo until it was time to come over here for dinner. Theo Soros?" We nodded that we knew who she meant. Her story about that part was just what Soros had told us. Then on to the Forstmans'— Fred and Patsy's—for supper at six thirty. George in his uniform and nothing unusual about him or anyone else.

"It took forever to get here," she said. "Half an hour or more. Then we went straight to the big room here and had drinks. They'd already started when we got here."

"And some drugs, I guess," Bud said, nonthreateningly. I stirred a little: it would have been better to wait for stuff like that.

And sure enough, it stopped her dead. "No, no drugs," she said. It didn't sound true. Hell, it wasn't true.

"Look, Alex," I said, reasonably, "this isn't a drug bust or anything. We're not gonna chase you for that. Let's not get off on the wrong foot. This is too serious to lie about little things. Obviously there were drugs; you can smell the grass and everyone looks like hell. C'mon."

She looked back and forth, then took a deep breath, made up her mind. "No. No drugs."

"Jesus, Miss," Bud rumbled, his face grave. "Bigelow is right: We can't fool around here. An' that big room, up there, smelled to high heaven. Don't fuss with lyin' about that. That's not what we're here for."

She did the same business as before, looked back and forth, but a little more pulled together this time. "No drugs. All night."

"Whoo!" Bud said, wiping his whole face with a big hand, a familiar gesture after a while. He sat back and we looked at each other. Then forged ahead—interviewing a key witness without a lawyer is too rare and wonderful an opportunity to miss.

"Forget that part, Alex," I said. "Go ahead." She didn't start right off. "You had drinks," I coaxed, "starting at what? Seven . . . ?" Eyebrows up, waiting, you know. So anxious to hear, to listen to her. To believe her and get her out of this mess. All right, here she goes again.

"We had drinks. We had a lot of drinks." She was going to admit all of that, but no more. No drugs. Fine. "Then dinner at seven thirty, I guess."

"Who was here?" Bud asked.

"Marion. Marion Robinson, who's a close friend of mine and George's. And the man Marion was with on the cruise, Johnny Stockwell. The two of them were staying on the Suttons' boat, but they stayed here because of the fog." She looked at me and I nodded: I knew them slightly. "The Suttons were supposed to come, too, but they begged off. We were with them the night before."

"So it was the six of you for dinner?" I asked.

"Yes. I thought George might try to get the Suttons later. He was all wound up, but he didn't . . . So we were just six."

"Was Theo invited?" I asked.

She frowned as if that question was a surprise. "He could have come, if he wanted, I guess, but he wouldn't have. He's George's business guy. He wouldn't come to a thing like this. Dinner was over by nine and the steward was dismissed. There was a full bar and everything in the saloon."

"That the guy we saw just now, the guy who brought us coffee?" I asked.

"Yes. Fred told him he could go for the evening and he did."

"Old Fred lock the door, did he?" Bud asked bluntly.

She looked up at him, startled by the question. "Yes," she said.

"Then what?"

She shook her head, vaguely, apparently thinking about what had happened next. "This next part is odd," she said, lowering her head and then looking up. "Around eleven, George got up and said he was going to do an errand."

"An errand?" Bud said.

"Yes. I assumed at first he was going to get something here on the boat, but then it was clear he meant to go out on the water. Which was ridiculous, of course. We were in the middle of the Tangles in the middle of the night, in the worst fog anyone had ever seen. We all protested. He just smiled and said he was going to 'get some more.' He'd be right back."

"More?" Bud said. "More dope?"

She shook her head. "He wouldn't tell. He put on his jacket and hat and left." She leaned forward to tell us this important part and her breasts moved against the ribbed cotton shirt. I literally looked away. She saw that and, so help me, she smiled.

She smiled, at the very point when she was laying down the heavy timbers of the story that were supposed to save them all . . . the story that George had got up, late in the evening, put on his hat, and headed out on the water. Where he was murdered, by "some other dude," not them. That's what criminal defense lawyers call it: the "some other dude" defense. That apparently was the idea here. And still—at this critical step in the story— there's this little smile as she notices me looking at her breasts.

"We were all pretty lit by then," she went on, "and we laughed at the idea. Like it was hysterical that he'd go off in the fog at this stage in the night. We told him, don't go. Or at least tell us where you're going. But he wouldn't."

"Did he say anything else?" I asked.

"No." She turned to me. She raised her hand to her hair. "He just looked pleased with himself. As if he had a wonderful secret. Then he left." She stopped and looked at us, as if she were as baffled as we were.

"Oh, he did say one thing. 'It'll be worth it,' or something like that." She had no idea what he meant.

There were a lot more questions and we tried a couple of times to get her to admit to the drugs, but she wouldn't and we didn't learn anything further. Bud took her through her story several times. He didn't accuse her of lying but his manner got darker. And Alex's got lighter, almost flip. It was a weird performance.

"Look, Alex," he said, finally, his face right up close to hers, "if you was foolin' around an' it got outta hand somehow . . . I don't know. The dope an' all . . . I can understand that." She was slowly shaking her head, not having it. For some reason, that made Bud angry and he reached over and took her by the shoulder, gave her a little shake, like a kid, that snapped her head back, made her hair go flying.

"Listen to me, for Christ's sake," he said sharply. "This is no time for horseshit an' stayin' with some dumb story you made up with that fuckin' Forstman. You're right up against it, Alex. Right up against it." And he gave her another shake, which made me uneasy; I am a Rules Guy and that kind of thing is not okay. "In a deal like this, someone always talks. Always! An' the first one gets the deal. The others go to prison. You be first, Alex. You'll come out a lot better. Won't she, Tim?"

"Guaranteed," I said. "And, think about this: your friends aren't hardened criminals. They'll talk, sure as hell. So you tell us what happened first, Alex, and we can look after you." Bud nodded his head and damned if he didn't start stroking her bare arm now. Not sensually but the way you would with a horse or a dog that was skittish.

"C'mon, old girl. Best get it done," he said softly. Then he waited.

She took a deep breath, looked back and forth at us, as if making up her mind. "I want a lawyer."

Bud sat back. Looked at her impassively for a long moment. "All right, old girl," he said, not unpleasantly. "You got a right. But, look, if this is just some foolishness about drugs, for God's sake speak up." He reached back and took a pair of handcuffs off his belt. "'Cause otherwise, you're goin' ashore. We'll take some o' your blood . . . get some urine. And we'll find out about all them drugs you didn't take." He waited a long minute. "If you want to try it one more time, I'm listenin'."

She waited a moment but then: "We had dinner on board. Drinks. No drugs. George left to get something and we went to bed. When he left here, there was nothing wrong with him. He never came back." Then she dropped her eyes to the handcuffs resting on Bud's knee and shrugged. As if to ask, *Now? Now do we do the cuffs?* And then she slowly held out her crossed wrists to him . . . for the cuffs, teasing.

I was mesmerized but Bud was disgusted. "All right, Doc," Bud said. "Put her in a separate room. I'll get the wife."

After Alex, Patsy Forstman was just a pretty woman. The electricity quietly leaked out of the room. Patsy's story was identical to what we had just heard, right down to George going to get "more" something, but no one knowing what. And she agreed that he was excited about it, that it was going to be some kind of a "treat," as she put it. And no drugs at all. We were at it a long time, but it didn't do a bit of good. I wondered what it was, made them so stubborn and seemingly dumb.

I wondered even more when we went to get Marion Robinson. She was interesting. Not because of her story; the story was the same. But she wasn't. In fact she was so very different from the others that it was hard to think that she was a friend of any of these people at all. She was softer and quieter, calmer. She looked like a quiet Darien housewife who didn't get into the city much. And that was about right, except for the fact that she'd been separated for six months, her husband had custody of the children, and she was here with a date, the sleepy Johnny Stockwell, who looked five years younger than she, and they were obviously lovers.

She was in her midthirties—about five foot three, trim but round, with dark hair, conservatively done. Her clothes looked odd on her, too chic. It turned out they were Alex's and they didn't fit. Her estranged husband, I vaguely remembered, was not a nice man. He was a long-time member of the club and a dreary, hard-drinking banker. No kind of companion for her.

She, too, looked as if she'd had a hell of a night. Even if she weren't that kind of woman. And she had been in tears over something . . . crying hard for quite a while. My immediate thought was that she was bound to be the weak link in this chain. Bud must have had the same instinct because we kept her there a long time and we bore down hard. But it was a waste of time. She just wasn't very interested. Not scared or hostile or anything . . . just not interested. I began to get the sense that she was sad about Minot. I didn't get that as much with Alex.

And certainly not from Patsy Forstman. But Marion was sad. That did not mean that she had not helped to kill him, you know. But, if she did, she sure felt low about it.

Stockwell looked like a bit player who'd walked into the wrong play, and that was about right. His story squared with the others, but he had gone to bed early, before Minot left. He was a bachelor in his early thirties who had a little place in Stamford for weekends. I don't know much Stamford society, but I'd bet that there are more than a few lonely or unhappy women up there and that Johnny Stockwell was a bottom-feeder, preying on the lonely and desperate.

Finally, we sent for Forstman. We'd been at it for quite a while by then, and Forstman looked marginally better, perhaps because the cocaine was wearing off. But his manner was the same: he was a tycoon and he was doing us a favor. Bud gave him the warnings and he waved them away, amused at the notion that he might need them, a man like him. Then we marched through the story again. It was identical to what we'd heard.

Bud took him through it twice, then sat back and gave him a long, speculative look. "You know, old boy," he said, "we been sittin' here, hearin' this same horseshit over an' over." Forstman's smile went a bit stiff. "I kinda assume that you're the fella that put it together for us, this bein' your boat an' all." Forstman scowled now. Then Bud gave Forstman the same shot at immunity he'd offered Alex. Forstman wasn't remotely interested.

"Bud. Please. Surely you don't think that I . . ."

"I don't know," Bud interrupted. "I just don't. But if you didn't do nothin', Jesus, quit lyin' to me. Quit this stupid business about no drugs, an' tell me what the hell happened."

"Bud, please. I assure you . . ."

"Stop it!" Bud stood up, and looked down at Forstman with a dark scowl. "Just, for Christ's sake, stop it, will ya? Someone's been murdered tonight. If you done it, you take the Fifth an' good luck to ya. But don't sit here an' give us this crap about how he went off somewheres in the night. An' you ain't done no drugs. What's the matter with you people? My heavens!" He just stood there a minute and Fred looked at him, maybe a little scared. Then Bud sat down again.

"All right, last chance. Do you want to tell me the truth or are we all goin' into town?"

Forstman sat there looking at Bud. I thought maybe he was going to tell us something. But instead, he pulled himself together and said, "Get the fuck off my boat!"

Bud said, quietly, "No, old boy." He stood up and took Forstman by the upper arm. "We're all gonna get the fuck off your boat, and then we'll see where we're at. Come on." And he gave him a little shove toward the door. Forstman stumbled and looked around, horrified, started to say something but thought better of it. He looked as if he had been slapped, and Bud looked very calm. For some reason, my Rules Guy sensibilities didn't cut in this time.

Next, we did the crew. We got nothing except that Mack, the captain, did see Minot leave at around 11:00 p.m. He didn't see or hear him return.

When we were done, Bud and I sat alone for a bit, talking it over. "Looks like we're gonna be at this awhile," Bud said.

"I guess so. These people sure as hell are lying about something, but I don't know what. Maybe he came back."

"Yup," Bud said, "yup," getting up. "They're certainly lyin'. So we'll let 'em spend the day in 'house arrest' as material witnesses. Get on with the rest of our people. Go after 'em this afternoon."

"They'll be all lawyered up by then," I said.

"Yes, they will," he agreed. "So we'll get a court order . . . search the boat. Get divers down in the meantime . . . search the bottom. And then drug test the lot of 'em. That'll move things along."

I was impressed with that and said so. "Yeah, well," Bud said with a small smile, "this ain't my first rodeo." It turns out that he had been a cop down in Portland for seven years and had been promoted very fast. In fact, he was a senior detective when he left to run for sheriff, back home in Hanson. He'd done a number of murders down in Portland. If our murderer had counted on having a rube for law enforcement, he'd had his first bit of bad luck.

It was full light by the time we were done, and there were a couple of lobster boats standing off Forstman's boat, waiting. Bud had radioed and they were here to take Forstman and his party to town. He was going to put them up at the old hotel, not the jail, but he was going to hold them as material witnesses. He had talked at length to the local district attorney.

When Forstman got the news, he was stunned. He started to shout and carry on as he was handed down into one of the lobster boats. Bud just looked at him, then said softly but ominously, "Shut up or I'll cuff ya." Forstman became quiet. But he looked at Bud with a cold anger that was eerie. Turns out there was more than one personality inside that baby-blue sweater.

CHAPTER 13

ON THE BEACH

After the Forstman people were sent ashore, Bud spent a lot of time on the ship-to-shore with the local district attorney—a man named B. T. Horton. He eventually decided to leave the Forstman group to Horton for a few hours while he, Bud, oversaw the beginning of the rest of the investigation. It was a painful decision because the Forstman group looked awfully promising. But, he said, Horton was able, and he himself couldn't just ignore the other five hundred people on the cruise. I told Bud to warn Horton that Forstman would have an army of good lawyers up here by midday, fighting like steers to stop him.

On the way back to *Java* in the fog, Bud admitted he wasn't so damn sure just what to do next. Some five hundred "suspects," on a remote island, in deep fog. Not so easy. But we both felt better after we'd been back on *Java*, talking to Harry for five minutes. Because—in our absence—Harry had turned his considerable powers to the problem and had devised an elaborate plan. Not a foolproof plan but not bad.

At about one that afternoon, all 503 of the remaining members, guests, and crew on the cruise were assembled, in deep fog, on the beach at Broken Island. Harry's plan was to tell them all what had happened. Then pass out a questionnaire he'd drafted, which Bud and I edited. They'd fill 'em out, right there on the beach. Then there'd be some follow-up interviews and some searches. Not many, but they didn't know that, and they seemed to take the questionnaires seriously.

It had been a hell of a job, listing all the boats and the people on the cruise, and getting 'em all on the beach for the announcements, but Harry had managed, with a lot of help from the club's very experienced launch men and Bud's people. The upshot was that, by one o'clock that afternoon, everyone on the cruise had made their way to the beach. There were scores of inflatables, pulled up on the sand, and some five hundred people standing around, in the fog, trying to see and hear Harry. Quite a scene.

"My friends," Harry began, using a loud-hailer. He was standing on a low rock, surrounded by this big crowd. In the fog, only about half of them could see him. "This is very hard. Last night, at around midnight, George Minot was killed." The crowd murmured at that. "I am horrified to say that in fact he was murdered . . . and that the murderer is still at large." Then there was a real murmur. One man near me said, "Wow!" and sat right down in the sand.

"The body was discovered in a dinghy at about three last night, at the work float, on *Java*'s port side. I was woken up and we called the Hanson County sheriff, Bud Wilkerson, right here." He pointed at Bud, standing there, with his huge gun on his hip and two of his deputies and four uniformed state policemen at his side. The state guys had arrived at about eleven that morning. They had those old-fashioned trooper hats tipped over their eyes, crisp gray uniforms, and shiny boots, but they were out of their element and looked it. Bud was very much in charge. Maybe Bud and Harry.

"This is an extraordinarily difficult situation for law enforcement, obviously. In these unprecedented circumstances, we've been working with Bud and his people to help them with their investigation. We are a little like a civilian posse, I guess. I have said that we'll do anything to help, anything he asks of us. All of us." Pause, as if to ask for dissent. There was none.

Then he explained about the questionnaires, and the possible interviews. Said how we all had to stick around for two days, regardless of inconvenience; if there were special problems, they should "come and see the law officer, my brother, Tim, whom most of you know. He was a prosecutor in New York and he's helping out."

That was it from Harry. But—in those few moments—he had done what we had set out to do: demonstrate to all that he, Harry, their commodore, was co-heading the investigation here, and that no one should think of him, for a single second, in any other capacity. Certainly not as a suspect. His presence, his wonderful voice, his competent seriousness . . . everything made the same point. Pretty good job. No wonder he'd worked so hard, pulling this odd meeting together.

Bud was a bit more blunt. "Commodore says you ain't to leave for two days. That's right. Anyone tries to leave without permission, our people will stop 'em, bind 'em over in the Hanson jail till we can get to the judge an' be heard. We're gonna have boats out here all the time. Radar can pick you up, goin' out the Cut, out the Tangles. We ain't got time to fool around on this. Any real problems, see me or one of my deputies or Tim Bigelow, like Harry said. But it better be damn serious."

The system of questionnaires and interviews was complex and kind of cool, but it didn't amount to much in the end. We spent hundreds of man-hours and some of our people worked late into the night, and we didn't learn squat. But it looked good.

What we learned, eventually, from questionnaires and interviews, was that there was a fair amount of invisible dinghy traffic in the early part of the evening but only a couple of boats after eleven. One dinghy was reported by a couple of people to have been motoring slowly—it was impossible to say where—in the fog. And one guy had briefly seen a dinghy just drifting. That was odd, but we couldn't make any sense of it. There were no gunshots. No screams. Nothing odd, except the damned fog.

The questionnaires, which took forever, were pretty much useless. We did create a list of about forty people who acknowledged knowing Minot fairly well, socially. They'd be interviewed, but no one had had any contact with him on the day/night of the murder. Still, we'd interview them. Maybe search their boats.

Bud's people did one other thing that at least looked substantive. They went around the Squadron in all that fog and put numbered marker buoys down at the bow of every boat. Then two men took the only lobster boat in town that had a GPS—I was surprised there were any—and logged the locations of each of them. So we could create a chart showing exactly where every boat in the Squadron was moored that night. Again, it looked serious. Putting aside the Forstman people, I began to think that looking good was the best we were going to do.

To give the whole thing a bit more substance, I had two associates sent up from my firm, to do what they could. They arrived late that afternoon. I asked Jayne Robinow, the more senior of the two, to stick with me and get involved with the Forstman people. I told David Bowen, the younger one, to help

Harry and the others with the questionnaires, interviews, and all that. They were both former prosecutors and super capable. It wasn't all show.

With all that in place, I suggested to Bud that he and I—and Jayne—head into town, see how our prisoners and the DA were doing. I thought that had to be the main show.

CHAPTER 14

GONE!

B. T. Horton, the district attorney, had an office in the 1880s courthouse in the middle of Hanson. The cupola and the flag and the statue of blind Justice, which I knew were up there someplace, were lost in the fog. What was clear was that it was a handsome building—built of stone, like all public buildings back in granite-quarrying days. It must have been about ten times bigger than they needed today, now that the sardine business was gone and granite quarrying and boat building were over. But it was well maintained. Some of those shrunken Maine towns—way down east—had fallen apart. Not this one.

Horton was sitting behind his desk and didn't get up. "Walk right in, for Christ's sake," he said irritably to Bud. "Bring your friends." He was in his late thirties, medium height and thin. He wore a cheap, dark suit, a white shirt, and plain tie . . . an American flag tie-clip. A young Richard Nixon. His desk was flanked by flags of the state of Maine and the Union.

"Evenin', B. T.," Bud said and introduced Jayne and me. He quickly said what we'd been doing out on Broke. Then asked, "The tests set up yet? How are your prisoners likin' it up t' the hotel?"

Horton waited a moment and seemed to be trying to summon his dignity. Then, "They ain't there."

"What?" Bud said, very sharp and clear.

"They ain't there. I agreed, late this afternoon, after a lot of negotiations and a long hearing before Judge Cruller, that they could go back to . . ."

"Oh, for Christ's sake," Bud started, his voice thick with anger. "You silly son of a bitch! One or more o' them birds probably murdered this fella, do you know that! That's our only lead. What the hell were you thinkin'? This is the stupidest thing you ever done in your life, B. T., an' you ain't been idle up till now."

"You just cut that horseshit out right now, an' listen to me, will you." Horton tried to sound as if he were in control here, which he was not. He would never be in control when Bud was in the room. "There's a lot you don't know. We had a gang of lawyers here, starting at eight o'clock. Lawyers from Portland, lawyers from New York . . . Ted Duffy here in town. We were before Judge Cruller before we knew it. You were out there fuckin' around in the fog. And Cruller made it damn clear that we didn't have any basis for . . ."

"Why didn't you call me, you damn fool?" Bud growled. "There's radios. Cruller knows me. Sweet Jesus, B. T., I can't believe you didn't send for me. *Jesus!*"

"I knew what you had, and that wasn't any good. 'Material witnesses' stuck up in the hotel, for Christ's sake . . . They didn't like that much, I'll tell you. Looked like Dogpatch."

"Who fuckin' cares what they like!"

"And the judge didn't care for it, neither," Horton said. "They had a motion on that, motion to quash. Motions on every damn thing you can imagine. So we negotiated with him and we got . . ."

"Yeah, tell us what ya negotiated, for lettin' 'em go, for Christ's sake," Bud said, deeply sarcastic but getting calmer. "Passel o' murderers, for Christ's sake. Bet ya done good." He and B. T. looked at one another for a long moment. "Believe I'll go to law school for a couple of weeks, take over your fuckin' job!"

"We did the best we were gonna do," B. T. said, putting both hands on his desk and leaning forward, a not-very-confidently aggressive pose. "They agreed you could search their boat, what is it . . . the *Endymion* . . . search their boat any time you want. And they'd stay in the country."

"Stay in the country?" I said. "You mean the county, right?"

"No," he said. "The country."

Bud shook his head, deeply disgusted, and Horton looked small.

"They've left the state?" Bud asked, knowing the answer.

"This afternoon," Horton said. "Three big limos, drove 'em down to New York. Or Boston . . . someplace outa this fuckin' fog."

"Did you talk about drug testin' at all?" Bud asked.

"Sure. Started to, anyway, but Cruller didn't care much for the sound of that neither . . . based on demeanor. Terrible Fifth Amendment problems. Fella, Barrow, from New York . . . he was all over that."

"William Barrow?" I asked.

"Yup, he did most of the talking. You know him?" Horton asked.

"Yes. Able guy," I said. "We're going to have a tough time from here on, Mr. Horton."

"We!" Horton was delighted to turn on me and quit facing Bud for a moment. "Who the fuck's *we*? Who are you, for

Christ's sake? Tellin' me what to do?" Horton had both hands on his desk again, for this little outburst.

I was not much taken with B. T. Horton but decided to go slow. "I'm Tim Bigelow, Mr. Horton, as Bud said. Law officer for the yacht club and a former prosecutor in the Southern District." Even in deepest Maine, the fella was going to know what the words *Southern District* meant. "I take a lot of the responsibility for what happened here. I did ask Bud to warn you but I should have come in and given you a hand. Those birds know how to put on a blitz."

"Yeah, they do," Horton said, a little mollified. "So who the hell are you now?"

"These days, I am a partner at Hazard, Davis in New York, and Jayne here is a senior associate." I could see that Horton knew the firm name, too—didn't necessarily love it but he knew it was serious. "We got another associate out on Broke, working on that part. Don't know what we can do at this point, but we're here to help any way we can. Whether you want to use it or not . . . that's up to you."

I stopped at that and waited. Horton just looked at me. Then he looked at Bud. He didn't like it—didn't like me, apparently. Certainly didn't like my suggesting that, if I had been there, none of this would have happened. But he really was stuck. And he had fucked up. Finally he said, "Okay, Mr. Bigelow. Sorry to be so touchy. This has not been a great day. Bud," he said, "you endorse these people?"

"Hell, no," Bud said quickly. "I don't know 'em from Adam. Just met Bigelow yesterday, Jayne today. But I can say he knows what he's doin', and he and his brother have been a lot of help already. And we need help, both of us." Horton started to say something but Bud held up his hand. "Only way." Horton didn't argue.

He sat there, an unhappy man. "All right," he said. "Let's do it. But now the question is, just what the hell can you do for us? My fault or not, these Forstman people are gone. We could summon 'em back to appear before a grand jury, but it will take time to create one. Then get 'em up here. Too late for the drug tests. Besides, they'd just assert their Fifth Amendment rights in the privacy of the grand jury. We'd be cooked. Squeezin' 'em on the drug stuff before they got their heads straight was a good idea, but that's out the window now."

Jayne spoke up. "Not so clear," she said, thoughtfully. "No way to impanel a grand jury up here in time. I get that. But maybe we can do something quick enough in New York. Suppose we go back to your judge. Get him some papers tonight . . . go see him early tomorrow. Give him a sense of how critical this is. Have Bud testify about the appearance of Forstman and the gang. If he's persuaded, we get him to issue a special order compelling tests, to be enforced by a New York State court immediately, down there. You swear us in—Tim, David, and me—as special assistant DAs here in your county and we'll go to New York and do it. Make sense, Tim?"

I thought for a minute. "Probably not, but shit . . . let's do it. Best idea so far. B. T., what do you think?" I asked.

B. T. thought for a long moment and then said, "So, what's the theory again, Jayne? We testin' 'em to indict 'em for coke possession, or what?"

"Not up front. We're gathering evidence in a murder investigation. Forstman's boat may be a murder scene; it was certainly the last place Minot was seen alive. It's clear to Bud and Tim that there was heavy drug use there, that night. That's the peg. And maybe we find some coke—in the big room, or on the bottom under the boat. But the witnesses all say there was none, which is a lie. We need to know what really went on there, that night. So we test 'em. As part of the murder investigation."

Not bad, I thought. Might work, if we got the right order from the Maine judge. And a good judge in New York.

"We could look like idiots," Horton said finally.

Jayne grinned. "Hate to be mean, Mr. Horton, but we already look like idiots; you took care of that part already." It was part of her rough charm that she could say something like that and get away with it. "Now, the trick is to make them look like idiots." Horton nodded and damned if he didn't agree. Got kind of excited, as a matter of fact. But Horton did want a cover-your-ass letter, which made sense.

"I want a letter, Bigelow," he said, "that spells out just exactly what the duties of you and your two associates are on this case as my special assistants. You have an exclusive duty to this office and to me. I want you to point out that someone in your club is likely the murderer. And recite that nasty speech the dead guy gave, and the wine-throwing thing, so it'll be obvious your brother probably killed the son of a bitch. And talk about his gun, which is supposed to have been down at his place in Massachusetts. I want all that shit in there. And the letter is an attachment to the papers that go to Judge Cruller. Make it clear that he's blessing the whole silly thing. So when it goes in the toilet, he gets to share the blame. All right?" I said it was perfect and we got to drafting.

While Jayne and I were working on those papers, I asked that Horton start immediately on the search warrants for Forstman's boat . . . or an agreement with their local lawyer. And I asked Bud if he could contact divers, tonight, and get them to start searching the bottom under Forstman's boat for drugs. Turns out he'd already done it, and they were at work. That Bud was an able guy.

Time, of course, was of the essence. The Forstman group had taken the drugs on Sunday; tomorrow was only Tuesday, which was not bad. But—even if all the procedural stuff worked—the soonest we'd get a hearing in New York would be Wednesday, and it was more likely it would be Thursday, with tests set for later that day. And the risk that the drugs would be out of their bodies by then was pretty high. Happily, I had a backup idea for all that, but I kept it to myself.

At nine the next morning, we were before Judge Henry S. Cruller of Hanson and an agreeably able man. I thought he'd made a dreadful mistake the day before, but it was still clear that he was an able guy. He was about sixty, he had been a judge for fifteen years, and he knew what he was doing. We had left our papers at his door at midnight and damned if he hadn't been up and read them carefully and gotten a fair sense of the issues. Had, in fact, been persuaded, it seemed to me.

"I guess you boys think I made an awful mistake yesterday, letting those folks go," he began, after the introductions and such. I started to say something polite but he waved me quiet. "Maybe, maybe not," he said. "But I'm willing to listen to you now."

Horton laid out our case for him. The judge asked what I thought—mostly just to get a look at me, I assumed. Then he agreed to have Horton question Bud about the appearance of the Forstman people . . . the likelihood that they'd been doing drugs so that the judge could partly base any order on his impression of Bud's "demeanor." Evaluating "demeanor evidence" is peculiarly the job of the trial court judge and cannot be second-guessed on appeal. Bud was terrific and Cruller obviously liked and believed him.

"You want to hear legal argument, Judge?" Horton asked, after Bud was done.

"No," Judge Cruller scowled. "I read your papers and managed to look at a couple of your cases. It may work. The only real question is about you, young man." He turned and looked hard at me.

"What I want, Mr. Bigelow, is to hear you talk for a while. Tell me a little about yourself. Why you're willing to do this. And why the hell you think you can carry water on both shoulders like this. Private lawyer and prosecutor at the same time. Let's hear about that."

I walked him through my background. Told him how this situation was unique for all kinds of reasons. Finally, I told him I thought this business of deputizing us in a murder case was obviously a terrible idea. That got his attention. The only thing worse was letting a murderer go free. Just because he'd had the good luck to do his work where law enforcement was so damn thin. The commodore, my brother, cared a lot about that, and so did I. We thought these drug tests were the best shot we had, and we were willing to stick our necks out and foot the bill. That was it.

The judge just looked at me for a long time. Then, with a sigh, "All right, all right. I'm going to do it, Mr. Bigelow. I hate it, but I'm going to do it." Then with a dramatic lean forward, over the bench, he looked at me. Very theatrical. "But let me tell you something. This is on your head, sir. We're going to have a shit storm here"—he realized he was on the record and waved a hand to the stenographer—"a storm. I saw that Forstman legal team and they're not lightweights. So we'll be tested. I'm relying on you not to make us all look like fools."

"We're not lightweights, either, Your Honor. No one's going to be embarrassed." That was a little boastful but my guess was he wanted to hear something like that. He nodded, apparently satisfied.

"Okay, Marjorie," he said to the steno, and we were off the record. Then Jayne and I were sworn in as temporary assistant DAs. He also signed the search warrant for *Endymion*. David would come in to be sworn later. Bud and I went back to *Java* to do the last interviews, starting with Theo Soros.

We assumed Soros could not have murdered his boss, because he was stuck on his boat without a dinghy, on the other side of the Squadron from *Java*. And almost as far from *Endymion*, out in the Tangles. Bud and I had talked about his swimming here and there, but that seemed mighty remote, especially in all that darkness and fog. We wanted him mostly for context.

There was another, important "procedural" step: Right after that session with the judge, I got Harry a lawyer, Jack Tiglio, a good friend of mine. I insisted that Harry have his own lawyer for several reasons. If I was going to be running around playing Deputy Dawg with Bud and B. T., Harry should at least have the appearance of a separate lawyer. But I was also slowly coming to grips with the notion that Harry might become a real suspect someday. Implausible but not inconceivable. So I wanted someone good to be watching this weird movie, on Harry's behalf, from the beginning. Jack was very good indeed. And his and my ties ran deep.

When I told Harry about it, he was reluctant. "C'mon, Tim. Almost the whole point here is for me not to look bad. Hiring a lawyer looks bad."

"Yup, but no one will know about it for a long time. And—in the end—looking bad may be the best of it. I'm beginning to sense that this could get serious. It's so damn odd, I just . . . I just don't get it. Which scares me. So I want you to have a lawyer." My voice and expression were deadly serious. Harry understood, didn't argue.

"He's pretty good?" he said. Small talk now.

"Way beyond that, he's as good as they get. He'll be sensible and invisible in the early stages. But, if things go sideways, he's as tough and smart as anyone you can get."

"Except you," Harry said, with a nice smile.

"Yuh, except me," I said breezily. "But you foolishly loaned me to the other side."

CHAPTER 15

SWINGS

Soros was waiting for us in the Race Committee room, and he didn't stand when we walked in. "Morning, Counselor, Sheriff. Thanks for getting my inflatable back." He leaned across to shake hands, casually. He was wonderfully composed.

"Glad to do it," Bud said. "Not much there for forensics, it turns out."

Soros was dressed in pleated, black linen pants, rope-soled espadrilles, and a black T-shirt. His hair was pomaded again, short on the sides and long on top, swept back dramatically. He was distinctly handsome, in a dark, Euro way. And athletic looking, too. I wondered how in the world I'd gotten my impression of a limping, timid bookkeeper. The man sitting across from us now was supremely self-confident . . . downright tough. In fact, if he hadn't been stuck all night on his boat with no dinghy, I would have said he was the most promising of all our "suspects" . . . the one who would have the stones to murder his boss and stick him full of pins.

After the warnings, Bud told him a little about the investigation thus far, including the fact that the Forstmans and the others were refusing to talk and had left the state. Soros snorted at that and said an odd thing.

"You people," he said, looking at me. "You do your killing in such remote places. Teddy Kennedy drowning that poor girl at Chappaquiddick. It's rough on the local police, isn't it, Sheriff?" He turned to Bud. "The 'Chappaquiddick Effect,' they should call it. All respect to you, Sheriff, but there's not much you can do, is there?"

"We'll do what we can, Mr. Soros," Bud said laconically. "We'll do what we can."

Then he started. "Tell us a little about your friend," he said. "Give me an idea the kind o' fella he was." Soros settled down a little and thought for a moment. Ran both hands over his face and through his dramatic hair, an odd echo of Bud's familiar, more homely gesture.

"Well," he began, "let's see. He was smart and driven. And he had amazing force. He could get people to do things. I don't actually know where his original fortune came from, but I do know he did some very big projects since I've been with him. Made a lot of money. Both real estate and pure financial. Huge amounts."

"He got any enemies from business, might've done this?" Bud asked.

"He wasn't like that in business. He was tough but he was direct. People always knew just where he was coming from. They may not have liked him but no one felt betrayed or humiliated or anything. He was a bull who charged straight." That again, the bull thing. I also wondered whether Osborne would have agreed about not feeling humiliated.

"How about a mob thing?" Bud asked. "Someone told one o' my people there might be mob connections."

"Please," Soros said, disgustedly. "That is such horseshit. People say all kinds of things about George, because he's foreign and exotic and so damned rich. But mob connections? No."

"What was your deal with him?" Bud asked.

"As I told you, he's a distant relative. He took me up, I had a gift, and eventually, I became his trusted aide."

"You his number-one guy?"

"Yes."

"Doin' okay?" Bud asked.

"He has made me very rich, by my standards. By any standards, really. Given me . . ." He stopped and looked up as if he couldn't think of what else to say. "Everything. He has given me everything."

"Do you know if he has a will?" I asked. "Who stands to inherit?"

"That's interesting," Soros said. "Unless there have been changes, a chunk will go to some Greek charities, some to the American Academy in Rome. I got him interested in that, frankly, because we're both interested in architecture. Some goes to the club—to endow a 'Minot Cup'—and quite a bit to other entities and individuals, here and in Greece."

"What individuals?" I asked.

He thought a moment. "Alex gets a piece. A couple of million. And the New York apartments, the furnishings . . . some other stuff. I think she gets a big chunk of the remainder, too. I also get a million, which was very kind; he'd already done so much. Smaller bequests to some others."

"What are the apartments worth?" I said.

"Oh, Counselor, don't bother. If Alex killed him, she didn't do it for money." He smiled as if he were thinking to himself, shook his head. Maybe thinking about Alex. I had the liveliest sense of that scene, with the two of them dancing. The idea of the two of them getting together to kill poor old Minot had an instant appeal. Cassie had said that Minot would have killed them if he'd suspected their relationship. She also said that maybe Minot saw him as a Theseus figure, the guy who slew the original Minotaur. If any of that was true—and if Alex and Theo were in fact lovers—that wasn't a bad motive for a murder. There were difficulties, of course, but I told Bud about it later and kept it in mind myself.

"What was their relationship?"

Soros blew out a breath, as if this would take a while. "Lovers, of course. Lovers from the time they met, years ago. Mentor/mentee." Shrug. "Father and daughter? Brother and sister? Help yourself. They were everything to each other. He used her for . . . let's see. He used her to seduce people, of course, for their 'swings.' A lot of that."

"Swings?" Bud said, confused.

Soros looked back and forth at us, a little surprised that we didn't know. "He was a very . . . sexual man. Intensely sexual." A little laugh. "An addict, not to put too fine a point on it. He loved women. He didn't mind men in a pinch, but that was rare. And he really loved fucking." I felt rather than saw Bud shift in his seat at the word. "And he sure fucked an awful lot of 'em. Including, lately, a number of the wives and daughters in the club. There's a lead for you, I guess. Chat with the fathers and husbands of all the women he's fucked, in and out of the club. Take a while, though. He's been at it for some time."

I was way back on my heels. "Swings?" I repeated.

"Yeah. I assumed you would have known about that by now. He wasn't content to fuck 'em one at a time. Wanted 'em stacked up. Rooms full, if he could. He'd seduce a woman . . . then get her to bring her husband or whatever. Or get Alex to do it. Like a chain letter. A daisy-chain letter," he said with a little laugh; he liked that. "Last couple of years, it amused him to recruit members from the club. Of all things."

"The club," I said flatly.

"Yup. Those Greenwich matrons, boy. Get one of them lift-ing her little shirtwaist dress up, with all those buttons. The soul of modesty but, you know, naked underneath. Shyly danc-ing around for everyone. Weird sight, let me tell you."

"You've seen this yourself?" I asked.

"Just once. Not quite my kind of thing."

"Forstman involved in all this?" Bud asked. Suddenly that evening flashed clear.

"Of course. I assumed you knew that, too. George and Alex nailed Pat last spring. That's Forstman's wife. Then old Fred. Ask Alex. Ask her about the whole thing. She'll tell you." He laughed again. "She was his little recruiting sergeant. Or the Little Drummer Girl. She and George went over on Sunday to fuck Pat and Fred," he said with another laugh. "The language . . . and the notion of Alex. It jolted me. Soros went on, "And Marion and what's his name. And anyone else in sight, I guess. Imagine an orgy with old Fred," he said.

"Funny thing to want to do," I said for some reason.

"Listen, if George's head had been half as original as his cock, he would have been a great architect as well as a great financier. But he was better off fucking. That was the highest and best use of George Minot: fucking him. And only about a thousand people knew it. Congratulations, Sherlock, you're making real progress." He was looking directly at Bud.

"So George was bisexual?" I asked.

Soros paused. "Not much. But he was an omnivore. He had a rapacious appetite and he'd take what was there. But men didn't much interest him. In fact, lately, he worried about AIDS. Even had private detectives checking on the men . . . weed out the gays and the bis from his events. Less of a risk in the Great Arcadia, of course. Maybe that's why he started hunting here." He seemed to be thinking about it some more. I wondered what Soros thought of the Great Arcadia . . . and wondered whether he was gay. Regardless of his relationship with Alex, he looked as if that could be true. Not that my eye for gay men was so remarkable.

"On the other hand," Soros went on, "if you told a shrink about all this, he'd see plenty of sexual ambiguity; orgies aren't exactly a line-drawing exercise." That was interesting; thoughtful man, our Theo Soros.

"The people on Forstman's boat all tell us he took off, around eleven, to get *more* o' somethin'. Make any sense to ya?" Bud asked.

"Make sense?" Soros thought it over. "I guess so. I mean, I have no idea if that's what happened, but, sure, George would be capable of taking off like that, fog and all. He was amazingly comfortable on the water . . . and in the night. Would he go off to get someone or something to crank it up even higher? Sure."

"So what'd he be gettin' more of?" Bud asked.

Soros didn't have to think at all for that one. "Women." He grinned. "More women to fuck. More likely, one special girl."

"Like who?" I asked.

"That's hard," Soros said. "Could be anybody. The two of them, he and Alex, could have lined up just about anyone they wanted, and I mostly wouldn't know about it." I thought about Alex's invitation to join them for supper; was this what we were being invited to? Wow! Theo mentioned that Bob Sutton and his wife were on his "active list"; we might think about them.

Bud said we were planning to see them soon.

I was blown sideways by the sexual business, could hardly believe it. But I got it together enough to ask one practical question. "Were there any deals pending, when George was shot? I remember he did some takeover stuff . . . was there anything like that in the works?"

"Not really," he said. "There was one takeover effort that may or may not go forward now. In recent times, George has been less interested in business and much more interested in racing and sex. His office staff had shrunk to ten people in New

York and a few in Greece; he didn't go to either office often. He had all the money in the world, of course, and he wasn't much interested in getting more. I've noticed over the years that there are periodic rises and falls in his sex life." Soros grinned now: "We've definitely been having an uptick, lately."

"On the business side," I pushed on, "was anyone in the club involved in anything that's going on now or in recent times?" Soros said there was not. No one in the club knew anything about his last deal or his business life in general.

"Does that include Alex?" I asked.

Soros shrugged, as if acknowledging a point. "No. I forgot about Alex. She might know. She knows everything. But she truly doesn't care. Not her world." I asked if he could tell me anything about the open transaction, and he said he couldn't. It was unlikely he'd try to go forward with it now, but just unwinding it was going to be tricky and confidentiality was of the essence.

That struck me as plausible but I was interested. "Have you and George taken a position yet?" I asked. "Bought any stock in the target company?"

He waited a moment, then said, "I may have given you an overbroad impression of my involvement in George's affairs," Soros said carefully. "I know a lot, but I was mostly on the edges on his takeover things. That was more between him and his bankers."

I noticed that, in his excitement to disabuse me of a mistaken impression, Soros had not answered my question. Happens all the time. But not to adequate trial lawyers.

"So, had you or George taken a position yet, or don't you know or what?" I tried again.

"George doesn't like me to talk about these things," he said, almost petulant all of a sudden. "I'm not to say anything about them."

"Yuh," I said, "but George is dead, and the only reason I ask is that it might help us catch his murderer." I had never heard of a "takeover murder," but it made perfect sense.

Soros smiled to show he wanted to be helpful. "Look, I really am out of my depth here. I'd feel more comfortable if you'd talk to his bankers."

"Fine," I said. "Who are they?"

"I don't think that would be appropriate," he said.

"Mr. Soros, for heaven's sake, don't fuck with us, will ya?" Bud said. "What possible harm could that do?"

He shrugged and said, "I guess that's right. It's Moran, Teichner. A man named Morris Sullivan. My apologies, but George was such a fanatic about security." I sympathized with that; leaks are the curse of the takeover business.

As soon as we were done, Bud and I grabbed David and Bud's son, Andy, and told them to have all our people, in all the interviews, ask a series of questions about anyone George might have been picking up for "romantic" reasons. The "More Woman" we called her. It was, I said, a major thread, and they were to treat it very seriously.

When we were done with Soros, I assumed we would go over to Peter Osborne's boat, the next witness on our list, but we didn't. One of Bud's guys had interrupted the Soros interview and talked to Bud, to one side. Apparently as a result of whatever he said, Bud grabbed me and we headed down the float to the *Betsy B*, and headed out into the fog.

We milled around for a while and finally pulled up in the middle of nowhere, beside a large, empty inflatable with a red-and-white "diver down" flag. Bud cut the engine, and soon two divers popped up beside our boat. They climbed into the inflatable and took off their masks and hoods . . . scratched their itches for a moment, the way you do. Bud told the two men who I was and one of them leaned over the side to get something out of the black storage tube, floating beside their dive flag. With a grin, he handed Bud a wet leather shaving kit. "There ya go," he said.

Bud said. "You both seen where it come from?"

The younger man said he'd seen it; he'd called over his friend and the two of them marked where it had been. "Just where it was s'posed to be."

"All right," Bud said. "Anythin' else down there?"

The older one said, "Doubt it. We woulda found it by now. We'll give it another hour, see what we see."

"How's the bottom?" Bud asked.

"Sand, clear as a bell." The diver grinned.

"No chance a gun or somethin' got dug in? Worked in durin' the last couple o' days?" Bud asked.

"Nope. No current. It ain't buried 'less someone buried it."

"Okay. D'you open this?" Bud asked. The younger diver said they had taken a quick peek but hadn't disturbed anything.

Bud put on thin plastic gloves—just like the TV—and unzipped the bag. It was a conventional shaving kit with a razor and such. And five little brown bottles, sealed with black plastic tops. And cocaine inside. Bud tested a bit on his tongue.

"There we go, Doc. Now, let's go see these fellas." He smiled.

"They moved their boat," Bud shouted over the engine. "The Suttons. We're gonna see them next." It was hard to hear; he said wait till we got to *Java*. When we were tied up to the float, he said, "One o' my fellas went to tell 'em they was gonna be interviewed today and noticed their boat wasn't in the right place. Their boat, *Spindrift*. We got it on our chart. But it weren't where it was s'posed to be."

I looked around at the impenetrable fog. "How in the world did they know?"

"No boat where this *Spindrift* was supposed to be. My fellas went out in the one boat that's got the GPS so they could go right to her. But she wasn't there. When they found her, she was a hundred yards away. We couldn't have made a mistake like that. So, they must've moved her. Moved the buoy, too. Now, why'd they do that? Get away from somethin', I thought. So, when they told me that this mornin', I had the boys look around on the bottom at the old location, an' this is what they got."

"Wow!"

"Yup, that's a break, old boy." On the way to the Race Committee room we quickly agreed how we'd use it.

CHAPTER 16

GREENWICH MATRONS

Bob Sutton was waiting for us in the Race Committee room, and his wife, Jane, was waiting outside. He asked if they couldn't do this together, save time. But no, they could not. Bob was a tall, nice-looking man in his early forties. Blond, pink pants, Greenwich, but pleasant looking. The last man on God's green earth you'd expect to see in a tangle like this. I knew him slightly and introduced Bud. I thanked him for sticking around, and he said that he and his wife had been fond of George and were glad to help. But in fact he wasn't glad to help; he was nervous as a cat.

Bud and I had agreed that I'd lead off. I gave Sutton the warnings in a casual way, making it obvious by my tone that this was boilerplate stuff that had little to do with a man like him. I did come down a little hard on the notion that lying in an investigation like this was a crime, as if that were an odd bit of information I'd come across in my life that might interest him. Mentioned casually that people with no problems at all sometimes wind up in terrible trouble because they lose track of the stakes . . . tell a lie to avoid a scandal and wind up in prison. And people should bear in mind, I said—a raconteur who talks too much—that prison is a lot worse than scandal. Risk almost any scandal before you risk being indicted. Being indicted for a crime makes such a hash of your life, that you should run naked through the Stock Exchange long before you risk it. I was just chatting, you know. About interesting things I had learned in my work.

I lobbed him a couple of gentle questions so he could settle down again. He gave us his résumé: born in Boston, went to St. George's School and Williams College. Then work, and business school, blah, blah, blah. And now, son of a gun, he was a partner in a venture-capital firm. And raking it in. There were two kids, thirteen and ten. House in Greenwich, pied-à-terre in town. Hell of a guy.

I am condescending, which is unfair. He'd chosen a perfectly reasonable life and had turned out to be good at it. If he'd stuck to it, he'd have been fine. But he hadn't.

"Are your children at home?" I asked.

"You mean do they go away to school?"

"No, just are they home? You know, they're not here, so are they home?"

"They're both at home. They don't really like to sail," he said after a pause. "Why do you ask?"

"I don't know. I guess I was just wondering about this trip."

"They come sometimes but they didn't come this time."

"So this was an adult cruise."

Pause. *What the hell is this all about?* "Yes."

"And Marion's husband didn't come."

"No. They're separated," Sutton said.

"Ah. So Marion, Johnny Stockwell, you, and your wife . . . the four of you, on your boat."

"Yes," he said.

"And you knew George fairly well, had seen a fair amount of him and Alex?"

"Some," he said, a little uneasy.

"Was it fun?" I asked.

"Yes, we had fun," he said. Longer pause this time.

"Boy-girl? Boy-boy? Girl-girl?" I asked. Bud moved in his chair.

"What are you talking about?" Sutton barked, almost angrily.

"Your children . . . Do you have boys or girls or what?"

He paused as if that were an entirely different matter. "Oh. Two girls." He was very attentive now, and way off balance.

"Okay," I said, "can we walk through the last couple of days, starting with the day of the race?"

"I thought you wanted to talk about Minot," Sutton said.

"I do but it's a help to fill in the background. Did you race?" I asked pleasantly.

"Yes. We came in seventh in the cruising canvas class. That means no spinnakers . . . not hard-core racing, as you know."

Ah, do you hear that? We have skirted some scary stuff, but now we're back in good water. How we reach out, in trying times, for the familiar and the good. How we reach back to that sunny, windy day when we were racing and shouting and trimming the sails in stiff winds, and coming in seventh in the cruising canvas class.

"We have an Alden 46, and that was pretty good for us," he said.

"Sailing short-handed, too. Had you four raced together before?"

"Not Marion. But she was all right. She'd sailed a lot and she could follow orders," he said, smugly.

"Could you see the 50s finish?" A comradely question: the finish of the Custom 50s—the hybrid class in which we had sailed—was already notorious.

"No," he smiled. "But I heard about it. Wasn't that something?"

"Absolutely. We were with Harry. A great race. Osborne didn't behave so well," I said. Then, in a lighter tone, "The early evening was nice, too, wasn't it? I saw you and Jane on *Java*. Great party."

"The best." He smiled again.

"And the dinner, too," I said. "Until it all got crazy."

He shook his head, as if he could barely believe it. "Imagine Mimi throwing her drink. I thought Harry would turn to stone."

"Then it really got crazy," I said.

"Everyone . . ." He laughed. "I think I saw you . . ."

"Please," I said, raising both hands. "Not in front of the sheriff." And we both laughed.

"What did George think of it?" I asked.

"Oh . . . he loved it. That's his scene, you know. He was all over the place. Great fun. He talked, he danced, he . . . well, you know him."

"I don't, really," I encouraged him.

"He was just out there. Took forever—" And he paused for just a beat. He hadn't meant to say that.

"To get him to leave?" I finished.

"Yes."

"And then off to your boat, I gather?" As if we all knew at least that much.

"Yes," he said a little uneasily. "The six of us: Jane and I. George and Alex. John and Marion."

"And stayed until three."

That hit him as being a little too much. "Oh, I don't think it was that late. I'd say . . ."

"Yes it was, Bob," I said softly. An entirely different manner now. Leaning forward. "Until three. Because you were all whacked on cocaine. And you couldn't sleep the next day, either. For the same reason."

"No. No," he said, ineffectually indignant. "There certainly weren't any drugs and, no, I doubt very much it was three. I . . ."

"Just stop, Bob," I said, a little stern now. "Don't do that anymore." I nodded to Bud. He reached under his chair and brought up a plain paper bag he'd set there. He tipped it upside down on the table and the wet leather shaving kit fell out.

Bud opened it, looking at Sutton the whole time, and dumped the contents. There was his razor. There was his shaving soap, there was his toothpaste. And there were his little brown bottles of cocaine. Sutton looked horrified. Then he deflated with a long sigh. A pause from me now, to let that sink in. But not too long. Not long enough to decide to stand up and get a lawyer, which is what he should have done at once. The whole point of what I had just gone through was to disorient poor Bob so he would not demand a lawyer.

"We're here for the murder, Bob, not the drugs," I said quietly. "But we're terribly serious about the murder. We'll arrest you for this. And try you. And wreck your life. Even if you don't say another word. Unless you tell us absolutely everything you know. Right now."

It's so interesting when a grown-up is "caught" like this. A man who hasn't been caught at anything since he was ten. And now he has no idea how to behave. Doesn't know what grown-ups do when their lives come tumbling down. There are no models for them and they react very slowly. So, like an idiot, he did not refuse to talk without a lawyer.

"So, let's go back," I said gently. "You go out to your boat. It's late. No one is particularly sober and my understanding is that . . . Well, you tell me." He stared a long moment at the things on the table, then another sigh. He was getting used to it. Getting used to the tremendous changes. But it was still hard.

Bud said, gently, "We know a lot o' this stuff, old fella. Best just go ahead, an' get it done. Hell, it ain't the worst thing I ever heard . . . 'less you fellas killed him."

Sutton jerked his head up. "Oh, of course we didn't kill him!" He looked back and forth quickly to see if we could possibly think that. I mean, it wasn't that bad.

"Well, good," Bud said, "I bet ya didn't. You don't look like that kind o' fella. But Tim is right: You gotta tell us everythin', so's we can catch this guy. Or else we're gonna grab ya for the dope. That's true." Shorter pause, then, "Anyhow, them two come on board . . . d'you do some dope?"

"Yuh," Sutton let it out with a little pop. "Yuh," again. "We did some dope, as soon as they came. The coke. That was the first thing we did. We didn't have drinks, we'd already had a lot. Just some coke." Pause again.

"Minot and Alex, too?" I asked.

"Sure, a little for both of 'em. Mostly the coke, to wake up some."

"An' I suppose," I said, "from what we been told, that folks started taking off their clothes, that right?" This was pure bluff and it worked fine.

"Yup," again, the little pop. "Yup, we started taking off our things. You see, we'd known them for a while." He stopped again, couldn't go on.

"We ain't doin' this for fun," Bud said softly. "Honest, we ain't. It's just that this stuff happened the night before the murder an' we got to know."

To get him started on an easy one, I asked how long it had gone on. He thought for a minute, head down. Then he looked up and, all of a sudden, gave us this sweet smile. "Not long," he said. "Didn't seem long, anyhow."

I was taken aback. Here was this decent man—this father of daughters, this owner of an Alden 46. Talking about painful stuff that could ruin him. And he smiled. He was remembering something nice, and he smiled.

"So what happened?"

"Oh, everything. I don't know, but everything." The dam broke and it was suddenly easy. "My wife pulled down the covers on the big bed in the main cabin. Alex started taking off Marion's clothes. And then, you know, just everything. It's all jumbled." He turned to me. "Suppose you've never done anything like this?"

"No. I . . ." I shrugged helplessly.

"Well"—he smiled again—"this wasn't a particularly wild night; it was already late and we were fading and couldn't keep it up for long. But it's always confusing. Everyone's all together." He stopped. Then he started over.

"You had to know George. Or Alex. She's the one you had to know. She was . . ." He shook his head. "She was something, that's all."

"Alex . . . ?" I prompted. I felt a fugitive, sexual twist, in spite of myself, starting down this road.

"Oh, Alex." He shook his head. "There's no end to her. She's like a kid who won't come out of the water." That was an odd way to put it. One saw a skinny little girl in an empty two-piece suit, loving the water, shivering. Her lips are blue. "If she had her way, I sometimes think it would never stop." Twist. And the smile again from him, thinking back.

"Went on for a couple of hours?" I asked, just to get started again.

"What? Yes. Less, actually. We were tired, as I say. And the fog was bad. They wanted to get back. I told them to stay with us . . . they'd never find their way. But they insisted. Roared off as if it were broad daylight. I was horrified, but I guess they made it. George knew more about the water than anyone."

We walked him through the whole night in as much detail as he could remember. When we seemed to have it all, I said,

"Anything unusual?" The words were out before I could hear what I was saying and all three of us started to laugh. Especially Bud. "Anything unusual?!" Well, I guess so.

When we stopped, I rephrased the question, and suddenly, it was obvious that poor Sutton was stuck again. He was trying to decide whether or not to tell us something.

There was a screwy intimacy among the three of us now and Bud said, gently, "Too late to figure an' scheme, old boy. Just tell us whatcha seen."

"It's not so heavy." Sutton came out of his reverie. "It's just that it makes Marion look funny, and I'm not sure that's fair."

"Yeah?" Bud said. "What happened?"

"There was this business between George and Marion."

"Yup."

"Well, Marion was absolutely fascinated by George . . . couldn't get enough of him. She wasn't a loose woman, you know. Hell, none of us were loose people, really. But she was particularly serious. Loved this stuff, loved him . . . couldn't take her eyes off him. And she didn't just like the sexual part. She was living for it . . . gave up her whole life for it and for him."

"Yup," Bud said again.

"She was upset because George wouldn't make love to her that night." Bud shifted in his chair. *Would he ever get used to this?* "He told her that he was saving himself for the next night. Wouldn't say what he had in mind, but implied it was a big deal and that she'd be part of it."

"So what was he talking about?" I asked.

"I never found out. I assume it was something that was supposed to happen on Forstman's boat the next night, where we were all supposed to be. As it turned out, my wife and I were so whipped we just couldn't do it. We'd had it."

"We heard somethin' special was supposed to happen," Bud said, "but we don't know what it was gonna be. You got any ideas?"

"Gee, I don't know. My assumption was that he had some marvelous new person. Or a bunch of them. Ask Alex, she'd know."

"Says she doesn't. Do you have any ideas at all?" I asked.

"None, I'm afraid. But she must have been someone pretty special. He wasn't one to save himself."

"A woman?" I said.

"Look, I don't know if it was a woman or a Saint Bernard. But from the fact that he was 'saving' himself, I'd say a woman."

I remember that I asked him—partly out of my own curiosity—about the emotional consequences of this stuff. I assumed that it put terrible pressure on people . . . ecstasy but terrible stress, too.

"Depends on the people," he said. "Some just can't stand it. Marion's husband went completely crazy. He did it once and they literally broke up the next day. Some people just can't take it," he said.

"So, yes," Sutton went on, "it can be horrendously dangerous. Sometimes, even with people who like it, there are little dustups: 'Why did you come with her, not me' . . . stuff like that. Some people are as cool as the stars. Like Alex. Some people talk about this as if it's Utopia, the real sex addicts. It's not. But I know what they mean."

Eventually we let him go and I brought in Sutton's wife, Jane, poor woman. In a flowered shirtwaist dress. It took her a while to get used to the idea that we knew. Then she told it all, with horror. Her story was the same as his. But one thing did become obvious, when she had finally relaxed and was just telling us what had happened. She loved it. Just like her husband. A couple of times in her account, she drifted back there in her mind. And smiled at what she saw, just like him.

Could they both have lied? Could George have come back, the next night, and they up and murdered him? I guess so. But I'd be awfully surprised. Bud, too.

CHAPTER 17

THE DRY SALVAGES

Osborne was a dull, humorless man, but he didn't look much like a murderer. We still spent a lot of time with him and with his crew. We learned that the crew didn't like him much and concluded that they were highly unlikely to lie for him. So he did not look like much of a suspect because they gave him a pretty strong alibi.

Osborne himself was mostly just furious. Furious that a man like him would have to be interviewed at all, you know. Furious that he'd had to wait on the tender while we talked to his crew. Furious that a man like Minot had ever appeared in his life. The one thing Osborne was most serious about was the idea that Minot was a gangster and this was a "mob hit." That was interesting. We asked him how he knew.

"Obvious," Osborne said. "The man's a thug. You can tell by looking at him. The manners of a guttersnipe." Been a while since I'd heard that word. "If we had real police on this thing," he said with a deliberate rudeness, "they'd be all over that line."

"Yeah, that'd be good," Bud said laconically. "But we gotta get along with what we got. So . . . anything solid on this gang-connection idea? Any specifics?"

"Yes, I have specifics. I have met the man. That's all the specifics I need. It's fucking obvious." It was also fucking obvious that Osborne had already been drinking, even though it was only late morning. "It was appalling that a man like that was a member of a gentlemen's club. He is precisely the kind of person you join a club like this to avoid. And making him commodore? My God! All your brother's fault, too, Bigelow. I don't know what he was thinking." I didn't mind that . . . didn't mind having Osborne tell Bud how close Minot and Harry were.

"What do you mean?" I asked.

"He literally got him in the club. Got a couple of his stooges to nominate him. But he put in the good word and snuck him through. After that, he moved him along . . . put him on various committees. Then," Osborne said with a fresh access of anger, "he put him in charge of the East River Station business. Dreadful. No stopping him after that."

That was interesting. The real key to Minot's success in the club was that he had made the club an absolute fortune. Made it one of the richest clubs in the world. The Arcadia had owned a piece of land on the East River that had been a "station" or docking spot for fancy commuter yachts in the 1920s. They commuted to and from the Gold Coast on Long Island Sound . . . Jay Gatsby country. It had been derelict for a long time, just like those yachts. Minot—who was a serious real estate player, among other things—put together a package, including the club property, and sold the whole business for a huge sum. The club made a ton on its own land, but Minot contrived to give the club a big chunk of what he made on the land he amassed beside it. It was that performance that put his feet on the path to becoming commodore.

We only had one more interview scheduled, and it was the weirdest of all. And the saddest. Dean Barker and his wife, Doris, had been waiting for quite a while. I apologized and asked Dean to come into the Race Committee room. We had talked to him for only five minutes when I saw why David wanted us to talk to him. Nothing Dean said was particularly interesting but there was a funny vibe. I took a flyer. I told him a little of what we had learned about Minot's swinging life and then—ridiculous though it seemed—asked Barker if he knew anything about that. He lowered his head, becomingly, and said, "Yes. Yes, I do." And then we were off.

Dean was seventy and Doris was thirty-seven, somewhere in there, when their adventures with George began. They'd been married for a dozen years and—he said—they were deeply in love with one another. He wanted to stress that that was true, despite the age difference. But Dean—a successful banker and outdoorsman—indicated, without going into details, that he was starting to come apart with age. Among other things, he said, he was becoming impotent. Once in a while he could rally, but not often.

"That was hard," he said, "because it was our sexual life that had brought us together." I had the sense that he wanted me to know that, at one time, he had been a hell of a guy. But no more, and it was driving him crazy. "I was embarrassed, frankly. Thought it was so unfair to her, a young woman like that. I actually suggested that we might want to think of a very amicable divorce so she could . . . get on with her life. She was indignant at that. Said we were in it for life, which was very handsome of her. Very."

He took a deep breath after that. This was not easy for him. Not one bit. Nor for me, I must confess.

"At some point George Minot picked up on something about Doris . . . came on to her a little. She turned him down, sharply. Told me about it, actually. Perhaps you can guess what happened," he said. "I gently suggested that perhaps it wouldn't be such a bad idea. George was known to be a womanizer . . . it wouldn't be 'personal.' Perhaps she should." Doris was indignant at first, said she wouldn't dream of it. But Dean kept bringing it up, at first jokingly—jokes at his own expense—and then more seriously. At length, it was silently understood that Doris was going to give it a try. They never discussed it, he said, but he knew.

One night when he was out of town, she went off with George. For a while, it was a happy arrangement. Dean both knew and did not know. They were exquisitely careful of one another and it looked as if they might have hit on an answer that would last a long time.

But then George started working Doris into some of his more complicated swings. She took to it with great pleasure and argued to herself that it entailed even less risk to her marriage because it was, in a way, so impersonal. Her intimate life with Dean also took an upturn as all this was going on, because she was on fire. One day, making love with him, she happily confessed all. She did so because she had determined that Dean should join her, that he should come, too, to one of these nights. He was much better now anyway, she said. They should give it a try.

"I, uh . . . I was very uneasy, as you might imagine. Interested, of course. I had been very, um, sexual, as a younger man and had often thought of such things. So I was excited about it. But nervous, too. It was going to be odd to have such an old chap at such an affair. Doris was wonderfully generous and encouraging, though . . . said I'd love it and be the star. We both laughed at that and off we went. It was not a success."

That was an understatement. The night of the swing started off with a normal-seeming buffet dinner. Dean was, of course, much the oldest man there, but there was a delicate effort to make him feel special, not foolish. Things took a turn when the cocaine came out at supper. Doris urged Dean to try it but there was something wrong with the membranes in his nose. First it hurt and then it made him sneeze like crazy.

He did manage to smoke some marijuana, but that didn't work, either. Then they went into the other room. He was, of course, fascinated to see the people, many of whom were very beautiful, and some of whom were now friends of his wife. But he was not necessarily aroused. He and Doris took off their clothes and she lay with him on the pillowed floor. Perhaps by prearrangement, another beautiful woman joined them. Dean found himself in the center of a soft, triple spoon, his wife behind, and the stranger in front. They started to move about, and Doris whispered wonderful things in his ear . . . reached around to the front of his stringy body and held him in her hand.

"But I was not aroused, sir," Dean said with as much dignity as he could muster. "The awful fact is that I mourned for my old self and . . . damned if I didn't start to cry. Worst moment of my life."

He told us that he wept quietly for a time and they tried to calm and comfort him. And then he began to sob aloud. He sobbed uncontrollably at last, and he could barely stand when Doris and the other woman walked him out of the room. Doris sat him down in a big armchair in the living room while she went back to get his clothes. Then she dressed him and clucked to him like a child while he sniveled and wept and tried to help by lifting an arm, a foot.

They got into a cab and he wept all the way home. He wept while she undressed him and when they went to bed until finally he fell asleep. Then she wept.

Dean had held himself together pretty well up to this point in the story, but now he lowered his forehead to the corner of the table for a minute. Then he pulled himself up, wiped his eyes, and said, with wonderful dignity, "You should know that I did not blame George for a moment. It was nothing to do with him. In fact, he treated me with great kindness. He insisted, a few days later, that we have a quiet drink. I agreed and he asked whether I thought it might ease things if I were to try again. It was his experience, he said, that sometimes those who have the hardest time are the greatest 'naturals,' as he called them.

"I thanked him. But I told him that I was old. And that I would die. And there was nothing that he or I or all the loving women in the city could do about it. After that, we saw him occasionally at the club, but neither Doris nor I returned to his circle. That is true despite the fact that Doris and I never made love again." A deep sigh now, in which I found myself joining. "But we get along."

He looked back and forth from me to David. "How shall we proceed?"

At that point, I was close to tears myself. I said we were done. We'd like to have our forensic people take a look at his boat, which was fine. And David would do a confirmatory interview with Doris, because Bud and I had to travel in the morning. Which was true. But the real reason was that I just couldn't listen to that story again.

In the corridor, Bud and I were mute for a moment, thinking on what we'd just heard. "Awful tough stuff, Bud," I said.

"Oh, my."

"But it's something to keep in mind: this is powerful and dangerous, what Minot and his pals were fooling with," I said. "I'm sorta getting used to it, but this is strong."

"Got him killed, is my guess," Bud said.

"Mine, too," I said. "Mine, too. Just a question of who got fucked up enough to finally do it."

I stopped to tell Harry about our day, before heading off with Bud. I was going to spend the night at Bud's house so we could get an early start for the hearing in New York. Harry had heard the short version of the "swings" story, after the Soros interview. He'd been pretty morose at that. He was a good deal more morose, now. He looked absolutely gray.

"We have to get out, Tim," he said when I was finished. "We just have to quit. You were right: this is no Paragon; everyone goes down with this one."

"Get out, Harry?" I said. "Good grief, we've only been at it for three days. And we've just started this ambitious program in New York. And we're not all 'going down' with this one. It's beyond bizarre but it has nothing to do with you and me. It's nasty and we may be smeared a little, but that's all."

"That's all, huh?" Harry said, as if I were an idiot. I said I understood how serious it could be but that we had no choice: at the very least, we had to finish the New York business. Which might—by the way—solve the murder. And if it didn't, we'd offer some help on the documents and then get the hell out.

He gave me a slightly dark look. "I guess that's right: Do the thing in New York. Maybe help them with documents. But have the associates do the documents. Let's you and me get out."

I agreed. As I headed to the door, he spoke again. "Timmy, when we get to New York, I'd like to get together and talk for a bit. When do you think that'll be?"

"If we lose, Thursday. If we win, next week."

"Okay."

"What the hell, Harry, talk now. What is it?"

"No, no." He was suddenly dismissive. "You focus on the hearings. No rush."

"Are you finally going to tell me about you and Minot, in the good old days?" I asked, lightly. He looked up so sharply at that, that I was almost alarmed. But then he quickly waved it aside.

"Look, don't worry. You have enough on your plate, we'll talk soon." In fact, we did not talk soon. We did not talk at all. Too bad.

The next morning, at Bud's house, we got some remarkably good news. The divers came by (at 6:00 a.m., if you please) to tell Bud that they had found cocaine during the night, out in the Tangles. Eight bottles, under *Endymion*, bigger than the ones under Sutton's boat. Right where the main saloon lay. That was huge. A little later, things got better. The state police techs who had swept *Endymion* called to say that they had found traces of coke in the carpet of the main saloon. Our New York motion was starting to look pretty good.

THE DRY SALVAGES

That same day, I tried to get Harry on *Java*. I wanted to tell him about the coke bottles and the drugs on *Endymion*. I got through to *Java*, but weirdly, Harry and Mimi had left. I got David Bowen on the phone and asked if he knew what was going on. He just said that the interview process had wound down and Harry had asked if he, David, thought it would be all right if he and Mimi left. David was a little nonplussed by that but said sure. And Harry and Mimi had gone, on their sailboat. I found that astonishing. The interviews may have been winding down but he was still in command, for heaven's sake. And he left? And he hadn't mentioned the possibility to me? What the hell?

"To Marblehead?" I asked. David didn't know but he asked one of the boatmen who had spoken to Harry and helped them put their stuff aboard. The boatman said Harry had mentioned the possibility of stopping in Rockport.

"Rockport, Maine?" I asked. David checked.

"Rockport, Massachusetts."

"Jesus!" I said. "Put him on." And David put the boatman on. "How come Rockport?" I asked. Rockport is a tiny fishing town on Cape Ann, on the other side of Gloucester. I used to sail there when I was a kid, but I couldn't imagine why Mimi and Harry would stop there now. It wasn't that far from home; why not stay outside Cape Ann and sail straight to Marblehead? The boatman had no idea. I asked him how long he thought it would take, though I had a pretty good idea, myself.

"They motor straight through, it'll be two days. They try to sail . . . God knows."

I thought about them often, over the next two days. I saw them sitting in that cockpit in the gray or the dark, side by side, the motor grinding away, hour after hour. Talking, I suppose. Endless talk, with long pauses. The stink of the diesel smoke sometimes being blown back into the cockpit. In impenetrable fog for two long days and nights. Especially the nights: with only two people on a sailboat, no one really sleeps. And Rockport? Jesus! Rockport is a small town with a long, granite mole offshore and a crowded harbor. There's a famous fishing shed that's been painted by artists about ten thousand times, and the picturesque twin lights on Thatcher Island, but that's it.

Well, there are also the rocks, the Dry Salvages. *Salvages* rhymes with *assuages*, by the way . . . emphasis on the second syllable. Lovely, haunting sound, isn't it? *The Dry Salvages.* It is the name of three rocks, well out to sea. And of the T. S. Eliot poem from *Four Quartets.* It's a corruption of the French name, "Les Trois Sauvages." Three rocks, three savages, in a canoe, humping their way toward Rockport. After God knows what atrocities. Indians were a horror on this coast in those days, when the rocks were named.

Eliot, like me, had sailed out that way as a kid. So the question crossed my mind: Was Harry sending some weird message? Almost certainly not, I thought, although he knew the poem. And if he was, he was sending it to himself. He was amusing himself by ringing a little bell in his own elegant mind.

It's quite a poem, actually, and contains more than one bell to be rung. It is about a boat as a metaphor for life. And about death. And about the Hindu god, Krishna, warning that death can come at any moment, and praising redemption through bleak resignation. I won't pretend that I got it; Eliot, like Harry, was too religious for me. But the Dry Salvages, huh? Harry, making for the Dry Salvages. Did I lose him right there?

CHAPTER 18

CASSIE AND THE SEXUAL LIFE

Three hours later, I was lying in bed in the dark, wracked with an anxiety which I could neither understand nor unwind. Couldn't begin to sleep, which was serious because I had this court date in the morning. Suddenly I reached out and called Cassie.

"Wow, long time no talk," she said. She sounded a little different, perhaps a little distant, but I couldn't put my finger on it.

"Well, four days. Seems like four weeks, but it's not. Anyhow, it's getting weird back here and I can't sleep. So I thought I'd bother you."

"Good," she said.

"Sorry not to have called sooner. I'm afraid it's been absolutely nuts up here, and I've got this odd role in it."

"What?" she asked, and I explained.

"Wow, you and Harry, man; you're really something. So you're leading the investigation, huh?" I said that we were by no means leading it; the sheriff was a very able guy. I was just helping out, but it was still a ton of work.

"But the thing that has me going nuts—and the reason I called you—is the turn the damn business has taken." I described what we had learned about the swings from Soros and the strong likelihood that the murder was rooted in sexual excesses. "What I am really worried about is Harry. This sexual stuff seems to have knocked him absolutely sideways; he thinks we are all going to be washed away in the scandal, no matter what. I thought you might have some insights." Cassie took a moment but then seemed to get it.

"I'm so sorry, Tim. I hadn't thought of that. But of course you're right. He is delicate that way. It hadn't occurred to me, but, yes, he could be hurt, and I am so sorry."

"Explain," I said. "You've been there, in a way, with Alex and George. Tell me."

"You fuck Alex yet?" she said, out of the blue.

Jesus, where did that come from. "Uh, no. I've been busy." Try to make it a joke.

"Yeah, well, I expect you'll get around to it. Or she will." Not a joke, apparently.

"Not going to dignify that with argument," I said, stiffly. "Tell me about the sexual life and Minot. Give me some context, for Christ's sake."

"Context, huh?" For some reason that amused her. Then she spoke, but in a different voice, concerned now. "Oh, Tim," she said. "I think . . ." She stopped again, then went ahead in a rush, as if she had thought about it a lot.

"What I think is that the sexual life is wild and deep. The currents run every which way. And some of them run awfully fast and they can carry people away. And now you're in 'em, you and Harry. Which may be okay for you. But I guess it's not so easy for Harry. As I say, I hadn't thought about that. But for him, getting mixed up with Alex and George and all, no matter how indirectly . . ." She let it trail off. Then, "They swim in fast waters, George and Alex. Which are a joy to them but a danger to others. I can see how Harry might not be able to bear it."

"My God," I said somberly. "So, we should . . . ?"

"Get out. Just like Harry says. Get out as fast as you can."

I didn't respond to that. Instead, I asked, "What did you make of George and Alex, out west? Were you tempted yourself?"

"No!" She did not have to think that one over. "Not for a second. I am lucky in the sexual life. You too; it's our bond, or part of it. But I am miles and miles from those two. I knew they were dangerous from the get-go. Far worse than what you saw at the dance or the race. He passes himself off as the Beast, the Minotaur . . . a joke. But it's not a joke. He is the Beast in the Labyrinth, or thinks he is, which may be the same thing for some purposes. He murders people, boasts about it. Back in Greece. He told us."

"Do you believe that?" I asked.

"Absolutely," she said with great certainty. "I *know* it."

"Wow. So you . . . what?"

"Got the hell out. When they hinted that we were all going to take our duds off and jump into the scrum, I just got in my truck and ran. My great mistake was not grabbing Don, getting him out, too. But Don refused. He was too fascinated with Alex. I warned him about the danger, but he simply didn't believe me."

"The Cassandra problem," I said, for some reason. The problem of seeing the future but no one believing you. "What about Don? You never said."

"No, and I'm not gonna. But he got banged around some in those currents. And it might have made him careless."

"Careless going over the fence?" I was asking if he had committed suicide.

"Maybe. I wasn't there but maybe. A pal of his was the sheriff and easily called it an accident. But Don was careful about guns. So maybe not."

"And basically Minot did it . . . killed him."

She paused for a beat. Then, cold, "Yes."

"You were talking a lot with George on the cruise . . . joking."

"I wanted to take a closer look."

"And?"

She didn't answer and we were quiet for a moment. Then I switched back to Harry.

"You were saying that there's going to be some kind of a public frenzy. Talk about that."

"Think about sex structurally for a sec," she began seriously, almost a little lecture. "There's this . . . this great, underground river in all our lives. Very powerful, very dark, and very seductive. But dangerous, too, like a whirlpool. Sometimes we love it . . . want to swim in it forever. But we're terrified of it, too . . . terrified that it will sweep us away and we'll drown. And people do drown, all the time. Like Don. Like that old guy you were talking about. Others romp, happy as otters. It's very, very complicated. And dangerous. So the public reaction to something like this, it could be violent. Probably will be. So, yeah, I think Harry's right: there's going to be a shit storm. And, for some reason, he's vulnerable."

"Come back east," I said suddenly.

She laughed. "Maybe. You work for a while and keep in touch. I do like you, you know. Even though I think you're an idiot about Alex." I started to object but she cut me off. "We'll worry about that when the time comes. For now, worry about Harry. And get out. I mean it: get out."

I thought two things, after we rang off. First, I realized that I was in love with her. I was uneasy about her and Minot. I didn't think that she killed him, you know, but I thought there had to be something. I loved her anyway. Second, she might be right about getting Harry out. I resolved to do so as soon as I could. In any event, it didn't matter. It was already too late.

CHAPTER 19

FARCE!

"Your Honor, this is a farce!" It was ten o'clock the next morning, court had just been convened, and Bill Barrow, Forstman's lawyer, was already on his feet. He was trying desperately to grab the attention of the Honorable James L. Tobin, a long-time New York State Supreme Court judge and the one who had caught our motion. Oddly enough, the "Supreme Court" is the trial level court in New York State, and Judge Tobin had heard a lot of passionate pleas in his day. But Judge Tobin did not see big deputations of Wall Street lawyers in his courtroom every day, and he was listening.

"Your Honor, dragging a man like Frederic Forstman into your courtroom on eighteen hours' notice. At the behest of a private lawyer for a yacht club! Who has been made a deputy like a cowboy in a Western. I am truly astonished. And appalled!"

Lawyers have to ration their rage in court, because judges hear so much of it. And because everything takes so damn long. You can't scream all day; judges won't have it. Especially state trial court judges in New York City. So Barrow, a good lawyer from a good firm, was taking a chance. Made sense though: his best shot was right now, on procedure. Once we got into the merits, he was toast. Because of those little brown bottles under *Endymion*. And the trace amounts in the rug. Hence Barrow's rage.

"Our first motion here," he went on with tight-lipped disdain, "is to get rid of Mr. Bigelow. Because of his obvious conflicts. And, of course, because it's absurd to think that a lawyer for a yacht club can be turned into a roving prosecutor in a murder case. This is not operetta!"

And so on. The histrionics aside, Barrow was good. And, of course, he knew that it would be all over, if he could get me thrown off the case. But so did the judge, so my part was easy. This whole business, I said, was a question of Maine law, and Judge Cruller's views were binding on questions of Maine law. I also planted the image of the Forstmans and their playmates, sitting in a fancy apartment uptown, swilling water as fast as they could. To get the damn drugs out of their systems.

Barrow, of course, was furious at all of this, too. Outraged that a man like Forstman could be accused of such things. But the judge was not a child and in the end he ruled our way on the motion to have me removed.

The hearing, after that, took forever, because Barrow was obviously dragging his feet, giving his clients more time to get the dope out of their systems. I did not make many objections. I had something else in mind. We were finally done at 2:00. At that point, we broke, so we could all get a delayed lunch and the judge could consider his opinion.

When he returned, Barrow leapt to his feet, all good cheer, to say that a ruling would not be necessary after all. His clients were now willing to go ahead with the urinalysis, if it could be agreed that the fact of the tests could be held in confidence unless they came back positive.

The judge looked grim at that. If there was no need for a hearing and an order, what the hell had we been doing all day? And for the two days before that? The answer, of course was that they thought they had gotten the dope out of their systems and were willing to rely on the tests coming back negative. Most important for us—and most foolishly for Barrow— they were going to rely entirely on the tests and waive their Constitutional rights. The judge looked at me: "Counselor?"

"Your Honor," I began, "I agree, with one condition. In view of the delay, I ask that Mr. Forstman and the others be brought into court immediately upon your judgment, with no prior notice of what is being sought, so that each of them can also give a series of hair samples as well as the urine."

"Hair samples!" Barrow was instantly on his feet.

"Let him finish, Mr. Barrow," sternly, from the judge.

"Hair samples which can then be tested for cocaine traces. And also perhaps matched to hair samples found on Minot's uniform." Barrow was back up on his feet, but the judge just held up his hand so I could finish. "It is a well-known technology, Your Honor, and a widely accepted one. With that one proviso, Mr. Barrow's suggestion seems fine to me." Then I sat down. Most reasonable man in the world.

Barrow, who apparently had taught himself a little about drug testing, went wild.

"Your Honor, the only relief mentioned until this moment was urinalysis. Now, at the last minute, Mr. Bigelow springs this outrageous request. This hair business is by no means 'accepted' as Mr. Bigelow blithely suggests. It purports to cover cocaine use for up to a year, especially for people with long hair like Mr. Forstman or the women. This is unconscionable. I object! I object most strenuously. This is an outrage!"

You know, it was an outrage. I had known all along that I was going to ask for hair samples. But I thought the request might be more warmly received if we waited until Mr. Barrow had jerked the judge around for a while, which he obligingly did.

Judge Tobin looked over at me. "Your Honor, the test is very simple. Not as intrusive as blood. As to questions about reliability, that can be argued to the court in Maine, when the time comes. Once we get the samples."

Barrow was on his feet again, raging, when Jayne whispered over my shoulder that one of Barrow's associates was leaving the courtroom.

I stood up in the middle of Barrow's tirade. "Forgive me, Your Honor. I hate to interrupt, but would it be appropriate to ask for an instruction that no one speak to the Forstmans until this matter is resolved. I only interrupt because it appears"— and I turned and called out—"Mr. James . . . could you hold up a minute?" Then back to the judge, "Because it appears that one of Mr. Barrow's colleagues is leaving the courtroom. Ordinarily, of course, there would be no concern, but, ah, in the circumstances . . ." I just stood there.

"Yes," the judge said, a little embarrassed. He raised his voice, "Uh, Mr. James. Would you hold on a minute," he said. "Is that all right, Mr. Barrow?"

Barrow said of course it was all right, as if it were not the most insulting thing that had ever happened to him in court. Mustn't jerk those trial court judges around; you never know. I thanked Barrow quietly and sat down, trying not to let the dizzying surge of pleasure show.

Eventually, Tobin said to Barrow, the way judges do when they're about to rule against you, "Anything else, Mr. Barrow?"

Barrow, who was a grown-up, after all, said, "No, Your Honor," and sat down for his beating. Which came about fifteen minutes later, after a short recess.

Judge Tobin had some notes. "Mr. Barrow, Mr. Bigelow," the judge began, "I have carefully considered your presentations and the testimony of the witnesses and . . ." Blah, blah, blah. The usual thing. But there was one pleasant note. "Most important was the testimony of Sheriff Wilkerson as to the appearance of Mr. Forstman that morning. I found him altogether credible and convincing." Fuck you, Barrow, for jerking my friend Bud around.

Fifteen minutes later, the big courtroom doors opened and in trooped Forstman and his wife, Pat; Alex; Johnny Stockwell; and Marion Robinson. They were quite a sight. Dressed to the nines and all ready to go pee in a bottle. In front of two lawyers. And then get a little haircut. It was a heady moment for me, vindictive chap that I am. Tobin had left and a "magistrate" was overseeing the proceedings.

Peeing in a vial is pretty bad, but in a way, the hair business was worse because it happened right there in the courtroom. Before anyone could think, the tester said, "Right here okay?" and Forstman said, "Fine," took off his suit coat, and sat down. We watched silently as the hair tester took three little samples. Each went into a plastic bag and was laboriously labeled.

When Forstman stood up, he did something nice for a change. He rolled his eyes as if to say, *Oh boy.* Then he turned to his wife and, shaking out his coat like a barber's cloth, said, "Next!" and grinned. His wife, Pat, didn't think he was funny.

Alex looked relaxed and elegant at the same time. A lovely little smile played around the edge of her mouth as she sat down. She shook out her hair, which was too short to shake much.

Then, just as the hair guy stepped forward, Alex stood up, looked over at me, and turned her chair around so that she faced me. While the man took the three little snips, she never took her eyes off me, and she smiled ever so slightly. When she was done, she came over to me and whispered, "I thought you'd like to watch."

CHAPTER 20

ET IN ARCADIA EGO

"Possible cocaine use by all five, Your Honor, according to the urinalysis results. Definite cocaine use by all five, according to the hair samples." I was reporting the results to the court at eleven the next morning, Friday. We'd had the tests done privately, overnight. The results would be forwarded to the court in Maine.

I gently suggested to the court that it now was obvious that the individuals could not be represented by one law firm; Barrow could not and did not argue the point. He said he'd been talking to the individuals and was arranging other counsel. He would keep Forstman as his firm's client but none of the others. Now I had no doubt that our basic plan would work: pretty soon, one or more of the individuals would cut a deal and talk to us. The great hope, of course, was that one of them would tell us that one or more of the others had killed Minot and we would be done. It would take a couple of days but it would happen; the whole thing would work.

While we had the sympathy of Judge Tobin, I asked him to issue a broad document subpoena, as well. That amused Tobin. Document production is not a normal incident of a murder investigation, as it is of business litigation. "Force of habit, Mr. Bigelow?" he asked.

"There's always money," I told the judge.

He laughed at that. "I guess there is, Mr. Bigelow. I guess there is." And he granted the order, at least as far as Minot's documents in the United States were concerned.

The only hitch was that Theo Soros's lawyers, who were in court for this part, made an impassioned argument against Soros's ever having to produce any documents at all. They fought particularly hard on bank records. Interesting.

The judge told us to file papers on Monday on the Soros documents, answers on Tuesday. He would have an answer for us promptly. He said that, if document production was ordered, the Soros bank documents and others would be due ten days from today. Good.

Outside the courtroom, afterward, I told Jayne to phone Citibank counsel, tell them about the argument and the ten-day deadline . . . get them working. And to be prepared, herself, to lead the document review. Jayne was a hound for documents. She grinned and said, "There's always money, Tim."

That afternoon, we were in a holiday mood. Bud couldn't get a plane to Maine until the next morning, so we decided to do something we'd both wanted to do for a while: go and see where Minot lived. Get a sense of the Beast in his Labyrinth.

It turns out that Minot had two apartments, the first a big, traditional spread on Fifth Avenue. The second was down in Tribeca where he apparently lived most of the time.

The uptown place was in an old building with a spiffy door-man and a handsome lobby. It would have suited most of my older partners. Four bedrooms, maids' quarters, library, a large dining room, and a big living room. Lots of traditional, brown furniture and some impressive art. A lovely Bonnard, a Degas, and a marvelous Picasso drawing of a bull. Also a wonderful Stubbs . . . a horse being attacked by a lion. I reminded myself to double-check the will: if Alex got the contents, as well as the apartments, it could amount to a fortune.

To me, the most interesting piece of art in the place was a large copy of the famous 1637 Poussin painting of a pastoral scene with a tomb: *Et in Arcadia Ego*, it is called. The original is in the Louvre. *Et in Arcadia Ego* was the name of the painting but also one of the most famous lines in classical Greece. It is best translated as: "Even in Arcadia, I am there." And it is pretty much agreed that the *I* is Death. Thus the tomb in the Poussin painting. So, the translation could be, "Even in Arcadia, there is Death." Minot had been so taken with that painting, or the thought, that he had this superb copy in his apartment. Interesting guy, as everyone said.

Downtown was a slightly different story. Minot had a half floor in a large loft building with a wrought-iron facade. It was mostly open space, with big new windows and old iron columns, facing west, toward the Hudson. There was a staircase going up to the roof, which he also owned. Except for one green door, there was not a spot of color in the main room. The most accessible thing on the walls was a huge Chuck Close portrait of someone, in black and white. There were also some tiny Robert Wilson drawings. Everything else was abstract, including a big, stern Agnes Martin painting—like a close-up of barbed wire on a gray background—which I knew I should admire but didn't. By comparison, the polished granite counters in the kitchen seemed positively sensual. This place was stark.

Not so, the enormous bedroom. You walked through a white door and were flooded in reds and purples and blues, and then more reds. The walls were lacquered in different shades of red. The vast bed was covered in a thickly woven red spread. There were ever so many red and purple pillows. It sounds hideous but it wasn't. It was wonderful. And incredibly lush. The bed was the largest I had ever seen, and the carpet was the thickest, most lavish you ever saw. You wouldn't hear a pin drop. Or a girl. Or a Saint Bernard. The lighting was very elaborate and as adjustable as a stage set. Jayne was delighted. "Orgy-Georgie," she said, and grinned.

There was a media room off the bedroom. Thick carpets here, too. There were ever so many videotapes in the shelves under a giant TV, and many of them had no labels on them. Jayne laughed aloud at the sight and Bud ran his hands through his hair.

Back in the main room, the only color was the dusty-green door on the far, right-hand wall. I went over and tried it, assuming it would be locked, but it wasn't. It opened into an enormous, music-filled loft—apparently the other half floor— with a fireplace, lush rugs all over the place, and more color than you could shake a stick at.

It was such a shift that it took me a second to realize that there, on a big mat, was Alex, dressed in spandex, doing exercises. She had stopped when we came in and was looking up, smiling, as if our wandering into her place were the most natural thing in the world. She tousled her damp hair, stood up, and walked toward us. She was soaked in sweat and her skin must have been hot. I didn't know where to look. She put her hand on my shoulder and kissed me on the cheek. "Hi," she said. "More haircuts?"

"Uh, no . . . we were inspecting George's apartment. I didn't know you were next door. I just tried the, uh, door," I said, stupidly, and then ground to a halt.

"It's never locked. Want to look around?"

I took a couple of steps into her place. Bud and Jayne were standing in the doorway behind me, gawking. We must have been a comical sight, and Alex did laugh. "All of you. How you doing, Sheriff?"

"Pretty good, Alex. Real nice place."

"Come take a look." And she gestured us in.

"We'd love to," I said, "but, uh, one of the things is, when you've got a lawyer, another lawyer can't talk to you unless he's here."

"I won't tell." She grinned conspiratorially.

"Well, thanks," I said, "but we better not." We started backing out, awkwardly.

"Talk to you soon," Alex said, waving as we closed the door.

Back on the other side of the door, Jayne said, "Wow!"

"Wow is right," I said.

Bud smiled. "Quite a girl, that Alex. I ain't seen so many times, Doc, when you ain't had nothin' to say. Was you takin' the Fifth back there, or what?"

I smiled ruefully. "A beautiful place."

"Yeah," Bud said, dryly. "That's prob'ly what done it. Awful nice place."

"And what a contrast. Cozy, natural, lived-in," Jayne said. "All that junk all over."

"I seen a cat," Bud said.

"And another Bonnard," Jayne chimed in. "Over the fireplace. She's a rich girl now."

CHAPTER 21

ENCHANTRESS

By eleven that night, Bud was asleep in my guest area and I was reading in bed when the phone rang. There was no intro-duction, no preamble, just Alex's low voice: "I fired my lawyer, Tim. Will you come down? I need to talk to you."

I waited a beat, then said, "I'll wake Bud and we'll . . ."

"No," she said. "Just you or I can't do it. This isn't easy for me, and I . . . I know you." I thought again for a moment. I asked about firing her lawyer and she said she hadn't had to. Barrow had said he could not represent her anymore. He gave her the names of other lawyers but she said she didn't want one. That had made Barrow crazy but she was very clear. She said he was fired and she didn't want anyone else. So, yes, she was "unrep-resented," she meant to stay that way, and Barrow knew it. I said fine, and that I'd be down as soon as I could.

I wanted to just run out the door, before she could change her mind, but I did two things first. I woke Bud—which took a minute—and told him what was going on. Told him I had to go alone.

"The hell with that. I'm goin' with ya," Bud said. "Lemme get dressed."

I put a hand on his shoulder, then went and got him a bathrobe. "Won't work, Bud. I know her a little and she will not talk if we both go." We went at it for a while, but eventually he understood and he agreed.

Next I called Jayne, at the office. And sure enough she was there, beavering away. I told her what was going on and asked her to write a memo, outlining our discussion of all the things I would say to Alex about the consequences of talking to me without her own lawyer. Jayne got it at once and said she was on it.

As I was turning to leave, Bud, who was now sitting at the kitchen table, said: "Be awful damn careful, Tim. Not just the legal horseshit . . . look out for yourself, too."

"What do you mean?"

"I mean she's about a third crazy on a good day, an' this ain't been a good day. She might just decide to kill ya."

I hadn't thought about that. "Want me to take your gun?" I joked.

"It wouldn't be so dumb," he said. "She ain't standard issue, I tell ya."

"No, she is not. I'll be careful. And if I'm not back by morning, boogie on down." I gave him the address.

Bud walked me to the door, patted my shoulder. "Good luck, Doc. An' if she asks to take a peek at your dick, you tell her no." I promised.

All of Bud's concerns—and mine—fluttered away when Alex opened the door. She had this lovely, welcoming look that no murderess could have worn. And of course she looked amazing.

She had on another of those ribbed, short-sleeved shirts, a short white skirt, and a quizzical smile. She was amused at the humor of the situation . . . She had quite the sense of humor, that Alex. She was barefoot, which for some reason made her look taller. "Come in." And she walked back into her apartment, not waiting for me, as if we had known each other for years. Her place looked different at night. The lighting made it look even warmer and more textured than it had in daylight. There were lights on the Bonnard over the fireplace, and on the wall of books and in the open study on the far left. It was dimmer in the main area where we were and almost dark way off to the right, in the bedroom area. It was an extraordinarily intimate place.

She went into the bright, half-open kitchen. "Drink?"

She was having Campari and soda and I said I'd have one of those. "Relax," Alex said, handing it to me with an amused smile. "I'm not a biter."

"I'm relieved to hear it," I said, taking a sip.

"And I'm not a murderer, either, Tim," she said softly. She held my eye for a long moment. I nodded, as if in agreement.

"Before we begin," I said, "let's talk about the rules."

She laughed at that. "For a girl who does not care much about the rules, I sure have heard a lot about them lately." She gave me a pleading look. "Do we have to? I'll swear that you told me everything you're supposed to tell me, honest I will."

Despite her protests, and later her amusement, I rang all the changes. By the time I was done, she looked almost glum.

"You make me miss Barrow," she said with a pout. "You're a real Rules Man, aren't you?"

"They're my life," I said lightly, as if it weren't true, which it was.

"Want another drink?"

I said no, and we began.

"Soooo," I said, "when did you meet George?"

She was amused at the sudden transition. In tone and content, but she went ahead.

"Five years ago this spring."

"Wow. And you were . . ."

"Twenty."

"That's awfully young, isn't it."

"Not in my case," she said quickly. "I wish he'd come sooner."

"Really? You make it sound, I don't know. I suppose he was almost forty then, and you . . . Were you close?"

"Yes. From the moment we met. As close as I will ever get."

A shrug and a sip, to show that she wasn't going to be maudlin.

It hadn't occurred to me before, and I said, "You loved him."

"In my way, absolutely."

It sounded true, but who in the world could know. Who knew anything, with a girl like Alex. And a man like Minot.

"Forgive me, but, all those other people. If you were close, why all of them?'"

"You know about that now?" she said.

"Soros told us. And we've interviewed some of the, uh, participants."

She looked at me with those gray-blue eyes for a long moment. "We aren't like you," she said at last. "Our world is not your world, and our 'values,' if you like, are not your values." She stopped. That was it. They were not like me. I guess not.

"I suppose that's one of the things that makes all this so hard," I finally said. "George was so utterly not like me, too. I probably miss things. Maybe we should just talk about him awhile, the way you know him."

"Knew him," she corrected me automatically. Then she took a moment to gather her thoughts. "Well, he was powerful, as you know. That's the first thing you saw, his strength." She sounded a little like Soros, didn't she? "You're used to that in your life, but my parents were academics; I'd never seen anything like it, the way he just cleared this big path ahead of himself. It was ugly, in a way, and ruthless, but I loved it." She grinned. "For a while, I took a terrible pleasure in being like that with him. A couple of thugs. I'd never been with a thug before."

"Where was the beginning? Where did you meet?"

"Some club, downtown. I was a twenty-year-old kid, down from Mount Holyoke. A tall, Mary McCarthy knockoff, or thought I was. I'd come to New York with a crowd of friends to see the bright lights and be bad. There was some dope— people were doing a lot of coke and, rarely, some Ecstasy—and we were all feeling decadent. Schoolgirls on the edge.

"Then this enormous man came up to me and started talking in this high, gentle voice. And I wasn't on the edge anymore. We talked for a while, but I don't remember that. There was this *thunk* of him falling into place in my life. In an hour we were down here. He'd just bought this building. There was just one big floor with a mattress, a stereo, and some lights. The bathroom worked but it was filthy. Like the bathroom in a bad gas station. It was the most romantic place I'd ever been. We stayed here, with little trips for food and air, for three days." She paused and smiled. "We made love all the time. The heaviest thing that had ever happened to me. And the best. There is absolutely nothing like George, making love. The force . . ." Then a little, helpless shrug with both shoulders, and a smile. She waited.

"Did you go back to school?" I asked.

"Yes, for about two weeks. Then I switched to Columbia. He arranged everything. I graduated, actually; he was a great believer in the life of the mind and insisted. Me, too; it was part of our bond. I hope you'll be impressed to hear that now I am working on my PhD. A kind of a homage, I suppose, to my academic parents."

"Wow. In what?"

"Classics. I have decent Latin and I'm making progress on Greek. Languages are easy for me. Actually, all academics are easy for me . . . a pleasure, not work. I'll do more of it now, I guess. Once I get used to all this."

"All this?"

"George being gone."

"Oh, of course." I felt clumsy. Then I got clumsier: "Was there talk about getting married?" I asked.

"Oh, Tim." She was genuinely amused; she leaned forward and patted my knee affectionately. "I was twenty! I was beginning my life. No, we did not discuss marriage. It wasn't like that. Nothing real."

Then she stopped and said, "We did talk about courses; that was real. There were a few things he felt passionate about. Architecture . . . ancient history. There were some courses we almost took together. He was awfully smart and had an astonishing *connaissance*. Especially about the classics. That was fun." She thought a moment. "And he insisted on taking over the financial aspects of my education, too. Paid for everything."

"What did your parents think?"

She laughed. "They were astonished. I mean, they wanted to meet him . . . Wanted to know what his 'intentions' were." She laughed again at that.

"Did they meet him?"

"No," she said demurely. "They would not exactly have understood." She looked at me levelly, her gray-blue eyes still. "But they let him . . . go ahead."

"With your education?"

"Well, the money, yes. It was such a blessed relief that they let themselves blink at that. And frankly I haven't been in touch with them a lot ever since. We talk but . . . they let him take me. Which is what I wanted. But after that, their . . . their rights? Their parental rights didn't rise so high, did they?"

"You moved in together?"

"Yes. We made this floor into two places. So we could have some privacy. But we did them together. He had the uptown place, too, but he only used it to entertain his business friends and sleep when it was more convenient. He gave me this one, in case anything happened to him."

"This place was yours before he died? His will gives it to you now."

"No, it's mine already." I made a mental note to check.

"Did you, uh, pick out the things in here?" I wasn't quite sure of the usage: did you "pick out" a Bonnard?

"We did this side together, me much more than him. The other side was almost all him. I used to kid him about his terrible Richard Meier phase. He always wanted to be an architect, as you may know."

"Is that really Richard Meier?" I asked, surprised.

"No, no. I was just teasing him. For his starkness. I didn't like it."

"What was it about him that . . ."

"Won my heart?" she said. I nodded. "Well," she began, matter-of-factly, "I should say . . ." She dragged out the word *say* jokily, as if laughing at the banality of the question. Then suddenly serious: "I should say it was his astonishing sensitivity to . . . longing. Maybe *sexuality* is closer, but I think longing is better. Sexual longing, but longing." Her manner of speaking was faintly academic, maybe those academic parents.

"He was so tuned to it," she said, and her voice warmed. "He heard it all around him, all the time. Louder here, softer there. But all the time."

I wasn't following. She saw that and leaned forward, her elbows on her knees, eager to tell me. Her shirt fell away from her breasts. They were brown. Golden, like her arms in that light. "Look, you know about his seducing all those women in your club, right?" I nodded that I did, although I was surprised that we were going to talk about that so soon. "Well, that's what that was all about." I looked at her blankly.

"Listen. He walked into that claustrophobic club atmosphere, people all dressed up in those 1950s clothes . . . all that dull talk. And all the while, he heard some of the women . . . humming in the wind like guitars." She liked that phrase . . . smiled. The rich, alto voice dropped a third. "Throbbing down there in their fur, under the Villager skirts and the panties, throbbing like the heartbeats of birds."

Wow!

"Not all of them, of course. Some women are cunt-dead." Jolt. She saw my shock and put her hand up to her mouth as if she had burped. "Oh dear, I forgot how new you are to all this." She patted my leg again, sweetly. "It'll be all right. It's nowhere near as strange as you think right now. And it's true, you know: a great many perfectly nice women are cunt-dead." Jolt again, to hear this magical creature say something like that. She didn't pause this time, didn't cover her mouth. "And God knows how many men. Usually the ones who touch you at parties and joke about 'tits and ass.' George didn't care about the dead ones. He just listened to the ones with the tiny timpanis, down in the fur, the humming . . ."

"The fur . . . ?" I wasn't sure I was hearing right.

She just looked at me. "Yes, in their cunts. In their fur." Oh, Lord . . . I was never going to catch up.

"He heard this music, in the fur, and wanted what? To conduct?" I ventured, cautiously.

"Yes." She smiled, perhaps glad to see me trying. "I suppose so. He was something of a control person, but that wasn't really it." She searched a second. "Mostly I think he just wanted to take the mutes out of their pussies . . . Oops! I forgot." And her hand went up again and she grinned. "Take the mutes out of them and listen. Wanted to bury his muzzle in their thighs or in their necks and listen to them. That's what it was. He had that wonderful ear for it, and he loved it so much. He wanted to hear it undistorted. It's not just sex, it's a whole different thing. The intensity, the purity of . . ."

"Was he ever violent?" I asked. "Was he coercive?"

She scowled at me, for being so dense. "Of course not. He was the polar opposite of that. He drew them out, their real selves. Their depth. Depth to depth . . . that's what it always was with George. That was the whole point. He was a violent man—an actual murderer back home, he said—but never about this. Never."

She rushed on, wanting to make sure I got it. "Think about Marion, Marion Robinson. She's the best example. He absolutely loved her. She was so pure, and so sweet. She'd lived for years with this complete idiot. Talk about 'cock-dead'! They lived in this lead box of a house in Darien, and he commuted back and forth, blind and cruel as a convict. And she was locked up, too, in that dreadful house. But all the while, she sang in her cage like the sea! Through all those numbing years."

Alex sat up, let her voice settle down a little. "Then, mercifully," she said, "George heard her. She was on the edge of a cluster of people at the club. No one was paying any attention to her; they never did. Her husband was bellowing away. But George heard. He was almost deafened, he said. She was like one of those powerful beams they send into outer space, just in case there's intelligent life? That little brown wren, sending out this extraordinary beam, all the time?" Her voice lifted at the end to draw me in. "And he heard her?" A rhetorical question. "The first one ever? And saved her?"

"She went off with him?" I asked, a little dumbly.

"Oh, yes. He followed her over to the buffet table and just put his hand on her shoulder—a way he has—and murmured something. She didn't turn around, didn't look. She just leaned back against him and made a little sound in her throat, a little groan. She told me all this later. It was a miracle for her.

"He told her where to meet the car. And, the next morning, there she was. In her regular clothes, but all clean, and with L'Air du Temps under her breasts. She never, never looked back." Alex was beaming. She rushed on again.

"She was amazing in the crowd scenes. I loved to lie with her, either at the beginning, when it was just starting. Get to her first and bring her in. Or in the middle, when she was soaked in sweat and barely knew who she was. I'd hug her and think I was at the center of the world. Nothing felt better than Marion's arms around you in the middle of that frenzy. I mean *nothing*. One of the most loving people I've ever touched. And I've touched a few."

Alex was radiant, but she paused, seeing my troubled, flushed face, and she reached over and patted my leg one more time. "It's okay. You'll see," she said gently. "We'll go. You and I."

"Together?" I said, dumbly, breathing through my mouth.

"Yup," she said, with a sweet smile. "Give me your hand."

"No," I said, but I didn't resist as she took it and gently placed it at the top of her brown leg, at the edge of . . . her fur. A wild surge ran through me. The current . . .

"Catch your breath," she said, gently, not moving. I felt as if I had been given sodium pentothal and we were sitting there, the two of us, waiting for it to work. I felt her against the edge of my hand, just barely stirred my knuckle at her lips. And waited for my heart to settle. Then slowly, slowly, I moved my hand away.

"Wow!" she said, gently. "You're something. Talk about Marion!" She grinned at me. "See? I can hear, too. Like George. I could hear you, that night at the dance. It wasn't his idea to get you . . . it was mine." I sat there, like an idiot, barely able to move. Like one of Odysseus's sailors, surging around Circe, the poor dopes, waiting to be turned into swine. Worth it, I would have said, in that brief moment. Worth it.

I didn't want to but I raised my hand to my face, smelled her intimacy, ever so faintly. She laughed. "Oh, my!" I closed my eyes, dropped my hand to my side and just sat there a minute. "Shall we finish?" she asked, kindly. I didn't quite shake myself like a dog coming out of the water, but almost.

"We were going to talk about George," I said at last. "That story was about Marion."

"No, no!" she said. "That was George! That was the point. He heard her . . . He could hear."

"And hear all the others."

"Yes." Eagerly again.

"And someone killed him for it," I said suddenly without thinking. She leapt to her feet, and I felt awful. She stood there a second, looking first this way, then that. Then just sat down again. It was strange. Then, like a parody of an uncomfortable man in a tight situation, I asked where the bathroom was. She laughed—we both laughed—and she sent me on my way, the tension carefully broken. Alex was in the kitchen getting another drink when I came back. A glass of wine this time. The sensuality that had hung so heavy in the air seemed quite gone. "Where do you want to start?" she asked from the brightly lit kitchen, her voice raised. "The night he was killed or what?"

"The night before, I guess. After the dance. We've talked to the Suttons, so I have some idea of what happened."

"I'm surprised they'd talk to you," Alex said, walking back with her wineglass. "Did you twist them a little, too?"

"Yes, as a matter of fact," I said. "There'd been some coke that night, and . . . well, we found it."

"Hmm," Alex said, interested. "Those poor people. They didn't really . . ." She stopped. "I was going to say they didn't belong in all this, but of course they did. They came running, once we began. Still, if George had one real perversion, it was his appetite for, um, innocence. I think of it as purity with Marion, but with the Suttons you might say innocence."

"Kind of rough, wasn't it?" I said without thinking.

"You could say that," she considered. "But no one had to do it."

I thought of poor Sutton and his wife. And of Cassie's husband, Don, who was not only "debauched" but dead. And for a moment I was angry. "The debauching of innocents has always been the business of people like George, hasn't it?"

She looked up. "You can be a little rough yourself, can't you?" she said, a bit stiff all of a sudden. "And you may be right, but I don't think so. It was the lucky innocents that we took. And they loved it. I mean loved it. Ask Jane Sutton. Ask Bob. Ask your girl, Cassie; she came this close," she said, holding up a finger and thumb. That stopped me. Alex went on in a gentler voice, "And now there's you, Tim," and she put her hand on my thigh. I felt suddenly warm.

"May I get myself a drink?" I asked, getting up to go into the kitchen.

She smiled at that . . . at me, running away. "Please."

"Did George do a lot of cocaine?" I asked, raising my voice so she could hear me from the kitchen area.

"No, not much. Some, to get things rolling, sometimes, but not much. Or to stay awake." I looked up and down the elegant granite counters for soda but didn't find any. Then I rooted around in the well-stocked fridge until I found some. More ice, too. Made myself at home . . . we were settling in.

"He'd had a little the night he was killed, apparently. The . . ." I was going to say the *autopsy*.

"Yes, some," she said. "They found it in his system?"

"Some. I just wondered if there were something unusual about that that might lead to anything . . ."

"I doubt it. He didn't have much, but it wasn't unusual for him to have some. Or anyone else. Forstman was practically an addict. And his wife and I had some. It's the lady's drug, as they say. Men, it turns their cocks into little Thompson seedless grapes." She grinned at that. "Their heads are as keen as ever, but their cocks turn into hard, little seedless grapes."

"You're very knowledgeable, Alex," I said with a smile.

"Oh, everyone knows about that."

"No they don't." I took a sip, went on. "Anything unusual about George the night of the ball? Apart from that speech of his?"

"Yuh, there was, actually. He was unusually full of himself that night, I must say. From the cocktail hour on *Java*, all through dinner and after. He wasn't usually that hyper. That speech was part of it, I think."

"Was he still hyper on Sutton's boat?" I asked.

"No, he was trying to rein himself in by that point . . ."

"Sutton mentioned something like that. He speculated that George was 'saving himself' for someone the next night. Does that make sense?"

"I've thought about that. It makes sense, in retrospect. Because of the business with the 'more woman' and all that. But I didn't think much about it at the time."

"Forgive me, but jump ahead for a sec: who was the More Woman?"

She stared at me, wide-eyed, perhaps a little apologetic. "I have no idea. You'd think I would, but I don't."

"Assuming it was someone new, would it be a woman?"

"Oh, for sure. That business about holding back, surely a woman."

"Sutton said that Marion was angry about that, his holding back."

"Not angry . . ." She considered. "It's just that the idea of holding back . . . She couldn't." Shrug.

"Was there a time during the night, Sunday, when she was away from the rest of you?" I asked.

Alex looked up quickly. "Oh, Tim, don't bother. She never, never killed him. I mean, never. I can get things wrong but there's no question on that one. She worshipped him."

"Isn't that all the more reason to worry about her?"

"No. She's like me." Alex instinctively took my hand for this part. "If George has found some extraordinary new woman . . . that's a delicacy for us, Tim. A delicacy." Oh.

"I'm sorry, I've been jumping around. What time did you two leave the dance to go to Sutton's?" I asked.

"Not long after you left, maybe around one thirty," she said.

I was surprised. "How in the world do you know when I left?" I asked.

She smiled nicely. "I have a sneaker for you, what do you think? I told you I could 'hear.'"

I swallowed. I almost gulped, and Alex looked at me so sweetly, so touchingly, that I almost forgot why I was there. But not quite. Also, I was not delusional: I did not assume that she was coming on to me without some motive.

"You got to Sutton's boat and . . . what?"

"It was very short, as those things go, because George wanted to go back, because of the next night, I assume. But Marion was up for it and the Suttons were raging. It had been quite a night at the dance, remember; pretty strong stuff and we were still wound up."

"We'd all been together before, too. So, boom, it just began. Sutton and his wife pulled back their bed and we . . ." She looked up and must have seen something troubled in my face. She grinned. "I'm going to turn you to stone, aren't I?" she said sympathetically.

I shrugged and smiled. "I'll have to do the best I can."

"Does this offend you? All this sex?"

"No," I said. "Consenting adults can do anything they want." I thought about the talk with Cassie and wondered if that was really true, but this was no time for that discussion.

"Okay. Well, we're on Sutton's new boat," she began, "down below. And we just began, Marion and I. The others watched for a minute. People are always fascinated to see us. I'm tall and sort of glamorous, you know. And Marion's darker and rounder and so still at first. A nice housewife. A young mum. I don't know what they fantasize, but people love to watch us. Even that experienced group."

The rest was what I'd already heard from the Suttons. It came out differently, but it was the same in the end. Except that she stressed the fog. She was excited about that, said they all were. "That fog," she said, "that fog may have triggered everything."

I skipped ahead to the next night, on Forstman's boat. I tried not to show it but I was hugely interested to hear this part. In the event, it was oddly disappointing. In fact, apart from the addition of drugs and the now-almost-familiar orgy, it was much the same as what I'd heard before. They ate and drank. Did some dope and made love . . . George still holding back some. He even dropped off to sleep at one point. Then at ten thirty or so, he astonished everyone by getting up, dressing, and leaving. Same exact story as before.

"Except he came back," I couldn't help coaxing her. My whole theory of the case turned on his coming back, and I wanted to make it easier for her to talk about it. "He came back?" I said again and looked at her hard.

But she just looked puzzled. "No, he didn't," she said, as if she couldn't imagine how I'd gotten that wrong. "He never came back. That was the thing." We stopped for a moment at that point, while I tried to decide how to go forward.

"That's clear?" I said.

"Of course." She looked at me funny, then went on. "I'll tell you what is different," she said, "something I did not tell you before." Pause. "I went looking for him. Out on the water."

"What?!" I tried to look calm but this was electrifying.

"I got uneasy for some reason. It was dumb in a way: no one was more at home or safer on the water than George. Maybe it was the dope; sometimes it makes you paranoid. Anyhow, I got worried. I got up and got dressed and told the others I was going to have a look. Marion wanted to come, too, but I said no. I just put on my stuff and went out the door . . . down to the place where the inflatables were and grabbed one."

"What time was this?" I asked. Calmly now, as if it were not the most important question of the investigation.

She startled me by smiling; this was going to be funny, apparently. "There was a big nautical clock in the saloon," she said. "It was loud and it rang eleven thirty, seven bells, just as I was going out the door. I stuck my head back in and said, 'Cinderella's off to the ball. I'll be back by midnight.'

"That was a joke, of course. I would not be back in half an hour. But I did come to my senses pretty fast, out there in the fog. I did make it out of the Tangles and found the Squadron, but quickly realized there was nothing sensible to do. I looked around for a few minutes, trying to spot George's dinghy, but that was ridiculous; I'd never find it in that big fleet in all that fog. So I turned around and—by some miracle—found my way back to the Tangles and *Endymion*. I walked back into the saloon just as the big clock struck twelve thirty, one bell. 'Cinderella's home by twelve thirty,' I said. 'Close enough.' They all laughed at that. And then, you'll perhaps be surprised to hear, I took my things off and we all began again."

"To make love?" I asked, genuinely astonished.

"To make love. It's my default action, maybe, when things are tense. We didn't do it for that long. We were in bed by two or so."

I tried to be casual but I had never been more alert. This was a huge admission: she had been out on the water when George was murdered. She could have murdered him herself. Or she and Theo could have linked up. But she gave herself a pretty good alibi, too. If that business with the maritime clock chimes held up—and I was positive it would, no one was going to forget an incident like that—she had only been gone for exactly one hour. Nowhere near time enough to find and murder George— with or without Theo—and get back to the Tangles.

Unless, of course, that part was a lie and they were all in on it. Unless this was the fallback position they had all agreed to, and this is where they would take their stand. But then the question arose, why would the others stand by the clock story if it weren't true and if she had been the only murderer? And— even if there were some explanation for that—I just didn't think this crew was up to putting together such an elaborate story at this point, even if they wanted to. And they'd surely fall apart, under close questioning. My guess—my disheartening guess— was that the seven bells/one bell story was true. And that she had been alone on the water for an hour. What in the world was one to make of that?

I did ask why she had gone along with Fred and his foolish no-drugs story. And failed to tell us earlier about her little trip.

She sighed at that, almost as if she were bored by it.

"Fred's a dope," she said. "A complete fool, actually." That certainly made sense.

"The fact is that he was terrified of his drug dealers. These three guys had come all the way up to Broke from Fall River or someplace to bring him a ton of dope. Real thugs, in a big Bertram. And they scared the hell out of all of us. But especially Fred. They told him that, if he even admitted that he had this dope—let alone identified them—they'd kill us all. Fred believed them and he convinced us. So we lied. We were a lot more afraid of the drug guys than we were of you." Maybe that made sense, but not much, it seemed to me.

"So this whole nonsense was about Fred being afraid of his dealers?" Good grief!

"Yup. I told you it was stupid. I should never have gone along with it; but I was so whipped by then I just let it ride."

"And then when we arrived and you learned George had been murdered . . . ?"

"My head was miles away by then. I just didn't care . . . just followed Fred's line, as we'd agreed."

"And your trip out on the water? How about not telling us that?"

"That was Fred, too. He just said we should keep it simple. I really didn't care much at that point. Just went along."

"But, Alex . . . you'd been out on the water. You were the principal suspect."

"That's silly," she said, serenely. "No one would have thought that."

"Are you nuts? Everyone thinks that. I think it right now, for Christ's sake."

"No, you don't," she said. "No one would. I just went along with Fred."

"You didn't just go along with Fred. You stuck to the line hard when we questioned you. For a long time. And then, by heaven, you joked about it," I said, with real astonishment in my voice. "You held your hands out for the handcuffs. How could you joke?" I asked.

She looked at me evenly, a small smile on her astonishingly beautiful face. "I am not like you," she said. "I am a jokey girl."

CHAPTER 22

DETECTIVES

Alex walked me out to the old freight elevator and I tried to think how you say good night after a session like that. I ended up giving her a companionable pat on the shoulder, as if we were some kind of pals, which was totally weird. She picked up on the humor of that instantly and patted me back, like another guy. Then she leaned forward and lapped my face. One long lick across my cheek and mouth, like a dog. Then, "G'night," in her rich alto voice. I stepped away, the elevator arrived, and I backed in, all in an instant. I was spinning.

Sex is hard, isn't it? The great joker in the deck. The whole deck, often enough. And still we play, night after night, absolutely riveted. As if life made sense. Cassie got all that right, didn't she?

It was late when I got home, and Bud was asleep. I made myself sit down and dictate the whole story over the phone to a gadget in the office. There would be a transcript on my desk, and Jayne's and David's, first thing in the morning. I asked that a copy be faxed to me at home, too, so Bud and I could read it over breakfast. Then I went to bed and slept until ten. Bud of course had been up for hours. He was sitting in the kitchen with a cup of coffee, the remains of some rolls, and the transcript of my memo beside him.

"Quite a night, old boy," Bud said laconically.

"Quite a night," I said, pouring myself a cup of coffee. There was a moment of silence.

"Why the hell did she do that?" Bud said at last . . . scowling.

"Do what . . . go out on the water or tell me about it?"

"Both, I guess, but mostly, why'd she drag you down there and tell you that? She headin' off somethin' worse? Gettin' her version out there?"

"Makes sense," I said. "That's what I assumed. Sooner or later, this was going to come out. One of those dopes would have said she'd left. Lord only knows if this story is true but one thing's sure: this is her 'final' fallback, her last version of what happened. The next version is, she killed him. Or she brought him back and they all did. And we aren't hearing that. Not from her, anyway."

"Nope. An' she's restin' everything on the one hour . . . on the others remembering the clock business. Think that'll hold up?"

"Of course it will. She's awful smart, and she wouldn't have staked everything on that if it wasn't going to stand up. That 'Cinderella' thing? I guarantee it. The big marine clock bangs out seven bells and she calls their attention to it . . . eleven thirty . . . and says she'll be back by midnight. When she does get back, the good old clock lets go again—one bell this time and everyone looks again: twelve thirty. Whether by chance or not, that is a very careful alibi."

"Sounds right," he agreed.

"And the worst is that I bet it's true. I don't think for a minute that she'd put her life in the hands of those bozos. They'd

fall apart in no time, and she has to know that. The great question for us is, could she have murdered him in that time?"

"That's what I been stewin' about, the last three hours,"
Bud said. "An' it don't look so good." He set down his cup and
squared around. "Think what she woulda had to do. She had
to go down an' get a strange dinghy offa the stern of the big
boat . . . figure out how to start an' get 'er goin'. That's a couple
o' minutes at least. Same on the other end, when she's back to
the Forstman's boat . . . tyin' up an' such . . . walkin' up to the
saloon. So there's five to seven minutes, just gettin' off an' tyin'
up. Once she gets powered up, she goes off in the dark o' night
in the thickest fog I've ever seen, to find old Minot. First, she's
gotta get out of the Tangles without knocking her propeller off
on a rock. That's a crawl. Then she has to find him. He's got to
be on a boat someplace, an' that's a hell of a problem. Even if
she knows what boat he's on, it's gotta take a while to find it.
A hell of a long while, is my guess. Twenty minutes would be
a miracle. Then she says howdy an' there's some foreplay—to
raise that dandy erection he had." I had to smile at that . . . at
a guy like Bud, trying to factor how long it would take Alex to
get Minot erect. "What?" he said, seeing me smile. "Is that a
dumb idea?"

"No," I said. "Go ahead."

"Then she has to kill him. Or maybe help someone else do
it . . ."

"Yup," I agreed.

"If there was two of 'em—she an' Theo, say—it gets a bit
more plausible," Bud said. "But not plausible enough. Anyhow,
she—or they—kill him an' stick pins in his dick. That has to
take some time."

"Then she's gotta pile him into the dinghy," I said.

"Two dinghies, of course. She had to pile him into his and
tow him over to *Java* with hers. Or the two of 'em. If there's
two, it's easier to get him into the dinghy but the time's still

mighty tight. And, if there's two, she has to bring Theo back to his boat before she goes out to find an' make her way through the Tangles again."

"Yeah," I said. "Then into the saloon on the dot of twelve thirty. And it's 'Hi, kids . . . I'm back. Let's boogie.'"

"She's quite a girl . . . ," Bud said speculatively.

"She'd have to be Wonder Woman to do all this."

Bud stopped to think for a minute. "Didn't happen, did it?"

"No," I said.

"Gotta get them others to talk," Bud said with a sigh. "But, if their story squares with hers—the chimes horseshit—it begins to look as if all this ain't gonna amount to much."

I didn't respond. It was too depressing.

That night, Harry finally called. He was in Rockport, he said, in a phone booth. He'd be in Marblehead tomorrow and New York the day after. "How are you doing?"

I didn't ask why he'd left or what the hell he thought he was up to. I just brought him up to date on everything that had happened.

He was silent for a long moment. Then, with all his old grace, he said, "You've done an amazing job, Tim. Absolutely terrific. But it hasn't worked, has it?" No, I said; it had not.

Another long pause. "Let's bail, then. Question the other Forstman people, obviously. And set your associates to helping with the documents. But otherwise, let's get the hell out. Suit you?" I said it did. Said I'd go to Maine on Monday and tell Bud and Horton we were done. See the judge.

There was one other loose end I did tie up. The copies of Minot's films had been sitting in my office for a while, and Jayne had been after me to take a look at them. Whether because I needed to or to embarrass me, I wasn't sure. Anyway, I put a handmade Do Not Disturb sign on my door, drew the blinds, and went to work.

It was not quite the erotic treat I might have thought. It was in color and the quality was fair. But the people were not miked for sound, so all you heard was the music in the background and the occasional grunt or cry of passion. And of course there was no story line. But still, it held my attention very closely indeed. Because Alex was in virtually every frame. She was a serious athlete, which was curiously erotic for me. Tall, ropy, and very strong. The things she did with her body were wonderful. And her energy and her capacity for joy was . . . fantastic. She was the great force in all the films, and I couldn't take my eyes off of her.

There was just one other interesting thing . . . there was this weird guy, in an elaborate bodysuit. Or maybe a superlight wet suit. It was bright green and blue and the colors ran along swooping, artistic lines. He looked like a comic-book hero. And of course he was the only one who wore anything at all. So he stood out. But he was very quiet, the whole time. He just sat on the edges and watched. I backed the film up several times whenever he appeared but didn't get anything . . . just the anomaly of it . . . this guy sitting there, on the edge. In disguise.

When I was finally done, that was the only thing I wanted to follow up on: who the hell was he. Without really thinking about it, I picked up the phone, called Alex. I started by explaining what I'd been doing, watching the films.

"Did you like me?" she broke in at once.

I was completely nonplussed by that but managed to joke, "Like you . . . I adored you," and laughed. "If I were free, I'd come over and curl up by your door like a golden retriever."

"You could come in," she said quickly. Suddenly serious. I didn't doubt it for a minute, and I felt a tug.

"Uh, I am deeply grateful but I am the Law Guy, as you know. For as long as this case goes on, I have to stay outside. But I do have one question." Then I asked about the guy in the wet suit or whatever. "Who is he?"

She paused for a minute and then said, "I don't know."

That had to be a lie. The tape was from about three years ago. Anyone who was there would remember that guy. My heart sank. "C'mon, Alex. Are we back to the 'no dope' period? Who is he?"

"I don't mean that I don't remember," she said. "Obviously I remember, but I don't know who he is. George found him and brought him. He showed up in that rig and just sat there the whole night. *Very weird.* My assumption was that maybe there was something wrong with him, sexually. Or that watching was his thing. Although that couldn't have been it; even then he'd have shown a physical reaction. He didn't. Either there was something wrong, or he had astonishing control or some damn thing. I asked George later, of course, but he blew me off . . . wouldn't say. I can say this: he never came back. Not in costume, anyway."

I didn't begin to believe all that but I couldn't figure out how to get a purchase . . . how to pry into it. I let it go and assumed I'd get another chance later.

She could see that I didn't believe her. "Look," she said. "I know it's implausible, but that's how it is. Maybe he's the president of the United States, but if so, I didn't recognize him."

That was it.

She asked if I wanted to have supper and I said sure, as if everything were fine. We were both downtown; we picked a place and met early. It was pleasant, in a weird way; it was, after all, dinner with a murder suspect. Not a strong suspect, maybe, but the best we had. And one who was still holding something back, I thought: the identity of the guy in the blue-and-green wet suit.

There was one tough moment. I was talking about getting the rest of the Forstman people to talk—which I was sure they would, now. I said I did not expect to learn anything and added, gratuitously: "They're a slightly odd bunch, but I can't see any of them killing George. Let alone that business with the pips."

"What pips?" she said, and I realized I had made a mistake. I sat still for a long minute but she said, "C'mon, what pips? What happened?" I still waited but didn't see a way around it. I slowly explained about the two bullet holes in his forehead, equally spaced, with a pip in each. Plus the one in his ear. I was still thinking about the fourth pip when she burst out:

"His cock. Did they put one on his cock?"

I was astonished at that but said, yes, they had.

"But it was the old hole, right?" she rushed, way ahead of me. "He had a hole in his foreskin and it was the old hole, wasn't it?" As if she wanted to be assured that he hadn't been tortured.

"Yes," I said, glad to tell her. "It was the old hole. It's like Bud said: apart from the shots, he wasn't hurt. He would never have felt a thing."

She sat silent after that, her face a mask. She wasn't looking at me, now. Just staring into the middle distance. Finally, I got my balance back and asked, gently: "Does that suggest anything to you?"

"No," she said. "Not a thing in the world."

The next day, Sunday, was one of the oddest yet. It turns out that it was a day of profound transition, although I wouldn't know it for a while. But the signs began to pile up. First, I couldn't reach Horton to say I was coming up to Maine to withdraw from the case. I called all day Sunday and into the evening. No luck. But I also couldn't get through to Bud. I spoke to Caroline once and she sounded downright odd. I didn't ask her what was the matter but I did ask her, urgently, to tell Bud to call me. He never did.

Next, the judge. I couldn't reach him, either. And his wife—like Caroline—sounded odd. Finally, Harry. No one answered the phone at home, no one picked up the cell. That was unusual. I decided to fly up the next morning anyway . . . find out what the hell was going on and tell them what I was going to do. I did stop at my office Monday morning. And there was a stranger waiting for me. A messenger from Sammy Cameron. That didn't fit in anywhere.

PART II

CHAPTER 23

THE DEER IN THE SWIMMING POOL

The messenger recognized me as I walked in. He stood up and handed me an envelope. Like a process server who had been lying in wait. But it wasn't a subpoena, it was a hand-written note from Sammy Cameron. I was going to take it into my office and read it in private, but the messenger asked if I could read it right there. It was very short, he said, and he was supposed to wait for the reply and get back to Mr. Cameron immediately.

Sammy Cameron? A note this urgent from Sammy Cameron? That didn't make a whisper of sense. Do you remember him? He was the lovely old guy at the party on *Java* who had been such a help to Harry. His great mentor, in fact. The note was short:

"Timmy, I understand you may be going to Maine today. Could you possibly break your trip in Boston? I need to talk to you and it would be hard for me to come to New York. I'd be grateful if you could alter your plans a little and come see me. At, say, eight this evening. I'll arrange a plane for Maine, first thing in the morning. The delay will not, I think, matter. And can this be between us? No need to bother Harry." That was chilling. Not bother Harry? . . . His great friend and my beloved brother? I thought about saying no, but then thought better of it: Sammy Cameron would not make a request like this for any but the best reasons. I told the messenger to tell Sammy I'd be there.

I got to Boston at the end of the afternoon and took a cab to the Salem and Canton Club on Beacon Hill. It's a very old-fashioned men's club, in a 1790s townhouse, just down the hill from Sammy's place. The name came from the conceit that its members had roots in the China Trade at the turn of the eighteenth century, when Salem rivaled Boston in importance, especially in the China Trade. Canton was the great trading port in China in those times. Some of the founders of the club surely did have roots in the China Trade, but most of them made their dough in the 1840s and '50s, when the big money came from the slightly less romantic and vastly more profitable cotton mills in Lawrence and Haverhill. Still, the club decor was Federalist and there were plenty of China Trade artifacts sprinkled around. Lovely ship models, maritime paintings, and some stunning china. Remarkably nice place.

Harry had insisted I join, and somewhat to my surprise, I loved it and always stayed there when I was in town. I was able to get my favorite room, on the third floor, which had a huge bathroom right in front. The bathroom must have been a bedroom at one time. But the result of the modernization was that you could sit in an immense, old tub and look right down on Boston Common.

I had an early dinner at the club. Not the best food in Boston but a wonderful dining room . . . and lovely, old Irish waitresses who had been there forever. Superb wine list, too. Harry and I dined there regularly. "The Bigelow Boys" tapping into their Boston roots: scrod . . . sometimes a lobster. Then Indian pudding. If you haven't grown up on Indian pudding, you probably won't like it. But if you have, oh boy.

At a little before eight I tried Harry again. No luck. I walked the few steps up Beacon Street to Sammy's house. He met me at the door himself; there didn't seem to be any servants around.

"Ah, Tim, you are so good to do this. It was going to be awfully hard for me to come to New York tonight, and I couldn't meet earlier."

I said no, it had been easy, and looked around. It was perhaps the most beautiful house in Boston, a match for the Salem and Canton Club but older, fancier, and better maintained. I suspected that it had been in Sammy's family since it was built. Actually, that may not be right. The "original" Boston aristocracy of the seventeenth and eighteenth century was heavily Tory and sailed away on British warships to Nova Scotia on March 17, 1776, after Henry Knox dragged the cannons down from Fort Ticonderoga and drove the British out. The fact is that of the famously haughty and puritanical Boston aristocrats of the nineteenth century many were new men, who had arrived or risen up after the revolution. Not all but a lot. Where the Camerons fit in that hierarchy I didn't know. Whatever . . . the Cameron house was beautiful and his roots were plenty deep enough for me.

The furniture may have been original to the house, even if the Cameron family was not. The poor Tories had not been able to take much on those British warships, and their successors—the Rebels—may have just walked into the furniture as well as the houses. I have always been fascinated by that transition. The Tories—and the British army—left on March 17,

1776, "Evacuation Day" in Boston ever since. But there was no wind for two weeks. So the poor devils had to sit in the harbor, jammed into those warships, and stare back at the royal lions on the Old State House. And at the roofs of their old homes. And their old lives, to which they would never return.

Sammy said he was having a bourbon and soda and would I join him. I would. We stood in a little butler's pantry off the kitchen while Sammy mixed. Then went upstairs to his study on the second floor. Like my wonderful bathroom at the Salem and Canton, it was right in the front of the building and would have served as the master bedroom in any modern house. It was paneled and book-lined and there was a wood fire burning in what was almost certainly a Samuel McIntire fireplace. My mother had lost track of a lot of things by the time I came along, but she knew her furniture and especially admired McIntire carving. The sheaves of wheat on the mantel were the giveaway.

I did not recognize any of the marine paintings, set out among the books, but it was no trick to pick out the authentic Revere bowl, which needed polishing, on a high shelf.

"Pretty nice spot, Sammy," I said with a smile; it was an amazing spot.

"'Tis nice, isn't it," he said, and I had the pleasant sense that he knew precisely how nice it was and was grateful, as some inheritors are not. I am less excited about "old money" than most because I have seen so much of it turn sour, including the portion that had come down to my parents. But it can do some remarkable things . . . such as creating a Sammy Cameron and a room like this one. Not trifling accomplishments.

"Harry stayed in this room for a few weeks," Sammy said as we sat down with our drinks. "We made it into a temporary bedroom for him, while we figured out what to do next. I can't tell you what a pleasure it was to have him here, even during that troubling time."

"Lucky Harry," I said with a small smile, looking around appreciatively.

"Well, yes and no, I guess," Sammy said. "It was a sad business, taken all around. But this part—his staying here with me—that was pretty good. The beginnings of a terrific, lifelong friendship. I was single then and I had a lot of time for him."

There was a brief pause while we settled down to whatever we were going to be doing.

"Okay," Sammy said at last. "As you know, I was one of the few who sailed out of Broken Harbor, two days after the ball. Marcie and I went through the fog, all the way to Marblehead, overnight."

"I remember," I said. "I knew it would not have been all that hard for you, in that boat, even in that weather."

"No, it wasn't," he agreed. "But that's not why we went, I'm afraid." I waited.

"We had stayed that night on *Java*, you know, so I heard about Minot early on. Didn't see the body, but I heard the story and knew he'd been down there, on the service float. Frankly, I was not anxious to talk to the police the next day, so we made our way over to our boat in the morning, pulled up anchor, and just took off. Fog or no."

"Ah . . ."

"There was fog all the way to Marblehead, but we made out well enough. We moored the boat and drove into town." A deep intake of breath at this point. "And I decided to move up a trip we'd been thinking about . . . to go to France for a while. We went the next day. I had hoped that the whole business would have blown over by the time we got back . . . that the murderer would have been caught and so on."

"But no," I offered.

"No," Sammy said. "In fact, Horton, the district attorney up there in Maine, has been in frantic touch with my office, trying to arrange an interview. He even threatened to come to France. At that point I decided to come back."

"Have you spoken to him yet?"

"On the phone. And I am going up there on Thursday. First a conference, with my lawyers and so on. And then right into the grand jury, I gather," Sammy said. "And I wanted to chat with you first." A grand jury? I hadn't heard about that.

A longish pause. Then: "Our cabin was on the port side, just where the gangway ran up from the work float."

"I see."

"Yup. And for some damned reason, I was looking out a porthole just before midnight . . . checking on the fog I guess, or maybe I heard something."

"And you saw . . ."

"Harry, coming up the gangway."

There you go. There goes my life. Mine and Harry's both. Done.

I paused for only a moment, then asked, perfectly calmly, "It was pretty clear, even with the fog, that it was Harry?"

"I'm afraid it was. His face was not two feet from mine. He didn't notice me and I didn't signal him, but it was Harry. He was dressed in normal sailing clothes . . . chinos, a peacoat, watch cap, and was walking normally."

"No gun?" I offered. "No bloodstains or whatnot?"

"No, no! Of course not," Sammy said impatiently. "He seemed perfectly normal. Except it was midnight. In dense fog. And he was coming up from the service float."

"You took a peek at your watch?"

"It was ten of twelve, exactly."

"Umph. Anything else?"

"No. But I suspect it may be enough to get them focused on him pretty hard. If they are not already. And I got the impression that Horton is indeed pretty heavily focused on him already. And I sensed that he knew a lot. To the extent I had been thinking about perjuring myself, I forgot about it."

I just nodded. Then, with a deep sigh, I sat there for a couple of minutes and didn't say a word. Sammy watched me closely, with a little sympathy, I thought.

"I didn't know," I said.

Sammy nodded. "Somehow, I didn't think you did. That's why I wanted to talk before you went up there. So you wouldn't get blindsided." He paused. "Horton also told me, on the phone, that they had had a tip and found what he assumes is the murder weapon . . . a ways off from Harry's sailboat, right on the track to *Java*. Don't know what to make of that at this point, but I assume it's serious." Now a long pause while we just sat there. I suppose that—at some level—I had had to know that something like this was conceivable, that Harry might have murdered Minot and lied to me and everyone else about it. But it had been buried pretty deep; I was stunned.

"So odd, Sammy," I said at last. "Why wouldn't he tell me, for heaven's sake?"

Sammy shrugged, didn't say anything, but I suppose the answer was obvious: Harry didn't tell me because he had murdered Minot in the night and thrown his gun into the sea. And what was I going to do about that? That wasn't the only explanation, but it was the only one I could think of on the spot.

I sat there and Sammy just watched me. Watched my life drift away.

"Pretty wild, Sammy," I said eventually. We did not know each other well, and we were not going to have a heart-to-heart, but I was so taken aback I had to say some damn thing. "And why in the world would he let me take the lead on the investigation? I would have thought . . ." I stalled out.

"That he would have protected you? Me too. He must have thought . . ."

I took a deep breath. "He must have thought he was doing the right thing." That notion hit me forcefully: if Harry thought he was doing "the right thing," he was capable of absolutely anything. Maybe including betraying me. A little hard to imagine, but there had to be some explanation. This might be it. We'd see, I guess.

Sammy tried to help: "He's a passionate man, I'm afraid. And he trusts his gut, which is not always his friend. Mostly but not always."

"And not violent, Sammy," I said quickly. "Not killing someone and putting pips in his cock." I fairly shuddered at that improbability. "I have never known him to do a violent thing in his life, have you?"

Sammy sat there for a long time. "I have, actually." Another pause. "I've been thinking about telling you this for a while. I am not at all sure why, but there is an old story that almost no one knows. But it might bear, and it might be best if you knew."

He paused, as if still making up his mind. I just looked at him.

"You remember—or maybe you don't—when he left home, I suppose?" I said I did, some of it. But go ahead.

"Well, he came over to my place back then. Stayed for a week and went home again. Then he left home for good a week or so later. Stayed with me for some time." I said I more or less knew that. Remembered it, in fact.

"Well," Sammy went on, "that first night, there was a violent turn." I waited; I did not know this. "He came home unexpectedly, and there was some kind of a dustup at your house. I don't know the details but Harry got into it."

"A 'dustup,' Sammy; what are you talking about?"

"I don't know but apparently he grabbed a friend of your parents for some reason . . . a big fella, and they got into it. Dragged him out of the house and across the lawn. Took him out by the garbage cans . . ." Sammy paused and looked at me.

I nodded. I knew where the garbage cans used to be. "And then he began to wail on him pretty hard. Punched him, kicked him, broke some ribs. Hell of a thing. The older man was a big, athletic chap but Harry was already good sized himself, and he just went to town."

"Why?"

"I have no idea. Happily, some people came out of the house, and put a stop to it. Which was a good thing, because Harry might have done him a real injury. Anyhow, the fella who broke it up knew me and knew that I was fond of Harry. So he just up and drove Harry over to my place."

"What was it all about? And why are you telling me now?"

"I don't know what it was about, and I'm telling you because I thought you should know that Harry had been quite violent, that one time, and there is a police report, which Horton may find. It was a long time ago, but it was serious business, and Horton may use it. I wanted you to know about this, just in case."

"I have never heard a whisper of any of this. What was he furious about? Who was this guy?"

Sammy shook his head, sadly. "I don't know. Your parents were terrific people in a lot of ways. The genuine article. But, as I guess you know, they got . . . a little lost. And some of those parties . . . there was drinking and things maybe got a little rough."

"Fights?" I said, incredulous.

Sammy just shrugged. "Apparently."

"And after that, Harry left home," I said.

"Pretty much," he said. "He stayed with me for ten days or so. Then he went back home for a week."

"Then he went back to you again and that was it," I said. "I remember that."

"Yup. The second time, he just showed up with his stuff and asked if he could stay for a while. I said he could."

"That's wild, Sammy," I said. "He just up and left home, and you took him in?"

"I guess it had gotten pretty bad at home. It was clear he wasn't going back again, and I thought I might be able to help. He asked me, did I have any ideas about work for him and so on. As you know, I did, and some friends and I were able to help. Found a place to stay, after a stretch with me. All that."

It occurred to me that there was more but that I was not going to find out about it that night. We sat in silence for several minutes.

"Do you know about the deer in the swimming pool?" I asked. Why I asked that, I cannot begin to say, but I did.

Sammy looked at me blankly. No, he didn't. But that didn't matter, for some reason; I soldiered on.

"I know this is odd but for some reason, it came strongly to mind, as you told me your story."

"Yes?" Sammy said, neutrally.

"Yes. One of the sharpest memories of my childhood is from that week, when Harry first left. A huge buck fell into our empty swimming pool and broke his neck, died. I told my parents but they seemed paralyzed. By Harry's leaving, by this fight you just told me about, I don't know. But for whatever reason, they didn't do anything. *Couldn't* do anything. It began to rot. And then it began to smell. Until, eventually, there was this horrendous stench all through the yard and even in the house. And still my parents didn't do anything. It was as if it were going to be there forever and they were going to live with that."

"Yes?" Sammy said.

"When Harry came home, he asked me about the smell, and I took him out to the pool. He took one look and called the cops. The desk cop said if it was on private property, we had to 'dispose' of it on our own. Harry said it was starting to fall apart and we couldn't. The cop said he couldn't help that. Then after a pause he hinted, 'If it was on the public road, now . . .'

"That evening, Harry got a rope and we tied the stinking body to the pickup truck. He put towels around the deer's neck to make a kind of harness . . . so the head would be less likely to tear off. Then he held the deer's head up and I ran the rope under it, tied it around his neck. Quite a responsibility for a six-year-old. The stench and sight, up close, were sickening. Then Harry made a kind of ramp, up the side of the pool, with some old boards and a pair of skis. He checked the knot and tied the other end to the truck. He drove; I stood and watched. Watched the neck stretch, the tongue squirt out, and the head go off at an odd angle as the line went taut. The body slowly inched out of the pool—it didn't come apart, thank God. Just inched up the ramp and across the grass and the lawn, leaving a trail of blood and slime all the way out to the street. He left it at the side of the road, near the garbage cans. In the morning, he called the same cop, said the carcass was in the street. The next day, it was gone.

"No one said anything," I went on. "A couple of days later, Harry and Mother and I were at breakfast and my mother said, very quietly, 'Thank you, Harry.' Harry didn't say a word. Just looked at her. The next day, he was gone."

"Interesting," Sammy said. "What do you make of it?"

"I don't know," I said. "But I was thinking of Harry dragging things across the lawn . . . wondered about connections. Harry cleaning up messes, maybe? Looking after Mother? I don't know."

Sammy nodded, noncommittal. Said that was interesting but he had no idea. Eventually I stood up and said I better get going, get to bed. I had that private plane in the morning, so I could set my own departure time, but I wanted to get there . . . find out what the hell was going on. Although now, I had a fair idea.

CHAPTER 24

STAND ASIDE NOW

I had a wretched sleep. No sleep, mostly. I finally gave up
around four, after a particularly vivid dream. In it I see Harry
coming up the gangway on *Java* in the fog, and opening his
cabin door. To find Mimi, naked and up to her armpits in blood
. . . with dead George spread across her lap. Harry walks in,
unsurprised, and starts wiping the gore off Mimi. Somehow,
George disappears and it is just the two of them . . . Mimi
sitting there, limp as a child, while he washes her hands and
face, her breasts, with a warm, wet cloth. Harry, the father . . .
cleaning up this appalling mess. Then this terrifying segue to
the head of the deer, with its tongue squirting out as the rope
tightens around its neck.

There was another scenario that I tried a couple of times
in my conscious mind, with the lights on, but I could not quite
manage it. I could not make myself see Harry sitting on his
boat with George's cock in his hand, scowling in the bad light

as he looked for the hole in the foreskin, the pip in his teeth like a sewing needle. I still couldn't see that one.

Bud was standing by his pickup truck waiting for me as usual when the plane got in. But he didn't look the same. Distant. He was very distant.

"Somethin' come up, we gotta go see the judge," he said, taking my bag and putting it in the back of the truck.

"What?" I asked, getting in.

"Be easier to do it all just once, over there," he said, "all of us together."

"Okay, but you look pretty tough . . ."

"Best hold up, Doc," he cut me off. "We can talk over there." There was silence after that. He did hand me a bag from the Hanson Donut. "You better tuck in if you ain't had breakfast . . . this could be a while." I took a peek into the bag. "I will tell ya," he said, "that we found a gun off the stern of Harry's boat, may have been the murder weapon."

"I saw Sammy Cameron last night," I began. "He told me about the gun, and some other things. Is this about him?"

"Bunch o' things. Best wait till we're all together," he said.

I sat there, eating glazed donuts and sipping coffee as we drove into town. There were patches of fog on the empty country road. When we got to the courthouse, the judge's clerk directed us to his courtroom, not his chambers. Horton was sitting stiffly at the counsel table on the left-hand side. He did not speak. The judge came in—in robes. He didn't speak, either. Then the court reporter, with her little black steno machine on a tripod.

The judge scarcely looked at us. Just a muttered, "Good morning," as he sat down. Then he fussed with some papers. He turned to the reporter, "Marjorie, you ready?" She was.

"The caption for this is 'In re: Grand Jury One,' this date. List those present," and he read off our names.

With a sigh, he turned to me. "Mr. Bigelow, it was not possible to give you notice of this proceeding and I apologize for that. That is not the way lawyers are normally treated in my court. But this is not a normal situation."

Another deep breath. "As you have perhaps heard, this has to do with your brother, Henry R. Bigelow." He looked down at a piece of paper to get the name right. That was Harry's formal name.

"Harry," I said.

"Harry," the judge agreed.

"The point," the judge went on, very heavy now and leaning forward in his chair, "is that a grand jury has been impaneled to weigh the possibility of indicting your brother for the murder of George Minot."

Everyone was silent for a moment, looking at me. I started to say something, I don't remember what. But the judge cut me off.

"No, Mr. Bigelow. You aren't expected to respond." I started to speak again, but he held up his hand. "There are some things we have to get on the record.

"I am told by Mr. Horton that there is every reason to believe that Harry Bigelow is about to be indicted for murder. And that raises grave questions about you. I don't know what you knew or when you knew it." He paused and looked at me over his glasses. "That's not this morning's business, either. I do understand from Mr. Horton that you may be indicted as a coconspirator or for obstruction. Or maybe not. Perhaps, as I tend to hope, you were an innocent dupe in this affair, like the rest of us." His voice softened a little at that.

"But frankly, that doesn't matter right now. Since Mr. Horton does not ask that you be taken into custody at this time"—a brief pause to let that sink in . . . that they had been thinking about putting me in jail this morning—"we have some housekeeping chores." He smiled faintly at the incongruity of those homely words. I was not to be put in prison this morning, so there were some housekeeping chores. Oh, of course.

"First, you and your firm must withdraw. I assume that's agreeable?"

"Well," I began, "if—as I cannot imagine—there is serious consideration of indicting Harry . . ."

"Very serious indeed, Mr. Bigelow," Horton cut in. "It will happen."

The judge said, without waiting for me to speak again, "All right, I accept your resignation." Then, turning to Horton, "What do you want to do about records in Mr. Bigelow's possession, Mr. Horton? He should get those up to you at once, I assume?"

"That's right, Your Honor. At least the interview notes and, uh, various videotapes they may have. There are masses of business documents that Bigelow and his people have been digging through for some reason. I don't think we'll need those. If you order that he preserve those intact until the conclusion of any trial, that would be fine."

"Suit you, Mr. Bigelow?" the judge asked.

"Of course, Your Honor. Actually, there are some important papers due to be produced soon." I turned around to Horton. "The Theo Soros papers from Citibank?"

Horton shook his head as if I were discussing disturbances on the moon. "Never mind those, Mr. Bigelow. I don't think we'll be interested in that anymore," he said sarcastically. "The case has taken a different turn."

"All right, then," the judge said, "that's 'so ordered,' too. And let's assume, Mr. Bigelow, that you or your people will have the notes and tapes delivered by, oh, the end of the week."

There's a certain rhythm to the housekeeping orders from the bench, after you lose a case, and this was oddly like that: tidying up at the end of our lives. Harry's and mine.

"You'll want access to Mr. Bigelow and his colleagues, Mr. Horton? Just in case?"

"Yes, Your Honor," said Horton, not very interested.

"All right, Mr. Bigelow?" That was fine and so was a raft of other arrangements.

"The next part, Mr. Bigelow, is particularly important. We have all been placed in an awkward position. To say the least. Maybe you were to blame, maybe not. But the 'appearances' of conflicts . . . well, they couldn't be much worse." He paused as if to consider for a moment just how bad they were.

"Accordingly, I am issuing an isolation order, effective immediately, that neither you nor anyone in your firm have any contact, direct or indirect, with your brother or his wife or their counsel. Or any other intermediaries."

"Is she being indicted, too?" I asked in astonishment.

"No, no," the judge said. "Just part of the separation from your brother."

Now he leaned forward, back on track and bearing down. "If there is any violation of that order, it will be contempt of this court and obstruction of justice. By you and by your brother, and your lawyers and his, if they are involved. And the violators will go to jail. Do you understand?"

I was reeling but I still managed to say that I objected strenuously to such an order. I had been Harry's principal lawyer for a long time . . . he would clearly want me on his legal team, "if this remarkable procedure is going forward."

"Oh, it's going forward, all right, Mr. Bigelow," Horton interjected, unpleasantly. "And the fact that your fundamental loyalty is to your brother is precisely why we're in this situation to begin with."

"That is exactly correct," the judge said, sternly. "You may be heard, right now, but I cannot conceive of a situation where you would be allowed to have further access to your brother or his legal team. I'm sure that he will have superb lawyers, but you will not be one of them. You can make a separate motion later, if you insist." I stood there, silent.

Then the judge asked if I happened to have my passport with me. I told him that I did; I always carried it.

"Fine," the judge said. "If you would be good enough to surrender that to the court, it will . . . well, it will save some fuss." I paused for a moment and the judge pointed out gently that the alternative would be to hold me in custody until we could have a hearing. I handed my passport to the clerk and the judge put another order on the record.

When that was done, he paused and looked down at me thoughtfully for a moment, as if he wanted to say more. But he thought better of it. "You may close the record, Marjorie."

The judge rose to leave and we all stood. I turned to Horton, who glared at me, snapped his briefcase shut, and walked out of the room. I turned to Bud, who just stood there looking at me, not unkindly but remote.

"Best you stay away for a while, Tim," he said quietly. "Stand aside and see how this plays out."

CHAPTER 25

EVERYTHING CHANGES

At this point, everything changes.

Harry, who had been the rock on which my life was built, was taken off to Maine in a rickety-looking little bus, with bars in the windows. He was in handcuffs, if you please. As if he might overpower the guards and go haring off, into the Maine woods. Maybe it was routine to treat him like that, maybe it was melodrama, cooked up by the endlessly rotten B. T. Horton. Whichever, I did not go down to see him off. I couldn't speak to him, anyway, but mostly I did not want to appear on TV, quite possibly in tears.

But I did see it from my place, and I did weep. I am not a weeper, but I wept for this. Funny feeling, at my age, to be sitting there in my comfortable Tribeca loft, watching television and weeping. I tried to choke it off at first, to swallow it, but it just broke through and there was this awkward blend of sobs and gasps and swallows. Until I just let it go, a long series of breaking sobs . . . little waves on the beach. I hadn't cried since Harry left that first time.

It didn't go on forever. By the end of the news clip, I'd stopped. And I probably sounded more or less normal when— as soon as the news piece ended—the phone rang and it was Cassie. To my great surprise. She was up early, she said, because her sister—who lived in Boston—knew of Cassie's connection and had called her. Cassie had been astounded at the news.

"He didn't do it," she said, almost the first thing. "You say I'm a witch and that I 'know' stuff. That's horseshit but I do know this: he didn't do it. I wanted you to know that." I didn't know what to say so I just said thank you. She repeated herself, I said thank you again, and there was a little dead space on the phone. Then we picked up . . . started talking normally. We talked for twenty minutes. We talked about Harry, of course, and the denial of bail . . . the kind of jail he'd go to and how long it would be before a trial. She was very concerned about that. Then I talked a little about the isolation order and what I might be able to do to help. That didn't take long either because I had so little to suggest at that point.

At the end, she said, "I love you," which she'd never said before. I hadn't exactly been thinking about that, but I said I loved her, too. Which, I realized with sudden force, I did. Where that might lead in these terrifying times, who knew. But it felt good. On a day when everything felt god-awful, it felt good. There is a lot in this story about sexuality, but as you know, love and sexuality travel different if sometimes parallel lines. Loving Cassie made things better. And much, much more complicated. Among those complications was a small, lingering unease I still had about her sudden decision to go home, just before the Minot murder. That was *so* weird. Well, I thought, Cassie was a slightly magical creature. What did I expect?

I got a few things done after we hung up. I told Jayne to make a careful copy of all the Minot documents and send them to my apartment. I told her what had happened and said that helping me could get her in trouble at the firm, but she was not concerned. "Without you around, no one's gonna make me a partner anyway. So fuck 'em. You'll have the docs tomorrow."

I also called Frank Butler. He was, if anything, more lost than I. I asked him if he'd come see me the next day. I might be trying to do some stuff, and I'd be grateful for his help.

"Anything," he said. "Absolutely anything." Just like Cassie. I wasn't so totally alone, after all.

One other thing I had going for me, an enormously important one: I got a hand-delivered note early that morning—no signature or sign of who it was from—telling me that Harry had arranged for a massive fortune to be transferred to me, irrevocably. I am talking about well over $100 million! Astonishing. The note did not sound as if he had written it but it purported to set out his views of the gift. He hoped that I would use it wholly to support my own life, however things turned out. The future was going to be very rough, it said, and it would be a huge comfort to Harry to know that I was more than taken care of, forever. Mimi had been taken care of, too, the note said . . . not like me but ample. Taxes had been paid, it was entirely legal. So, with the stroke of a pen apparently, I was a wildly rich man. The note had said I was to use the money for myself, not for Harry, who was more than amply provided for. But that wish was obviously not enforceable. Lord knows what I was going to do for him, with no access to the legal system, but money is a weapon and I would think of some damn thing.

At about seven, I was running on empty . . . obsessing about Harry but to no effect. Then there was this loud knocking on the door, and a woman's voice. I opened up and there—to my astonishment—was Cassie. No suitcase, just a handbag and a raincoat over her arm and the dress that she wore. She must have gone straight from our phone call to the airport. Talk about a magical creature.

"There are a couple of other things," she said, still standing in the hall. I said never mind, and took her in my arms. Hugged her hard.

"Miss ya, baby," she said. "Awful sorry about this." Then she leaned back and gave me a close look. "You okay?" Then that amazing smile. In the midst of all this crap. "I was worried about you," she said.

"I guess you were," said. "But you should know I'm poison these days, and gonna be for a long, long time."

She looked impatient, almost annoyed. "You think I care about that? Who the hell do you think I am?"

Now I smiled. "I know who you are, but I'm still a little surprised that you're here."

"Yuh, well . . . it turns out I care for you." Sweet shrug and a smile. "So here I am."

Then she kicked the door shut with her heel and walked me backward toward my bedroom. We tumbled onto the bed. Made love. First with a kind of gentleness, as if of reassurance. And then with a ferociousness that we had not known before.

Later, we showered and she got back into the same dress until I persuaded her to put on a robe. We dug around for something to eat and then settled down to talk. She was pretty organized; I suppose she'd been thinking about it, on that long plane ride.

"A couple of things, babe," she began. Uh, okay. Why in the world would she have an agenda, at a time like this?

"First," she said, looking at me hard, "let me say again, Harry didn't do it. You can count on that as you do whatever you manage to do with this 'isolation order' or whatever."

"How do you know?" I blurted out.

"I just do," she said without missing a beat. "You say I'm a witch . . ."

"A seer."

"Okay, a seer. I do see stuff, more clearly than some. Anyhow, Harry did not do this. You can count on it.

"Second"—and now she reached over and rocked me a little by the shoulder, as if she had to be more emphatic for this one—"you have to protect yourself. That's really why I'm here. I want to make sure you don't get swallowed up by this." Okay, I said, although I had no idea what she was talking about.

"You can worry about Harry all you want: that's your job. But you gotta worry about who *you* are, too. Gotta hang on to that hard. If there's no *you*, there's no Harry or me or anything." I just sat there, not understanding, my face neutral.

That wasn't good enough for her. "No!" she said flatly. "I mean it." She gave me a little shake. "You cannot imagine how deep this can go, even for a solid guy like you. An existential threat, baby. You can be undone. I was when Don died, and I never really got over it. And you can be, too. I don't want that for you. That's the main reason I came: I want you to *know* that it is going to work out all right. You gotta do your job . . . do whatever you can do. But you don't have to tear yourself to pieces over it; he's going to be okay."

"How in the world do you know that?" This was starting to sound strange, as if maybe she'd been hit pretty hard by this, too.

She waved off my question. "I just do. You can count on it. So don't go falling apart."

"Uh, okay. Anything else?"

"Nope, not now."

Then she sat back, suddenly relaxed. "That's really all I came for, to tell you that. 'Cause you and Harry are scary-close, and you could be hurt." As if that weren't obvious. "I'll fix it myself, if I have to."

"*You!*" I said, puzzled. "What can you do?" I didn't mean to be rude, but what the hell?

She just smiled sweetly, sadly. "I don't know. I'll think of something."

I didn't take that seriously, but it was awfully nice . . . part of a new intimacy in our connection. After that, things got more normal. I talked about my wafer-thin "plans" for helping Harry. I said that I really had no plans except to make some "radical tacks."

"Do you remember radical tacks, from this summer?" I asked.

"Sure," she said. "The crazy tacks you take, when you're fucked and it doesn't matter."

I laughed at that. She was *blunt*, wasn't she? "You got it," I said. "They seldom work, but that's all I can do. Even if it's stupid."

"Not stupid," she said, suddenly thoughtful. "I've thought about it, too, and this case is not going to go the normal way. Radical tacks could make all the difference. Because the 'winds' are going to shift a lot, I just know that."

"A prediction from Cassandra is magical," I said lightly.

She just shrugged. "Could be." That was it for substance. She left early the next day. Weird trip but, oddly, it grounded me some . . . gave me hope. Her plan, probably.

CHAPTER 26

WHO ARE YOU?

One thing about her visit: that stuff about "who you are" had a funny resonance for me. Because "who I was" was the least bit complicated.

A few people have their own "creation myths," stories they tell themselves about who they are and how they came to be that way. You've already heard mine: I grew up in a troubled household but had the great good luck to be raised, as a little kid, by a magical older brother, Harry. And later, to be rescued by him . . . plucked up and taken away to safety. For the rest of my life I would be wrapped in that story . . . wrapped in the great cloak of Harry's love, his enormous wealth, and his decency. As a result, I was a solid and more or less decent man myself—optimistic, happy, and deeply committed to a decent life in a sunlit world. I was a bit austere because of my almost weird commitment to the rule of law, but basically I was easy. I was the well-liked litigation partner in the very good law firm; the loving pursuer of too many women; and the rock-solid support to my brother. At heart, I was a lawyer ... the practical navigator, as Harry liked to tease me. But he appreciated it, too. We were a balance and it had real-world benefits. Harry was amazingly fast and almost always magically insightful. I was slower but not pathetically so. I walked us through whatever it was more slowly and carefully, and we both felt more secure. I was the navigator, keeping us safe, as he jokingly said. Together, we were quite a team.

I liked that story and used to tell it often. Not about what a hell of a guy I was but about the rescue part. It was true, too, which was nice. But by no means complete. Because I had done a lot of my growing up during the ten long years when Harry was not around and I was mostly alone. That was a much rougher business, and magic played no part. Nor decency nor optimism nor sunlight. Nor the rule of law. It was a story of alcoholism and loneliness. And, sometimes, terror and a dreadful resolve.

The thing about alcoholics, from a kid's point of view, is that they are just not there. They may be in the house, some place, but attention is not paid, meals are not prepared, and lunch money does not appear. The norm is solitude: no one knows or much cares who or where you are. There is a public shame, too, which is baffling to a little kid. Everyone seems to know about your parents, and you carry some of the stigma. Even when you are six years old. You are the son of the drunks in the big house on Peaches Point, and there's probably something wrong with you, too. Other kids keep their distance. You are beaten up more, until you learn to take care of yourself. And soon enough, you are the one keeping the distance and they don't have to bother. You go cold. In lieu of self-esteem, you have cold. And you turn inward. Your default thought is, *Fuck 'em, I'll be fine.* And you are. I was, anyhow. Pretty much. You learn to be alone. And unloved. You learn to live in a darkness. The thing about Harry was that he lived in a great circle of light; before that, during those ten years, there was a darkness.

It wasn't all bad, by any means. I lived a kind of Huckleberry Finn existence during some of that time, and kids envied that. I could, after all, do whatever I wanted. But none, I think, would have swapped with me when it was time to go home to supper. I could go home, too, but not to supper. Not often, anyway. My parents were not destitute, and there was food in the house, when Mother remembered. And, to be fair, she had great charm when she was sober. But I did not trust her. Not for one minute. Because when she was not sober, she was a corpse. And that was terrifying. Until I got over it and over her. Our occasional conversations after that were like conversations between cynical adults, with deep veins of skepticism and dark humor. I liked that, actually. Liked her. But it did not occur to me to try to rescue her the way poor Harry did. Or to seek her love. In the same vein, I was not devastated by her eventual death; it was all of a piece to me.

At her core, I think she had been a loving and basically good woman. I saw glints of that from time to time, and a terrible sadness. Heartbroken acts of kindness to me. Little gifts, little votaries, sometimes given with tears. Because of who she'd become. But less and less. The alcohol ate her away like acid. And only the bones remained.

"Home" mostly meant the empty third floor of the Marblehead house. With books and dogs. I was a reader, from the earliest days. The six Newfies had their own rounds and lives but we were together a lot, too. Up on the third floor, lying around and reading.

There were odd shifts, especially in the early years. When she was all right, Mother—who had a lovely singing voice—liked to sing lullabies, which she had learned from her mother. Do you remember this one? "Old crow, go crow; baby's sleeping sou . . . ound. And the wild plums grow in the jungle. Only a penny a pound. Only a penny a pound, Baa ba-ah. Only a penny a pound." So mysterious, so ineffably sweet. It's Kipling and I loved it. Still do.

But when she was drunk the repertoire was a little different. Heavy on an almost snarling Marianne Faithfull . . . especially the one about the blond who realized that she would never ride through Paris in a sports car with the warm wind in her hair. So she threw herself off a building somewhere in the Midwest. Sleep did not drop down so gently on nights like that.

She did one critical kindness. At one point, when I was seven or eight, I began to get angry at Harry: Why had he left us? Where was he? And why didn't he love us? For once in her life, she was absolutely terrific . . . jumped on that hard. "No, no, no," she insisted. "Harry adores you. He always has and he always will. He just cannot come back now, is all. It is not his fault. He wants to be with you. He loves you very much. But he just cannot. You'll understand in time."

It worked and I stopped being angry at him. Put him on that pedestal and tucked him away. For that kindness—from the depths of the fog of her life—she deserves great credit, and I am grateful.

I took to the water early on. There was a battered rowboat down by our dock and I rowed all over the place. I had a kind of route. I avoided other kids but there were offbeat grown-ups I'd drop in on. Timmy, the old guy in the cloth cap and the stub of a cigar, who had the hot-dog shed on Devereux Beach. The only place that stayed open when it turned cold; he had no other life. The shutters came down and you had to go inside to order. But there was a potbellied stove and a few crappy chairs for his geezer friends. And an overturned box for me. I was invisible there and got to hear them talk about everything: wars, death, crooked cops, crooked women. An education, a dark one. I hung out in sail lofts and boatyards, too . . . with younger but also eccentric men.

When I was twelve, I taught myself to sail the junker sailboat that Harry had fixed up. Pretty good-sized sailboat, actually, but Harry must have taught me something, because it was easy for me. By the time I was thirteen, I was sailing fairly far afield . . . over to Manchester, up to Gloucester, through the Annisquam Canal, which was tricky. I got myself some charts and learned to do "dead reckoning," which is good enough for coastal navigation. I was into it and enjoyed it a lot. I liked being competent, always would.

When I was fourteen, I went up as far as the Isles of Shoals, off the coast of New Hampshire, and spent the night. Not shoals of rock, by the way, shoals of cod . . . so plentiful in the seventeenth century you could almost walk on them. Then into Portsmouth, which was really tricky when there was a standing wave in the narrows, as there often was. I hung around the waterfront for days. Met some okay people. And ran away *hard* from some others. Not always hard enough. I hurt a man once, a man who took me out to his powerboat. He did things I'd just as soon not talk about. Then he turned his back on me, at last, and I hurt him. With a kitchen knife. And ran. I doubt if I killed him but I wasn't sure. And I didn't care. I was most assuredly not a Rules Guy in those days; he deserved what he got. No sane parent would have allowed any of this, of course, but mine had no idea. I became alarmingly self-reliant, practical, and wary. Very, very wary.

Despite all that, when Harry came and got me, I was delighted and deeply grateful. As I say, my mother gets some credit for that. In any event, I was not so far gone in solitude and suspicion that I didn't see the magic and warmth of him at once, and revel in it. I had loved him deeply as a little kid; I had managed to hold him in my heart when he was gone. And I fell back in with him, easily and without reserve, when he came for me. That was a miracle. I could so easily have gone the other way and told him to go fuck himself. Instead, I blossomed in his warmth, became the sunny person in my myth and his.

But not completely. That cold-eyed little kid was always there, watching. And thinking things over. Tough little sucker, too, and a bit ruthless. More than a bit ruthless. And wary. That, also, was "who I was." If Cassie had known about that, she might not have been so worried.

CHAPTER 27

EARLY DAYS

When Cassie left, early the next morning, I settled down to business. I had hired a Maine lawyer to keep me informed of every development (and every rumor) in Harry's case. He faxed me a copy of the indictment immediately after it came out. It was mostly a "bare bones" indictment, as they are called, just the conclusory facts and the charges, not many details. It did mention "the murder weapon" which, as Bud had told me, had been found on the bottom, just twenty yards off the stern of Harry's sailboat, on the way to *Java*. It also mentioned the pips, for some reason, including the one through poor George's cock. Horton's hunger for publicity, I assumed. He certainly got it. By the end of the week, there wasn't a person in the country over the age of ten who did not know about George's cock. And Harry's disgrace, of course. It was astonishing that someone like Harry had committed murder. But the notion that a man like Harry had done that to George's cock. *Well!*

There was less interest in me, at first, but I got my share. Horton—at his first press conference—went into detail about the dreadful things I had done to co-opt the investigation. It made him look like an awful buffoon, of course, but he must have figured that it was best to take that hit now, while he was riding high from the indictment. He also said that I would very likely be indicted, too. In the meantime, he was relieved to say, Judge Cruller had *cauterized* the situation—B. T.'s odd word— by forbidding me from any contact with Harry, his wife, or his legal team. The press loved it.

It did have a certain charm: a slick Wall Street lawyer insinuates himself into the trust of a decent Maine lobster-man/sheriff and the DA to take over the investigation of a murder committed by his own brother. Oh, my!

After digesting all that, I settled down to the business of considering what I might do in all this . . . what odd, dark role I might play. If any.

For the first two days, I mostly just sat and thought . . . made outlines of nonsense plans. On the third day, I actually went to work. I went to the City Bar Association library on Forty-Fourth Street and spent a week of very long days, immersing myself in Maine criminal law and procedure.

A couple of things came out of it. First, as I studied Maine's "speedy trial" law, I had an important insight. All states give criminal defendants the right to a speedy trial. Which sounds good, but no one with a decent lawyer takes advantage of it. Everyone believes that delay is in favor of the defendant, which is true. Ordinarily, a well-advised client like Harry—with deep pockets—would not be tried for a year or more. But my instinct was that Harry would not follow that advice and that the trial could be as soon as late fall. I made my own plans on that assumption, which turned out to be right. (The trial began in late October.) I had no idea what I was going to do, but I decided that I didn't have much time to do it in. That turned out to be a help.

The only other thing was that Maine was oddly pro-prosecution on questions of *Brady Material*. Brady Material is "exculpatory" stuff that a prosecutor learns which may be helpful to the defense. Prosecutors have to turn over material that helps the defense, to ensure the fairness of the trial. Weirdly, Maine had a string of cases, dating back to the 1950s, that gave the prosecutor a much stronger hand than in most states. They were only obliged to turn over the most blatantly exculpatory stuff, and even then they could do it at the last moment. "Trial by ambush!" the defense bar screamed, and in time, Maine practice fell in line with most states. But those odd cases had never been overturned. Would Horton do something cheesy like that? Of course he would.

After the study of the law, I turned to some traditional fact gathering—interviewing witnesses. Except it wasn't traditional at all, because the only people I spoke to were way off "on the margin," to which I was relegated. I was not looking for evidence for the trial; these people would never testify. I was just looking for background. Most of it was a total waste. One interview was not.

After talking to about thirty people in New York, I went up to the Marblehead house and started to talk to some of Harry's early Marblehead friends. Again, nothing. Except his first wife, Julia Stone. The one to whom he had been married for about six weeks when they got separated and Harry went crazy.

I didn't think she'd see me if I called, so I just showed up at her door. She had remarried, not long after Harry, and clearly she and her family were doing well; they had a handsome, late-eighteenth-century house, beautifully maintained. She flinched when she saw it was me, almost shut the door. But I am not scary looking, and she had a lingering affection for Harry. So, after a careful exchange, she let me in and we went and sat in the low-ceilinged kitchen. There was still a huge eighteenth-century fireplace with cooking hobs and the like. And the usual collection of wildly expensive modern appliances.

It was interesting, how much she looked like our mother. And like Mimi, of course, though almost a decade older. She was a nice woman and she seemed to be "together," although she was certainly nervous to have me sitting in her kitchen. She had clearly been fond of Harry and we fell in together easily, after her first unease. Still, it was almost two hours before we got down to it.

"This is awfully hard," she finally began, "but perhaps you ought to know . . ." And then she came to a complete stop.

"I ought to know . . . ," I began again and leaned in just the least bit.

Deep breath now, and she sat up straight: "Harry was impotent."

There was almost nothing she could have said that would have surprised me more. But I sat there totally calm, totally reassuring. "I thought there might be something like that," I said. Which was an appalling lie. I never lie but I did this time, to make it easier for her to go on.

"Well," she laughed nervously, "you're a lot more insightful than I. Or maybe Harry. He must have had some idea. He'd been careful to have us wait until after the ceremony. But I'm not sure. He seemed as astonished as I was."

"What did you do?"

"Oh, Lord . . . I can't say. But we waited. We tried stuff. Neither of us had any idea in the world; we weren't that old or sophisticated. After a week, Harry couldn't bear to try any more, it was just too awful. I said, 'Let's go see someone,' but he wouldn't. Then, to my astonishment, he began to drink. A lot. He never drank, as you know, but now he did. And it was terrifying. I went home, told my poor parents what had happened. And, in no time, they had the marriage annulled."

"Did you see Harry again?"

"He wouldn't see me. Then there was a stretch when, I gather, he wouldn't see anyone. He was in New York, of course, and I was up here. I never saw him again. Which makes me sad." And, sure enough, there were tears in her eyes, even after all this time. "I loved him." I carefully put my arm around her and said I did too. Which was why I was doing all this stuff.

"Is he going to be all right?"

I wanted to comfort her but there was no sense in that. "I don't know. He has a superb lawyer, one of my closest friends. But I don't know what facts anyone has. What I can say is, I will do absolutely anything in my power to see him out of this. But it's such a mystery. And what you just told me makes it even weirder." We stood up and I put my arms around her, gave her a gentle hug. "If I learn anything, I'll tell you."

Driving away, I thought: If I didn't know *that* about Harry, what else didn't I know? I dreaded to think.

This next bit turned out to be surprisingly lucky. I hired a detective, a terrific one. I turned to a guy I knew named Peter Dole, who had started the world's fanciest and most successful detective agency. His great insight had been that—in the era of high-stakes takeover battles and the like—there was a need for a much more sophisticated level of detective services for corporations and the very rich, and that price wouldn't matter. He hired the usual former cops and FBI agents but his innovation was to hire some of the very ablest lawyers and accountants from leading firms and turn them into investigators, alongside the cops. He paid them lavishly and now he was on his way to becoming the best detective agency in the world. We'd known each other in the Southern District, and his greeting was warm. His company had just moved into elegant new offices.

"Pretty fancy, Peter," I said, reaching over to shake hands as I was led in.

He grinned at that and turned, open armed, to take in his new office. "We're rich, by heaven. Wanna join me? I'd love it. And it's a lot more fun than regular practice." Peter of course knew what had happened to Harry and me. And he was still going out of his way to make me feel comfortable. I appreciated that a lot.

"You bet," I said, "but right now I have a problem and need your help."

"You want one of my villains to try to find out what's going on with the prosecution . . . and the defense? That's not a strength of ours," he began but I interrupted him. Said that's not what I had in mind. I was playing a longer game. I wanted him to find out absolutely everything about George Minot, here but especially in Greece. "Then everything you can learn about his Greek sidekick, a guy named Theo Soros. And then everyone else in the case." I took a pad and pen and wrote out some names. "If there's time, I'd particularly love to know whatever there is on his girlfriend—who may also be Theo Soros's girlfriend—Alexis Andrews."

He looked at the list, nodded. Looked up. "We can do this but we don't testify, you know," Peter said. I said I knew that and it was fine. "And we cost a fortune," he went on ruefully. "I'm happy to cut you an old pal's discount but this is big money, no matter what. Can you manage that?"

I told him that money was the very least of my problems. Thanks to Harry, I was an extremely wealthy man. "*Extremely*," I repeated, to be sure he heard and to get him used to the notion that I really wanted him to go flat out on this. Did he have anyone really good whom he could put on this? At his full rates? He said he did. Somebody perfect in fact.

Two years before, Peter had hired a young litigator away from one of the best firms in New York, and he turned out to have a remarkable gift for Peter's kind of work. "He'll be running all of Europe soon. May succeed me, in time. And the best part"—he paused, positively twinkling—"is he is Greek. He's operating out of Athens and Dubai. He knows Greece cold, of course, and he's a lovely guy. You are in luck."

His name was Paul Kazanstakis, and his per diem was startling. But I said that was fine . . . let's go. Peter picked up the phone and called Dubai, even though it was after midnight there. "At our prices, you get twenty-four-hour service," Peter said.

Paul K. had a ton of charm and we got along easily from the get-go. Partly, he was genuinely fascinated by the assignment. He had never met either Minot or Soros but he'd heard a lot about both and was fascinated by George in particular. "He's a legend in Greece," he said.

"A Minotaur-in-his-Labyrinth legend?" I asked; I had told them how George thought of himself.

"I don't know about that," Paul said with a laugh. "But maybe. Let me sniff around and I'll let you know."

Paul went on to give me a caution that Greece was a deeply secretive and corrupt society, and a guy like Minot would be hard to track, even dead. Greece had been occupied by the Turks for four hundred years and lying to the government (and everyone else) had been the essence of patriotism for a long, long time. There was also an ancient tradition of robbery and lawlessness. So I was not to expect too much. I said that was fine; do the best you can.

CHAPTER 28

CLEOPATRA'S BARGE

Here's where things get particularly weird. I was getting a little weird myself, partly on purpose (to open my head up to novel approaches) and partly just from being alone all the time. I warmly embraced my oddest ideas. None was odder than spending two days at the Peabody Essex Museum in Salem, the town where Harry and I were born.

The Peabody Essex is the great museum of the China Trade and one of the great museums of the early Republic in general. Harry and I had loved it as kids, especially Harry. When I started, I was looking for traces of Harry. What I found were traces of myself.

Harry's great focus in our days at the museum was on the life and times of one George Crowninshield, an inspiration. Which made sense because George Crowninshield was a Hero and a Rescuer, just like Harry. He had made a fortune in the China Trade in the early 1800s and doubled it as a privateer in the War of 1812. He was one of the richest men in the country, but what he was really known for was his rescues. He twice leapt into the freezing waters of Salem Harbor in winter to rescue drowning men and, once, rescued a woman and her children from a burning building. He was also known for having sailed to Halifax, during the war, to rescue the body of an American captain who had been killed in the battle between the frigates *Chesapeake* and *Shannon*.

But the thing for which he was most famous was the creation of the astonishing hermaphrodite brig, *Cleopatra's Barge*. She was a yacht, ostensibly . . . the first yacht ever built in America. She had beautiful lines, the work of Salem's Retire Beckett; and she was amazingly fast, even by the standards of a town where they built privateers. A thousand people a day came down to Crowninshield Wharf to marvel at her lines, at the many gun ports (yachts had guns in those days), at the nonmatching trim along her port and starboard gunnels . . . at her great cost.

The good people of Salem also marveled at the ship's lavish interior, part of which is reproduced in the museum. They wondered at her curiously Napoleonic decor. The imperial eagles and the colors in the cabin. Napoleon's colors. The very name, *Cleopatra's Barge*, had a Napoleonic ring to it, because it was Napoleon who had lately opened Egypt and made all things Egyptian the rage. Later there was a box with a lock of the emperor's hair, the gift of Bonaparte's mother, a tough little Corsican lady with certain expectations. The captain who had rescued Napoleon from Elba—his first island of exile—was part of Crowninshield's crew.

This was all in 1816–17 when Napoleon had been safely tucked away on the tiny island of St. Helena, a thousand miles off the coast of Africa, after his defeat at Waterloo in 1815. But people in Salem—and with the British fleet at Malta and in Whitehall—wondered just how secure that exile really was. Because they suspected that George Crowninshield had built and manned *Cleopatra's Barge* for nothing less than . . . the rescue of Napoleon.

If that's true, he might have pulled it off. The British fleet was far away. The garrison was small, five hundred men, and he had a lot of money for bribes. The *Barge* was faster than anything the British could have set to catch her, and Napoleon's supporters had acquired vast tracts of land in Louisiana where he could have set up shop, perhaps started a new country. It was not a silly idea: the world was much more open in those days.

Alas, Crowninshield died on board—in Salem, actually— in November of 1817, before he could pull it off. But the story had a wonderful resonance for Harry and now for me.

For us as kids, it was the derring-do that fascinated. For me—all these years later—it was a little different. The thing that held me now was the fact that Crowninshield had become a criminal. Not by his own lights but certainly as a matter of English law and even the laws of the United States. If he had been caught, he would have been hanged.

That fascinated me. Here was this regular establishment figure, the great hero, and—in his passion—he rose above questions of law and custom, and became a criminal. It occurred to me how often the Hero rises above the law . . . answers to a higher call to commit crimes. Which was fine. Because, by definition, there are things a criminal can do that others cannot. And they might be a tremendous help. I was not talking about breaking Harry out of jail, like Crowninshield; that wouldn't work now. But other things would come up that might work as well. The best lawyer in the world will not commit crimes for you. Would I do it to rescue Harry? . . . Of course. That alarming notion was oddly liberating. I was drawing on my old self, the kid who knifed the guy on the boat. And it felt fine . . . a little cold, a little ruthless, to be sure, but fine.

CHAPTER 29

HANSON, MAINE

There was not a lot of structure to what I was doing. Knowing that I had to operate "on the margin," and had to leave the central and obvious things to the regular lawyers, I was uncharacteristically quick to follow instinct or whim, like spending all that time in the Peabody Essex Museum. That was the goofiest example, but there were others, and I let myself follow them. So, when I got a strong sense that I should go next to Hanson, I didn't think about it a lot, I just went.

One of the things I had decided, before I got there, was that I wanted a *base*. In this new, rootless life, I wanted a solid base in Maine, and I could easily create that with Harry's money. I got up there on a Saturday afternoon in mid-September, and went straight to the old Hanson Hotel. I'd told old Bill Needham, the owner, that I was coming and wanted to talk to him. I gave him an idea what I was up to on the phone, but it didn't really sink in. Because he was old and what I wanted was so outside the range of his experience that it was going to take a while.

What I wanted was to rent the top two floors of the Hanson Hotel for a year. With an option to renew for another year. And an option to buy in the end. I also wanted the right to remodel those floors. Including new wiring, new furniture, and a lot of office equipment, which I only hoped I would need. Bill shrank back, appalled at the idea, and was already shaking his head no. Then I told him what I was willing to pay, and he quit shaking his head. Didn't agree quite yet, but he did pause long enough to take in the notion of that much money. A lot of it in cash, right now, or as soon as we could get papers drawn up. Then I told him I wanted him to continue to run the place, but I might have some security concerns he'd have to accommodate. At first he could not believe his luck. And then he could. And then—old Yankee that he was—he started to negotiate. I laughed aloud at that and old Bill grinned a little sheepishly. I told him to get over himself, this was by far the best deal he would see in his lifetime. Take it or leave it. He took it.

I suppose it crossed his mind that he was about to cut a deal with a guy who was a major pariah here in town, and maybe a murderer. In fact I alerted him to that risk. He just grinned, the old rascal. Made sense: the rental deal alone was worth more than the hotel. To make him a little easier, I told him that in fact I hadn't murdered anyone and didn't know a thing about it; I was just here to help my brother. I don't know what he thought of that, he just nodded.

Next, I called Frank Butler, told him what I'd done, and asked if he felt like coming up and giving me a hand with the redo and the new furniture and all. I said we were going to create a little "law office" for ourselves—among other things—and I hoped he'd equip it. He said of course.

"What are we going to be doing?" he asked.

"I have no idea," I said.

"Good," he said. "Sounds good. Fully equipped law office with all the fixins," he said, "for a handful of people?"

I said that was exactly right. Maybe just two. State of the art, especially security and communication stuff. He said he'd spend a couple of days in New York, thinking about it, and then buy the major pieces down there. He'd be in Maine on Monday or Tuesday.

The next morning, Sunday, there was a tricky thing to take care of. I dressed in a suit and tie and walked to the other end of town, up the hill to Judge Cruller's house. It was a nice walk and I appreciated the chance to see the village without the fog, for once. It really was a lovely spot, one of the prettiest on the coast. It was a shadow of what it had been a hundred years ago, to be sure—back in granite-quarrying and ship-building days. But, like an old lady with good bones, it carried its shrunken size and importance gracefully.

The stores and commercial buildings on Main Street weren't busy but they were well kept. And so were the streets and the sidewalks sloping down to the harbor. There were lovely old elm trees everywhere. Dutch elm disease, which had left the streets so cruelly bare back home, had not yet come this far north. It was coming, I was told, but like cancer in an old man, it was moving slowly and there were these tall, graceful elms all over town. How I loved that. There was a time when Salem had the best elms in America. Now it was probably Hanson, Maine.

Judge Cruller was astonished to find me at his door, worried about ex parte contact, even at this early stage. I said it was nothing substantive . . . just a courtesy call to let him know I was in town. He braced at that . . . maybe thought about turning me away. But he was a decent guy, we had a history, and he asked me in. No offers of coffee, you know, but we went into his study and sat down. I said I wanted to let him know that I had taken rooms at the hotel and would be in and out of town over the next months. And for the trial.

"I'm more or less moving into the hotel for a while, and I got a fella to help me with various things. Given all that, I just wanted you to know that I fully understand the importance of your order," I said, "and that I will honor it closely." That went down reasonably well, I thought, so I took a little chance. "I also wanted to say to you, personally, that there was never a time—when I was acting for the state—when I knew anything that suggested that my brother had done anything wrong." Going down that road clearly made him uneasy, as it should have, and he started to speak. I just raised my hands and said, "I wanted you to know. Just between us." I stood up and he showed me to the door.

It was a beautiful day and I wanted to go out to *Nellie* but I'd left the Whitehall in Bud's barn. I didn't want to embarrass him, but I had to get the damn boat sometime and today was as good as any. So I changed and walked the two miles to Bud's house. It turns out that he was away at some law-enforcement conference, but Caroline was there. She was startled to see me, but inevitably, she was welcoming . . . gave me coffee and insisted on giving me a hand, taking the boat out of the barn and muscling it across the lawn and down to the water. She said it'd leak some, like any wooden boat, "before she gets swole up." She loaned me a bucket and a big sponge to bail with, too. "You oughta be able to keep up, with that bucket." Then she laughed: "Best stay close to shore, though, just in case." She insisted on lending me a life jacket, too. I took off my shoes and socks and rolled up my pant legs, got ready to wade out in the surf.

She put her hand on my sleeve. "Bud don't believe you done any o' that stuff, Tim. He don't know about your brother, he says, but he knows about you." Damned if that didn't bring tears to my eyes. I thanked her, gave her a hug. I said Bud was right: I hadn't done any of that stuff. She just nodded, as if she'd known it, too. Then I walked the boat out into the low breakers, climbed aboard, and quickly pulled through the surf. Then rowed north toward the harbor.

It was a sweet pull, past a few small houses like Bud's, with dories pulled up in the side yards, lobster pots piled up near sheds. Flagpoles with American flags and MIA pennants flying. I rowed to Hanson Point, then turned left into the harbor. Past the lobster boats, and past *Ariadne* and *Endymion* and *Celene*, all of them more or less together now, in one part of the harbor. And finally, *Java*, standing alone in the middle. I had been surprised to see her there the day before. Wasn't sure there was deep enough water for her. But obviously there was, and there she sat, stunningly beautiful.

Finally, there was *Nellie*, off to one side as usual. I tied up and clambered aboard. Everything looked fine on deck and in the rigging. Down below, it was dank, as you'd expect, but neat as a pin. I looked at the bunks and the cold fireplace. I thought how cozy my old boat was. And that segued almost at once into the "sight" of Cassie, lying naked and warm, in the big bed, in front of the fire. The green frog. Then damned if it wasn't Alex lying there. *Jesus!* I thought. Is there any end to sexual craziness? No, I thought. No, there is not. Not in this lifetime.

I started the engine to charge the batteries and puttered around in the cabin. Then went up on deck and sat while the batteries charged. I saw that someone—Bud or his son, I assumed—had gone up the mast and rigged one of those whirligigs to keep the gulls off so they wouldn't shit on the deck. It had worked pretty well. I scrubbed the deck anyway, out of habit, and then got in the Whitehall and took a quick pass at the topsides. They didn't need it, either; the water's clean up here. I came back aboard, put out the big American flag on the stern and, after a moment's pause, ran the Arcadia Club burgee on a jack staff to the top of the mast. A sailboat looks funny without a burgee. Reason enough to join a yacht club.

Then I put out some cushions and just sat there—watched as the currents moved us this way and that. I felt okay. I don't know why but I felt pretty good. Maybe some obscure signal that I was doing the right thing. When finally it began to get chilly and dark, I got back in the Whitehall and rowed over to the town dock. I pulled the boat up on the float and walked up to the hotel. I stuck the bronze oarlocks in my pockets, cold against my legs, and put the curved, varnished oars over my shoulder. It's not fair to tempt kids with a boat like that, leaving the oars and oarlocks on the dock.

CHAPTER 30

ON THE MARGIN

One of the reasons I had come to Maine was that I had this bee in my bonnet. It struck me that—somewhere at the heart of all this mess—there had to be a navigation problem. Of course, if Harry had done it, the problem went away. His *Silver Girl* lay just some fifty yards away from *Java*, and he could have found his way out there and back with his eyes closed. But if it was not . . . if "some other dude done it," as criminal defense lawyers put it . . . then that person had almost certainly had a hell of a navigational problem. Getting to wherever he killed Minot, towing him over to *Java*, and getting away again. Not easy. And if by any chance the Other Dude had to get back and forth to Forstman's *Endymion*, way-to-hell out there in the Tangles, well, that was all but impossible. So, a navigation problem. And it seemed obvious to me that, if I were going to solve that, I'd have to do it right here. Or, more accurately, out on Broken Island.

Just how I was going to go about all this I had no idea. What I did was to go down to Bangor and buy a ton of diving gear: both a wet suit and a dry suit (for prolonged immersion in cold water) and a regulator, an alarming knife, diving buoys, and all the toys I could think of for whatever might come up. The main expense was a big, hard-bottomed inflatable with a 15-horsepower engine (and a trailer) to use as a dive boat and to go back and forth to the town at speed, to refill my air tanks. I didn't care if the people in town saw what I was up to; that was part of my plan.

I was out on Broke, on *Nellie*, for three weeks. I had several things in mind. I wanted, first, to get a detailed sense of how long it took to get from this place to that on the surface, in all kinds of weather. And then in the water, both on the surface or on the bottom, with flippers or whatever. Next, I wanted to learn the bottom of the harbor like the palm of my hand. Distances and times, the nature of the bottom . . . everything. Just in case. It occurred to me that if you knew the bottom and had a big lamp, you could find your way around easily, regardless of the fog. Except, of course, it would take forever, which probably ruled it out.

Finally, I was curious about sound—the sound of guns— on the water. I couldn't replicate the fog—which might have muffled the sound some—but I could maybe get an idea. So, in addition to the inflatable and the diving gear, I had bought some guns. Three Ruger .22s, just like Harry's. Why three? First, I was going to test for sound. But then I meant to run some half-baked "tests" for the effect of corrosion in salt water on that particular gun, over time. My notion was that, if some other dude had planted the "murder weapon" long after the actual murder, it might be obvious to an expert that the alleged murder weapon had not been in the water long enough, there wasn't enough corrosion. It wasn't a very promising lead, and it didn't go anywhere. But it was the kind of thing I had to try.

Finally I bought a Sig Sauer P226, a 9 mm automatic. For my own protection, I guess. I very much doubted that I'd ever need it but I'd always wanted a handgun. So, what the hell. I was playing cops and robbers out here—might as well have a gun.

The diving came first. Almost the first thing I did, after getting comfortable with all that diving gear, was to go down and take a look at the spot where the so-called murder weapon had allegedly been found. *That* was a revelation, a joyous one. Because what I found didn't make a bit of sense. On the contrary, it made it look as if Harry had been framed.

When I got out to Broke, I anchored *Nellie* right where she had been last summer. I knew because I had a copy of the map that was made back then, with the aid of the GPS gadget on the one lobster boat which had one. Bud and his people had been very meticulous about that, thank heaven. The map showed just where every boat in the Squadron had been. The harbor was still full of the red buoys, which Bud's people had put down, to mark the position of every boat. But now there was a new one, bright green instead of red, which I assumed marked the place where they had found Harry's gun. Just looking at the buoys, it was weird. The green buoy was not more than thirty yards from the buoy that marked where Harry's *Silver Girl* had been. And it was directly on the path from there to where *Java* had been, another thirty yards along. Harry would have had to be awfully stupid to leave it right on the path, between the two boats. And Harry was not stupid. Even if he was upset by what he had just done, he would never make a mistake like that.

But when I dove down below, the murder-weapon story got much better. For us. Because the little lead anchor, under the green buoy, was sitting in glaring, plain sight, on top of the only open rock for many acres around. Served up on a silver platter, really, and life doesn't work like that. Not on the bottom of Broken Harbor, where most of the bottom was thick and black with kelp, several feet deep. There was in fact only one big, flat rock in that sea of kelp in that area. And damned if Harry's gun wasn't sitting right in the middle of it. If it had landed anywhere but there, it would have sunk into the seaweed and never been seen again. Did I believe that? Well, no, I did not. Not for a second. I believed that someone had come along, long after the murder. A diver, who had gotten his mitts on a gun like Harry's. And he had fluttered down, found the one open rock, and set the gun down there so it was sure to be found. At that point, he must have called Horton or Bud and told them where to look. And *bingo*, there it was. *That* was too good to be true. Somehow I would get word to Tiglio and he would make good use of it.

For the rest of my time on Broke, there was nothing else that important. I just went meticulously about my business of learning the bottom—and the surface—of Broken Harbor. It was soon clear that one could readily learn the bottom and swim or walk around it with confidence, in any fog. The trouble was that either swimming or walking on the bottom took forever. Interestingly, I could swim among the nearer boats on the surface, just barely fast enough. But swimming underwater was much slower. And you had to be on the bottom to be able to "find your way." It was not a practical technique, given the time frames.

Most of my days were spent on the navigation problem, and they were pretty much wasted. But I also found time to fool around with the guns. That was mildly interesting. The thing about the guns was the noise. All the boats that mattered were fairly close together, except for *Endymion*. And, I instantly learned, the noise of a gun shooting .22 Magnums was very sharp. And loud. So loud, in fact, that any gunshot out of doors had to be audible for a good long way, regardless of the fog. Which suggested—if anything—that the murder had occurred deep in the interior of a big boat. Not necessarily as big as *Java* or Forstman's *Endymion*, but big. Interesting.

The one other thing I learned was how to shoot handguns. Silly, I thought, but a nice change from all that swimming. And surprisingly good fun. Because it turned out I had a little flair for it, and I could actually hit stuff. Not like Cassie, you know, but pretty good. I went over to the field above the beach on Broke, near the abandoned boathouse. I lined targets up against its thick, stone wall and blasted away, some two hundred rounds a day. The wall was over ten feet high; even in the early stages I wasn't going to miss by ten feet and kill some lobsterman. I spent a shameful amount of time practicing. At the end of two weeks, I was a good shot. A *very* good shot. Learning to shoot and finding the "murder weapon" rock were the most important things I did out there. But I didn't mind. I loved the whole business of learning the surface and the bottom. Loved lolling around, down below. I had always been oddly comfortable on the water.

Back in town, Frank had done a wonderful job up at the old hotel. The place was clean, the new furniture looked good and was comfortable. The office and security toys—which Frank happily explained to me—were impressive, as was the planned rewiring of the place. I am a nest builder. It was going to be operating on the wild side, but—all the same—I had managed to rig up a remarkably cozy nest. Like a particularly well-funded spy.

The time out on Broke had not been hard, so I was rested and alert when Frank and I turned to the next order of business, digging into the Minot documents—all thirty-one boxes of them. After a moment's hesitation, I asked Frank to help, which was a good idea. He was good at it.

I have spent a ton of time reading financial documents, and have a nose for corrupt deals . . . for *rot*. What I have learned is that there are often cracks in crooked deals—places where rot forms—that let you in on some interesting secrets. What would I learn? I didn't know but maybe something that I could turn to account.

One deal that started to smell increasingly funny was the hostile takeover of a mining company, code-named the "Sweet Rocks Tender." There was a small takeover "group" but it was mostly George's money. His and a couple of others.

Two things seemed odd: the market price of the stock of the target company was surprisingly low. The planned premium for the offer was barely 10 percent over the market price. Usually a takeover bid has to be some 25 percent above market price in order to work. What did George and his little friends know that made them confident that such a low bid would work? My nose started to twitch.

I began to think that maybe there was some "parking" going on, and that the deal was locked up, no matter what. Parking? Well, it goes like this. There are strict limits to how much stock in the target company a takeover group can buy before they declare their intent to make a public offer. So, unscrupulous investors "park" shares of stock with their friends, to get around the limit and make sure the deal works. Sadly, it is a serious crime, which is hard on the takeover fraternity. No matter, they try it all the time. And sometimes they get caught and go to prison. Hard to think a man as rich as George would take such risks in a relatively small deal, but George was a pirate from way back; perhaps he just couldn't resist.

What I thought was that maybe George parked a chunk of stock with his man Theo Soros. That is, he gave Theo a pile of money to invest in the target, which he'd have to give back later. Perhaps with a large fee in thanks for his committing this crime for his master. If that were true—or even if it could be made to *seem* true—that might very well get Harry out of jail. On the theory that Soros had a big chunk of his boss's money (given to him to "park"). Which he could simply keep, if something happened to George. If, for example, he were murdered as a result of some nonsense arising out of his sex life. Just a thought, at this point, but not bad. If it were not true, I might think about committing some crimes to make it look true. By now, I was ready for that. Quite a change, wasn't it?

CHAPTER 31

CASSIE TO MAINE

After I'd been in Maine for a month, Cassie said she wanted to come east. Just for a couple of days. I was delighted.

When she stepped out of the tiny plane at the little Hanson airport, she was wearing a simple dress with a touch of cowgirl in it and flat-heeled shoes. A soft wind stirred the hem of her dress around her bare legs as she waited a moment at the top of the portable stairs. Then this big, slow smile. A touch of sadness in it now—the whole world had turned sadder since the summer—but still that astonishing warmth.

She walked down the stairs and into my arms. We hugged for a long moment. Then we walked over to the car and drove up to the old hotel. Frank had thoughtfully made arrangements to be down in Portland for the weekend, so we had the place to ourselves. Cassie was charmed and amused by the notion that I had taken over the two floors. She was complimentary about how Frank had done it up and how cozy my rooms were.

I showed her "her" room, if she ever wanted to get away. She said that was unlikely.

At that point I wanted to build a fire, make drinks, and eat the stuff I'd prepared. But she had plans . . . We took off our duds and rolled around together for quite a while. Not as crazy as it had been in New York, but awfully good. When we were done, we lay there looking at each other. "Just keeping you sane, baby," she said with a grin. "That's my job here, keeping you sane."

"You're amazing at it," I said. And she was.

She was intensely curious about what I had learned and what I was up to. She loved the story of the murder gun turning up on a "silver platter" out on Broke. She saw at once how that cut. I did not burden her with all my plans and doings. I especially held back my criminal thoughts about making it look as if George had been parking with Theo. But there was still a lot to tell. For example, I told her about my visit to Harry's first wife and his impotence. I asked what she made of that.

She shrugged. "Harry's complicated. He pretends he's not but he is. Like you, perhaps."

"Yuh, but this?"

She shrugged. "Apparently."

Then I blurted out, "Do you think the impotence makes him more of a suspect?"

"No," she said quick and flat. "He didn't do it. I told you that, you can count on it."

"So, does it matter?" I asked. "The impotence?"

"It makes him more complicated, is all. We talked before about how the sexual life moves in fast waters. And this is just another current. A crosscurrent, maybe."

I guess I looked glum at that. She saw it and said, "Harry's still Harry, Tim. You still know him best. He did not do it.

That's the one thing I want to bring home to you. Keep working because he is innocent. He will not be convicted. Or, at least the conviction will not stand." Then she smiled as if she were comforting a little kid.

Next, I told her what I'd just learned from Paul K., the detective in Greece. I had gone down to Boston just a few days before to see him. He would only report in person; people like that have a horror of electronic communications. So we each took a room at the Ritz and talked most of a day in mine. I brought Gussie, the Newfie, with me, and one of the nice things about Paul was that he got down and roughhoused with him for a minute, before we went to work.

I repeated to Cassie what I had learned. George had popped up, in his early twenties, in a little town on the coast of Greece, up near classic Thebes. He was already rich and he apparently had uncanny business skills. Not just for someone his age, for *anyone*. "He was wildly precocious," Paul had said, "and wildly rich. Already." All that was still a deep mystery.

He grew his fortune by starting an investment business, first in Greece, then all over Europe. Again, he was very successful. But the most interesting thing to me, I said to Cassie, was that he developed an odd reputation for violence. He went out of his way to foment the notion—in Greece, anyhow—that he literally killed people. To make himself more scary. And, yes, Paul had said, he did begin to raise some version of the Minotaur story to heighten the effect. That was very vague, Paul had said, but it was definitely out there. "He was a scary guy," I said.

"Scary, all right," Cassie said. "I got a good sense of that."

Cassie asked if Paul had learned anything about Theo and I said he had.

"Theo was from this tiny town, Perivoli, way up north. He was a distant relative of George's and very bright. His mother sent him to George, who took a real shine to him. Sent him to a good school in Greece where he starred. Then to college in the States where he himself was spending more time. He went to work for George, and in less than a decade, he became George's right-hand man."

"He must have been awfully young," Cassie said.

"Sure, but George had been awfully young himself; he liked that. The other big thing," I said, "is that Paul is sure that there's a ton of Minot money in Greece. He was rumored to have been a billionaire. And Paul thinks Theo may know how to get his mitts on it. Which, of course, gives Theo a ton of motive for killing George."

"I'll say," Cassie said. She was thoughtful a moment, frowned. "I'm sure you've already thought this, but you represent a terrible threat to Theo now. And, if he's the killer—or even if he isn't but he's stolen a lot of dough—he may be wildly dangerous to you. You're the only one who's still looking, still a threat to him. You gotta watch him like a hawk."

I said I understood that, though in fact I hadn't given it much thought. I told her about getting the Sig and learning to use it.

"That's good," she said, "but that may not be enough."

"Uh-huh," I said, a little puzzled.

"Do you want me to stay . . . watch your back?"

"What?"

"I'm a cowgirl, remember? And a good shot." She smiled but she was absolutely serious. "I brought a gun."

"You brought a gun *here*? My God, how?"

"In my checked luggage. Want to see it?" She stood up and went over to her suitcase. I just sat there, dumbfounded. She dug around and brought out a package in a heavy, oiled cloth, unwrapped it.

"Cowgirls don't just get the blues, baby," she said, smiling and handing me a big black revolver, "they pack."

"My God," I said. "You, Cassie, are quite a girl, I'll tell you."

"Yes, I am. So . . . do you want me to stick around or not? I know you got Frank, and he may be a gun guy. But he's not a patch on me."

I just looked at her, still smiling. "I've never had an offer like that before. Can I sleep on it?"

"Okeydoke," she said and took the gun back, started to wrap it up again.

"What is that damn thing, anyway? It looks huge, like a .45."

"Nope. A .22 Magnum, but on a .38 frame. Heavy, great aim. No kick. But I can hit stuff with this. And it'd hurt."

"I bet it would," I said, mildly. "I bet it would." My head was spinning.

A couple of days later, we had breakfast in our suite and Cassie was packing to leave. I had declined her offer to stay and watch my back, but promised I'd carry my Sig when I went out at night. She was still standing with her back to me, putting stuff in her suitcase, when she startled me by saying, "D'you fuck Alex yet?"

"Jesus, Cassie, are you nuts? Fuck Alex? Of course not."

"Good," she said. "But I can see how that might happen . . . you wandering around 'on the margin' and all, looking for an edge. She could help, and I bet she would. But you'd have to fuck her first; that's how she'd work. But if you do it, watch yourself. She's dangerous."

I didn't know what to say to that so I just shrugged. She gave me a steady look, to drive her point home, then finished her packing.

As I handed over her bag at the airport in Bangor, we hugged, and she said, "Take care of yourself, baby. I care about you."

CHAPTER 32

COUNTRY COURTROOM

There's something nice about a country courtroom. A good one is like a Congregational church back home . . . simple, even austere, but with good lines, and useful. The courtroom in Hanson was a beauty. It was fair sized, which was good for a trial like this. The walls were white and the railings around the jury box and around the "well" where the lawyers stand were mahogany, stained dark. The judge's high bench, like the witness box, was clad in "beaded" boards, painted off-white, and the cornices and his desk were dark mahogany. The flags of Maine and the Union flanked his black leather chair. Nice room.

Frank and I were the first people there, early in the morning, the day the trial began. We must have been there by eight. The courtroom should have been locked overnight so loonies couldn't come in and wire it for bombs, but they weren't thinking that way yet up in Hanson. Like the elms, it was going to take a little longer for assumptions about decency to die off up here. This trial should help.

The defendant's first entrance always creates a stir, and that was certainly true that day. When everyone was in the room but the judge, Harry came in, guarded, through a side door. He was immaculately dressed in a double-breasted suit, dark blue tie, black shoes . . . a white handkerchief in his pocket. His carriage was as erect and fine as ever I'd seen it. His handsome face was grave, but he smiled and nodded, restrainedly, at people he knew. Our eyes met for a long moment and he gave the nicest smile. *I'm fine,* he was saying, *I'm fine.* I nodded; glad to hear it. Me too. We were not fine, of course; we'd each lost some weight, and for good reason. But it was a nice moment. *Mercy,* how I loved him.

Judge Cruller came into the courtroom on the dot of nine: "All rise." He looked and acted very much the judge as he greeted and addressed the jury. Very balanced and judicial. But I couldn't help thinking back to the cozy sessions with the prosecutor, back when I was part of the prosecution team. That coziness with the prosecution—not uncommon—was bad enough. But he also had to be furious at Harry and me for making such a fool of him. Cruller was the last man Harry would want to run this trial. On the other hand, he was still a Law Man, and I counted on that in the end.

B. T. was a better lawyer than I would have thought. I expected him to be a bit cheap and theatrical but he wasn't. He was serious, correct, and persuasive. Occasionally his language would sharpen and his distaste for these rich, depraved outsiders would show through. But he was good. He did not go at the sexual motive directly, but he dangled it out there. Wonderfully prissy about it, too, in his opening statement.

"Ladies and gentlemen," he said, "this is a murder case, which makes it terrible enough. But there are aspects to the murder that are especially disturbing. Things that people like you should not have to hear about." He didn't quite purse his lips but he managed to convey his distaste. Some of the jurors leaned forward, some leaned back.

B. T. almost shriveled with disapproval as he described the way in which Minot had been decorated. "Penis," he called it, and he said that George had not been circumcised.

"You may conclude that the deceased was not"—he paused—"a wholesome man." I thought that was fair. "Like some of our own children, he had a pierced ear, for an earring. But he also had a pierced foreskin. That is, the murderer did not have to make a hole in the foreskin when he attached the pip to it because Minot already had a hole in his foreskin, presumably for, uh, attaching earrings and so on." There was a buzz in the courtroom at that and a giggle from somewhere in the back.

Judge Cruller promptly banged his gavel and said, "Ladies and gentlemen, there will be a lot of sexual material in the course of this trial. I understand your reaction. But I warn you, I will not have any outbursts when these things come up. I will clear the room if I must. All right, Mr. Horton."

"Thank you, Your Honor," he said, contrite as a deacon addressing a bishop. He hated it, you know, but he would go on. "There will be evidence," B. T. said, "that the dead man was not only extremely active, sexually, but that he was perverted in various ways. Having his penis pierced, to carry a ring or other ornament, was part of a larger pattern. The state will offer evidence that he was a notorious philanderer." That was an old-fashioned word for George: he was a philanderer. I guess he was. "He particularly liked orgies where groups of people of both sexes gathered to have sex and drugs. He recruited members of his yacht club to participate in these activities.

"He had been at such an orgy the night before he was killed and he was at another, on a huge cabin cruiser, the night he was killed. But it is clear that he was not killed at the orgy.

At approximately eleven o'clock, he left the big powerboat. It was understood by his companions that he was going to fetch another person to participate in the orgy. Minot had only told his companions that he was going to get 'more' of something. It was understood that he meant a woman, and during the investigation, she came to be referred to as 'the More Woman.'"

Horton took a drink of water. "It is not known who the More Woman was. It is known that the defendant's wife, Mimi, began sleeping alone that week on the defendant's yacht, *Silver Girl*, and that the defendant stayed on the club's flagship, the steam yacht, *Java*. But on the night of the murder, it was the other way around for some reason." He turned and pointed at Harry, who was sitting forward, both arms on the railing now, interested in all this. "No one was there, but it is the prosecution's contention that, on the night of the murder, it was the defendant, Harry Bigelow, who was alone on *Silver Girl* and his wife who was back on the steamer." B. T. stopped a long moment, let them think that one over.

"It is the position of the state that Minot went to *Silver Girl* that night. That he went on board and was confronted by Harry Bigelow. And that Harry Bigelow took the .22-caliber revolver which he had brought with him from the flagship. And murdered George Minot. When that was done, he took the pips, the very symbols of Minot's obnoxious success in the club. He took them off the dead man's epaulets, and inserted them in holes in the dead man's body. Two holes he found, ready-made: the left ear and the penis. Two he made himself. With his revolver. Then he put the dead man on the bottom of the inflatable dinghy and towed that dinghy back to the steamer, where it was found a couple of hours later. Along the way, he tossed his revolver into the sea, where it was eventually found by divers, on the path from his boat back to *Java*." Horton took another drink of water, ran his eye back and forth over the jurors. He had 'em, no question.

He started his peroration; you could hear the shift in his voice. "Murders are usually done in the dark when no one is around. This time it was not only dark, there was fog. The worst fog in years. No one saw Minot go on board Bigelow's boat. No one saw Bigelow go on board, either. And no one saw Bigelow bring the two inflatables back, in the fog. But there are many things to suggest, irresistibly, that that is indeed what happened. Including the devastating fact that one of Bigelow's closest friends saw him coming up the gangplank, from the service float where Minot was found, in the middle of the night." There was a buzz at that, all right.

"The state submits that, when Minot appeared at Bigelow's boat that night, for whatever reason, Bigelow shot him. And mutilated his corpse. Then returned to the steamer *Java*. Where he was clearly seen by one of his closest friends. If you agree, then you must return a verdict of guilty of murder in the first degree."

Harry watched Horton, speculatively. As if he were thinking it over, that interesting proposition. And as if he were a little surprised to learn that that was what we were all here for. Wonderfully dignified man, my Harry. Even at a time like this.

I called Cassie that night. I was calling her a lot, during this stretch. She was intensely interested in how Horton had done . . . what I thought of his case, his demeanor, and so on. She also cared very much about Harry: how was he weathering all this? I got the nice sense that we were very much in this together, even though we were two thousand miles apart. She cared. She cared like crazy, and that felt good.

CHAPTER 33

BILLY COLLINS ON CROSS

As his first witness, Horton called Billy Collins, the poor devil who had found the body.

Collins was only thirty-four, but he was a caricature of a club man from an earlier age: not the smartest man in the world, a bit pompous, and more than a bit dull. He had a wonderful, haughty accent . . . what people used to call "Locust Valley lockjaw." Lots of syllables and even whole words got lost in something that sounded like, *waugh, waugh, waugh.* I think they must have taught that at places like St. Paul's School years ago. Not that Billy could have gotten into St. Paul's. He was a perfect first witness for Horton: show the jury just who these people were.

Billy was obliged to testify in detail about his great adventure with Sally Pringle, out in the fog. You could see that he was terribly torn as he went through it. On the one hand he hated to talk about such a thing; on the other he was rather proud of himself and loved this rare moment of serious attention. He told about it with a smug restraint that had to offend almost everyone in the courtroom. Horton took a long time with him, walking him in detail through his making love with Sally Pringle in the inflatable, letting the jury get a good look at these people and their ways. Then his getting lost in the fog.

Billy had had a lot to drink, he testified, and because the fog was the thickest he'd ever seen, it had taken him forever to find his way back to *Java*. Perhaps an hour. It was so foggy that he actually hit the service float before he saw the steamer, and he almost fell in. So foggy that he almost didn't see the other two dinghies on the float, or the man in the bottom of one of them. But he did.

He was "damned concerned," Billy said with a little frown, "to think of some poor chap, sleeping it off in the fog like that. I was sure that was it, you know. Awful lot of drinking on a foggy night like that. Has to be." He didn't explain that rule, but it made sense to me.

Billy testified about how he had stepped in to try to help. "I remember saying to him as I got in: 'Come on, old boy; no good sleeping out here in the fog.' Then I pulled him out from under the seat.

"I, uh, noticed right away it was Minot, and thought it was funny. Not much of a drinker, Minot. And he was damned cold. I noticed that," Billy said, as if this were a little test and he'd gotten that part right. "And there was a funny smell to him." Billy shrugged at that anomaly. "Then, uh, I saw a pip, you know. Two pips, stuck to his forehead." Horton had him describe for the jury what a pip was and then passed one around. A fresh one, he said, not one from the body.

Billy explained how he thought it was a joke at first, that someone had pasted them on somehow. "And, uh, I reached up and took one off. But there was a black spot there . . . a hole, and it was wet; and someone had just, uh, stuck the pip in the goo."

Billy paused, straight-faced, and looked around. There were horrified smiles in the room; not the first time in his life Billy had made an unintentional joke. He hurried on. "Uh, the hole. Anyway, I, uh, . . . I put it back." He came to a halt at that one, and Horton had to nudge him along.

"You put the pip back in the hole? Back in the goo, you said?"

"Yes, I did," Billy said, pompously. "Scene of the crime, you know. Wanted to leave things as they were, uh . . ."

"Then what?"

Billy didn't like to talk about this. "I, uh, I saw that his dick was out of his trousers. Penis," he corrected himself quickly. "Swollen up like the devil, and there was a pip on it, too."

"Did you take that off?" Horton asked.

"Of course not," Billy said, horrified. "Certainly not."

"Then what?" Horton asked.

Billy was relieved that this was almost over. "Stuffed him back under the seat and went to get the commodore, of course. Minot was dead so I didn't go to the doctor; wasn't sure where he was anyway."

"You stuffed him back under the seat?" Horton asked, as if he were surprised. He probably thought he had to ask, to satisfy the jury's curiosity.

"I thought it was best," Billy said, "scene of the crime, as I say. The pips, uh, didn't fall out," he said with satisfaction. "I was pretty careful."

"And then you went to get Commodore Bigelow, is that right?"

That was right. Horton glossed over the scene of getting Harry. He did ask whether Billy had noticed anything unusual about Harry, but he had not. Horton pointed out, with questions, that Billy had had an awful lot to drink and that he'd had quite a shock, so he hadn't paid much attention to how Harry had looked. Then it was Tiglio's witness.

Tiglio stayed seated for a moment, at the counsel table, as if he were thinking over what he had just heard, and as if he were terribly interested. And puzzled. Then he lumbered slowly to his feet. He was a big, heavyset man, and he moved ponderously. He had a short white beard and hair, and hooded eyes, and he was careless about his clothes. For the first time, it occurred to me that Jack—one of my closest friends—carried a touch of menace in court. He scowled as he walked slowly toward Billy, and Billy seemed to shrink back ever so slightly in the witness chair.

Tiglio has a thick Jersey City accent, which is heightened by his husky voice. Not "dese" and "dose" but rough. In that Maine courtroom it was almost a caricature, like Billy's. But it wasn't funny. There was nothing funny about Jack.

He stood there in front of Billy for a long minute, looking at him; then: "D'you take a bottle with ya, out in the dinghy?"

"What?" Billy said.

"You take a bottle," Jack repeated, a little impatient, "out in the dinghy, when you took your friend's wife out there? Sally?"

"No." Billy was scared.

"What time was it when the guy passed out, you notice?"

"No, around two or so."

"You sure? Coulda been earlier?"

"I'm not sure."

"Okay, the guy passes out. You two talk a little, right?" That was right. "Then the two of you go over the side to the dinghy and fool around, right?"

"We were going to get some air . . . ," Billy began.

"To sober up a little?" Jack asked, sharply.

"Yes," Billy said.

"So, you sober up a little out there on the water, then you start to fool around. Take all your clothes off?" he asked, kind of interested in how this would be done.

"Uh, no. Partly. Uh, the pants and shoes and all. And loosened the rest."

"Underpants off?" he asked.

"Yes, both of us."

"Cold," Jack said.

"What?" Billy said.

"The side o' the dinghy must have been wet. Was it cold?"

"Uh, it was, a little. She said that. And I put my coat down and she did too, her sweater, on the sidewall."

"Not many clothes left on, then, it sounds like."

"No," Billy said, a bit cautiously, "just my shirt and socks."

"She the same?" his voice still gruff, not in the least salacious.

"Yes, but her shirt was open." Jack nodded at that.

"How long did it take you, making love like that, out there on the water?"

Billy shrugged, and I wondered what was going through his mind. Had he come too quickly? Had she come at all? Did he know or care? "About twenty minutes," he finally said.

"Twenty minutes," Jack repeated. Then he shrugged speculatively, as if he were thinking that over, thinking over Billy's performance. "Coulda been longer?" he asked, not dubious you know, but wanting to give Billy the benefit of the doubt.

"Yes," he said. "Could have been half an hour." Jack nodded at that.

"That must have sobered you up some, out there in the night with your clothes off, making love in the fog. That wet boat. Did you sober up a little? That half hour?"

"Yes, of course." Now it was clear enough where he was going.

Jack walked him slowly through the trip back to the sailboat where he dropped Sally Pringle, through the endless search in the fog for *Java*, and finally the jolt of finding the dead body. No matter how much he had had to drink, Jack was

saying, he'd had an awfully long time out in the cold, and at
least two sobering experiences.

"So, when you got to Bigelow's door, you weren't really
drunk anymore, were you?" he asked. He was not, Billy
conceded.

"Okay, now, in your opinion, when he came to the door,
had the commodore been asleep?"

Objection. Overruled. "Yes, I thought so."

"Took a minute to turn on the light?" Yes. "To open the
door?" Yes. "Looked as if he'd been sound asleep?" Yes. And so
on. Jack had Billy back on his heels and the answers came out
just the way he wanted them to.

The essence of it was that Harry seemed to have been asleep
and that, once he woke up, he was his normal, commanding
self, and it wouldn't have occurred to anyone who saw him or
knew him to think that he might have done the murder.

Then there was this bit. Jack said, "This is a trial, Mr.
Collins, about things that apparently took place out on the
water. Maybe in a big boat, maybe not. You took off your
clothes, you and this girl, in a little rubber boat, in the middle
of the harbor and made love." Pause. "Was it hard?"

Billy sat there, nonplussed. "No. Not hard. I mean, no. We
managed."

"Was it fun?"

"Yes."

"You went out, made love for twenty or thirty minutes, and
had fun. Anyone see you?"

"No."

"D'you worry they would?"

"No. No one could see us in that fog."

"You could have done anything out there, in that little
boat?"

"Yes."

"You kill Minot?"

"Of course not"—shocked—"I hardly knew the man."

"But you could have."

"No. That's ridiculous."

"I don't mean you really did," Jack said, patiently, "but you could have. Even in that little boat? In the fog?"

"Yes, I guess we could have, but . . ."

"There was room?"

"Yes."

"To kill him and fool around with the pips, like you did later, in the other dinghy?"

"Yes."

"And time enough."

"I guess so. I don't know how long it would take."

Jack walked very close to Billy and paused a long moment. "Let's see," he said. "Let's try something, just to get a rough idea." Then he pointed a cocked finger at Billy's forehead, not touching him but very close. "This isn't going to hurt," he said with a little smile, "we're just doing it for the time." Then, softly, but sharp: "Bang . . ." Billy flinched. Horton got to his feet but the judge gestured, no. Jack slowly dragged his finger across the arc of Billy's forehead to the other side. Even softer, but a sharp puff of air from his lips: "Bang." Long pause, while they looked at each other.

"Now the pips," Jack said. He very slowly pantomimed taking the epaulet off of Billy's shoulder, never touching him but never taking his eyes off him, either. Looked at him while he took the invisible pips off the invisible epaulet. Then he took one and placed it, ever so carefully, into the bullet hole on the left side of Billy's forehead. He picked up another and placed it . . . slow, slow, slow, into the other hole in Billy's forehead. Then the third, with both hands now, into his right earlobe. He picked up the fourth pip a bit suddenly, and Billy twisted sideways and crossed his legs. But Jack didn't do anything with that one. He just stood there with the pip cupped in both hands at his waist, waiting, for almost a minute.

"How about it?" Jack asked softly.

"How about what?" Billy said, just as softly.

"Would it take longer to do that . . . than it took you and the girl to take off your clothes . . . your pants, your underpants, put your jacket under her . . . and make love?"

"No. Of course not."

"No," Jack repeated, deeply satisfied now. "No. On a night like that," he said, very slow, with dramatic pauses, "on a night like that . . . anyone . . . could do anything . . . anywhere." It wasn't a question, and it hung in the air a moment before Horton objected, and Billy said yes.

Horton didn't look so good. He had had a little lesson in advocacy and he had not cared for it.

CHAPTER 34

WITNESSES

The next witness was the coroner, and that was pretty easy going. Minot had been shot twice in the head—with hollow-point .22s—and that had not done him any good. As to the massive erection, that was more than odd but the doctor had no explanation.

Then Horton called one of the divers, T. J. Cousins, to testify about finding the revolver. He had dived under Harry's boat, soon after the murder, and found nothing. But, about a month later, Horton had told him to look again, in a wider orbit. And there it was, about twenty yards away from *Silver Girl*, in the direction of *Java*. The gun itself, with its "Exhibit A" tag, was identified and passed around.

When Horton was done, Tiglio stood up. "Just a couple of questions." After that business with Billy Collins, the jury was watching him intently as he walked over to stand in front of the witness chair. "Mr. Cousins, you're a lobsterman and a diver, is that right?" Yes, that was right. "And part of your business is to put out these traps, put them down on the bottom, and catch lobsters that walk into them, is that right?"

"Yes, I do," he testified.

"And you been doing that, how long?"

"All my life, since I was a boy," he said. "Geez, maybe twenty-five years ago was the start."

"So twenty-five years, working the bottom for lobsters. You have to know something about the bottom to be a good lobsterman?"

Cousins nodded and said laconically, "Yes, it's best to have some idea what you're doin'."

"You put the bait in the trap, is that right? And then you pick a spot, and put the traps over the side where you think lobsters'll walk into 'em?" At the prosecution table, Horton was twitching impatiently at this nonsense, started to get up and sat down again. Jack turned on him. "Yes? You have something, Mr. Horton?" he growled at Horton, very menacing now. Horton had to stand up, or look as if he were afraid.

"Your Honor," Horton said, contemptuously, trying to put Jack down in front of judge and jury, "this little aside about lobstering may be helpful to out-of-state counsel, but I doubt if the jury is learning anything new. Or relevant."

Jack broke in sharply. "Oh, no," he said, as if to get that deep misconception cleared up right away. "Oh, no, Mr. Horton," he growled. "This is going to be very relevant. I'm afraid you're going to find this goes to the heart of your case." And he stopped, let it hang there.

The judge broke in and undid the moment: "Mr. Tiglio, if you would . . . please address your objections and responses to the court, not to Mr. Horton. I know you understand." It is one of the salutary rules of court etiquette: all remarks have to be addressed to the court, not the adversary. It does a great deal to preserve decorum. Jack of course knew that perfectly well, but he risked this bit of drama, to set a tone for the jury and put a little fear into Horton.

"All right, Mr. Cousins, you been working the bottom for lobsters for twenty-five years, and you been diving down there for fifteen, is that right?" Yes, that was still right.

"If that gun had been down there, under the boat, or even ten yards off that first time, you think you'd have found it?"

"Prob'ly."

"Even with all the kelp, Mr. Cousins? You sure?"

"Pretty sure."

"But a month later, you look again, and, all of a sudden, there it is, is that right?"

"Yep. But a little farther off."

"So, how'd you happen to go back a month later? Did you maybe get an anonymous tip that you should look again, maybe look a few yards farther to the left this time?"

"Objection! May we approach the bench?"

"Approach the bench, gentlemen." Good judges don't like "sidebar" conferences; they break the rhythm of the examination and annoy the jurors, who don't get to hear. Good judges care quite a lot about their jurors. But sidebars are a regular part of trials and this was the first request.

After some back and forth, the lawyers went back to their places and the judge turned to the jury. "Ladies and gentlemen, Mr. Horton has informed me for the record that, in fact, his office received an anonymous phone call urging a further search for the gun near Mr. Bigelow's boat. The search was resumed and the gun found later that day. No specific suggestions as to where to search were made in the phone call."

Jack stood there, looking disgusted at Horton for hiding this critical piece of evidence. Jack turned back to the witness. "Where'd he tell you to look?"

"Who?"

"Who!" Jack said, almost angrily. "Horton, of course."

"Toward the big boat."

"And there it was."

"That's right."

Jack went back to the counsel table and got sets of photographs and passed them to Horton and the clerk, then showed them to Cousins. "You put out a green buoy to mark where you found the gun, is that right?" It was. "Look about like this?" It did.

The next photo was an underwater picture of the lead weight on the rock, the line going up toward the surface. "We sent some divers out to Broke. They found the green buoy, and went below. The weight was on a rock. This is a picture of it. This where you found the gun?"

Cousins looked at it a moment. "Looks right, yes."

"My divers say there's thick weeds, or kelp, all over the place, for acres and acres, under the boat and all the way over to *Java*. You agree with that?"

"Yes, pretty much."

"But there's one rock, sticking out of the weeds, right here?" Cousins agreed.

"And the gun's sitting right there, on that bare rock. Is that right?" That was right.

"Served up on a silver platter."

Objection. Sustained. Jack paused.

"The gun, when you went back, and saw it sitting on the flat rock . . . you recognized it, did you, as a gun?"

"Yes, sure." Cousins frowned.

"It wasn't so encrusted with barnacles that you couldn't recognize it as a gun?"

"No, no barnacles at all," Cousins said.

"It wasn't overgrown with kelp, either?"

"No, it was lying on that bare rock."

"So did it look as if it might have been set down there in the last few days? Maybe the day before Horton, there, got the phone call to go and pick it up?"

"Objection!" Horton said, fast and loud. Jack went on anyway:

"One day? Two?"

"Objection," Horton broke in. "This man is no oxidation expert." And so on. There was some back and forth but the witness was finally allowed to testify. He said he couldn't tell, one way or the other, how long the gun had been in the water ... days or weeks. Jack looked at the jury, with a look of disgust on his face. He was saying that this was a set up and he, Jack, was disgusted. Pretty good.

CHAPTER 35

SAMMY CAMERON

The next witness was Sammy Cameron, and that was not so good. He was dressed in business clothes and he looked like . . . Well, he looked like himself, which was terrific.

"Mr. Cameron, you are a former commodore of the Great Arcadia, yes?" He was. "And you and your wife had a large room on the steamer *Java* that night." They did. "Was that partly because you were so close to Harry Bigelow, do you think, that you had the honor of a big cabin on *Java*?"

"Oh, I don't know, Mr. Horton. I've been around the club for a while, in various capacities. I might have been invited to sleep on board regardless." A very modest warning to Horton.

"But it wouldn't hurt?"

"I doubt if it would hurt, if anyone thought about it, one way or another."

"You woke up in the night, toward midnight?" He had.

"Went to look out the porthole." Yes.

"And your porthole was right by the gangway, is that right?" It was.

"What did you see?"

A deep breath. "I saw Harry Bigelow, walking up the gangway."

"I take it you were surprised."

Sammy shrugged. "It was late at night, in fog. He was coming up from the service float . . . Yes, I was surprised."

"And what was so odd about all that?" Horton asked. "The fact that the commodore was coming up from the service float?"

"Well, members mostly don't use the service float."

"And why is that, sir? Don't want to be confused with the working people?" Horton asked. He couldn't help but be nasty. Any more than Sammy could help being decent.

"No, no, man," Sammy said, annoyed. "Not that kind of a place. It's just an old convention of the sea, originally to keep out of the way of the people who were working the ship. It's just good manners."

"I see," Horton said, superciliously.

"The day after the murder and the day after that, were you aware that an investigation was going forward, under the direction of Sheriff Wilkerson?"

"I was."

"And you filled out a form, is that right?" It was.

Horton went to the prosecution table and picked up a document. "Is this that form?"

Sammy looked at it briefly. "It is."

"Question four reads, 'Did you see anyone board or leave your boat—or move between other boats—after 10 p.m. last night?'"

"Yes."

"And you checked *no*, is that correct?"

"I did."

"Why?"

"Well, I comforted myself at the time that I had not actually seen Harry come on board, so technically I did not have to answer *yes*. But, frankly, that was a little thin. The real reason was that I was aware of the foolishness with Mimi, throwing wine at Minot, and I thought it might cause Harry needless difficulty. It was inconceivable that he was involved."

"You were fond of Harry, and didn't want to cause him needless trouble."

"That's correct."

"Did you know at that time that Mr. Bigelow had told us that he had not left the boat all night?"

"No."

"But you learned that later?"

"I was told that by you, sir."

Horton tried to act offended. "Did you trust my word, Mr. Cameron?"

"I don't know anything about your word, Mr. Horton."

Horton wisely let that sit, but he wasn't liking it.

"In any event, you decided to tell the truth this time?"

"I testified truthfully."

Then Horton did a dumb thing. "Isn't it true, Mr. Cameron, that you told the truth this time because you realized that this was serious. Because your friend had murdered George Minot?"

"No, Mr. Horton. I have known Harry Bigelow intimately for over twenty years and that was absolutely inconceivable to me." Not such a good idea to ask a dumb question to a man like Sammy Cameron.

Horton tried to handle it with a smirk. "Very loyal of you, Mr. Cameron. That's all I have."

Jack had no questions, and that was it for the morning.

I wandered outside again at the lunch break. I went and sat on a granite bench by the cannons, under the Civil War statue. I was lost in thought when I looked up and realized Alex had come and sat beside me. It was the first time I had seen her since the summer. She looked as she always looked . . . absolutely stunning. I quickly got to my feet and we slipped into each other's arms. No hesitation, no remembering what we might have been to one another, no worrying on my part about Cassie; we just fell into each other's arms.

I confess that I had known that Alex was in town and I thought there was a good chance that I would see her, if not that day then soon. I was counting on it. The dark fact is that Alex was also the key to another, entirely different scheme that I had been working on . . . out there "on the margin." As you can imagine, after the report from Paul K., and Cassie's remarks, Soros was my great focus. I didn't know how I was going to get him, but I thought I could. And I thought—for various reasons—that Alex might be willing to help me.

I slipped easily into the role of her deep admirer. It wasn't hard; I had been captivated from the time I first laid eyes on her, as she well knew. And now here she was, and that attraction had not changed. I knew that a woman like Alex would pick up on that attraction in an instant and know if it was real. It was.

We stood there, holding each other, for only a moment. But the current between us was strong.

"We should not be seen to touch, before you testify," I said, after a minute. "That dreadful Horton will use it."

She smiled at that . . . shook her head. "He's been interviewing me, of course," she said. "He is dreadful, isn't he?"

"He is." Then she asked how long I had been here, in Hanson.

"Weeks," I said. "I have a suite up at the hotel. You?"

"Marion and I got here yesterday. The town's full, so we rented a little house up the coast, a few miles outside of town. Come see us."

I grinned at that: come see Alex and Marion. Oh boy!

"What have you been doing?" I asked. "These months since George died? Are you okay?"

She was amused at the question. "Yes, I've been fine. George was not my whole life, you know; I did not spend all my time going from orgy to orgy." She smiled but there was a little edge, too.

"So what did you do?" I asked.

"I cranked it up some, my work on my PhD at Columbia." I must have looked nonplussed because she went on. "I thought I told you. After I got that undergraduate degree, I was fascinated by the classics . . . I had decent Latin and learned some Greek. Decided to get myself a doctorate in classical studies."

"Wow. Does it still interest you?" What I meant but did not say was, does it still interest you, now that George is dead.

"More all the time. I also amused myself redoing George's place, next to mine downtown. I combined 'em. Awfully nice spot now. Come see me." Again the smile, the ambiguity.

"I bet it is. And I surely will," I said, "after you testify." She nodded, smiled. Looked forward to it.

"How's it going?" she asked. "The trial?"

I shook my head. "Hard for me to tell," I said. "I am not allowed to talk to either side." I explained the isolation order and she sympathized at how awful that must be for Harry and me.

"Do you hate it?" she said.

"Oh, yes, the whole thing."

She put her arms around me again, said into my shoulder, "They'll never convict him, Tim. He didn't do it." Alex knew that, too, huh? Everyone seemed to know Harry was innocent, except for Horton, the state of Maine, and the press.

"Yes" is all I said. She ran her hand up and down my back, comforting me.

"I'm going to be called tomorrow or the next day. I . . ."

"Tell the truth," I said, automatically, standing back. That's what you always say. So the witness can dutifully report it, when asked on the stand about your conversation. "Tell the truth."

CHAPTER 36

ORGIES

Bud was the first witness the next morning. He wasn't on for long because Horton didn't trust him. Almost treated him like a hostile witness. Horton did ask him to describe his arrival on *Java* the night of the murder. He bored in on Bud's two interviews with Harry and the fact that Harry had lied about where he'd been, both times. Mimi, too, of course. On cross, Jack got Bud to say that the case would probably have been dropped without Harry's and my help. There was a nice bit toward the end.

"To the best of your knowledge, Sheriff," Jack asked, "was Mr. Tim Bigelow sincere in his efforts to help solve the crime?"

"No question about it," Bud said simply.

"Obviously, Mr. Harry Bigelow lied to you." Yes, he had.

"Looking back, do you think there was ever a time when Tim Bigelow lied to you?"

"No, there was not."

"He was straight with you throughout the investigation?"

"Straightest lawyer I ever met." That got a laugh. "No, I mean it. He worked like the devil, an' his people, too. If he knew different . . . Well, I just don't believe it. I read all that stuff in the papers, but that's the bunk." Horton just sat there looking disgusted; there was no redirect. Horton hated it, of course, but he knew Bud could look after himself, and he was no fool.

I'm afraid that, two hours later, no one on the jury could have told you a word Bud had said, because they'd been sitting on the edge of their seats, listening to Bob Sutton talk about his little walk on the wild side. Poor Sutton was in agony as Horton took him through it, the orgies, his wife, the drugs. It was sad, watching Sutton's life go swirling down the drain. He had already been fired by his firm by that time, sold the big house in Greenwich, and worse was probably to come.

When Horton finally sat down, Jack was on his feet in a second. No pause, no gathering up his notes.

"Mr. Sutton: You testified you were with George Minot on half a dozen occasions when there were sexual goings on. Was Mrs. Bigelow ever present on any of those occasions?"

"No, she was not."

"Was Mr. Bigelow ever present on any of those occasions?"

"No, he was not."

"Okay," Jack said, then a long pause to let that sink in. After that, in a much softer voice, he said, "Let's turn to something else. You and your wife were in these . . . sexual events a number of times." Yes, they were. "And your wife made love to George Minot several times while you were there, is that right?" It was.

A long pause now. Then, Jack asked softly, "What's that like?"

There were no objections, interestingly enough, and poor Sutton had to sit there, in front of the world, and think what it was like. I understood Jack's imperatives, but it was a cruel moment.

Finally, Sutton said, "I can't say. It's very complicated. All kinds of things are going on. You'd really have to be there to understand."

Jack stood there in front of Sutton, slowly shaking his head. Then, softly, "We can't do that, Mr. Sutton; we can't be there. So, let me ask you, weren't there moments when you wanted to kill him? Just pull him off your wife and kill him?"

Sutton scowled for a second and said, "No, it was never like that."

"And you and your wife . . . Did the two of you ever have any regrets? Ever sit together, man and wife, and mourn for your old life together, the way you were before all this began?"

Sutton seemed to be really thinking about it. "I suppose there were times when we had regrets," he said finally. Then, as if he were sure of it, now that he thought about it, "Yes, there were times when my wife and I had regrets."

"But it's your testimony that he did not come back, that night in the fog?"

"No."

"To try to get you to come out one more time."

"No."

"And you and your wife, torn with regret . . . you didn't take him aboard. And kill him. For what he'd done?"

"No."

Jack paused, looked at him, quizzically: "Why not?"

Pause. Objection. Sustained. A buzz from the courtroom.

It was cruel stuff but Jack wasn't doing it for fun. He was doing it to show the jurors that these were extraordinary events, that extraordinary emotions had to be involved. And that every single man or woman who had been through it had been under tremendous pressure. And might just have killed

George Minot, as a result. Rough stuff, as I say, but utterly justifiable.

Then Stockwell and the Forstmans. It was all more or less the same. None of them had seen Harry or Mimi. And they told the same story about Alex and her going out in the night. And being back, exactly an hour later.

Then Marion. The jury let out a silent gasp, it seemed to me, when they realized that this dignified little woman was up to her armpits in this business. My word! Horton waded into Marion with particular relish. He had her outline her prior life in surprising detail, then had her describe her recruitment and the destruction of her family. It turned out that she had lost custody of the boy and did not have much to live on. Then Horton spent a long time on her life with George and Alex. Through it all, Marion was calm, a Darien housewife whose life had taken a little turn.

Horton went on at length about the fact that George was all excited when he left to get "more." Did she know what "more" was? She did not. Did she think it was another woman? She didn't know but she assumed so. He got her to tell how upset she was that George hadn't made love to her the night before . . . because he was saving himself for someone else. He even made her tell about the time when she was coming and turned away from George because he wasn't really with her. Then back to the More Woman.

"Did you think it could be Mimi Bigelow?"

She paused for a long moment and Horton asked again, "Was it Mimi?"

"I thought it might be, but I didn't know."

"Why did you think it might be, did he say anything?"

"No. But . . . it seemed possible."

"Despite the wine-throwing and all that . . ."

"Because of the wine-throwing . . . She was fighting it."

"Fighting the temptation to come to him . . . to Minot?"

"It seemed possible to me, but I didn't know."

"To join the . . . activities."

"Yes."

"To join the group."

"Yes."

He wisely let go at that point. Then he talked about how Alex left and he got Marion to say it was inconceivable to her that Alex would hurt George . . . just totally inconceivable. Then he had her talk about Alex coming back at twelve thirty, taking her clothes off, and starting up the sexual roundabout all over again.

In response to questions, Marion said, "Alex and I took our clothes off and made love to each other. I was upset and she comforted me. The Forstmans were beside us."

"Could I call that an orgy?"

"If you like," Marion said simply.

I saw Alex again, outside. I explained again that anything we did might come up in court, so we were circumspect. But there was that unmistakable current between us. We'd be together after she testified, I said. I did that in cold blood, led her to me. Ruthless, one could say. Well, of course.

Alex was Horton's last witness, the next day, and then it was going to be the weekend. She was wonderful looking, of course, but her testimony was anticlimactic . . . more of the same. Horton was particularly unpleasant but he didn't challenge her account in any way. Unlike Marion, she said it had not crossed her mind that Mimi might have been the More Woman.

When she was done, the judge left the bench, and Alex walked outside. The jury left and the lawyers deliberately packed their stuff into their yawning black litigation bags. Harry stood, in his elegant, bespoke suit and waited for the attendants to take him back to the Hanson jail. No one was looking and we caught each other's eyes. I gave him a broad grin, made a thumbs-up sign. Then blew him a quick, two-handed kiss. He grinned and did the same . . . turned and made his way out of the room. He looked good. In all this horror, he looked good, the dear, brave man.

Alex was waiting when I did come out, a few minutes later.

"Good job, Alex," I said, giving her a light hug and a kiss on the cheek.

"Thanks. I don't like that guy much, Horton."

"No one does," I said.

"Okay," she changed the subject. "I've testified. Shall we have supper?" I had thought about it, of course, and said yes. It was such a perfect day, I said, how about having supper on *Nellie*, down in the harbor. Would she like to do that? She would.

CHAPTER 37

ARIADNE AUF NAXOS

Late that afternoon, I launched the Whitehall and slowly rowed out to *Nellie* in the soft fall air. The surface was completely still, mirroring the buildings on the shore. Blankets of bright leaves covered the black water, close to shore, and then in patches farther out . . . then single leaves, all the way to the boat. The slow swirls from my oars rippled the reflections of the stone warehouses on the water and the steeples of the town.

On the sailboat, I put out the big American flag, raised the burgee. Then walked around the deck, the way you do, coming home. I went below and put away the groceries. I had picked up some flowers. I found a jar and put them on the table. It's good to have flowers on a sailboat in port. I put some wine on ice, too. Then back up into the cockpit.

I took a book but didn't read. Just sat, looking back at the town. The tide was out and you could see under its skirts . . . under the pilings and the tall docks along the shore. See the kelp beds and the barnacled rocks. And the dories and lobster boats, careened in the mud. The smells, too, the strong smells off the mudflats. Some people don't like that smell; I love it.

There's a small river that empties into the sea at Hanson, the Kennequod. Back in granite-quarrying days, the town built itself a lovely, stone sluice to carry the Kennequod the last fifty yards down to the cove. The sluice feeds into a granite "pond," also man-made. Then over the falls and into the harbor. The falls get louder as the tide goes out. I could almost tell the tide from that sound. Tonight it was very low.

I saw Alex come walking carefully down the steeply tilted ramp to the town float, holding on to the railing on one side. She had a little paper bag in one hand and a canvas duffel over her shoulder. I watched her select a big, wooden dory, tip the water out of it, and the dead leaves, then manhandle it into the water . . . put in a pair of oars. She climbed in and headed out toward me. She rowed well . . . long, slow strokes, not the choppy strokes of the landsman. And she pulled straight, which isn't so common. Straight out to me, without having to turn around and look many times. Alongside, she smiled but didn't say anything. Then gracefully shipped her oars and came aboard. She tied the dory off the stern herself and didn't let it bang the hull.

She'd changed into blue jeans and a heavy, blue CPO shirt. A watch cap and dark down vest, too. It was going to get colder and she was dressed for it. With her light brown hair under her blue watch cap she looked . . . Well, she looked amazing.

We didn't say anything, just, "What can I get you," and "Some white wine would be good." Then for a while we sat up there in the cockpit, cushions at our backs, looking at the darkening town. Watched the yellow lights come on in the houses and listened to the fall of the Kennequod, out of the stony hills and into the stony sea.

We sat silent for a while. Then she put her hand on mine and said, softly: "It's getting cold up here, Tim."

I nodded and we went below. I got out some more things to eat. She said, "Make a fire," and I did. She got the paper bag and fished out some grapes, an onion, a lemon, and a screw-top jar of what turned out to be caviar. "Surprise." She smiled, and went to chop up the onion. I lit the kerosene lanterns, and we sat side by side on the bunk by the fire. The mahogany-paneled cabin was warm now, and she took off her heavy shirt. Turned out she had on another of those ribbed shirts I'd liked so much. Long sleeves, this time. Lilac again, and made of light wool, but the effect, and her breasts, were the same.

I thought the caviar tasted funny, but didn't say so. It was miracle enough that she'd found it at all. I was a little nervous and was wolfing it down.

"Don't eat too much," she said, putting her hand on my arm gently. My body gave a little lurch at that: we were not to eat too much because soon, she was saying, we would be doing things for which we did not want full bellies. We would be rolling over and over in each other's arms, and we did not want full bellies then. No, no, no.

She got up and washed the grapes and got the bottle of wine. She filled my glass. "Have a couple of these," and she handed me grapes. Then the wine. As if there were some ritual here. Wafers with caviar, the grapes and the wine. Little sips. We sat there like that, side by side, for a long time, not touching.

And then—her mouth still cold from a last sip of wine—she leaned over. And kissed me softly on the cheek . . . nuzzled slowly down my neck. Then tilted back for a moment, and gave me a calm, careful look, a thousand years of intimacy in her eyes. Then, with the faintest smile, she gracefully crossed her hands and reached down to the hem of her shirt, as if to quickly draw it over her head. Which she did.

There are things which I cannot describe. Making love with Alex is one of them. I can only say that it was the most astonishing, the most wonderful, the most transcendent thing that had ever happened to me or ever will. We labored slowly up high mountain passes. We flew down the other side. We came and came and then started again, when that seemed impossible. We rocked and hugged and soared for hours. The most remarkable night of my life. Ecstasy piled on ecstasy.

There was also some guilt. I was not "bespoke" with Cassie but close enough. Sleeping with other women—especially Alex—was not part of our tacit understanding, even if Cassie anticipated it. But it was part of the *Cleopatra's Barge* phenomenon, part of my willingness to do anything to rescue Harry. I needed Alex's help, urgently, with Theo.

And—like Cassie—I was pretty sure that, for Alex, trust had to be rooted in intimacy, deep, physical intimacy; that's just who she was. So here we were. Not much of a sacrifice, you may say, and that's certainly true; I have never experienced bliss so intense. But it was a serious sacrifice in another. I had not been the kind of guy who betrays friends and lovers. And now I was.

The whole experience was extraordinary, magical, from the beginning. But at one stage, our passion—already intense—was radically ramped up. The amazing feel of her body became much, much more so . . . almost unbearably sweet. I could not get close enough, could not hug her tight enough or get my arms far enough around. Then it got really strange: the lights in the little cabin began to pulse, ever so gently. The flowers on the table became inexplicably bright. And they started to pulse, too. Her touch, already extraordinary, became much, much more so. I had never had pleasure so intense. Then the whole cabin began to throb and glow.

Which is when I finally got it. "Ecstasy!" I said to her, astonished, leaning back. "You little rascal, you put Ecstasy in the caviar! That's why it tasted funny . . . As if your gifts weren't wonder enough! What in the world?" I really was dumbfounded. I laughed out loud, amused and astonished.

She looked a little sheepish but mostly pleased with herself. "I wanted to be sure you . . . liked it. Liked me. Besides, I'm a jokey girl." She smiled more broadly at that. "As you know."

"As I know." I howled at that. The idea that she would need any stimulants to draw me to her or to intensify my experience was beyond me. I had actually had Ecstasy once before, making love, but it had been nothing like this. It was Alex, not the drugs, and I wished, in a way, she'd skipped it. Still, it was hard to complain. I had just gone to places where I had never been before . . . not even close. But now everything calmed a little. The laughter brought me down, brought us both down. Which was fine. It was time.

We were lying now side by side on the wide bed, companionable and easy. She pulled the tangled sheet up, to wipe her face. Lay back again. At rest, after that astonishing trip. Then Alex began, and I was surprised at the direction she took.

"You're with Cassie now?" she asked, as if it were a matter of mild interest. A bit of casual conversation.

"Yes," I said, at length. "We are . . . together. Although no one has said quite what that means."

"Probably not this," Alex said, with a smile and a little push of her . . . her fur against my leg. As profoundly sated as I was, I stirred at that. She was amazing. But we didn't take that turn . . . kept on talking.

"Who knows?" I said. "Cassie is . . . very wise. And very, very complicated."

A little frown now from Alex, as she went on. "Did George drive her husband to suicide?" she said.

"Whoo! I don't know. Did he? The story I heard is that he was climbing over a fence with a gun and, you know . . ." Actually, of course, Cassie had finally said that he had committed suicide but I did not feel free to tell her that. Besides, this was an opening.

"Yeah, I know about the fence. But was it suicide?" she asked.

"I don't think anyone ultimately knows. Does it make sense?"

She sat for a moment. "Maybe."

"Like?"

"Like that night took a funny turn. George is amazingly sensitive, as I told you. And he picked up on something with Don that interested him. Or amused him . . . I don't know. And he gave the night a homoerotic turn. Quite a powerful homoerotic turn. Don had assumed that he'd been drawn to me; that was the idea. But George knew. And Don found himself . . . well, he found himself in a new space. And he liked it quite a bit. So George took it further, much further. And Don found himself doing things—and having things done to him—which he had surely never imagined. Hard-core, homosexual lovemaking. Hard-core. Which could have shaken an older man like Don, later."

She was oddly calm about that. And I was impatient. Angry in fact. The man was dead, after all, almost certainly at their reckless hands. Because they were so incredibly deep into any intimacy, any sexuality, and were amused to see how far down they could take him. It made it easier for me to do what I was doing.

"Let's not talk about that now," I said. "We've got other things to do."

Now she looked the least bit wary. "Like what?"

"Saving Harry." A pause. "Saving you."

There was the slightest tightening around her eyes: "From what?"

"From Theo Soros, I assume." Here we go. Now her eyes did tighten.

"Look, let me tell you some things I know. Then you decide what you want to do." She didn't say anything, and I began.

"I have been scuttling around on the edges of this business for months. I can't talk to Harry or any of his people. But I have gotten a curiously good idea of exactly what happened. I know better than Harry's lawyers, better than Horton. Better than anyone." Pause. "Except you, Alex. You and Theo." I paused a moment. "I also know why you're afraid."

She started to say something, but I just shook my head and went on. "I can help. And I will. That's why I am here. Not just to make love to you, profound joy though it was. And certainly not to turn you over to the cops or any of that. I am not the Law Man anymore; I won't do that. Ever." I squeezed her shoulder gently, to make the point. "Never, Alex, no matter what." Long wait now, to let that sink in. "I will help you, partly because I need your help, for Harry. But also . . ." Another pause and I closed my eyes a moment. "Because I have been in love with you from the beginning and I won't see you hurt. I just won't. You may or may not believe that . . ."

"I believe it," she said. "That's the kind of thing I know." I saw that she did believe it. And now it was going to be easy. "And don't be so sure that we won't end up together." She smiled. "I have my ways." She smiled more broadly, rolled over on top of me, partway. I smiled, too, and put my arms around her. But we did not start making love again. We kept on talking. It was the reason we were here now, and we both knew it. I went on:

"I will go to any lengths to see you safe. But I need your help, to be able to help you. And to save Harry."

"I won't go back to court," she said quickly, almost stiffening on the bed. "I won't go to prison."

"Not for an instant," I said. "It won't work that way. You are going to leave the country for a while, and I'll do everything. But I have to know where I am in this darkness. I need the thread, Alex. I need to know how it was done. How . . ."

"There is no thread!" she interrupted angrily. "My God . . . 'Ariadne's thread.' Spare me! That was always nonsense, and now you? Jesus!"

I was startled by her vehemence. She went on: "George started the Minotaur nonsense to scare the yokels back home but then he started to believe it himself. Which was stupid. Then your brother, for heaven's sake. But you! I thought you were the sane one . . . the one who could really save me."

"I can," I said quickly and pulled her over, on top of me. "That is exactly what I will do: I will keep you safe, thread or no." I paused, looking up at her. "You could have slain a hundred men, Alex . . . I do not care. I only need Theo. And I will see you safe. No matter what."

"Safe," she said. Not a question, just the word. As if she were holding it in her hand, maybe weighing it. She rolled off of me, just lay there a moment. I raised up on one elbow to go on.

"Yes. That's why you came to me, isn't it, way back when, at the dance? You were thinking, even then, that you might need a refuge, and that I might do. Even when you and Theo were still together. Theo was telling you that George was going crazy and might kill you both. And he was going to kill George instead. Which made sense but terrified you, too. Partly because you loved George, for all the threat he might be. But also Theo: if he'd do that, what wouldn't he do?"

Again she started to speak and I shook my head.

"Once he'd done it—once he'd actually killed George— your fears started to build. Theo started to go crazy but in a whole new way . . . things you hadn't seen. Before, you'd been lovers, enormously close, and that was the whole point, as it should have been. But then he almost lost interest in you and was completely into the money. And his grand life plan, to go back home and be king. With Minot's gold. And you were ancillary to that, if you were to be involved at all. And then it occurred to you that maybe you weren't so ancillary, that maybe you were a threat. It was hard to know, but maybe. In which case . . ." She rolled to me, snuggled down against my chest. She didn't say I had it right but there she was. That was enough.

"But now something else has happened. I don't know what, but you are different. It was unmistakable, you're really scared now, which is unlike you. And you've turned again to me." I didn't know where I had gotten all that, but I believed it. And now, with her lying tucked against me, I was sure of it.

I tipped up her head, so I could look into her eyes. "What happened?" I said. "What did he do?"

A long wait and then she buried her face against my chest again. She spoke so softly, it was almost hard to hear. "He wanted to kill Marion," she said.

"What?! My God! Whatever for?"

She was shaken but relieved, too. She wanted to talk. "He thought she was beginning to suspect it was him, not Harry. I'm not sure where he got that idea, but it's the kind of thing he might have been right about. And now he wanted to kill her, before she went to Horton, or whatever."

"Great God! What did you tell him?"

"That I'd sooner kill him," she said, simply. "Which I would. I would have killed him in an instant. Then he laughed, as if it were all a joke."

"But it was not."

"No, it was not."

I drew her into my arms again. Held her tight . . . a kid who had woken up scared in the night. "No wonder you're scared. Jesus! Now you're both the threat, you and Marion together." And we lay like that for a long moment, thinking about where we were now.

We had been circling one another, ever since the dance that night on Broke. And now, here we were: conspirators and lovers at last. In that lovely cabin. In the firelight and the kerosene lanterns, and the smell of the pines and the sea. And the gentle rocking of the good sloop *Nellie* . . . way east on the coast of Maine. What did the fella say? Et in Arcadia ego? Even in Arcadia, I am there. Well, I guess so! All of us now. And Alex and I were holding on to each other, trying hard to find a way out, a way up.

"Shall we begin?" I asked, at last.

With a touch of what looked like sadness, she leaned up and kissed me, on the tip of my nose. Then she went, naked, over to the other bunk, got her little backpack, and came back to bed. Dumped it out.

There were various things, but the thing she was looking for and the thing that held my eye was a black, electronic-looking device, the likes of which I had never seen before. Or heard about or imagined. It took a minute for it to sink in, what it was. Then I got it.

It was a lovely design. It was triangle-shaped, smooth-edged, and jet black . . . about an inch thick and three inches long, with a little Trimble logo. It weighed about half a pound. I turned it on, and it powered up in an instant and it knew just where we were. The windows for the numbers were big and the words, telling you *Go right* or *Go left* or *Go back* were wonderfully legible, and they lit up. There were no edges and it felt good in your hand. It was obviously waterproof, too, and would lead you through the deepest fog or darkest night. Not underwater; it wouldn't work unless it could "see" the satellites. But it would when you came to the surface, to check.

I had had no idea there was such a thing. The GPS on *Nellie* was the state of the art, as far as I knew. It cost as much as a Volkswagen and was almost as big. Not really, but big. It had simply not occurred to me that it could be miniaturized into a device like this. I was astounded.

"It's a prototype," Alex said. "George found out about 'em somehow and got one for each of us. His and hers." Then she just watched me take it in.

The gadget was obviously real. But to me—having never imagined such a thing and still reeling from the Ecstasy and the night—to me it was magical. Like Alex herself. And, back on that earlier night, in the fog, a girl who knew her way around on the water. A girl like Alex, say, with one of these magic devices in her hand. Why, she could go anywhere. Pretty fast, too. And never, never get lost. Not for a moment. And certainly not for an hour.

She could, for example, have come—straight as an arrow—from Forstman's boat to Theo's, by prearrangement, while he and Minot sat there. Could have come aboard and slipped off her clothes. And ridden George one last time, while clever Theo watched. One last canter on her hugely swollen lover. Or taken him in her mouth again. To get him ready. For the bullet. And the pip. Was it like that? I have no idea. But I saw those pictures in my head, as we lay there, my murderess and me.

"Ariadne's thread," I said, with a small smile.

She smiled too but was scornful. "Don't be stupid. It's an electrical gadget, not a magic thread."

"I've never even heard of such a thing. How did he get it?"

"George just knew, went to the manufacturer. Maybe bribed them. Everyone'll have 'em soon, he said."

"Did you give it to Theo?"

"Yes."

"And he used it that night to get around."

"Yes. He didn't say so, but obviously." I did not ask her when she had given it to him. I had a fair idea but I didn't want to know. I only needed Theo, for my purposes, not both of them. I needed her as my ally, not as a murderer. Which she may have been.

"How'd you get it back?"

"He gave it to me later. He had George's by then."

"May I have it?"

"Of course. That's the point, isn't it?"

I nodded. "Thank you, Alex." And I took it.

I smiled, reached out for her. We hugged. Then I sat up, swung my feet down onto the cabin sole. "Want supper?"

"Sure, I'm ravenous. You gonna cook?" And I was. It took a while but not forever. I had some more hors d'oeuvres. We did not dip back into the caviar. She gave a wistful look at the jar and then up at me. "I guess we've had enough of that for tonight," she said. "Pity." She said it with a seductive grin. That Alex, boy; she would have done it in a heartbeat. A little kid who won't come out of the water, even though her lips were blue. I have said that Marion was the wonder . . . the great goddess of intimacy. But that's not right. Alex was the Olympian. There was nothing like Alex. Absolutely nothing.

Comparisons are odious and never more so than here. But, in a sense, Cassie was not her peer in intimacy. She was at the same broad level but it was entirely different. Because, with Cassie, love and caring were at the heart of it, and that is an entirely different experience. Cassie would take you into her life, a magical honor. But Alex would fly you to the moon and the stars. No one makes that trip . . . almost no one. It is a joy beyond comprehending. And here's another odd thing. It's nonsense but I had the overwhelming sense that—if I had taken a quarter turn to the right or left . . . said just the right thing at that moment, touched her in a certain way—she and I would have been together forever. And it would have been a profound pleasure and privilege. Did I consider it? Nope, not for a second. Not then. But later? When my life went to hell? Yes.

Back to business. "One last thing, Alex," I said. "Do you know about a deal they referred to as the Sweet Rocks Tender?" That, you'll remember, was the deal that smelled funny to me from the documents . . . the deal where I thought some "parking" might be going on.

She smiled at that, as if it were amusing that I had tumbled to that. "Yup, good for you. The tender offer where George gave Theo all that money to invest."

"What do you mean?" In fact I knew exactly what she meant or at least I had deep suspicions. Because of all the time I'd spent with the Minot records.

"Theo was all excited about it. Apparently George gave him a chunk of money—I remember seventeen million—for Theo to invest in the deal. I don't know why George didn't just invest in it himself but there were reasons. Anyhow, Theo said that, if anything happened to George—that's how he spoke about it—'if anything happened to George,' that money would simply be his. Or his and mine, I guess; we were talking about being equal partners." Alex was not very excited about this. I, on the other hand, was very excited indeed.

"Are you reasonably sure about that number?" I asked casually.

She frowned, as if that were a funny question but then said, "Yes. I have a good head for numbers, for some reason. It was seventeen million . . . quite a lot." I thanked her, said that was all I needed. Then I said, "This is going to work."

"Because of that money?" she asked.

"Yes, partly because of that money. And the GPS. I now think it is more or less certain to work. It will take a little while for it to kick in; it will be later in the trial, if we use it. But it will work. In the meantime, I worry about Theo. He is a violent guy and he knows you know a lot. I want you and Marion to get out of the country. Like today or tomorrow. I have a guy whom I will set to looking after you." I told her about Paul K. and said I would put him in touch with her this morning. He would set a serious guard to look after her the next few weeks. But, soon, my permanent plan would cut in and Theo would cease to be a problem.

"You're sure," she said; she was worried.

"Very," I said. "Going to take a while but very sure."

In the morning, all I could find was coffee and a single corn muffin, which I warmed in butter, on the stove. Half for her, half for me. Juice, a whole quart, thank God. We drank all of that. Then I gave her contact information for Paul K. and said I'd be in touch with him. Then we went back to bed. Irresistible, I'm afraid. And amazing.

Later, we got up and dressed. Alex pulled her things together. She put on her vest, and the woolen watch cap. Tucked her hair up. She would get Marion and go to New York as soon as they could pack, she said. Then Europe, as soon as the next day. Did she have enough money, I asked? She laughed at that, patted my face. "Yes, you darling. I have plenty of money. But thanks. I like it that you think like that."

"I said I would take care of you," I said, "and I will. Are you going to Greece?"

"Eventually, perhaps," she said.

"I get the sense from Paul K. that there are mountains of Minot gold out there, much of it yours. I'll see that you get your share. He'll help."

She shrugged, didn't care. "I'll take a look but I have way more than enough now. My parents were academics, remember. I don't care much about money." Pause. Then, "Where do you go now?"

"Back to watch the rest of that dreadful trial, I'm afraid. Less dreadful for me, now. Now that you have given me this"—patting the Trimble—"and that business about the seventeen million."

"Use it carefully," she said. I promised I would. "Then Cassie?" she asked.

"Yes," I said. "As far as I can tell now, anyway, although it's not entirely clear. There's something . . ."

"What?" she said.

"I don't know. There are mysteries." She nodded, interested but not deeply troubled. Shifting romantic alliances were nothing new to her.

"Fine," she said. "If that's what you want. But do keep in mind, she is . . . dangerous."

"How do you mean?" That was a surprise.

"Well, she's a great moralist, you know. Like your brother. Like you, maybe, although you . . . not so much now. But Cassie for sure, and she's scary. Moralists are dangerous. They see things with a terrible clarity—black and white. Cassie sees things with a terrible clarity. And she acts on what she sees.

"She saw George, for instance, that night in Montana, or thought she did. She thought he was 'the Beast' and she tried desperately to get her husband to leave with her. She was almost screaming, right in front of us. 'He will kill you. And me!' Her husband smiled, embarrassed. Didn't believe her for a second. Which only made her crazier. Finally, she gave up in a fury and stormed out of the house. It was something."

"I can see that," I said. "But she was right about George, wasn't she?"

"I guess. But the thing for you to remember is that people who see things with that certainty are . . . dangerous, as I say. Not evil. She's a deeply virtuous woman. But that has its dangers, too. 'Virtue armed' . . . not safe."

A long pause. Then she said: "If ever you're . . . troubled, Tim. Or she's not enough." She waited and smiled. Again, a thousand years of intimacy in her gray-blue eyes. "Come to me."

"Thank you, Alex." A quarter turn . . . no.

Then we both went up on deck. I offered to row her into town but she said she could manage, which was certainly true. She stopped a second. "I didn't kill a hundred men, Tim. I didn't kill one." I just nodded. She reached up and gave me a last kiss. And I wondered if that could be true . . . that she hadn't killed anyone. I had long since decided that I just didn't need to know. What I needed was an ally to help me save Harry, and I had one.

She stood there a moment, with the line in her hand. "Look after me," she said. I promised I would. Then she sat down on the gunnel, lowered herself into the dory, and rowed away.

I stood on deck, watching her all the way. Watched her pull the dory up on the float . . . set the oars down and head up the gangway, almost level with the dock now, at high tide. Watched her walk up the hill into town and the morning. I felt a terrible pull, I yearned to jump into the Whitehall right now and follow her. But I did not.

Alex flew to New York that day, with Marion. Then on to Paris the day after. I was in touch with Paul K. and he met her in Paris; they made security arrangements, he told me. Then, he said, she went on to Rome for a week, to the Hassler at the head of the Spanish Steps. From there she went to Athens—still with Marion—where, Paul was alarmed to say, he lost her. He said he knew she had gone down into the islands and he'd find her soon. He mentioned Mykonos, his favorite. And Patmos, which is very chic these days.

But that's not where I would go, if I were looking for her. I would go to Naxos, where Ariadne had gone. And where I thought Alex might go. To wait for a lover. For a Dionysus, whose powers and gift for passion were far, far greater than my own.

CHAPTER 38

CREATING THE BARGE

As soon as Alex left, I cleaned up and hurried into town; I had a lot to do. Alex had given me not one but two invaluable threads. First, the GPS, which would have solved the navigation problems. And second, the $17 million story, which made my speculation about a crooked Sweet Rocks Tender infinitely more appealing. There had been parking all right. But—miraculously and stupidly—a huge chunk of the dough ($17 million) had been parked with Theo. That was incredibly reckless on George's part; there was a high risk that the SEC would check the accounts of an associate like Theo, even though he was not technically part of the takeover group. In any case, Minot had apparently done it and that made everything radically better for me.

The point was that—for the parking to work—Theo had to have been given all the indicia of actual ownership of the $17 million, even though he and George knew he had to give it back, once the deal went through. But the beauty part was that—if George happened to die while Theo was "seized" of the money—why, Theo could simply keep it. Which was an incredible motive for murder, wasn't it? The $17 million was only part of what Theo might logically expect to get; there was all the Minot gold in Greece, too. But this was an instant fortune-on-hand which would make the rest of his search much, much easier and more certain. And give him an almost irresistible motive for murder.

Again, I couldn't prove any of this legitimately. But I had a pretty clear idea of how to do so illegitimately.

I grabbed Frank, told him what I had learned, and we set about getting ready. Which was mostly a matter of drafting papers that we might or might not ever use. The papers would mostly rely on real documents from the Minot trove. That would give the whole thing verisimilitude. But the key on which all else hinged was not in the Minot trove, because it did not exist. The document to suggest that Minot had given Theo the $17 million and that Theo was to invest it in Sweet Rocks was to be a forgery. Forgery—especially forgery of evidence—is the ultimate sin for a trial lawyer. Would I do that for Harry? In a heartbeat.

The draft documents would also allege that Theo had a miniature GPS, which solved his navigation problems. So, in a sense, the motions would rest on two forgeries or fakes: a memo of some kind about the $17 million and the GPS, which I had gotten from Alex but that I would "plant" on Theo somehow. Frank and I labored hard all weekend on preliminary papers. Later—if we ever had to use them—we would put them in final form.

Frank and I had become close, during all our work together. We became so close that at one point Frank decided to take me into his confidence on something we'd never talked about.

He asked, casually, one night while we were having supper in my suite, if I wanted to hear the story of Harry's gun. My heart skipped a beat, but I said sure. And Frank went ahead.

Harry had told the sheriff that he thought his .22 was still down in the Marblehead house, and he sent Frank, by limo, to get it. But that, Frank said, wasn't really necessary. Because Frank had the gun all along.

"I was out on deck when Harry came back that night," Frank began.

"You knew he would be there?" I asked.

He ignored that and said, "I was there. And Harry handed me the gun. Said to get rid of it. He hadn't used it, he said, but he never wanted to be tempted again."

"Do you think that was true?" I asked. "That he really hadn't used it? Or was he just trying to give you some cover?"

"Dunno. Anyhow, I took it down to the galley. And popped it into a big pot of lobster chowder that I had simmering on the stove. I'd planned ahead."

"The lobster chowder, huh?" That Frank.

"Yup. All during the searches that the sheriff's people and then the state police did. The next day, I fished it out and went to Marblehead to 'find' the .22 and bring it up to Maine, but first I had to get rid of the old one. I had the driver stop on that long, low bridge, outside Belfast so I could walk for a few minutes; I was a little carsick, I told him. Asked him to wait on the other side. I threw the gun in the river. When I got to Marblehead, I got in touch with some rough friends, from the old days, and had them get me one like it. I had the serial number so I knew what vintage to try to get. Told 'em money didn't matter, and they had it to me in two days. Clean as a whistle and ready for the ride back to Maine." Frank smiled, delighted with himself.

"Hollow points, Frank? In Harry's gun?"

He waited a beat and said, "I didn't look." Of course he looked, but there were still things we were not going to share.

"A couple of rounds fired?" I asked. He didn't answer that, either.

In the morning, I went back to putting the almost-finishing touches on Cleopatra's Barge. I had told Frank about George Crowninshield and that's what we called the forgery, Cleopatra's Barge. It was not a document . . . not a "forgery" in that familiar sense. It was a shiny pocket computer, which would eventually carry a critical message. The computer and its message were the forgery. That was Cleopatra's Barge.

I had learned that Minot had such a computer, and I knew that it had never been produced. He apparently used it to keep personal notes of important events and he had it with him, almost all the time. I had the make and model and sent Frank to get one just like it. Then he and I reconstructed it with dates and other information, from the real records. What we did not do was put in the final, critical note. That would be the last step, running out the tiny guns on Cleopatra's Barge.

CHAPTER 39

THE DEFENSE

Jack's case went in smoothly and I thought it was devastating.
It was interesting for me. And weird . . . sitting there, listening
to a story of the murder that was so deeply at odds with what I
now knew. But it was satisfying, just the same.

First, he put on his own ballistics expert, who rebutted
B. T.'s man. Then he tore into the notion that the "murder
weapon"—which no expert could say was in fact the murder
weapon—just turned up "on a silver platter," in the midst of
all that deep, black kelp. By the time he was done, the "murder
weapon" business was part of his story, not Horton's . . . part
of the notion that there was "some other dude" out there who
planted the gun. And killed George. Pretty good.

Then Jack drove his advantage with a long line of George's
people, from the orgies. Had them talk about their experiences.
And then testify that none of them had ever seen Harry or
Mimi at any of these events. There were so many that it almost

got boring. But not the payoff question: did you ever see Harry or Mimi? They had not. Pretty strong stuff.

I seriously believed that Jack could have rested right there and gotten an acquittal. But he didn't. Harry wouldn't let him, I suspect. Harry was playing a longer game. He wanted to be vindicated, and for that he needed to testify. And he wanted Mimi to testify, too. He wanted them to be restored to their old selves. Not a particularly promising notion, it seemed to me, even if it had gone well. It didn't.

Harry went first. That made a sort of sense, if one were going to do this at all. He could lay down all the heavy timbers and Mimi could just say, "Yes, that's the way it was."

Harry, of course, was superb. He went through his curriculum vitae with an attractive offhandedness, but Jack made him slow down for the best parts. For example, a few months back, the president himself had sounded him out about becoming undersecretary of the Treasury, with a view to becoming secretary later on. Harry had been very tight-lipped about that at the time, but now he had no choice.

He talked, too, about some private charities that even I had never heard about. It turns out that he had sent five poor young men from New England off to college. Not a formal charity, no tax breaks . . . just a secret kindness to kids who must have reminded him of himself.

Harry's presence during all this was the main thing. He was so utterly himself: strong, decent, and wise. It was all but inconceivable, listening to him and hearing that voice, that he had been part of any of this.

Jack turned at last to the night of the ball, the speeches and the incident with the wine. Harry's tone on Minot's speech was just right: "I was irked, obviously," he said. "I was reaching out to him, trying to have some continuity between his term and mine. Then he made those unpleasant remarks. I wasn't particularly surprised, frankly. I was sorry; but he was who he was."

Jack asked, "Did your wife think it was a big deal?"

Harry surprised me by giving his most charming smile. "She did. And I must say, when I thought about it later, it was awfully good of her to care so much. Didn't surprise or bother me, as I say; Minot had his flaws. But it made her furious."

"You weren't upset?" Jack asked.

"No, not really. But I was embarrassed, and I was sore at Mimi for having risen to his bait." Jack asked what happened next. "I stood up and more or less rushed her out of the room. Looking back, I shouldn't have. I wish I'd just apologized to him and kissed her on the spot. She was . . . terrific." He said it with real caring, and you saw the jury warm to him.

"That night, when you two were alone, Mr. Bigelow," Jack asked, "did you discuss it?"

"Yes. I'm sorry to say that I was still angry. I said she had made us both look like idiots. Then she was angry because, as she said, she had done it for me."

"And the next night?" Jack asked.

"The same thing. Someone made some mild crack just as we were going to bed, and I got sore all over again. We had sharp words, and for the first time in our married life, I stormed out of our bedroom. I got up, got dressed, and went down to the float, took an inflatable and went out to my boat. My intention was to sleep there. It was foolish.

"Anyway," he went on, "I couldn't sleep a wink. Sat on the bunk for a while, stewing about it. Then I realized I was being ridiculous. I got up and took the dinghy back to *Java*. Mimi was as wide-awake as I had been. I apologized, we both laughed, and we went to sleep."

"You used the service float when you came back," Jack said. "The jury's been told that 'isn't done.' Why did you do it that night?"

Harry gave another of his warmest smiles. "I'm sure there will be members of the club who will be more troubled by this than by the charges of murder." A smile and a shrug; he couldn't help that. "But the fact is I deliberately went up that way because I was consciously saying 'the hell with it.' The hell with a lot of things that didn't really matter." He paused, then, "That's it." Jack let a moment pass, let the jury savor it. Then with an audible sigh, he began again:

"Did you sneak up that side of the steamer, Mr. Bigelow, so you would not be seen?"

"No." Strong, definitive.

"Did you come up that way because you had just left a body down on that float?" Jack asked.

"No," Harry snorted. "That's nonsense."

Again, Jack waited, then went on. "Mr. Bigelow, Mr. Horton has gone to a lot of trouble to suggest—without formally alleging—that your wife was involved with George Minot and was going to meet him that night. To the best of your knowledge, is either of those things true?"

"Absolutely not," Harry said, grimly. On that note, Jack rested.

Horton picked away at Harry for a while on cross. He had to, really, after that. But it didn't amount to anything. Harry was solid as a rock.

CHAPTER 40

THE ALICE CLUB

There was a break after Harry's testimony during which Jack and his team caucused. Maybe they were debating, one last time, whether to call her at all. But they did and she was called to the stand. She is a stunning woman, Mimi, and she never looked more beautiful than that morning. But very nervous, if you knew her. She sat straight, with her hands working in her lap and bright patches of color in her cheeks.

Jack started slowly and gave her some time before turning to anything substantive. At first, she tossed her head in a scary way, jerking herself around to look at the judge, then back to the jury, then Jack. Her lovely blond hair was conservatively done, but it flipped around as she moved. Harry was smiling at her the whole time, and that seemed to calm her down. One of the nicest moments of the whole business occurred when she caught his eye in the middle of some early answer. She just stopped and looked at him, smiling sweetly and forgetting the pending question. "I'm sorry"—remembering where she was—"what did you ask?"

Jack walked her quickly through the night of the ball. Her indignation at Minot was sharp and clear. At that point her delicacy was a help, helped explain how an elegant woman like that could have been so upset over a slur that she would throw her drink and curse him.

She was good, too, on Harry's reaction, walking her out of the ball and giving her hell. "That wasn't fair," she said, still upset. "I'd only done it for him. Harry should have stood up for me." She stopped and looked up at Jack, a little lost in where she was. Then, "I loved him," she said, simply. Jack paused, then asked her about Harry leaving their bedroom the next night.

"Did you try to get him to stay?" Jack asked.

"Yes. But he was very stern, very cold." Then, astonishingly, she gave a good imitation of his business voice, right there in the courtroom: "'Mimi, I am very upset about this. I will see you in the morning.'" Then she grinned. "It was no good talking to him when he was like that." A couple of people on the jury laughed. Such a good sign.

"Did you sleep?" Jack asked.

"Of course not," she said. "I didn't even turn the light off."

"And eventually he returned."

"Yes."

"How soon."

"I don't know. It seemed a long time but I suppose it was an hour or two. I don't know."

"And what was he like when he returned?"

She thought. "He was himself again. He apologized for being stern and got into bed. We hugged and it was over. We . . . well, we went to sleep." One had the distinct sense they had made love, but we weren't going to hear about that.

"Were his clothes disheveled or torn or anything?"

"No."

"Bloodstains, Mrs. Bigelow?"

"No. Nothing like that."

"Was he distracted or 'crazy' in any way?"

"No, no. He was himself. He's very calm, you know. He was gentle, he apologized. He was nice."

"Mrs. Bigelow, were you ever involved in any way with George Minot?"

"No." Sharp and clear.

"Were you having an affair with him?"

"No."

"Were you planning to meet him, later that night, on *Silver Girl* so you could join him at a party on some other boat?"

"No."

"Had you ever been romantically or sexually involved in any way with George Minot?"

"No." Long pause while Jack looked at the jury and they looked at her.

"That's all I have, Your Honor."

Horton didn't quite smirk when he began, but there was that hint in his manner. He started, "Mrs. Bigelow, my name is Robert Horton. I represent the state of Maine in these proceedings. May I call you Mimi, by the way?"

"No, you're not our friend. You may call me Mrs. Bigelow," she said evenly.

"As you like." He smiled, as if this were amusing. "Mrs. Bigelow, one witness has testified that she thought that George Minot might be going to meet you the night he was killed. Her assumption was that he was going to pick you up and take you to an evening of sexual activities. I take it you deny that, Mrs. Bigelow?"

"Of course," she said, quickly.

He spoke softly, confidently, "And you deny, too, Mrs. Bigelow, that you had ever been involved with Mr. Minot, is that right?"

"Yes."

"Never met alone with him?"

"No."

"Never kissed him?"

"No."

"Never made love to him."

"No."

"And you never told your husband, that night, that you had been planning to go to Minot."

"Of course not."

Horton walked away from her a little, toward the jury. "Mrs. Bigelow, you are a Boston girl, is that right?" Yes, she had been born and brought up in Boston. "Went to Concord Academy?" Yes. "And to Wellesley to college." Yes. "And you worked at a publishing house in Boston?" Yes. Little, Brown. "And lived on Beacon Hill?" Yes.

"But you have not always lived in Boston, Mrs. Bigelow, have you?"

"I lived in New York for . . . just over a year. And again after we were married."

"Lived back then"—he looked at a yellow pad that was covered with notes—"on Seventy-Third Street, between Second and Third Avenue, at number . . . What was the number, Mrs. Bigelow?"

"I don't remember," Mimi said, her voice a little funny.

"Was it 220?" Horton asked.

"I don't know," she said.

"No matter. But you shared an apartment with a classmate, Debs Stoddard, is that right?"

"Yes, Debs Stoddard." A deep breath and her head thrown back, ready for the next question.

"And you dated, that year."

"Yes, some."

"And went to restaurants in the neighborhood?" Yes.

"And to some downtown." Yes.

"Including"—he paused and looked at his yellow pad— "let's see: the Odeon? Do I pronounce that correctly?"

"Yes, the Odeon, that's right."

"And Montrachet, is that right?"

"Yes, Montrachet."

"And clubs, too, I suppose. You went to clubs, downtown, too, Mrs. Bigelow."

"Sometimes. Not much."

"Not too much. Did you go to Nell's?"

"Yes."

"And"—he looked at the yellow pad—"Area?"

"Yes."

A long pause now, a long look at the notes—"Mrs. Bigelow, what is the Alice Club?"—not looking at her.

Mimi flinched and stuttered, "I don't know."

"Are you sure, Mrs. Bigelow?" He looked up. "It's a private club, isn't it? Downtown?" Now he walked toward her. "A very private club, named after one of the people in that old movie, *Bob & Carol & Ted & Alice*? Isn't that right?" He paused, and Mimi said nothing, just looked down at her hands in her lap. "That was an old movie about wife-swapping or some such thing, wasn't it, Mrs. Bigelow?"

"I never saw it."

"The club or the movie?" he said quickly.

"I never saw it," she said again. He let it go.

"A very private place . . . more a group of friends than a club. On the second floor of a building on Greene Street, does that refresh your recollection?"

"No. I wasn't there." But she looked down, and one knew with a terrible certainty that that wasn't true.

Horton turned and the next question rang out sharply: "Do you have pierced ears, Mrs. Bigelow?"

"Oh, that's awful!" Mimi said, standing up in the witness box. She looked around wildly as if to see if someone wouldn't make him stop. She looked at the judge, looked at Jack. Looked at Harry, but now Harry was looking at his hands, very abstractedly.

"All I asked was whether you have pierced ears, madam. Do you?"

"I don't know," she almost barked, "I . . ."

"Oh, sure you do, Mrs. Bigelow," Horton sneered. Then, soft and sinister, "Reach up and feel it, if you like . . . You can feel it with your finger and your thumb." And he waited, a long pause. "But you don't have to do that, do you, Mrs. Bigelow. You know, don't you?"

Still no answer. She was on the verge of tears or hysterics. "Don't you?"

"Yes," barely audible.

"You have pierced ears."

"Yes."

Long pause. "And the lips of your vagina, too," he went on quietly, standing next to her now. "They are pierced, too, aren't they, Mimi?"

"No." And she started to cry.

"Mimi, we can get the judge to order a doctor to examine you right now—I have one standing by outside—and everyone will know. It will only take a moment to . . ." He paused. "Let's not do that, Mimi. Just tell us. One of your lips is pierced, isn't it?"

She wept and nodded, yes.

"Yes," Horton said. "And George did it, didn't he? And put rings in you there."

She cried out or moaned at that and then, in awful tears, "Yes!"

"And you did go to the Alice Club on Greene Street with him, didn't you?"

"Yes." More tears.

"In fact, you were together a long time, back then, you and Minot. A good many months of those nights."

"No."

"People saw you, Mimi. The people who knew about your rings. It was months, wasn't it?" Horton was stern, matter-of-fact.

"Yes."

"And last summer. In the fog. It was you he was coming for, wasn't it?"

"Yes," she said desperately.

"But Harry guessed, didn't he? And told you to stay . . . he would go."

"Yes," she sobbed. But then she looked up anxiously: "But only to scare him," she said.

"That's why he took the gun?" Horton asked quickly.

And Mimi said, "Yes, to scare him away," before she could think.

Then quickly tried to take it back: "No, I don't remember if he took the gun. I just knew he was going to scare him."

"Oh, please, Mimi." Horton was disgusted. "Of course he took the gun. How else was he going to scare a giant like Minot? And you saw it, didn't you?"

"Yes." She was sobbing again. "He was going to scare him. He had it just to scare him."

"And he certainly did, didn't he? Then he came back and told you that he'd murdered Minot, didn't he?"

"No!" Mimi shouted. "He never said anything like that. And he didn't do it. It's not true."

But of course it had to be true. And every horrified soul in that courtroom knew it. Harry sat there looking at his wife with a faint, empty smile on his handsome face, as if he had just lost his mind.

Horton was silent a long time, looked as if he might just sit down and leave the poor sobbing creature alone. He walked away from her, almost back to his seat. Then stopped and turned. As if he had just thought of one last question.

"Did George ever put a pip on you down there," he asked, curious about that one last point.

"No," she whispered. "No pip."

"Ah, well, something else, I suppose." And sat down.

CHAPTER 41

RESCUE

It had been a rescue, of course. A botched rescue from long ago. And the very opposite of what I had always assumed: that Mimi had saved Harry. Not at all. It was Harry who was the Rescuer, as always. And he rescued Mimi. From Minot, many years ago. But again last summer. Because Minot wasn't quite done. And Mimi, either. She wanted to go back, one last time, to George and his dark pleasures.

To the Minotaur himself. To the great, dark creature in the Labyrinth, calling up with his bull-bodied strength, the aching sensuality and the exquisite, the appalling, the irresistible taboo. The sweetness of women lying with beasts. That's what poor Harry had managed to unwind, all those years ago. And what he sought to unwind again, last summer. Once and for all.

The story, or enough of it to piece together, came out over the next two days. Horton, the little cheat, had three "rebuttal witnesses," a woman and two men, all set to go, the minute Jack rested. And they knew everything; they had been in George's circle, back at the time. The testimony was choppy and confusing, as always, but the basic story was clear enough. It was a good deal clearer to me, actually, than to the court, because I knew so much. Even so, I was astonished.

Mimi came to George first. He had found her, that year in New York, when she was twenty, right out of college. He had picked her up like a child, and carried her down to the mare's nest of his life . . . to the Labyrinth. It had been the time for that kind of thing and a lot of people were doing it. Plato's Retreat and all that. Not like George, to be sure, but it was in the air. Anyway, Mimi adored it. The drugs; the wet, muzzling crowds; the thunderous music in darkened lofts. And especially the lunatic sex. As George had of course sensed, she had a special gift for it. More than a gift . . . she was wonderful. She was in the Labyrinth and she loved it. She loved George, too, almost the way Marion did. The way a young girl loves horses. She was only twenty, remember.

They had been together for some months and she was at the heart of George's life, when she went to Boston for a month. And Harry appeared. Harry and Minot came together, as I knew, just as Harry's disastrous first marriage was coming apart and as Harry himself—for reasons I did not know at the time—was also coming apart. Drinking, drugs, and not showing up at work. Terrifyingly uncharacteristic behavior.

Harry knew Minot from sailing and a huge investment they had done together. But Harry's collapse caught Minot's attention. With his incredible sensitivity to such things, Minot knew that something was terribly wrong, that it was sexual, and it interested him. He must have drawn Harry out and then somehow brought him into his sexual life. As a solution to Harry's impotence. That part—Harry's impotence—did not come out, but all the rest of it.

This story is full of rescues: the first was Minot rescuing Harry, if you can see it that way. Whatever, it worked, in its own frantic way. As the rebuttal witnesses testified at lurid length, Harry lunged, passionately, into the orgiastic life. The witnesses were experienced themselves, but they were much impressed by Harry. He threw himself into it with an energy and intensity that was almost alarming. Minot, they testified, was delighted. Harry was one of his triumphs, and it went on like that for several weeks. Mimi had not been there during that time, and she was not part of it; she had been back in Boston.

But then she reappeared. And everything changed, once again, for Harry. First he was simply awed. Here came this great beauty, this perfect Boston girl . . . tall, athletic, slender. Scarcely more than a child and already an eager sensualist. In the confusion of those days, she suddenly was everything to Harry. Harry, that most romantic of men, saw something astonishing, and nothing would ever be the same. Did he focus on the fact that she looked so much like our mother? Probably not, but that must have had plenty to do with it. What he did know was that she was perfect and that he must be with her. Must rescue her, in fact.

The witnesses described that first night that Mimi came back. She had missed Minot and the orgies very much. She fairly glowed as she walked into the room. At the Alice Club, as a matter of fact. She glowed, in her youth and her beauty and her eagerness for it all to begin. She started with Minot but then the others . . . one by one, and two by two. Harry was so fascinated, he could barely blink. It was one of the most intense nights of his life. Mimi was deep into it from the get-go, and she often laughed aloud, for sheer pleasure . . . like Alex whom in some ways she also resembled. That night and for many nights thereafter, he had her. Alone and with others. On and on . . . again and again.

But not the way the others did . . . not just as part of an orgy night. No. He saw her—naked in the scrum, mouth open, body soaked in sweat—twisting this way and that. And he heard a little silver bell.

He heard a little silver bell, and for him, the scrum—in all its tremulous squalor—simply disappeared. The two of them could just as well have been standing alone in the hayfield over Broken Harbor, holding hands, the warm wind in their hair. In an instant, he was done. He shook off the Circean drug and determined to take her up out of that darkness, into what would be their bright, new life, together. He would rescue her. The rescue of his life.

For Mimi, not so clear that silver bell. It was soon obvious to the witnesses—as it must have been clear to Minot—that Harry wanted to take her away. But she was not quite ready. She was deeply taken with Harry, they said, with his force, his handsomeness, and his tremendous passion. That makes sense, of course. And I am sure she was taken by his offer . . . by the idea of coming up into the light. She was an old Boston girl, after all, and had to have had some reservations about the life she was living. But she loved it, too, and loved Minot. She went back and forth.

It was during that time that George pierced her nether lip and gave her a ring to wear . . . marked her in his own way. Imagine her coming home, one gray morning, to Harry, her hair and clothes a mess, her makeup gone. Like a cat come home in the middle of the night with a matted coat and a torn ear. Not a torn ear, exactly; that ring. Poor Harry. Poor everyone.

But he kept at it. And eventually, he won.

The witnesses didn't know what actually happened except that Harry and Mimi simply disappeared. It was Harry's greatest rescue, and it quickly turned his life around, too. I remembered that part with great clarity. He simply became himself again, to my massive relief. He and Mimi became the golden couple in New York, Boston, and Maine, and he took up his old life of success and leadership as if he had never been away. It was a remarkable change. And the rescue of Mimi was obviously at the heart of it. Or their rescue of each other. It didn't occur to me for a while but it was mutual . . . it must have been, to work. They had rescued each other. And they were eternally bound to each other. Almost.

There was no testimony about this but there must have been some understanding that George would continue to be part of Harry's life. But only his sailing life, now. And the club, I imagine. That must have been interesting. At that time, George was very different from what he would become . . . much rougher, just as poor Osborne had remembered. One imagines him, around the club, experimenting amusedly with his weird, new accent, his elaborate manners. He was a brilliant man, of course, and he must have learned quickly, but learning a whole culture is not so easy, and his new ways cannot have run deep. And he was half beast, of course; that didn't make things easier. I can see Harry, trying to help. Telling Minot where to go to get those custom-tailored uniforms. And perhaps a custom-made version of that little visored cap, to go on his enormous head. An odd fit in every way.

But a decade later, the deal came apart. The creature began to stir, and George's animal nature called out hard. He wanted what the Minotaur always wants: he wanted the girl back and the hero dead. He wanted everything. Others who heard Minot's speech that night at the ball thought it was amusing and odd, maybe tasteless and even cruel. Harry knew it was much, much worse. That it was terrifying in fact. The beast was getting loose.

So, as everyone in that courtroom now assumed, Harry took Mimi back to *Java*, got her to admit what he had already guessed, and went to the sailboat in her place. With his gun. Minot had come and Harry had killed him and taken his revenge with the pips. That must have been what happened. Horton was beyond smug. He had a few more witnesses, but his work was done.

Jack Tiglio made motions for a mistrial, with each of the rebuttal witnesses. He said it was "trial by ambush" and that Horton had had a duty to put them on as part of his case in chief. Not a bad motion, but Judge Cruller denied it from the bench. The tide was running too hard the other way: Harry was guilty. Everyone knew it. And Cruller was not going to turn it around on a technicality. This was all on a Friday, so Jack would only have until Monday to save his defense. In the alternative to a full mistrial, Jack asked for a two-week adjournment so he could deal with the damage. Cruller gave him two days: the trial would resume on Wednesday. No one thought that two days—or two weeks—would make a bit of difference.

Harry had listened to the rebuttal witnesses with fading intensity. At first, he was electrified. Horrified, perhaps. But as it went on, the life drained out of him. By the time of these procedural arguments, he was no longer listening at all. He smiled vaguely, once in a while, for no particular reason that I could see. But mostly he just sat there and stared and stared. At what, one dreads to think. At his life spinning away.

CHAPTER 42

CLEOPATRA'S BARGE, ARMED

I left the courthouse, grabbed Frank, and the two of us went to work. Jack's excellent defense had failed, spectacularly, and it was time for desperate measures. It was time to arm and launch Cleopatra's Barge. Which was a matter of preparing some false papers and somehow getting Judge Cruller to look at them.

There were two sets of papers. I had previously drafted a memo, which I meant to give only to Judge Cruller, outlining the theory. Now I revised that, carefully. Frank and I had also put together a set of draft motion papers. The memo was designed to persuade Cruller to issue an extraordinary discovery order. The motion papers were designed to scare the shit out of B. T. Horton. Neither would ever be filed in court, but they would be the most important papers I would ever draft in my life.

We had already spent a lot of time on them, but finalizing everything still took a while, because we wanted the papers to be as perfect and up-to-date as they could be, within obvious limitations. It was a motion for a mistrial, grounded on prosecutorial misconduct. The misconduct was Horton's corrupt deal with Theo Soros to put on the rebuttal witnesses, to *not* put Theo on the stand and *not* to delve into or disclose anything about Theo's financial affairs. The guts of the motion was the story of the $17 million Theo would get to keep if Minot died—or was murdered. I did not expressly accuse Theo of the murder, but reading them, that was all you could think about. It was an extremely powerful motion. Except, of course, for the fact that it was based in part on a forgery.

The serious editing—the new part—turned around the forgery. There was the reference to Minot's "daily" computer. And to the little black navigator, the Trimble GPS. What Frank and I both now called Cleopatra's Barge. He had bought the computer and helped me to "fill it up" to look like George's personal device. But this was the first Frank was hearing about the Trimble GPS. He was as astonished as I had been and as impressed.

"How in the world . . . ," he started.

"Secret, I'm afraid. I swore a mighty oath that I'd never tell." He just shrugged, went back to typing. Then he looked up: "Alex?" I just looked at him, shrugged. He was a smart man, that Frank. He let it go, went back to work.

Then the memo. We'd go through a couple of drafts, but it wasn't that hard.

"This is pretty good," Frank said at one point.

"Not bad," I said. "But the session with the judge is going to be tricky. We'll see."

The last step was arming Cleopatra's Barge, putting in the final entry. It wasn't complicated. It read:

SWEET ROCKS TENDER. $17 MILL. THEO.
200K UP OR DOWN. SETTLE 9/16.

Which was meant to suggest, to the knowledgeable reader, that George had given Theo $17 million. And that Theo was to invest the money in the stock of Rockledge Builders, target of the Sweet Rocks Tender. In the end, George would get back his $17 million—together with a 15 percent profit, assuming the takeover went through. But the real point was to make sure that the tender did go through. For his role in this fraud, Theo was to get $200,000, regardless of what happened. Their accounts were to be settled on September 16, which happens to be my birthday. A marker, if I ever needed it, which was not likely. The $200,000 was not much money, really, considering what Minot stood to make and the risk poor Theo was taking. Never mind, it sounded plausible.

A little before ten that night, I put on a warm peacoat and a watch cap. Put the little computer in one pocket and the Trimble in the other and went down to the lobby and out a side door. I was heading down to the harbor. I took the short-cut, down a narrow alley behind the courthouse that passes Horton's offices. I was thinking hard—about what I was about to do—so I was taken completely by surprise when the back door of Horton's office suddenly opened into the alley. And out stepped Theo Soros, in the light of the doorway.

That was interesting. He had not been in town for a single day of the trial, as far as anyone knew. He had not been a witness, which was surprising. And here he was, walking out of Horton's office at eleven o'clock at night, when Horton had to be busily preparing. And he was absolutely horrified that I had seen him. I remembered Cassie's warnings and reached behind me to put my hand on the gun. But he did not come at me. Instead, he just pulled back against the wall, and his elbows shot up. He went right up on his toes and arched his back. Like a toreador, when the bull's pass is very close. And he snarled, as if he were in danger. But he did not produce a gun or a sword, and I did not draw my gun.

In an instant, he composed himself. He wiped the grimace from his handsome face, let his arms down and shook his hands, as if he had just put on his jacket and were shaking out the sleeves. And smiled at me sardonically. "How you doing, Counselor?" he said in a normal voice. Then he walked quickly toward the parking lot and his car. He tried to appear calm, but he must have thought that a dreadful secret—his role in the trial as Horton's guide—had just been revealed. His calm lapsed in the car, and he spun his tires as he tore away.

In fact, his cooperation with Horton was not really a secret to me. I had guessed a lot about Theo by then, including the fact that he had to be the source of Horton's information. The tip about where to find the gun . . . the devastating fact that Mimi was on her way to be with Minot that night . . . the names of the rebuttal witnesses from all those years ago. Only Theo could have told Horton all that. And probably only Theo could have prevailed upon the rebuttal witnesses to appear. How did he do it? I don't know, but the stakes for him were huge. If he had paid them a million dollars apiece, it would have been a good investment. However he did it, I thought it was him. And that was a major part of what the memo for Judge Cruller and the draft motion papers were all about . . . a corrupt deal between Horton and Soros. To nail Harry and keep Theo out of it.

I walked down to the harbor, to the float where the Whitehall was pulled up. There was fog again. The usual stuff, not like last summer. But thick enough so I wasn't too worried that I'd be seen. I put the skiff into the water and quietly rowed out to *Nellie*. No fire in the little stove tonight, even though it was pretty cold. No lights, either. Just a single candle while I climbed into my wet suit. Then I carefully lowered myself into the Whitehall, again, checked my bearings one last time, and tumbled over backward into the icy water. I didn't bother with the dry suit; I wouldn't be down that long.

I knew the way to Theo's boat, on the bottom. I had made the trip a few times, though I'd never been aboard. All I needed was a waterproof flashlight and a compass to take me to his rental mooring. An engine block, with a chain around it. Folks up here use anything heavy for moorings.

I slowly went up the mooring line and put my ear to the hull. There were no sounds; I did not expect any. Theo had not been aboard once, as far as I knew, since his boat was brought into the harbor by Bud's people. I swam around to the stern. There was a swim platform there, as I knew, and I carefully hoisted myself aboard. Slow, so as not to splash. And sat there a moment in the dark, calming down. And making sure, again, that there was no one on board. Then I stepped over the low transom and into the cockpit.

I took off the flippers and set down the tank and the hood and the gloves and the mask on the cabin sole. Then the wet suit itself. I put on surgeon's gloves so as not to leave prints. In fact, for an amateur, I thought I was quite the burglar: jimmies, screwdrivers, my dark watch cap. The works. There was a small, chromium padlock on the cabin door, which I could easily have broken with the jimmy. But I didn't do that. I carefully unscrewed the hinges and put the screws, one by one, into my cap. Once inside, I silently pulled it closed.

Down in the cabin, I turned on my tiny penlight and went around and drew all the blinds. Then I turned on my big, waterproof five-cell, and had a look. I was terribly tempted to take the damned computer out of its waterproof wrapping, plant it and the Trimble, and get back in the water. But I made myself look around, which turned out to be a good idea. There were things I had not noticed the one time I had been there before, with Bud. Or had not understood.

Theo was a diver. And his boat wasn't just an adjunct to George's yachting life. It was a dive boat. There was a good-sized compressor down in the engine compartment with hoses that led to built-in racks, ahead of the V-berth. There was state-of-the-art diving gear up there, too. And several wet suits, even a dry suit, like mine.

And, stuffed way back in a stow locker under the V-berth, down almost on the floor, there was an incredibly thin, light-weight suit that I might not have focused on. Except that I'd seen it before. It was a striking blue with ornate green mark-ings, and the mask had separate holes for the eyes, nose, and mouth. Theo was the man in the blue-and-green wet suit in some of the orgy-scene movies. Theo, the dancing man, had a costume for those dances.

Coincidences abound. I found a little computer in the side pocket of one of Minot's uniform jackets, just like the one I had brought with me. It had been completely cleared. I set it on a bunk. I found Theo's laptop as well. That, too, had been completely erased.

I thought hard for a long moment to make sure I was doing this right. Then put George's little computer inside my wet suit. And stuck my version into George's pocket. Tiny Cleopatra's Barge, her guns carefully charged and run out for engagement. Then I took the Trimble and stuck it in an open stow locker, just inside the companionway, on the starboard side.

I went back on deck and screwed the hasp back on, very careful not to make any scratches, any marks on the wood or the metal. I put on my gear, and crawled awkwardly, silently, over the transom. Then slipped into the black water and away.

CHAPTER 43

JUDGE CRULLER

The next morning, Sunday, I slept late and had a good breakfast with Frank. He had the delicacy not to ask how I'd done the night before, but it was clear enough that we were in business. Depending on how this next part went.

Then I put on a blue suit and tie, black shoes, and walked up the hill to the judge's house. He was in his shirtsleeves, with suspenders, like a judge in a 1940s movie, and he was plenty concerned to find me standing on his front porch. Approaching a judge, ex parte, in the midst of a trial, is one of the great taboos in the law. But I was ready for that. I quickly told him a couple of things that caught his attention. He just stood there, holding the door, thinking for a minute. Then said, "Come in." He showed me into his old-fashioned office, off the front parlor, where I had been before. It was a nice, Victorian room, full of papers—another old movie. He did not invite me to sit.

First, I walked him through the highlights . . . a short version of the $17 million business. Then I handed him the ten-page memo, telling the same story in slightly more detail ... with a few key documents attached. The best parts—the references to the Barge and the Trimble—were speculation now, but they were intended to whet his appetite for what I wanted him to do. It was a very good memo, frankly, and it held him. He was only a few pages in when he stopped and said, "Let's go and sit down."

He read it carefully. Then I walked him through the story again, orally . . . fed him more documents. He didn't know much about the securities laws, but he was a judge and a bright man; he got it.

"Why doesn't Horton know about all this," he asked at last. "It was his job to chase all this down. If it's true."

"That's the bad part, Your Honor. He made a deal with Soros. He dropped the document demand on Citibank and he never even picked up the documents that were sitting at my old law firm. He agreed not to pursue that line or call Soros as a witness. Of course Horton had no notion of the $17 million, then or now. Or so I assume. But he agreed not to pursue the document side, or call Soros, because Soros promised to hand him the case you heard over the last two days. Soros told him the story of Minot coming for Mimi and Harry finding out . . . all that. Which may be true, for all I know. I heard it for the first time when you heard it in court, and was astonished, but I believe it. My brother has led a far more . . . complicated life than I had ever imagined. And I believe that Soros told Horton that he could provide the rebuttal witnesses. They were all ready to go. Primed and ready. And my guess is he had already told Horton about the gun, which gave him a certain credibility."

"What about that?"

"I don't know, but my guess is that Soros planted it. Soros turns out to be a very experienced diver and he could have done it easily. But we don't have to think about that now. That wasn't the point, when they made the deal. The point was that Soros was going to hand B. T. an almost rock-solid case against Harry. And he might even be able to come after me, later. You know Horton far better than I. But he was enormously vulnerable to the attractions of going after someone like Harry or me. So he made the deal."

"That testimony was awful damn strong," Cruller said. "And credible. And it makes a powerful case against your brother."

"It was strong, for sure. And it was proof that both Harry and Mimi had lied and Harry had a hell of a motive to kill Minot. Which, conceivably, he did. My guess is that Soros got there first, but you have to assume it could have been Harry. Obviously, that is possible.

"But what is not possible," I said, bearing down, "is to go forward with this trial without putting this whole string of other possibilities—the evidence that Soros may have done it, to make a fortune, and made this deal with Horton—into the record. No matter what, this business with Soros and Horton just won't stand."

"If it's true," the judge said.

"If it's true," I agreed.

"Say it again," the judge said. It is so hard to remember, when you're arguing a case, that your audience doesn't know it cold the way you do. They are not dumb, it's just new to them. And it takes time.

"Soros would provide hard evidence, witnesses. And B. T. wouldn't fuss with the financial stuff. Or call Soros as a witness. The first part wasn't that bad; he was just agreeing not to pursue a line of inquiry that no longer interested him much; he had Harry, after all. But not calling Soros. Or telling Tiglio about him. Well, that was pretty raw."

"You can't prove this."

"No. But I know it's true. And think about this, Your Honor. Supposing you do nothing. Then, after the criminal case is over and my brother has been sent off to prison for life, your gag order will lapse. And Harry and I will bring a civil action against Soros that will curl your hair. Soros will likely be out of the country by then, but we won't care. We're not in it for the money. As for proof, a story like this $17 million story—if it's true—cannot be buried deep enough to withstand a well-funded search. It will all come out. Soros may be untouchable by then, because he understands this as well as you and I do, and he'll run. But the story will be public. It will reek to high heaven. And the administration of justice in the state of Maine—in your court—will look ridiculous. If not corrupt."

The judge's face closed down hard at that and he growled, angrily, "Are you threatening me, Mr. Bigelow? Here in my own house, in my own jurisdiction? You had better be very careful, sir. You don't want to threaten me."

"I certainly do not, and you can bet I am not. I have come to have tremendous respect for you, Judge. More than you can imagine, I think. Or I would have simply violated the order, and given this to Tiglio. I would have done that for my brother. But that would have caused a dreadful mess. Besides, I happen to think that you, sir, are a Law Man, and your respect for the law runs deep. As does mine." That was a bold thing for me to say, in the midst of this great crime I was committing. But I thought it would have a certain resonance for the judge. "I think that you will do the right thing, no matter how painful." That was almost too smarmy but I thought it was true, actually, and that Cruller saw himself in precisely that light. I recognized it because I used to see myself in that light. "I came to you, because I trust you to do the hard thing. To restore order in your court."

He paused and looked at me, speculatively, for a long moment. Then the smallest smile. "You are a wild boy, Mr.

Bigelow. I thought that New York business was nuts. But this! This is . . . well, I don't know what to call it. Crazy to start. Just what would you have me do, again, may I ask?" His voice was scornful, but I sensed a break in the room . . . sensed that we were beginning to think about "our" problem.

"I have a couple of ideas."

"I am not surprised, sir."

"I have informants, too, Your Honor. Like B. T. And I'll disclose them down the road, if necessary. But what I know, right now—as the memo says—is that Soros is surprisingly vulnerable to a sudden search. Of his boat and maybe the place he's staying, up in Emery. I am told, by someone whom I trust completely—someone who would know—that he has that little pocket computer on his boat right here in Hanson Harbor. It was supposed to have been produced to us before but it was not. It belonged to Minot, as you know, and it outlines his deal to park the $17 million. The same source—a very good source indeed—tells me that Soros also has the little handheld navigation device—the Trimble—on his boat, too."

"What the hell is this thing, again?"

"A navigation device, the size of a deck of cards. A GPS, if you know the term, that navigates by satellite. Bud and I had focused on Soros back in the beginning, but we assumed he couldn't have made those trips in that fog, that night. But with this gadget, he could. Both in the dinghy and swimming away, afterward. Soros is a diver, as I say."

"So this gadget, and the little computer. They're at the heart of the case you're making to me. And you want me to have Bud go after 'em."

"Yup. The time window may be damned small. It will close the instant Soros learns about our knowledge. So my recommendation is, get 'em all in here, first thing tomorrow morning. Soros, B. T., the sheriff, Tiglio, me. All of us. And tell 'em that you are considering issuing an order, on your own motion, to hit Soros's boat and his cottage up here, immediately. Don't let 'em leave the room. Listen to arguments and so on. Then do it. Send Bud to search the boat. I promise you, it will work. Then you take a look at what Bud finds. You decide where to go from there."

"That's nuts," he said, "there's no probable cause." But he said it with a little smile.

"Maybe. But it is a hell of a lot better than the alternative. If you trust what those limited documents tell you about the $17 million. And if you trust me a little bit . . . well, you might just want to do it. If what I say is right, there'll be a mess, I grant you. But you can issue orders to get it straightened out. And get the administration of justice back on track. Not to put too fine a point on it, you'll be hero of this mess, not the goat. But mostly, it's the right thing to do."

I'd gone too far. "Don't condescend to me, Mr. Bigelow. Or try to blow smoke up my butt; I'm not the type."

I smiled at that. "No, sir, you are not. But the one who's blowing smoke around here is Horton, not me. You and I . . . this may be presumptuous, but I think you and I have the beginnings of an understanding."

He shook his head, appalled at the idea. But I could tell; he was going to do it. I just sat back and waited for him to raise questions. One of the most critical things in litigation is knowing when to stop arguing. I stopped and waited for him.

The questions came but about details, not the basic concept. We spent another hour and a half going over this and that. Drafting the goofy order, mandating that the sheriff conduct the search. Going back and forth about what Horton could have been thinking. And speculating, nervously, about the fact that Soros was very likely a hard-core murderer and an extremely dangerous man. It was interesting.

At about two, he phoned, first Horton, and then Tiglio to say he was going to put over the motions he'd scheduled for the next morning in other cases, and that he wanted them in court at nine for a special session. If either of them had access to Theo Soros, they should bring him, too. No details, he told them; they'd have plenty of time the next day. When he hung up, I asked if he'd call Bud. He paused. He knew that Horton had kept Bud out of the case since the indictment. But Bud had to execute the search order, if it were issued. And, I said, there might be some real security concerns. "Bud and that great damn revolver of his might be a comfort."

He smiled at that, too. "Great God Almighty! You've got me in a movie."

I shrugged. "Pretty good part, though, Judge." That was saucy of me. But he smiled. We were in this together now. Quite a change from the last time I appeared before him.

From Cruller's house, I walked the two miles over to Bud's. He and Caroline were watching the Patriots, and I sat down to watch for a minute. Bud offered me a beer but I said no, there was stuff going down that night that might call for a clear head. I said I knew Judge Cruller had called him. I'd been there and it had been my idea. He gave me a slow look and suggested we go out and take a look at the peapod.

Out in the barn, I told him that Theo was in town, that I'd seen him coming out of Horton's late at night. That was part of how I knew they were working together. Which Bud actually knew. He'd wanted terribly to tell me about it, because it made him uneasy. But he hadn't because B. T. warned him not to. Said it would violate an agreement he had with Theo—which had been blessed by the judge—that Theo's role would be kept secret.

I told him that that part was nonsense. The judge had no idea. Didn't much care for it, in fact. Then I told him everything I'd told the judge and about the hearing the next morning.

When I was done, I asked what he thought. He stood there for a long moment, musing. Then shrugged. "I guess we'll see, tomorrow."

"Yes, we will," I said, "but I've got an idea that might move things along." And I proposed a little adventure to him.

When I was done, he asked if it was illegal, what I was suggesting. I said no, I didn't think so. But it could make him look awful bad, if I were wrong.

"Well, hell," he said with that nice grin, "I don't look so good right now. Let's go."

There was a crowd in Cruller's chambers next morning because Horton and Tiglio—having no idea what was going on—had each brought a couple of lawyers, just in case. Then Bud and I, of course, and a court reporter. Horton and his man were the last to get there, and he was horrified to see me. He started to sputter but the judge, who was already at his desk, just held up his hand. "It's okay, B. T., I know what you're gonna say, an' just hold it a minute. Let me tell ya what's goin' on." Poor Horton could barely bring himself to sit there, but he did.

I had planned to stand up at the outset and tell everyone what had happened the night before. But the judge—to be fair to Horton, I guess—just held up his hand again and said to me, "You wait, too, Mr. Bigelow. We got plenty o' time here."

Then he carefully explained what we'd been over the day before and said he was issuing an order, sua sponte—that means, *on his own motion*—to search Theo's boat. To look for computers, financial documents. Anything that might bear on this business of theft as a motive. He said he meant to reinstate the Citibank and other document demands as well.

Before the judge was quite done, Horton stood up, visibly shaken, and said, "Your Honor, this is an absolute outrage. I don't want to be in the same room with that man"—pointing dramatically at me—"this jeopardizes the entire trial, which is just what he wants."

"Calm down, B. T.," Bud said. "Wait'll ya hear where we're at so ya don't sound foolish."

That just made Horton more furious and he spun on Bud. "That man's had his tongue so far up your ass, you can't shit without he says so." He turned back to the judge. "All of us. He's had us coming and going. Doing everything to fuck up this case. Now he's back, an' you're gonna issue this order? That's crazy!"

The judge didn't like that much. He was "one of the boys," you know, but he'd been a judge a long time, and you don't talk that way to a judge. Cruller slapped his hand down hard on his desk. "All right, B. T.," he said coldly, "that's enough of that. You're in my chambers. And on the record." Horton mumbled something but he was too hot to apologize.

The judge stared at him hard, then said, "Why don't you take a minute now and just tell us what this Soros was doing. How he was helping out."

"In front of him?" B. T. asked, appalled.

"Yes, I'd say so," the judge said laconically. "Trial's 'most over. I don't see that it'll hurt. We'll issue orders later, if we have to."

B. T. hated it, of course, but he didn't have much choice. He took a deep breath and began.

"Shortly before I impaneled the grand jury, Soros called me. He called me first to say what he suspected about the gun, off the stern of Bigelow's boat. But he said he was coming to Maine the next day, to tell me much, much more. He came up and he gave me the lot. That Minot himself had told him that he was going off to fuck Bigelow's wife that night."

"Take it easy, Mr. Horton," the judge. "We're on the record here."

"Sorry, Your Honor," Horton said, flustered. "I get so upset..."

"Go on," the judge said, a bit dark.

"He had to see me alone. Because this Bigelow had Bud tied up in knots." He paused, thinking about the court reporter. "That is, he thought Bigelow had co-opted Sheriff Wilkerson, here, with luxury trips to New York, dinners and so on . . . got him into Bigelow's camp. He insisted that the sheriff know nothing about it." He nodded unpleasantly toward Bud. "He told me that Minot had said that he was going to pick up Bigelow's wife off their sailboat. He was going to take her out to Forstman's boat and . . . for the sex orgy."

"And he knew," I said, "about the pierced lip? And the prior history with Minot?"

"Yes," Horton said unpleasantly. "He knew all that. And about the people we used on rebuttal. To nail him down."

"So why didn't you put him on the stand? And give us some notice that this was the guts of your case?" Tiglio said, speaking for the first time, a dark rumble. "Just to surprise us?"

"No," Horton said. "Soros wasn't proud of being part of all this . . . filth," he said, looking at me, for some reason. "It was part of the deal I made to break the case: I would only call him on rebuttal. And only if I needed him."

"Your Honor," Tiglio began, angrily, but the judge cut him off.

"Another day, Mr. Tiglio. What else, Mr. Horton?"

"By coincidence," Horton went on, "at about that time, the witness, Samuel Cameron, got back in town. I subpoenaed him . . . made him come to Maine . . . and he finally admitted that he'd seen Bigelow comin' up the gangway from the work float." He shrugged. "Case closed." There was a silence and then the judge looked at me.

"Anything to add, Mr. Bigelow?"

"Well, yes," I said. "It's obvious but remember that all this was just days before Citibank was going to have to turn over certain of Theo Soros's banking records. And a couple of days after an anonymous call to tell you where to go get the gun. Is that right, Mr. Horton?"

Horton rephrased it, but yes, that was right. "Okay," I said. "Let me talk a little about parking stock, before a takeover."

After I'd talked for a while, Horton was back on his feet . . . broke in angrily. "Parking stock!" he shrieked. "This is a murder trial, for Christ's sake, not an SEC investigation." Horton was furious. He turned back to the judge. "I get the theory, all right, Judge. But what does he actually know? This is all to stop the trial."

He was about to go on when Bud spoke up from the back of the room. "Judge, we shoulda told ya before . . . save us some time."

"Yes?" B. T. snapped at the interruption.

"Caroline called Soros last night, up in Emery where he's stayin'. Told him there was gonna be a session in court this mornin'. About searchin' his boat for computers and such? He could be here if he liked."

Horton scowled and looked around, as if Soros might suddenly appear.

"No, he ain't comin' this mornin', B. T.," Bud said. "He come last night . . . around one o'clock."

CHAPTER 44

THEO COMES OUT

Caroline was nervous as a cat. She got the giggles once and Bud and I had to wait almost five minutes before we could begin again. But by the time she actually called Theo Soros from the kitchen, she sounded like herself, which is all she had to do.

"Mr. Soros? I'm calling for Judge Cruller? Here in Hanson?" Bud and I couldn't hear Soros but there was only a brief pause.

"Yes. And I'm to tell ya there's a hearin' tomorrow, nine o'clock. An' you can be there if you want. Or send your lawyer." Brief pause.

"I don't have papers. But they wanted you to know, 'cause it's about a search? Of your boat, there? The *Celene*? Yes. I don't know that. All I know is, it's about computers or somethin'. An' maybe a wet suit, I think he said. For divin'." That had not been part of the presentation to Cruller. We'd added it to Caroline's script to alarm Soros.

There was a long delay. "I just don't know, Mr. Soros. I'm sorry. That's all I got." Pause. "No. Can't call any of 'em, I was told. See 'em in the mornin'. An' don't be upset, now. That's all the notice any of 'em got. Yes. Yes. Sorry to call so late. G'night."

She looked exhausted, as if she'd been on the phone for hours. But she was pleased with herself, too, as she looked up at us.

"Awful good, Caroline," I said. "That was awful good."

"Well, thank you," she said, "but I'll tell ya, I don't wanna do it again real soon."

"You won't have to, old girl," Bud said and gave her a squeeze.

We were dressed warmly, and Bud had a special belt, big enough to go outside his jacket, for that huge pistol. I had mine, too, the 9 mm Sig Sauer, in a holster in the small of my back. For a long time, I'd just kept it in my pocket but that's awful clumsy. I felt like a dope, wearing a holster, but it was better than having the damn thing in my pocket.

"We got maybe twenty minutes, Doc. Let's get crackin'."

It looked for a while as if Theo wasn't going to take the bait. Three hours later, around one o'clock, Bud and I were lying side by side in the bottom of a dory in the fog, wishing we'd thought of a bunch of things. Like something to drink or eat. And more warm clothes. And of course we began to stew that Theo wasn't coming and wondered all kinds of things about that. But, no matter what, we were going to stay until morning to be sure. We'd feel like awful fools if he snuck out after we were gone.

We were whispering when Bud said hush, he'd maybe heard something. We listened hard. And then we heard the slow sound of oars. And barely saw a boat, moving through the fog. If he hadn't been sitting backward, rowing, he might have seen us, too. Or sensed us, the way you do. But I suppose he wasn't thinking that way. He quietly pulled up alongside *Celene* and tied up his dory. Then went aboard.

In our boat, Bud had already pulled up our little anchor, hand over hand, and set it silently dripping in the bow. The instant Soros went below, Bud took an oar and carefully paddled us over to the back of *Celene*. He pointed to me to hold on to the transom, and we both stood up.

We stayed frozen like that for maybe five minutes while Soros did whatever he was doing, down below. Then I heard rather than saw Soros fooling with the lock. Closing up again.

And Bud, that great damn gun in one hand, growled, "Don'tcha take a goddamn step!" There was complete silence for a second.

"Stop! Dammit!" And then there were two tremendous explosions. One right after the other. Bud had fired his gun in the air.

Mine was not pointed in the air. It was pointed right at Soros. And that was not good for him. I had fired perhaps two thousand rounds with that gun, out there on Broke, and I'd gotten very handy with it. I could have walked down the buttons of his coat . . . *bing, bing, bing.* And I was sorely tempted. There would be only one version of the story, mine. I took up the little bit of play that is built into the trigger of the Sig Sauer, and now it was just a question of going tap, tap. But I didn't do that. Because I am a practical man and I had thought it all through; this would not be the best way. I wanted to arrest him and take him ashore; my story would hold up long enough to rescue Harry, no matter what, and I wouldn't have killed anyone. But I sure was tempted, I'll tell you.

"Drop that shit, Soros!" Bud said. "Or I'll kill ya dead. So help me God, I will!" Soros stopped but didn't drop anything. Then suddenly his right hand flipped out . . . there was a splash . . . and just as quick, he reached toward his hip pocket.

"Stop, you damn fool!" Bud shouted. But Theo was in the grip of some craziness and kept moving. And then there were two sharp cracks—*Paff! Paff!*—lighter than the first two but plenty loud. My Sig. And Theo gave a horrible scream. He dropped what turned out to be a small gun and fell to the deck, clutching his leg with both hands.

"You shot me!" Theo grunted, as if that were unbelievable. In fact, I had shot him. Twice. In the thigh.

"Been worse if it'd been me," Bud said. "I'd've taken your fucking head off. Ya done?" He still held the huge gun on him.

Theo choked out that he was done, and Bud walked over carefully and picked up Theo's gun, a .32-caliber Beretta, checked the safety, and put it in his pocket. Then cuffed Theo's hands behind his back.

Bud looked down at him in disgust. "For a smart fella, that was about the dumbest thing I ever seen. Jesus!" Then to me, "Let's get the son of a bitch ashore . . . don't want him to bleed to death on us."

Bud had a knife and cut open Soros's pant leg to look at the wound. "You're in luck, Theo. Looks like no bone. May even walk again."

Bud said we should put a tourniquet on him and I found a piece of rope, tied it on tight. "That may do more harm than good," Bud said. "Let's get him ashore real quick."

We carefully put Soros, swearing now and in real pain, into the stern of our dinghy, his leg out straight and his hands behind him. I asked Bud if he wanted me to stay behind and dive for whatever Theo had thrown in the drink. Bud said no. We'd come back. That was actually better for me: my forgery would melt away in the salt water. And we didn't need it now. Soros had as good as confessed.

I started rowing and Soros looked around, as if he were thinking about jumping in.

"Jesus, don't do it, Soros," Bud said. "Give ya credit for grit, but the best man in the world ain't swimmin' in them cuffs, and his leg fucked up. You just sit there, like a good fella . . . let us get you some help."

Soros, to his eternal credit, managed a tight smile. "You've helped enough, Sheriff," he said.

I laughed aloud at that, and Bud did, too. "I suppose we have, old boy. I suppose we have."

For a long moment, the only sound was the clicking of the oars in the oarlocks, the soft swish of the oars themselves in the water, and Theo's occasional moans. It was a strangely intimate moment. As I rocked forward and back, Theo's head and mine almost touched at the catch.

I whispered, "Was it really Mimi?"

For all the pain he was in, Theo managed to grunt out, "Of course. She'd come back tonight, if he was here."

"And you used it all. You, the Great Trickster."

"Oh, yes," he said. He was unmistakably pleased with himself. Even now. "Oh, yes."

CHAPTER 45

GOING HOME

Things went pretty fast, after that. Mostly because the judge was so damn sore at Horton. "I am declaring a mistrial, sir," he said to B. T., when Bud and I were done. "I don't know what you think you were doing, this deal with Soros. And no notice to the defense, for God's sake? And all this money lying around! Good grief!" He had to make himself stop before he said too much. In the pause, Jack stood up and moved for a dismissal with prejudice. That would mean that Harry could never be tried again on these charges. The judge thought for a moment, and damn near did it. But he was too much of a judge for that. He'd get there pretty soon, we all knew, but not this morning.

But he did grant Harry's immediate release, without bail, which wasn't bad. Harry was to be released into Jack's custody and the local counsel's. Everyone knew he would never be tried again.

Horton just sat there. Didn't move or say a word. The judge was about to smack him again when he stopped suddenly and said, "That's enough. Let's go off the record. Come into my chambers." He stood up, abruptly, and we followed him.

He went and sat behind his big oak desk, and we took chairs in a half circle around him. His anger had come down a couple of notches, but he was still plenty sore. It wasn't just that he thought B. T. had made him personally look like an idiot. He also cared about "the administration of justice," and he thought B. T. had brought the administration of justice in Maine into grave disrepute, right here in his courtroom. He was furious at that.

But mostly he wanted to talk about Soros and what was to be done with him. His appetite for another trial into all this hellish activity was nil. All the lawyers in the room knew that the record was a hideous mess, now, and there was at least a chance that Soros would be acquitted, for all that we had him dead to rights, at least as far as the money was concerned. Of course, they did not yet know about the GPS, which would soon be found on Theo's boat. I did, and I had no question that Theo could be arraigned, tried, and found guilty. But the judge did not want that. He wanted Horton to give Soros a mighty scare, and then have him plead out to some damn thing. Second-degree murder or manslaughter, even. He would approve anything within reason—with as little as seven years in prison—but not another trial like this one. Never! "So, Mr. Horton . . . this is your mess. Fix it. Right now."

We all knew that seven years was a laughably short sentence (more like five, with good behavior), for the theft of $17 million alone, to say nothing of murder. But it suited me. All I wanted was to have this resolved and Harry vindicated. And that was going to happen. Theo would plead, if he were smart, and he was. He would do so, regardless of whether or not he had actually killed Minot. That was one of the beauties of it, from my point of view. I wasn't in the justice business on this one. I was in the business of rescuing Harry, and that I had done.

There was some more talk about further investigation and Swiss and Greek banking secrecy laws and so on. I offered to help with that. For once, Horton was genuinely grateful. We were starting to get into details about that when I broke in to ask if I could be excused and go get Harry out of jail.

The judge said, "Oh, Jesus," as if he'd left something burning on the stove. "Of course. You get right to it. We'll meet again tomorrow. And listen . . . it doesn't amount to much but tell him . . . Tell him I'll be apologizing to him in person before long. And wish him good luck."

The one thing we did before we left was to ask the judge for a warrant to search Theo's boat, which we'd do, after we'd seen Harry.

Harry was below ground, in a large stone room in the corner of the jail. Bigger than a cell, it looked like—maybe a holding pen. They probably needed a bigger room for all the meetings with Harry's legal team. There was no one else in the jail.

It was a dark place. There were pools of light under mesh-covered light bulbs, but there were not enough of them. It must have been hell, wiring that old, stone building at all. It had been built before electricity. There were shadows everywhere. In the corridor, in the cells, in the holding pen.

Harry was sitting in the light of one bare bulb, such as it was. There were four chairs in his cell, a desk, and a cot. He was sitting in one of the chairs, with his back to us, and his feet up on the cot, reading. He was in street clothes, by the way: a sport coat, jeans, and loafers. No tie. And not the handsome, bespoke suits he wore to court. He was not going to court today, so I suppose he was dressed for the weekend. Or whatever it was, down here.

I have said that he was very quick, my brother Harry, and that is true. But when he looked around and saw the three of us walking across the stone floor toward him, he couldn't make sense of it. Jack, that made sense; he saw him every day. But why Bud? And more than anything, why me? I suppose he did not let himself think about radically good news. His face was composed, just waiting to see. And he said in a neutral, expectant voice, "Timmy?"

Then Bud unlocked the door, and I walked in. Walked over to him. He stood and I hugged him, both arms around, as hard as I could. "It's over, Harry," I said quietly, over his big shoulder. "It's over. We're going home." And damned if I didn't start to weep.

We leaned back, hands on each other's shoulders, and took a look. My voice was unsteady. "It's a mistrial for now, Harry," I managed to say. "But it's over. Soros will be tried for the murder. And for framing you, from the beginning. Or, rather, he'll make a deal. And you will never come back here again. Never in this world." Harry just looked at me. Then a slow smile began on his handsome face, then a cautious grin. "Yes?" he said, tentatively.

"Yes," I said. And we hugged again. Then, "Let's get out of here. We are done with this place."

When Harry walked into my study at the old hotel, he took in the thirty-odd file boxes and the storm of notes and papers all over the place. He got it at once and positively grinned.

"You've been at it all along, Timmy," he said delightedly. "They said you couldn't help but you've been at it the whole time, haven't you?" I nodded. I had. He loved that notion, absolutely loved it. He was a romantic man, my brother. Hugged me again and said, "Thank you, thank you." By which time we were both in tears.

Jack broke in at this point to say, "It was all Tim, Harry. Every bit of it. We worked mighty hard on the regular case, and it would have worked, if Horton hadn't gotten up to those shenanigans. But this part was all Tim, it really was." Harry nodded, I thanked him. And Jack got a bit of a hug, too.

Frank walked in, in the middle of that. Went over to Harry and hugged him, too. Not much of a hugger, Frank, but he did it this time, for quite a while. I told Harry how Frank had helped tremendously, and Harry grinned at him. "Not a bit surprised, Frank. Thanks an awful lot." Frank just grinned back, but it was a nice moment. And Frank deserved it.

Eventually, Harry and I went over and sat in the big stuffed chairs in the bay window. Jack, Bud, and Frank pulled up straight backs. Bud said it was okay if we wanted to be alone but Harry said no, this was fine. We should all be together for this part.

"So, what did you do?" Harry asked. "What happened?" And I told him . . . an edited version. And when I'd been through it once, he asked me to go through it again, slower. Because he loved it so. And because he had been so deep in that jail . . . and so deep in despair, after Mimi's testimony . . . that he had trouble believing that it was over. And that he was free. And that we really were going home. He loved my story, loved me for what I had done. Couldn't get enough.

Then suddenly Harry stood up to go and stand at the window, look down into the street. It was an odd moment and we were suddenly quiet, too. Watched him and waited.

"I want Mimi," he said at last, his back still to us. No one spoke. Harry turned around and looked at us. "I want Mimi here." Jack slipped out of the room.

She looked like hell. As if she hadn't stopped crying for days. And scared, too, as she walked in, looking at Harry. Scared to death about what Harry would say or do, I imagine. But Harry just walked over and took her in his arms and hugged her as hard as he could. And she hugged him. A long time. Both of their faces smeared with tears.

Then Harry said, over her shoulder, "Maybe you'd leave us alone for a little." Which we did. As I ushered the others out of the room, I looked back for an instant. They were sitting on the bed, looking at one another, holding hands.

CHAPTER 46

THEO'S SONG

Horton sat down with Theo's lawyers and they quickly worked out a guilty plea and a deal. Theo pleaded to some lesser degree of murder—the Maine version of second-degree murder—and was sentenced to seven years in prison. Everyone knew he'd only serve five. He had to put back the $17 million, of course; the rat never gets to keep the cheese. But I knew that the real payoff—and Theo's reason for pleading—was that the *big* money, "Minot's Gold," was back in Greece. What shape it was in, I had no idea, but I bet Theo did. And he would take steps from prison to secure it as best he could. When he got out, he would scoop it up, a lot of it, anyway. Live like a king, in some city in Greece. Five years was nothing against that background, but I was satisfied. He'd been punished quite a bit: disgrace (in America, anyway), five years in prison, and he'd never dance again. Fine.

Theo had to "allocute" to his crimes. After an agreement like this, the criminal has to stand up in court and tell the story of what he has done, under oath—an extended and detailed confession. And then he has to promise to, you know, never do it again. That's an allocution. It is a ritualistic affair, done after the deal is all agreed to, but the law is full of rituals, and sometimes they matter. Actually, the judge couldn't bear to do this one in court but he directed B. T. and Bud—and me, somewhat surprisingly—to do it, on the record in jail, and submit a sworn transcript to him. I suppose he wanted me there to make sure that Horton's little peccadillos were duly noted.

So, a couple of days after the deal was struck, B. T., Bud, and I and Theo's lawyer trooped back to the jail and Theo sang his song. He had been well prepared by that time and knew what his job was. It should have been a dull affair, but Theo was a storyteller and he made it interesting. The justification for the lenient sentence was that Theo was acting in fear for his life. Not pure self-defense; he couldn't get that far, because theft was so obviously a key part of it. But he could go pretty far, and Theo really got into it.

He said that Minot came to his, Theo's, boat that night in an inflatable and that he was scary-crazy. He said that Minot had gotten his snoot into some very fancy Balinese, psychedelic mushrooms. This was new information and made us all nervous for a moment, but in fact it was a wonderful touch. Indeed, it was so good that I thought it might well be true. These Balinese mushrooms were a super aphrodisiac, Theo said, but they also made you feel all-powerful. As if Minot needed that. They had a strong smell, by the way; that's what Bud and the doctor had smelled on Minot, the night of the murder. That gave the whole story a certain credibility; we all remembered that smell, and it was tidy to have that explained. And it was a particular comfort to me: no matter what, Theo had been *there*, whoever had pulled the trigger.

Anyhow, Minot had come back to Theo's boat to get some more of this Balinese stuff for the upcoming orgy. But he was already crazy on what he'd taken so far. Theo had always feared that Minot was going to kill him eventually—it was the ancient Minotaur myth about killing the tribute children. Or, in this case, getting rid of someone who knew too much. But tonight it looked as if it might happen right now. You had to be there, he said, but Minot—cranked on the mushrooms—was, in effect, pawing the ground before a charge. So Theo killed him. Then he popped him back into Minot's inflatable (Theo was athletic and strong so that wasn't hard for him) and drove him very slowly over to *Java* and tied him up to the service float. Then he swam back to his boat.

The little GPS—"Ariadne's thread"—was a key to the whole thing. It was that which let him motor, unerringly, the half mile from his boat to *Java* in Minot's dinghy. Then, after he tied Minot's dinghy to the float, it was the key to the much more difficult business of swimming back, in the blackness and the fog, to his boat. He was in his wet suit the whole time, but he stayed on the surface for the swim because it was faster. The GPS was waterproof but it only worked on the surface. It could "see" the satellites through clouds and fog but not through water. So he swam—silently but straight as an arrow—back to his boat. "Took me twenty minutes," he said. I said that seemed fast. He said it wasn't: "Slower than average for a decent swimmer like me, because I had to keep looking at the GPS every ten strokes or so. But that's what made it possible: holding a course in the fog and the dark. I might never have made it without it."

As for the actual murder, Theo painted a crazed Minot, sitting there in that cabin in the half-light, stroking his huge cock through his trousers; he was on a sexual tear, Theo said—getting ready to pick up the More Woman—and his mind was running that way. So he stroked himself and smiled at Theo with a terrible menace. As if he might rape him and then kill him on the spot. When Theo said he was scared, it had a real

ring, and you could imagine it. You could imagine Theo shooting Minot out of sheer terror. And, of course, he said that's
what he did.

Theo stressed that he had acted alone, by the way. "No
Alex, no Harry, no Cassie," he said. That he included that last
name was a jolt: no one had suggested any involvement with
Cassie since the first day. So why did he include her in his list?
It was creepy. I saw that Bud gave the slightest stir, too.

But his testimony was fine. I had been involved in the last
phase of his preparation and carefully nudged him to say he
had acted alone. Nothing that Horton would pick up on, but
Theo knew at once what I was signaling. Knew it was part
of my price for the deal. It obviously didn't bother him a bit.
And—for all I know—it was true. He never said where he got
the GPS. Horton never asked. As for mentioning Cassie, I was
content to assume that he was just giving me a little needle, for
his own amusement. To say that I did not trust Theo, even at
this stage, is a wild understatement.

As for the pips, Horton asked if Theo had thought that up
on the spur of the moment. Theo said, no, he had been thinking about killing Minot for a while, and clicked onto the notion
of framing Harry, early on. He had thought of the pips as part
of that. He already knew about Harry's and Mimi's orgiastic
past, presumably from Minot. He had dug around, earlier that
summer, to line up the surprise witnesses to testify about it,
just in case. Spent a ton of money and time on them so that
they would be all set to go, if he ever had to pull the trigger.
He hoped that he wouldn't need to . . . that the investigation
would just peter out for lack of prosecution. Alas, Harry and
I got involved, and that didn't happen. So—as I closed in on
the Citibank documents—Theo went to Maine and planted the
"murder weapon." Theo was a diver, of course, so that was easy.
He said that he knew that putting it on the flat rock strained
credulity, but he wanted to be sure it was found. Then he cut

his crooked deal with Horton. Horton didn't enjoy that part of the allocution much, and the judge eventually used it to drive him out of office. But it pulled the story together. And showed dramatically that Harry had been deliberately and skillfully framed.

Theo came across as an extremely resourceful and dangerous guy; that part was not an act. He had been a formidable opponent and I was freshly relieved that he was in custody and pleading to all his crimes.

CHAPTER 47

TRIUMPH

The weeks and months after the trial were a period of massive relief and ease for us all, or so it appeared to me. Harry and Mimi stuck around in Hanson for a few days, mostly to keep me company. Cassie flew east to join in the general celebration. Cassie had been deeply worried about Harry, and her pleasure and relief at his release and vindication was striking. She kept coming back to just how relieved she was and actually hugged him quite a lot. Harry took that pretty well, the dear man, and Cassie fairly glowed. Harry's own relief—and Mimi's—was profound, and his gratitude to me in particular was a nice thing to see. I began to think that maybe he was going to be okay. That in fact we were all going to be okay.

At one point, I took the risk of bringing up the subject to Harry of how changed his situation would be, despite the vindication in court. The underlying story was not going away, and Harry was most assuredly not going to be assistant secretary of the Treasury. Harry shrugged that off as if he were barely interested. "A few months in prison, Tim, is a great teacher in resetting priorities. My great priority for now is rejoicing in being free. After that?" He shrugged. "We're clever chaps, you and I. We'll think of something."

Pretty good. And so much like Harry. It didn't last, you know, but a nice moment.

Harry saw that it wouldn't do to go back to New York right away—while the publicity was still so fierce—so he and Mimi went on a long ski trip, out west. Cassie and I joined them for ten days. Cassie turned out to be a terrific skier. Naturally. She and I spent a shameful amount of time rolling about in the feathers and liked it. There was a little hitch, it seemed to me, in our relationship, now that everything was about to get real and she would have to make some heavy decisions. But that didn't reach us in the feathers. Harry and Mimi teased us, but they liked it, too, liked that we were close. It was one of the truly magical times in my life, and I began to plan, *hard*, for a life together. I had some reservations and some questions . . . things that we had never talked about. But I decided to let all that go, and see if we could make this happen. I had not lost my mind but I was very much in love with her, had great respect for her, and doubted that I'd ever find anyone who suited me so well. With certain caveats that didn't really matter anymore. Not with Theo settling down peacefully to a five-year stretch in a Maine prison.

After the ski trip, Harry and Mimi decided to spend a couple of months in Europe; it still wasn't time to go back to New York. They took a lovely house down in the Dordogne— we went and stayed with them there, too—and just chilled for another stretch. By the time they got back to New York in late May, they both looked terrific and seemed restored. How deep that went, one could not know, but it looked good and I felt free to get back to my own life and the practice of law. I was nervous about that and about how it would affect Cassie, but I was going to give it a shot and so was she. Frankly, I was not all that optimistic about us in the long run: she was, after all, deeply committed to her life in the West and it was hard to envision a divided life that would suit us both. But we were going to give it a mighty shot.

There was a bizarre development, early on, that made my life—and my return to the law—much easier. The coverage of the trial and the acquittal was truly intense and it didn't let up for weeks. The weird thing was that, all of a sudden, I was the great hero of the whole affair.

It turned out that Judge Cruller, God bless him, had taken the extraordinary step of granting an interview to a pretty, young reporter from the Bangor TV station. Debbie something; Debbie Borden . . . that was her name. The judge gave Debbie Borden a version of what happened with Soros. And then, by heaven, he reached way out to give me all the credit for catching Soros and averting "a terrible miscarriage of justice." He said—if you can imagine a sitting judge saying such a thing—that the circumstances were extraordinary and that I had done "the best piece of lawyering I've ever seen. And maybe the bravest." Astonishing.

Good old Debbie took that story, got some more nice quotes from Bud, and put together a terrific little documentary, which ran on her TV station. A feel-good story about the triumph of justice in the face of terrible adversity. Starring me, if you please. It was picked up and excerpted by others around the country, including the networks.

After that, the story had a life of its own; I was a hell of a guy, and everyone wanted to be my friend. Even Horton tried to climb aboard at one point and he, too, gave me some good press. Little good though it did him. I was happy to let bygones be bygones, but Judge Cruller was not. I went to see the judge to thank him, and he told me his plans to get rid of poor Horton. I put in a good word for him but Cruller just shook his head.

"Sorry, Tim. I'll let him know you tried, but he has to go." The judge single-handedly hounded him out of office, a little while later. These days Horton's a solo practitioner, earning about as much as a lobsterman up in Hanson. Maybe a little less. I also thanked the judge for his extraordinary kindness, on the TV show. "That was astonishingly generous."

"Thank Harry," he said.

"What do you mean?"

"I asked him to come and see me, after the dismissal with prejudice, and he did. I apologized for the breakdown of the system and so on. I was particularly apologetic about the refusal of bail; that really was a mistake. Vindictive, to be honest, and I was ashamed of it. Harry was graceful about all of it but asked if I'd consider doing him a favor. His great regret, he said, was that he had dragged you into all this. And especially without telling you any of the bad things. Which, of course, was inexcusable. But, he said, no one was going to believe that you had not known. He asked if there was anything I could do, so that you could practice law again. I said maybe I could."

"I guess you did, Judge. You surely did. I could not be more grateful."

That made my transition back to work wonderfully easy. Not only had I been exonerated, I was the very model of probity and lawyerly responsibility. Ridiculous, of course—given what I'd been up to—but I managed to live with it. One ironic thing: I became known for a certain relentless integrity in legal circles, because of my struggles in the Minot case. And individuals and companies in serious trouble, who needed a person of unimpeachable integrity to front for them, came to me in droves.

I should perhaps say in my defense that, while I had done some awful things, I had not managed to commit any crimes. Forgery is the *publication* of a forged document, not its creation. In the old cases, it is called "uttering a forgery." I never uttered mine: Theo pitched it into the drink before I had a chance.

What did not go so well, as I had feared, was my relationship with Cassie. During the early, euphoric days, when she was so happy for me and so relieved for Harry, it was wonderful. We made love all the time, we chattered like magpies, and we said we loved each other. Cassie in particular had an extraordinary gift for intimacy. Lying with her, you felt you were lying at the warm center of the world. I *loved* it, and seriously pressed for our being together for the long term. But the geographical difficulties started to loom larger.

That, by the way, is the only thing I focused on, the geography. Not the unease that had bothered me all along . . . about Cassie's sudden disappearance on the day of the murder. On that subject, I had resolutely turned my back. Told myself I didn't care, although that was not entirely true.

When I went back to work—even part time—it became clear that Cassie's and my union wasn't going to be easy. I would have my old life, but she would not. She would be stuck without her ranch, which had become her life. And that would be intolerable. She handled it beautifully for a while. She did have eastern roots, after all, and knew how to behave. But the East was no longer her place, and it was not her. It began to be clear that the problem ran deep and that there was nothing to be done about it. We talked about various options. Part time, East and West. Me working in the West. That just made her laugh. "Have you ever been to Butte?" I had not. "Well," she said, still smiling, "it ain't you, babe. Not gonna happen." We talked about one idea after another but none of them was promising.

As serious as the problem obviously was, I was still stunned, one morning, when I woke up to find her already up, dressed, and drinking coffee. Her bags were packed and at the door. I looked around, took it in. Looked at her.

"Going home, babe," she said, with real sadness. "We're done here, and I gotta go." I poured a cup of coffee and sat with her in silence at the breakfast table. We were teary-eyed, but she'd made up her mind.

"I love you, you know," I said. "I can live with *anything*, to be with you." She squinted for just a microsecond at that . . . at whatever I was talking about. I had stressed the "live with *anything*" and she had gotten it. But she did not rise . . . just let it go.

"I appreciate that, Tim. But, no." She leaned in and gave me a serious kiss. Then she stood up. "Gonna miss ya. Love you so much." And that—bluntly and suddenly—was that. I helped her take her stuff down to the cab, waved her out of sight. It was a great sadness. And a slight relief.

CHAPTER 48

THEO: SIDEBAR

A few weeks later, Theo got in touch with me, from prison. He said that he wanted to see me and that it was urgent; it affected both Cassie and Alex. That was good enough. I flew to Maine the next day, rented a car and drove to Thomaston, to the ancient state prison. We had a private room, thanks to my Maine lawyer, and Theo looked relaxed. But he did not look good. He was smiling his usual, cocky smile, but it lacked conviction. Also, of course, he was in chains and his left leg obviously pained him a good deal. And he looked sick. Very, very sick.

"Thanks for coming, Counselor; I appreciate it."

"I hope you're not going to try to re-trade your deal so soon, Theo," I began, seriously. I meant to keep him back on his heels in whatever he was up to.

"Not for a second, Counselor. You were more than generous. And I know it was you who put the plea together, by the way, and I am grateful to you. Five years for my sins is beyond generous. But you and I have some other business." I just waited, not liking it.

"First, let's talk a minute about just who we are, you and I," he said.

It's been a recurring theme in this story, hasn't it? Who we are. And especially who *I* am. But I'd had more than enough of it now and I certainly didn't need to go into it with Theo. "You allocuted as to who you are, Theo," I said coldly. "As to who I am, that doesn't concern you anymore."

He nodded as if that made good sense. But then he went on smoothly, almost as if I hadn't spoken. "I did allocute," he said. "But obviously it wasn't quite true, as you know." I started to interrupt but he put up his hand. "This will only take a minute. I lied about who I was and what I'd done. And so did you. I see that you are the great public hero now, which amuses and pleases me; I always rather liked you, Tim, and I don't begrudge you a bit of it. I really don't. But—just between us—I think we need a bit of candor." He waited, watched me . . . went on. "First, there was no Minot computer," he said. "I found the original and wiped it clean. So the one I found on my boat that night was a forgery. And you were the forger." He was not back on his heels, was he?

"This is pointless, Theo. That little computer went into the sea and was really wiped clean. Why make up this stuff?"

"You know it's not made-up. And you can relax: I don't want much." Again, I let him go on.

"The Trimble GPS," he said. "Of course that wasn't really mine, either. Alex gave me one, and it made all the difference. But I gave it back to her when I was done . . . used George's after that, and then threw it into the sea. You must have gotten that one from Alex and planted it on my boat. I am impressed, I must say; it did not occur to me that you might seduce Alex away from me, too. Not bad."

"You made it easy, Theo; she thought you were going to kill her . . . her and Marion."

He shrugged. "I know I mentioned it, but I could never have done it."

"She was understandably concerned," I said, dryly.

"I guess." He shrugged, not very interested. Then went on. "Next, there was your 'theory of the case,' the parking of the seventeen million. Where in the world did you get that? It's true, but where did you get it? Maybe out of George's documents but I bet not. I suppose that was Alex, too. Or maybe Cassie.

"But here's the big one, Tim." And he hunched toward me, rattling his chains slightly against the edge of the table. "I did not murder George, as you perhaps know." He waited for a reaction; I hope there was none.

"I lied about that, for both our sakes. And to get this very modest prison sentence. The murder plea was your price for the sentence, of course. So Harry would go free. And I was happy to pay it. Five years is a joke for the kind of money I'm going to get. And, back in Greece, being a 'murderer' isn't such a bad credential. George taught me that."

Another long silence and finally I made myself say, "Who did kill him, then, if not you?" I spoke with a twist of sarcasm, as if I didn't believe him.

He sat back at that, to enjoy the moment. "Well, it's interesting, isn't it? Assuming it was not me—and it was not—the next best candidate is your brother, of course. Without me as scapegoat, he's irresistible." I stirred in my chair, ready to get up.

"Don't worry, Tim," he said. "It wasn't him, either." Another pause.

"So?"

"So . . . on to the girls, I guess. Maybe Alex?" He brightened at that with a pert little smile, as if that were amusing. But he dropped it at once. "But I don't think so. Because, if it was Alex, it would almost certainly have to be *me* and Alex. She could never have killed George on her own. And it wasn't me."

"Yuh?"

"Yuh." Pregnant pause. "That leaves your girl, Cassie, doesn't it?" A serious look from Theo this time. He wasn't taunting anymore, just deadly serious. "She's the one I like, Tim. I like her very much."

I couldn't help myself. I blurted out, "She was in a hotel at Logan outside Boston, Theo. And on a plane early the next morning to Montana. We checked."

"I bet you did," Theo said, "responsible chap that you are. But you can't have checked very hard. Because someone was at that hotel, but it wasn't her. Maybe her Boston sister; do you know about her?" I nodded that I did and he nodded back, as if surprised. "Ah. Good for you. You are thorough. I don't actually know if it was the sister at the hotel," he went on, "but what I *can* tell you is that it wasn't Cassie. Because she came out to *me* that night, Tim, in Maine. In an inflatable, in the fog. Close to midnight. Someone had left it for her in Hanson Cove, a ways below the town."

I couldn't help myself. "How could she . . . ?" And I stopped.

"Minot. He did it. And there was a tiny GPS, all set up to take her through the Cut. To the stone boathouse."

That's when it hit, the great gut punch. *The stone boathouse!* Of course. How could I have been so stupid! *That's* where she had sat, the "More Woman," waiting in the boathouse, waiting for the beast to come. Suddenly, those little doubts about Cassie, which I'd managed to tamp down, swam to the surface, like motes of phosphorus in dark water. Lit up everything. Again, I hope I didn't show it, but I was reeling.

"That's where she shot him," he said, very solemn now. "Then she took his inflatable in tow and brought him out to my boat. Wanted me to be involved . . . wanted me to get rid of the body, in fact. You really didn't know that?" He looked at me with real interest, surprised that I didn't know. Because it was obvious that I did not. A little smile began playing around the corners of Theo's mouth. The Great Trickster . . . he was amused by all this treachery. Treachery that reached into my life, now. Amusing.

"That's quite a story," I said at last. As if I didn't believe him.

"Quite a story?" Theo said, amused again. "You should have been there, Counselor. I was asleep and there was this banging on the hull. I came up on deck, naked. And there she was, this beautiful woman standing calmly in a dinghy, holding on to my boat with one hand. And holding this big pistol on my nuts with the other. And there was dead Minot, right behind her, curled up in the other dinghy, with these wet holes in his head.

"'He had an accident,' she said with a faint smile. She was tough, Counselor. Very, very tough. And righteous. Justice flying through the night, man, and that's the worst kind of tough. 'And you could have an accident, too,' she said, 'if you don't listen carefully.' I didn't doubt it for a second. I even stopped *thinking*—which is rare for me—and did what I was told. Scary."

Then he laughed, as if remembering something funny. "I asked her if I could put some pants on. She said, 'No. This is fine.' It wasn't fine for me, I'll tell you. Then she asked if I had known that Minot was coming to get her that night. Without thinking, I said that I had. She nodded. 'That's why I'm here,' she said. 'I want you to forget about that. And anything else about me. Or I'll shove that seventeen million so far up your ass you'll be shitting thousand-dollar bills for the rest of your life.'

"Imagine an elegant woman like that, saying something that rough. It made the whole thing even more surreal. And alarming. As to the seventeen million, I have no idea how she knew about that, but she did, and that was scary, too. Then she handed me the line to Minot's dinghy. 'You're part of this now,' she said. 'Put him someplace clever. That's what you're good at, isn't it? Clever?' Then she just pushed off and said, 'Do it right. And don't even *think* about fucking with me.' And that terrifying smile again."

"And the proof of all this?" I asked, as if I still had doubts.

"There is none. And I'm not telling anyone else, no matter what you decide. It ends right here, regardless. I'm not threatening you. I'm just doing you a favor. Telling you stuff. In hopes you'll do me a favor in return."

"You're not doing me much of a favor, Theo, making these astonishing claims about a woman whom I may be about to marry."

"Oh?" He was apparently a little surprised by that. "Interesting. I would have thought you were a little more wary than that. Well . . . do what you must. But do be careful. That's my little gift to you: telling you to be careful. I am sure she really loves you, but she is the great heroine. In time, she will do what she must. And, if you're in the way . . . tough shit, Counselor. Very, very tough shit."

I ignored that . . . certainly didn't want to talk to *him* about it. I changed the subject. "Did you do the pips?" I asked suddenly.

He was surprised, but after the shortest pause, he said, "Yes, just as I testified. Cassie had nothing to do with framing Harry, you may be pleased to hear. She knew nothing about it. But I'd been planning on killing George—and framing Harry as a fallback—for some time. The pips were always part of that."

"Okay," I said, finally. "What do you want?"

"It's easy," he said. "First, your guy, Kazanstakis, is starting to sniff for Minot's gold in Greece. I thought our 'deal' was that I'd have a free hand in Greece. That's what was in it for me, really. So I want you to call him off." I nodded, and he went on. "Second, if you could get a decent doctor up here to look at this leg, I'd be grateful. The local docs don't seem to have done a very good job." He stretched his leg, painfully, and looked down at it, his face suddenly blank as he thought what it might mean. That's what he really wanted, I now saw. Someone to save his life. And I just might be able to do that.

"That's it?"

"Yes. Simple, isn't it?"

This had come mighty fast, but I did have one thought.

"There's an ocean of money out there, Theo. More than enough for two," I said.

He raised his eyebrows at that. "You disappoint me, Counselor. I thought you were better than that."

"I *am* better than that; it's for Alex. I said I'd take care of her, and I will. I want her to get half, which is probably less than Minot intended. The Naxos Trust. He certainly didn't intend it to go to you. And I want Paul Kazanstakis to pull the money together, account for it, and divvy it up between you, just to keep everyone honest. Even after paying him a handsome commission and giving Alex her half, you'll wind up with more than if you try to do it alone. Because in five years, the little mice will have gotten at it: crooked Greek lawyers and bankers who know you're in prison. Suit you?"

He smiled, pleasantly. "Sure," he said quickly. "And that's more like you, Tim. Justice for Alex, in the midst of all this crap. Aren't you the one! I assume we don't need a writing for this," he said, and grinned.

"No." I smiled back. "No writing among thieves. But you'll find it's highly enforceable. Do anything unpleasant to Alex or Cassie or me and you will be killed. In prison or out." I didn't smile during that part.

Theo nodded, interested. "I must say, you continue to amaze, Tim. Calmly dividing up Minot's gold, threatening me with murder. Quite a different guy now, aren't you. Can you really make that happen?"

"Of course. I've met some terrible people in my practice. And, before we wrapped up our original deal, I took some precautions. Do something wrong and you'd be dead in a week. Maybe less; speed is of the essence in a thing like this." A pause while I gave him a chance to think about that. Then, "So, do we have a deal?"

"Yes," Theo said easily. "As you say, I'll probably do better with you than on my own. How about the leg?"

I said I'd get someone good, but there were no guarantees.

"That's okay," he said, "but you better hurry. It's pretty bad." I said I would.

As we stood to shake hands, I smelled something and realized it was Theo's leg, which had begun to rot. I didn't say anything, but I made an involuntary face.

Theo smiled at that, which I thought was game of him. "Better hurry, as I say?" He went on: "And, Counselor, I only say this because of some odd affection for you: do watch it with Cassie. She'd kill you if she had to."

"No, she wouldn't," I said. "I'd know."

He smiled broadly this time. "Good for you. Hope you're right. But, just the same, I'd watch my ass, if I were you." I just smiled.

"We'll see," I said.

CHAPTER 49

JUSTICE

I decided not to speak to Cassie. It didn't matter anymore, I told myself; we'd already split. And—whatever she had done or not done to me and Harry—I was still deeply fond of her. And persuaded of her core decency. Odd, perhaps, but true.

Theo had said, when I was doubting him, "Go ask Cassie. She's the great Truth Teller." I thought that was right, but I didn't care . . . didn't want to know, perhaps. I was prepared to let the whole business drift off into the fog that seemed to rise up off almost everything to do with the Minot affair.

Then Harry committed suicide that July, and everything shifted. Not that I suddenly wanted justice after all, or to see Cassie in prison. Certainly not that. But I had this weird hunger for clarity. The main thing was that I simply didn't understand why Harry had committed suicide, and that drove me crazy. We'd have worked something out together, he and I.

We'd have come up with a new life and a new plan. And he—with his astonishing gifts—would have made it work. So his killing himself drove me absolutely crazy. Now I wanted clarity instead of fog. As if that might throw some light on Harry. I meant to start with Cassie.

The day Harry shot himself, I went to Hanson, as you know. I arranged a plane for Mimi, arranged the cremation and all of that. But I called Cassie, too. Told her what had happened, told her I wanted her there and had made arrangements for her travel. So she could be there for Harry's burial at sea.

She didn't want to come. She was shocked at what Harry had done . . . deeply upset. "I had no idea," she kept saying. "I never saw this coming . . . I never imagined . . . I'm so sorry," and so on. She meant it, too. What she really wanted to say, I'm sure, is that she had never thought about any consequences involving Harry—certainly not his suicide—when she set out to kill Minot. But she couldn't say that, of course. Or didn't know she could.

But she sure didn't want to come east. "Oh, Tim . . . I don't know about that . . ." I could almost feel her shudder at the idea. I was not surprised. But I was not sympathetic.

"I'd be grateful, Cassie. And I think you owe it to him." I put it bluntly, my voice hard. There was a long silence after that.

"There are things you don't know . . . ," she began.

"No, there aren't," I said. "We'll talk when you get here."

Stony silence on her end. Then, "All right."

She got in around four the next day. No smile as big as Montana this time. No tumbling into bed. We went to the hotel, put her stuff away in "her room," and went and sat in my study.

"What do you want?" she said, blunt as ever.

"I want to know everything now. Including everything about you."

"You saw Theo?" she said.

"I did."

"Weak sister," she said impatiently. Odd thing to say about Theo but she was stern, wasn't she? "What did he say?"

"He told me about the inflatable in Hanson Cove. And you towing Minot out to his boat. And he said I should ask you, and you would tell me. Is that right?"

"Yes," she said. Flat, no hesitation. "Of course."

"You should know," I said, "that I will never use this against you or tell anyone. Ever."

"*Please*," she said with an impatient wave of her hand—and a little scowl, almost angry. As if such an assurance were beneath us, which it was. "I will tell you everything and you do what you must."

"And you don't care," I said.

She smiled pleasantly. "Baby, I do not. I am not wired that way, as I guess you know."

Now I smiled. "As I guess I do." Then, "Let's start at the beginning, then. You coming east. Was that all a charade? Was it about killing George all along?"

"Oh no, Tim, no," she said immediately, her face melting into real concern; she took my hand. "You and I met entirely by chance. I took a lovely shine to you and I came east just to see where it would go. It went very far and very fast. I fell in love with you. Still am, to tell the truth. Not that it's going to do us much good now. It had nothing to do with George."

"But . . ."

"There is no *but*. I thought Minot might be there but that was . . . collateral."

"Collateral for a while, I guess," I said.

She stopped at that, dropped my hand, and looked almost apologetic. "That's true, of course. When I actually saw him,

I'm afraid I more or less went crazy. And he wasn't collateral anymore."

"Talk about that."

She paused, then began. "I hadn't thought about Minot at all when I was falling in love with you. But—when I saw him there that night, in all his animal force and cruelty—I'm afraid I just went nuts, and that was all I saw. I am sorry, but that's how it took me. I am . . . I am the type I guess . . . black and white. I believed Minot raped Don and killed him. Not literally: he seduced Don and Don killed himself. But Minot knew exactly what he was doing and might as well have pulled the trigger himself. I knew that with perfect certainty—just as I knew he had killed others back in Greece—and I meant to kill him for it. Right now.

"It wasn't just mystical 'seer' stuff, by the way. It was perfectly clear that something dreadful had happened to Don, when I got back. It took a while—it was agony for him—but eventually he talked to me about it, told me what happened. Minot saw something in Don, something sexual and odd. Something gay. That interested him, for some creepy reason, and he slowly, slowly pulled Don in. Caressed him, talked to him about who he really was. Then got him to do things that astonished and appalled Don at first. And then they didn't. Then he liked it very much indeed. And was even more horrified. Basically, he went through a profound sexual change. That line must have always been there. I was well aware of his feminine side. Liked it a lot. But didn't see just how deep it ran. Neither had Don. This was the first he'd really known about it. On the one hand, it delighted him. On the other, it literally tore him apart. And me, too, I'm afraid. Not because I hate gays or any of that; but because of us. He saw—we both saw—that it would put an end to us. Not for sure but probably. Which hurt a lot. You have to remember that we were deeply in love with one another, we really were. So this was horrendous. Neither of us could see how we were going to handle it. Short of just running in opposite directions.

"I didn't want that. Told him that maybe we could find a way. Sex had never been a key to our relationship. Not like you and me. So I thought maybe we could maneuver around it. I didn't know how, but something short of chucking everything we had. I thought . . . if we really tried."

"Did he believe that?" I asked.

She smiled ruefully. "Not for a second. You could tell. But he said he'd try; we'd find out. But it was clear that he was just humoring me and that he was desolate. Undone. I wasn't thinking suicide at that point: hell, it wasn't that bad. We could always just go on to new lives apart. By the way, it wasn't the homosexuality that ate at me. I wasn't horrified, the way he was. But he was a different generation and he *was* horrified. I missed that. Didn't see just how profoundly it tore him up. And suicide? . . . Never crossed my mind. I would never have left him alone and gone down to Boise that weekend, if I'd thought about that. When I got back, he was gone."

"And you knew?"

"Oh, sure. He wasn't the kind of guy who'd be careless going over a fence. So, sure I knew. Then I went out to the place where it happened, with the sheriff. He was my pal, too, as well as Don's. So we never talked about suicide. For Don's sake. But it was clear as day."

"And it was clear to you that Minot had done it," I said.

"Utterly. I almost got a plane next day. To go east, lure him out and kill him. But I got control of myself. Said I wasn't going to ruin my life, too, over this. That's the way I felt until I actually saw him on the cruise. Thought of Don literally in his hands. And then I went crazy."

I just nodded, let it sink in. Said, "I guess." Then, "Did it feel crazy? Did you feel out of control?"

She smiled and shook her head no. "The exact opposite. I felt cold as ice and absolutely in control. He could have been a mountain lion in the hills: I had made up my mind to stalk him, and he was as good as dead. I mean it. And it felt wonderful. Destroy the son of a bitch."

I thought for a minute after that. Sighed and said, "So you seduced him that night, on *Java?*"

"Yup, and at the ball. And it was easy. He was incredibly wound up, for some reason, and jumped on it at once. I said I'd been thinking about him, the past year. Which was true, but not the way he thought." She smiled for a second at that. "Then I said I wanted to come to the next 'event.' He loved that idea, just loved it. Took my hand with great intimacy, great force. Even I—who knew him and meant to kill him—was overwhelmed by his intensity. *He was something.*

"He said the next 'event' was the very next night, and it'd be perfect. I was shocked at that . . . that it would be so soon. How could I possibly do it? But I was glad rather than concerned. 'Fine,' I said. I'd have killed him that night, if I could." She stopped and apparently thought about it.

"Keep going," I said.

"He had the whole thing planned out in an instant: my leaving the cruise, and then circling back, the little boat in the cove and the tiny GPS. He had people on the mainland. He'd arrange everything. He was uncannily smart and quick, and I bought it on the spot."

"And I disappeared," I said.

"No," she said with a nice look. "Not at all. But I had my work to do, now. And I had to be about it. Whatever was left of us had to wait."

"Forever, it turns out."

"Perhaps," she said. "But I simply didn't think about that. All I saw was him and what I had to do."

"'Justice flying through the night.' That's what Theo said about you."

She smiled at that. "Yes, I guess. I didn't think of it that way but sure. That's what I was doing, and it meant everything to me. Justice for Don and myself. And for Harry and Mimi, too."

That took me by surprise. "Harry and Mimi? Why them?"

"George took me totally in his confidence, once we began to plan. He told me with great pleasure that Mimi was coming, too. Told me as if I'd enjoy it, as he did. Which was utterly weird. I almost stumbled on that one. But instead, I just smiled and nodded. I did ask, 'What about Harry?' And he said, with the coldest look you ever saw, that it would kill Harry. And it was clear that that was just what he wanted. It was to be the great climax of that part of his life. No question about it. Just like Don. Men were different for Minot. He was well able to murder men. Whether directly, the way he used to do in Greece. Or by twisted torments, as with Don and Harry."

"What did you make of that?"

"It made everything clearer and stiffened my resolve. Not that I needed it."

"Mmm." Pause. "Talk about the details. How did you get the gun? What about that hotel room at Logan; we did check, of course. Was it your sister?"

That surprised her. "You knew about her?"

"You told me about her. And later—in the fall when I was stuck—I checked. You're almost identical."

"You checked on my sister?" She scowled, didn't like it.

"Look, there were bizarre coincidences in your story, Cassie, from the outset. Once I started working alone on the case—and *desperate* about Harry—I told Kazanstakis to take a look. Just get a photo of her. So I'd know. It would never go further."

"Yeah? But you'd set me up so you could use me, if Theo didn't work out, right?" She made it sound very nasty indeed. Fair enough. It was nasty.

"It never got that far," I said.

"But if it had, you would."

"No. It wouldn't have come to that, would it? As you promised me that first night when you flew to New York and burst into my apartment. Harry didn't do it, you said, and you'd save him yourself, if you had to. Made no sense at the time, but it did by last fall. You would have come forward, if he'd been convicted, wouldn't you?" She just started to nod, calming down. "It's who you are in the end, isn't it?"

"Yup," she said. And then gave this sweet, rather wide smile. "That's me, babe. That's what you get. Not enough, maybe, but that's what you get: I do the right thing. I could live with Harry being in jail and denied bail. That was not so awful. He had meant to kill Minot, after all, so he was hardly innocent. But really convicted? No. I wouldn't have allowed that."

I nodded. It was obviously quite true. I put my arm around her, close for a minute. Then I stepped back . . . wanted to hear the rest. "How about the gun? Was that Minot, too?"

"Of course not. Why would he do that? But I often travel with a revolver, as you know. I had one—a .22 Magnum. It was perfect."

"And the sister."

"I called her, as you guessed. Or as Theo told you. We were close and she'd do anything for me without explanation. I told her to get the room and check in. That was all she had to do. I'd drive all night, check out in the morning, as if I'd spent the night. On Sunday, after you dropped me off, I drove south for an hour or so. Had lunch at Just Barb's in Searsport, as you suggested. Amazing lobster chowder, by the way." We both smiled at that. "Then I turned around. The fog was thick, so it took a while to find the right place but I did. And there was the dinghy and all that. George and I weren't to meet until ten or eleven o'clock, so I had plenty of time to look over the boat and fool around with the engine and the gadget, see how they worked. I'm good at that sort of stuff, so it was easy. Then I set out at dusk. I went very slowly, but the little gizmo worked like a charm. I thought about you, bringing me in in *Nellie* with *your* GPS, which you were so proud of. And I was sad for the first time, almost paused . . . almost thought, *What the hell am I doing?* But I didn't. The passion, the rage, was too strong, and I got caught up again. I hit the Cut and then followed the shoreline."

"To . . . ?"

"To the stone boathouse, on the beach."

I sighed at that, appalled that I had missed it. But all I said was, "Tell me about that."

She gave a hint of a smile, almost wistful. "I loved it. I got there early and sat there, in the rubber boat in darkness with my pistol in my lap, rocking on the gentle swells. I was the hunter, waiting in a blind. I know how to do that. I could have waited forever."

"Felt good?"

"Very."

"And he came," I said.

"Yup. I heard him, coming pretty fast until he got close, then he slowed down suddenly. He must have had his own GPS. He cut his engine and drifted silently through the fog into the mouth of the big boathouse, toward me, deep inside.

"He was standing up now and I was, too. I had a big three-cell. I turned it on and blinded him for a moment. I said, 'Hi, George. I've been waiting for you.' I let his eyes adjust so he'd see the gun. The smile melted away, his big face went slack and he went pale. That was the best moment. Then I shot him, twice, fast . . . *Paff! Paff!* That was it." A long pause. I waited, saw it in my mind's eye. Then said, softly:

"Pretty good shots."

"Oh, yes, pretty good shots." She smiled, thinking back to it. "As big as he was, he was dead before he hit the floorboards. And I was enormously proud."

"You checked that he was dead?"

"Of course. You always check dead game. Especially the dangerous ones. Like George."

"And that's when you did the pips?" I said. I was trying it on, which was cheap of me. In case Theo had lied, as part of the deal. But he hadn't.

"The pips?" she said, puzzled. "No. That wasn't me. That wouldn't have occurred to me. That was Theo. Or Theo and Alex."

"My God, were they there?" I was not thinking straight.

"Of course not, but later. Theo, not Alex. He probably told you this part. I wanted to get my arms around him."

"You towed George out to him, he told me."

"Yes. That was the hardest part of the whole thing, by the way . . . finding fucking Theo's boat; it wasn't on the GPS. It took half an hour." She laughed. "But I knew roughly where he was, I had a compass, and I did it . . . found him and dragged him into the game, kicking and squealing. Left him the body to deal with." She grinned at that, too. Liked to remember it.

She paused for a second. Then went on. "Anyhow, I went back to the cove and went ashore. I set the inflatable motoring very slowly out to sea, with the tiller tied down. I shot holes in it when it was about to disappear in the fog. It's on the bottom there now, if you want to find it. Evidence . . . tell Bud." She grinned at that and I just smiled, shook my head. "Then I got in the car, drove to Boston. Long ride. And I was just humming, all the way. I went to the hotel and signed out. Then got on the plane."

"Jesus, Cassie . . . you are *something*." She gave the faintest of smiles. Yes, she was saying. Yes, she was something.

Then she stood up, said we were done and she was going to bed. Didn't reach out to me or anything but gave me the most intense look. "Gonna miss you, babe. I love you."

I stood, too. "Gonna miss *you*, Cassie. And love you."

"Well, there ya go," she said.

She went off to bed and so did I. Deeply troubled. Almost physically clumsy. Like a man struggling ashore in heavy surf.

The next day, we buried Harry at sea, out on Broke. Then I drove Cassie down to Bangor. We didn't talk, just sat there in the car, in silence. At the airport, I set her stuff down on the sidewalk, said, "Miss you," almost formally. She picked up her case, gave me a funny look, and said, "I guess."

Then I surprised myself by putting my hand on her shoulder and saying, "You know, it's just possible we could . . ." I couldn't finish . . . couldn't find the words. "Some damn thing," I finished weakly. "I'm not the Law Guy anymore."

She seemed to like that. But then she narrowed her eyes ever so slightly and said, deadly serious, "Yes, you are."

CHAPTER 50

BEACON HILL

Back in New York, I thought all the time about Cassie, of course. It was torturous, and I obsessed about it. Obsessed about the scene in the boathouse. It will stay with me forever.

But I didn't think about *doing* anything. That was not on my mind. Besides, my mind was turning back to Harry. And then I *really* obsessed. Because his suicide still didn't make sense to me, and I couldn't let it go. There had to be a piece missing. Something I didn't know, and it bothered me terribly. It was like leaving the hero unburied in Greek myth: you simply don't do that. Ever.

So I forced myself to put Cassie out of my mind and focused entirely on Harry. In the end, I did an odd thing. I went to Paul Kazanstakis, again, and asked him to have his people reconstruct the events of the night Harry left home at sixteen, all those years ago. Harry had harkened back to that night a couple of times during the last month of his life, and I thought maybe there might be a clue there for me. I told Paul to spend whatever he had to but to dig hard, get names and so on. And he did. At that late stage, I learned some things that were remarkably interesting. And as sad as anything in this sad story. Sadder, really.

I had trouble deciding what, if anything, to do with what I had learned. So—as I sometimes do—I decided to go off for a couple of days, on the boat, think it over. I told Frank, and he was worried. "Don't go blowing your brains out, like your fucking brother," he said. I promised I wouldn't. Said I wasn't the type. I got a hug for that. I asked him to keep Gussie and headed off.

I took *Nellie* through the Cape Cod Canal and down into the Elizabeth Islands. Down to Cuttyhunk for an afternoon and a night. Then over to tiny Menemsha on Martha's Vineyard and the little seafood shack on the dock. Had oysters and white wine in the cockpit. Read for hours, down below. Thought hard. Thought some more. Slept.

When I woke up, it was clear. I raised the sails, raised the anchor, and ghosted out the narrow harbor entrance . . . just enough wind to maintain way. Then I turned north in a freshening breeze. You have to motor through the canal, but on the other side I put up the sails again and soon caught a strong wind—a steady 20 knots from the southwest—that took me all the way across Massachusetts Bay to Marblehead.

I had called to say I was coming and that I hoped to be there by early evening. I left the boat on the mooring in front of our old house and drove to Boston. I got my usual room at the Salem and Canton Club, bathed, and walked up Beacon Hill. To Sammy Cameron's house.

He welcomed me warmly, but he was a little wary. That made sense; it was a very sudden visit, and I had not explained. We went up to his dining room where a cold supper had been laid. We didn't get into anything during the meal. Then Sammy grabbed a bottle of wine and herded me up to his study. He was old, you will remember, in his early eighties. And he looked it, with his grizzled face and bushy eyebrows, and that gruff voice. He must have been a smoker at one time, like most people of his generation. But his age was not what you noticed. What you noticed was his great force and his character. Harry used to say he was like one of those bronze statues, out in Boston Garden and along Commonwealth Avenue, heroes of the Civil War and "the New England Renaissance." Sammy might wind up in bronze himself, one day. But not yet. For now, he was still flesh and blood, just like you and me. Just like Harry, when all this crap was going on.

He came right to the point in his wonderfully direct way. "I guess that something's up, Tim. Is it serious? Is there something I need to know?"

"Pretty serious, I guess," I said. "And something you already know."

"All right," he said and waited.

"You were there, Sammy," I said, flat-voiced. He did not move. I waited a long moment.

"I recently hired people to look into it, and you were there, in the Marblehead house, the night that Harry came home at sixteen and found a room full of naked people." Again, not a quiver. "I know it was unlike you, but I'm afraid you lied to me, when you said that others brought Harry to your house, after whatever happened. And that you and I would never really know. That was not true. You knew exactly what happened, because you saw it with your own eyes." Now he did stir . . . uncrossed his legs to face me more directly but still he did not speak.

"You were there in our living room, against the wall, watching everything. And before that, you had been down in the scrum yourself. The oldest man in the room, by far, but a man of extraordinary energy. You were there and you were into it. My information is that you did not make love to our mother, which is a mercy," I said, with an involuntary tic of distaste. "But you made love to several others and liked it quite a lot."

He just sat there, staring hard. Making up his mind, I suppose. I made it easier for him . . . turned over more cards.

"You came with Susan Tinsley, who had been there before, with others. It was that long 'single' stretch in your life, after the death of your first wife, and I guess you were experimenting. This was Susan's idea, but you did not resist. For which I do not blame you for one second, I would have done exactly the same thing. Maybe not today, but . . . a year ago? Absolutely.

"But we are in a different place now and we have to see it—as is so often the case with the sexual life—from a different angle and with different eyes. Harry's eyes, this time. And you have to tell me what Harry saw."

Still he sat there, perhaps unable to embrace this great shift. Not so easy, at eighty-something, after you'd been Sammy Cameron all your life. Well, he should have thought about that before. We should all think about everything before. But we don't.

"It's time, Sammy."

Sammy's face softened at that, and he looked ineffably sad. I reached over and took one of his hands in mine. Presumptuous, given the difference in our ages and our stations in life, but it seemed right. And, sure enough, he squeezed my hand back. And began.

"I did lie to you, Tim. Not for myself or because I was ashamed of what I had done that night—although I certainly wish I had not been there. But because Harry made me promise. That very night. He was urgent about it, about protecting you. I am sorry I lied to you, but I felt honor bound. Anyhow, there is no need to keep that promise now."

He paused again . . . thought. "May I say we were not debauched people, your parents and I and the others. It was the sixties. The 'dawning of the age of Aquarius' and all that. This stuff was the 'done thing,' at least among some of the avant-garde. And your mother was very avant-garde indeed. Your poor father was not really part of it. He had gotten into drink by then, and . . . well. I'm sure you know all that.

"What you may not know is that he was an awfully good guy, your father. An honest-to-God hero himself who had seen far too much during the war. He was a decorated carrier pilot. Won a Navy Cross, in fact, which is rare." I didn't interrupt to tell Sammy about the honor guard at the cemetery. "Beyond that, he was a lovely man . . . smart, decent, and enormously charming. But he had seen some dreadful things during the war, and in the end they consumed him. People didn't talk about emotional damage after World War II, but it happened a lot, people being consumed by the dreadful things they had seen and done.

"Sarah was as remarkable as he, in her way. And she stood by him in his troubles. But she was restless, looking for a new life, too, as he drifted away. She was still a great beauty and had great energy and charm. She turned to this 'new age' of the sixties with tremendous enthusiasm and hope. Which did not make her a fool, by the way. A lot of awfully good people were doing the same thing, as odd as it looks today."

"Back to the story . . . ," I nudged gently.

"Yup." He took a deep breath. "There were a dozen of us. They'd all been together before. Been in your house, as a matter of fact. There were drinks and some dope, a few things to eat. And the wonderful music of the day. I was old for that room, as you say, but I still remember the music . . . 'Don't you want somebody to love?' . . . Gracie Slick." Sammy smiled at himself . . . saw the humor of an old Boston gent, remembering Gracie Slick. "Mercy, she was good.

"The others were seasoned and knew what to do. They lowered the lights . . . helped each other pull the furniture back, as if for a dance. Then got the mattresses. And then people paired and tripled and so on. Danced. And then lay down. It was my first and only time and I was . . . astounded. I have never known pleasure so intense."

"And Harry . . . ?"

"Yup. Yup." He was reluctant but he was going to do it. "There was a lull in the evening at one point. Most of the people were resting around the sides. I was completely spent, for example. But then Sarah and some others began again. If there was a star in that room—and there was—it was Sarah. She was the great beauty. Extraordinary energy. Just like you and Harry, of course. She was in the center of the room, with two men and a woman around her, and they began again. The other woman was wiping Sarah's brow, kissing her. More than kissing her. Another guy came in. Everyone else was coming back to life, leaning in to watch.

"Then the front door opened. God knows why it wasn't locked, but it wasn't. And Harry walked in."

"The poor dear man," I said.

"The poor dear man," Sammy agreed. "Awful bad luck. And the worst thing is that no one noticed him. The room was dim, the music was loud, and we were all deeply into what was going on. No one noticed him. Certainly not Sarah. Sarah was in a rapture . . . the sex, the drugs, the music.

"So Harry just stood there for a moment, looking around the room. Saw his father in the corner; saw me, I suppose. But mostly he saw your mother. He strode across the darkened room. Looked down for a long, awful moment. Then pulled the big man off her, before anyone knew what was happening. Pushed the second man away, shoved the woman aside. Then he paused. And looked down at your mother for a long moment. Looking for . . . well.

"She had no idea at first. She was so gone that she just assumed that Harry was the next guy. And she reached out to him, with her eyes almost closed, smiling, yearning up to him.

She reached up her lovely arms—in all the sweat and the beat and the darkness—to draw him down."

"Oh, Lord," I could not help murmuring. "Did he . . . ?"

"No, no. Not that. He didn't do anything. Finally, she saw. And she jerked herself into a ball, from which, I suppose, she never recovered."

"So it was not incest," I said. "I had been afraid . . ."

"Almost," he said softly. "Almost."

"What he did," Sammy went on, "was suddenly to rise up, grab the guy, and drag him across the room and out the door . . . dragged him across the lawn to the garbage cans.

"He started to beat him. Would have killed him, I believe, if he hadn't been stopped. But by then, I—and a couple of others—had come out, half-dressed, and intervened. He wanted to go back inside, get Sarah perhaps. Or—like Odysseus among the suitors—kill 'em all, who knows. But I thought we'd had enough of that. So I got him into my car. Took him home."

"I am surprised he went, Sammy. You were part of it."

"Yes, but he did. I told him, right away, that it was my only time and that I had never been with your mother."

"A blessing," I said with a bit of sarcasm. "That must have been an odd moment."

"They were all odd moments that night, Timmy, believe me. Anyhow, he chose to set me apart. And I resolved on the spot to make him a major focus of my life. Didn't tell him that. But I did."

"He was lucky, Sammy," I said and meant it. "You did a huge amount. You were both lucky."

"Oh, incredibly so," he said. "But not lucky enough. He pulled himself together miraculously, after that night. Miraculously, but he never got past it. Never got over it. You know about his first marriage, I suppose."

"Not really, but I was recently told, by his first wife, that he had been impotent. Is that true?"

"Yes, and I am certain that it dates back to that night. I am not sure he was aware of it himself until he got married. He had not been sexual before and apparently hadn't thought about it. Hard to believe, these days, but true. That's what he told me, anyway."

"He told you?" I said with some surprise.

"Yes. We were awfully close and—when it first happened, the impotence—he came to me. Before the actual divorce."

"What did you do?"

"Got him a shrink." Sammy laughed. "But before he visited the fella, he had made his own arrangements. Got a divorce and started to drink. To fall apart. It was absolutely terrifying."

"I remember," I said. "And then Minot picked up on it and offered his own, marvelous solution."

"Yes. All I know about that, really, is what we all learned at the trial, but, yes, Minot led him into . . . what did they call it? . . . his Labyrinth, I guess."

"Was Minot another mentor?" I asked. "Perhaps an evil one?"

"Was Minot a mentor? I wouldn't have put it that way, but maybe. And evil? I'm not sure the word applies to a creature like that. He is the beast in the jungle; he does what he does."

"But then Mimi showed up and saved him," I said. "Or he saved her."

"I dare say they saved each other," Sammy said.

"Harry was saved from his impotence and immobility," I said. "Mimi and Harry were saved from sexual addiction. And then . . . rose up into an amazing new life."

"And it was amazing," Sammy said. "He was not just his old self, he was more than his old self. He absolutely shone. The power, the optimism. Mimi, too, in her way. She was not a force, like Harry, obviously. And not the brightest woman in the world, but terrific in her own right. No one ever asks if Helen of Troy was smart; that was not her job. It wasn't Mimi's job, either. Her job was to receive his love. And return it. And that she did superbly.

"The Power of Redemptive Love," he said with a smile, as if quoting something. "Not to be scorned."

"That's wild, Sammy," I said. "Are you sure of this?"

"No, but I think it's right."

"After all that," I said, "why did Harry keep Minot around?"

"That's interesting. I asked the same question and he had two answers. He was actually impatient with me for not seeing it myself. First, he said, he was deep in Minot's debt, for Mimi, and for that first, huge, financial deal, other things. But also, he was absolutely fascinated by him. Just liked to watch him, see what he'd do."

"There's a fatal attraction for you," I said. I thought of Harry, that day in the Race Committee meeting, just watching Minot. "And Minot agreed not to come after Mimi?"

"It was implied, I suppose. And for years he did not."

"And then he did," I said.

"And then he did," Sammy said. "I would guess that his 'essential animal nature' reasserted itself, wouldn't you? His essential evil, if you prefer. I suppose he'd grown tired of his fancy new manners and all that, and wanted to pillage and burn. He certainly wanted Mimi. And the sad thing is that Mimi wanted him. Harry had offered her romantic love. But Minot offered sexual addiction. Addiction is very different, and she wanted it. Do you know anything about sexual addiction, Timmy?"

"A little," I said.

"I thought you might. Anyhow, Mimi loved Harry but she wanted to go back, too. Harry—with that lightning insight of his—saw that. And decided to kill him."

"He told you that?"

"Oh, yes. After the fact, of course. But he saw the whole thing instantly in mythic terms . . . the Hero and the Monster.

He'd caught Minot's psychosis, perhaps. Or maybe he just saw that Minot would never give up. Or Mimi, either. Maybe he saw that Minot was actually determined to kill him, which he may have been. Anyhow, he didn't hesitate."

"I know it's true but I still find that astonishing, even now," I said.

"Well, he didn't do it in the end. Because he didn't have to. But my guess is he had made up his mind. And it didn't bother him one bit."

"But someone else got there first," I said.

"Yes," Sammy said. "And then it got complicated."

We were silent for a long time after that.

I began again. "So why did he kill himself?"

Sammy looked at me with a little smile, and turned his hands up, as if it were obvious and I were a little dim. "Don't you see?"

"No."

"Well," he said, "the basic thing had to be that night and your mother. You have followed the thread to first causes, and that has to be it. His descent into . . . into what? The Labyrinth? As good a word as any, I guess. After a lifetime of struggle, he was sucked down into the Labyrinth and there he would stay, in the public mind. When that became clear, he just couldn't bear it. Or it might be easier to say it was the pips."

"The pips!" I said, almost angrily. "What the hell are you talking about?" I hated the pips by now.

Sammy paused, thought about how to get at it. Then picked up again. "Harry came to Boston, just before his last trip to Maine."

"I know. You'd set him up with some people who might have taken him in as a partner in their start-up merchant bank. Set his feet back on the path toward a normal life."

"Yes. They were very good people, too, and it was going to work. But at the end of the meeting, Harry's mind seemed to wander and he later said it wasn't quite right. I was sorry about that. But it was Harry's choice.

"Afterward, he and I drove down to spend the night in Marblehead at your house, as we'd intended; it was a beautiful evening and we wanted to be on the water. We lingered over drinks in those big Adirondack chairs, out on the lawn, looked out at the harbor. He sure has done a remarkable job with that place, Timmy; I hope you'll keep it up."

"I will," I said. "What next?"

"I said something about how beautiful it was," Sammy went on, "and how lucky we were. I said that today's meeting hadn't worked out, but the next one would. And our lives were awful damn good. I wanted to encourage him, of course, to lighten up and get on with his life. But he just gave me this wintry smile, as if I were the most naive creature on earth. I remember what he said, word for word:

"'You want to know something, Sammy?' he said. 'It's nice here, as you say. But if I step off this lawn, it all goes straight to nightmare.' Those were the words: 'Straight to nightmare.' Then he went on to say that—when we had been sitting in that office in Boston, with those young bankers—he felt that they saw him naked. That everyone saw him naked all the time. When he walked down Federal Street or Broadway, he said, he felt as if everyone saw him and his mother, naked as Adam and Eve, driven out of the Garden. Only much, much worse.

"That gave me a little shiver," Sammy said. "His reference to your mother. We'd never talked about her before. 'Sometimes,' Harry said, 'I feel as if I were carrying dead Minot over my shoulder. And his dick is dangling down. And the pip catches the light.' He had leaned forward to tell me that last, biting off the words. Then he eased back in his chair again and said, in that elegant, restrained voice of his, 'I'm not so sure I can live with that.'"

"And that was it?" I said.

"I believe so." We were silent for a while. Then Sammy shook his head. "We're funny little animals, aren't we?"

"I guess we are," I said. Then, after another silence, I said: "So, what do we do now?"

It was a rhetorical question but Sammy chose to stand up, think seriously for a moment. Then nodded his head, as if he had finally gotten the answer. "I think," he said, "I think we had better switch to brandy."

We both laughed, as if it were the funniest thing we'd ever heard. Then he left and was gone for almost ten minutes. He came back with glasses and a dusty bottle that must have been a hundred years old. "Took me a while to put my hands on this. My old man bought it," he said. "Saved it for an occasion that never came around in his lifetime. I think it has come in ours, don't you?"

"I do. I surely do."

He poured. "Let's see," Sammy said. "Guess we oughta have a toast." He paused. Sammy must have given a thousand toasts in his life, and he was good at it. "Try this," he said.

"Here is to your beloved brother and my . . . my son, really. Here's to Harry. Whose great gift it was to come out of a darkness, like all of us, and create this shining version of himself. This hero in all our lives. Until, finally, the darkness rose again. And he chose to slip away, untouched, as only true heroes can do, with all his honor intact."

"Oh, Sammy," I said, standing, teary-eyed . . . hugging him. "That is exactly right. Exactly right."

EPILOGUE

That winter, New York

It's going to snow tonight, maybe a blizzard. They're talking about a foot and a half, with wind and heavy drifts. I know it'll make a mess, but I love it, love extreme weather. It is seven o'clock on a Saturday night, and I have been up here in my office, working away on this damn brief, since ten this morning. It's just a regular commercial case, but I still care like crazy, thank God. It's saving my life. For now, at least.

Anyhow, I've got this one in hand: I have "picked my line." That is, I have figured out the version of the truth and the law for which I will fight and with which I will live, for the rest of the case. Picking your line is the most important and intricate thing you do in big, complex litigation. And in life, too, I suppose. But my expertise does not extend so far. In the law, picking your line is a kind of navigation, so I'd expect to be good at it. In life, not so much.

But now I sit, contentedly, in my lovely corner office on the forty-fourth floor, looking down through the snow at the East

River, the Brooklyn Bridge, and the yellow lights of the River Café. The café sits on a barge on the river, just under the bridge. One of the nicest things to do in New York is have an elegant meal there by the light of the tiny lamps on every table. And watch the ferocious, black water of the East River go tearing by, right outside the windows.

It's interesting: The River Café sits just a few feet from where Washington embarked nine thousand men one night (and morning) in August 1776, to escape some thirty thousand British and Hessian troops camped a few hundred yards away. He did so with the help of a miraculous fog, which masked his flight; a wind, which kept the British fleet in the bay; and the help of my townsman and collateral relative, John Glover. Colonel—later General—Glover was the one who led his Marblehead fishermen in small boats, laden to the gunnels, back and forth over that wild river, a mile across, all night long. Washington sat on his great horse at the water's edge, softly urging the men to hurry, setting the order of their going, telling them not to make a sound. While Glover ran the river. Not a man was lost. A retreat to rival Dunkirk. If Washington had been caught, the revolution would have ended right there. There's a small stone monument to Washington and Glover by the water's edge. There should be. "Where are my Marbleheaders?" Washington used to shout, after that. At the crossing of the Delaware, other places.

It's good to have people who are handy in boats. And heroes.

But I am done with heroes now. I have had enough of them to last a lifetime. Harry and Cassie; Alex, in her way. George Crowninshield, of course. Heroes lift us up, sometimes into an ecstasy, and they are great fomenters of change. Sometimes for the good, like Washington and Glover. Sometimes not. It would not have been so great, after all, if Crowninshield had

been able to set Napoleon up in Louisiana in 1817. And sometimes, they are much, much worse. Heroes are often criminals,
as I said: they raze cities, slaughter innocents, if they must.
And still they have this pull. Like Harry. Like Alex. Like Cassie.
I was something of a hero myself for a time and I liked it
quite a lot. *Quite* a lot. But it wasn't really me. I was too wary, as
Harry would say. Too uneasy with absolutes. And with crime.
So, in *recovery*, I guess you could call it, I am the practical navigator once again, making my careful way from one low island
to the next, keeping people off the rocks. Doing my measured
best. And it feels fine, natural. But I must confess that my line
in life is still not clear, even now. There are still things that
throw me off, draw me away. Creatures who come to me in
dreams.

Alex sometimes. But mostly Cassie herself. The great heroine, the great assassin. She drifts down silently, a magical
bird out of a darkness, and comes into my arms. Her beautiful
feathers are soaked in blood, but in my arms, she is as warm
and sweet smelling as a child. And as real as the bed itself, as
real as my socks on the floor. Her sins, if such they are, drift
away. And we lie together at great ease. We roll softly, a sound
boat in good water. We make love, and after, she whispers, "I
am your Labyrinth, baby." She smiles at that, amused by herself. Then she nestles down into my chest, and says it again,
softer now: "I am your Labyrinth." And fades away.

You know what I want after nights like that? I want to be one
of those people who . . . in the face of endless ambiguity, in the
face of everything, really . . . is steady enough to make some
damn choice, hold a course no matter what. And brave enough
to stay on board until the very end. Stay until the boilers blow.
And then go flying through the night, my skin flayed off by the
steam. My crooked lover in my burning arms.

ACKNOWLEDGMENT/

This list could be a lot longer, but these few shine out.

Terry Considine has been a deeply devoted fan of the book—and read too many versions, without a whisper of complaint. Beyond that, he has simply made it happen. No details but it was an amazing kindness. Consistent with his close friendship over the last fifty years.

Cathy Milkey has overseen the entire enterprise from the beginning, first finding and then coordinating *everything* with Girl Friday Productions. She is wonderfully able and has been a joy to work with. I hope she is in my life forever. Or at least as long as I can manage.

Melissa Coleman, a terrific writer, spent a tremendous amount of time going over drafts. Her one piece of advice, always: Go deeper. Then go deeper again. Excellent advice indeed.

Joan Crowley is the model for everything that's good about Cassie—and nothing that's bad.

Michael Robinson—like Terry, one of the smartest people I know—was a profound and wonderfully supportive reader.

The late Harry Lodge—my partner in writing *Younger Next Year* and no connection to the Harry in the book—was a steady and loving fan.

The late Jim Salter, a truly great writer, read a lot of stuff and kept my spirits up by saying at one point—not very seriously—that I was "the Satchel Paige of serious writers." You could look it up.

Ann Marvin, my baby sister, has been perhaps the most passionate and supportive reader over the years. She insists that I read it aloud to her whenever we're together.

My beloved wife, Hilary, and our children, Chris, Tim, and Ranie, have been a constant, indispensable help. Hilary in particular has a sharp eye for stuff that's "off." She is hugely supportive, and I trust her judgment without reserve.

Warm thanks to my agent, Carol Mann. And to my particular pals at Workman Publishing, Susan Bolotin and Bruce Tracy.

Finally, profound thanks to everyone on the astonishing team at Girl Friday Productions, who managed the entire production. Special thanks to Paul Barrett who designed the whole book and the perfect cover. The boat, incidentally, is not the *Java* of the book. The cover boat is older and smaller. But it—and the cover generally—perfectly reflect the book. Sara Addicott straw-bossed the whole gang and couldn't have been better. I have been edited by remarkable pros over the years. The Girl Friday folks were absolutely their peers.

ABOUT THE AUTHOR

Chris Crowley is the author (with the late Henry S. Lodge, MD) of *Younger Next Year*, the *New York Times* bestseller, with over two million copies sold in twenty-three languages. There are now six books in the *Younger* series, including *The Younger Next Year Back Book* (2018), written with Aspen friend and healer, Jeremy James. In addition, Chris's work has appeared in various periodicals, including the *New Yorker*.

Before all that, Chris was a litigation partner at a leading Wall Street law firm, Davis Polk & Wardwell. For twenty-five years, he led teams in the usual run of big cases for major companies. And he brought a pro bono suit against the City of New York—and successfully argued it in the Supreme Court—to compel the hiring and promotion of more African American and Hispanic police in the NYPD. He truly loved the law, he says. But he quit a little early "because I wanted to live more than one life." He moved to Aspen for five years with his wife, the portrait artist Hilary Cooper, skied a hundred days a year, lived the outdoor life . . . and wrote.

The Practical Navigator is his dream project. "I am crazy about *Younger*," he says. "But *The Practical Navigator* is my great love. I am particularly fond of the devoted brothers. I never had a brother, so that was fun. And the two women? Well, as I hope you can see, I simply love them both. As for the parents in the book, I should perhaps mention that my own parents were utterly loving and solid. Neither of them drank at all, and I rather doubt they had even heard about the kind of sexual goings-on that come up in the book. When you write your debut novel in your eighties, it is not exactly a coming-of-age book."

Chris was born in Salem, Massachusetts, and grew up in Marblehead and Peabody. He graduated from Exeter, Harvard College, and the University of Virginia Law School. He has three children and six grandchildren. He and Hilary live in Lakeville, Connecticut, and New York City and spend time in Aspen. They are avid skiers, bikers, and sailors.

Made in the USA
Middletown, DE
21 April 2022